Mabon
And
Pomegranate

I hope you
enjoy—

K. V.

Mabon And Pomegranate

by
Kimberly Richardson

Mabon and Pomegranate

Published by
Kerlak Enterprises, Inc.
Kerlak Publishing
Memphis, TN
www.kerlakpublishing.com

ISBN 13: 978-1-937035-17-4
Trade paper
Library of Congress Control Number: 2012944817
First Printing: 2012

Special thanks to everyone at Kerlak Publishing for all of the encouragement and assistance.

This book is printed on acid free paper.

Printed in the United States of America

Dedication:

To my family, as always.

To my dearest friends: you know who you are.

To the Tuatha De Danann. Thank you.

Table of Contents

Mabon

Chapter One

Monica stared at the account numbers on her computer screen, wondering for the third time in the past hour why she had to review them. Were they taking part in fraudulent matters, or perhaps they needed to be sent to another department? She sighed then leafed through her small stack of papers on her desk, trying to find anything remotely related to the accounts on her screen. After a few minutes of rustling and drawn out sighs, she finally realized that the accounts on her screen had nothing to do with the pile of papers. She stared at the accounts again and realized that she had pulled them up for the purpose of answering a question her supervisor had posed to her over an hour ago. She reviewed her e-mail on her other monitor screen, located the question and then reviewed the accounts once more to find the answer. Thankfully, her supervisor was lenient on work matters and did not feel the need to be a hovering manager; someone else would have sent her a string of e-mails five minutes after sending the initial one, asking her when she anticipated completing the project. As she typed out her answer for her supervisor, she sighed again; today was Monday and already it was going to be a long week.

Monica had no face; she easily blended into the wallpaper of Life while staring out at the world that she was not a part of. She had very few friends, no significant other and her relationship with her parents was simply there with nothing more. She lived day by day in a blank haze, filled to the brim with junk of the ordinary, the mundane and the simple. It wasn't what she wanted, but it was what she got and kept close to herself for no other reason than for comfort. However, there was another side to her, the side that no one knew about. She was a wild child, yearning for things that had no name and desiring something better than what she had. She wanted to listen to the inner voice that told her of things that could be hers if only she took the time to seek them out. She refused to show this side to others and played the wallpaper girl to its full effect; that was what people could understand. Anything outside of that would simply terrify them. Monica also enjoyed her closet title of a bibliophile. She spent most of her free time away from work at a bookstore or library, pouring through different genres while seeking out new authors and titles. She attended book signings, literary festivals and even tried her hand at some poetry that she later put in a box for fear of anyone wanting to read it. Her poems were her way of trying to express emotions that she normally kept bottled up from society. On paper, she could scream to the world that she hated her life and wanted out of it, but did not know how to do such an act in her world. Monica was a walking conflict; she wanted something different and could even feel that difference, but had no clue as to get to said difference. A Catch-22 beyond scope and reason yet strangely enough it suited her in her unraveling madness.

She sent off her e-mail and relaxed for a moment in her chair, wondering what to tackle next on her desk. The past weekend of reading her books and enjoying the quiet of her apartment quickly fizzled to nothing when she reached her office that morning; to this day, she still wondered why she took the job at Indigo Trident, an accounting firm. Although the pay and benefits were very good, the constant dredge of the work made her feel like a small cog lost in a machine that did not care about its parts nor did it want to. To them, she was only a social security number, but at least she got weekends and major holidays off.

Monica stared at the clock on one of her computer screens; the time read 11:15am. She took a deep breath and exhaled it through her nose; only an hour and 45 minutes until her lunch break that consisted of going to a secluded area outside and finishing off her latest novel, *The Beautiful and Damned* by F. Scott Fitzgerald. She tried to read some of it last night, but her eyes kept closing due to fatigue and her comfortable bed. She pulled out her book from her messenger bag and thumbed through it, feeling the cool and musty smelling breeze wafting from the pages while the smell of the paper rushed through her senses. She closed her eyes and smiled, wanting right then and there to read. She opened her eyes when the new e-mail sound alarmed on her computer, the daydream of her book quickly fizzling away.

Monica opened the e-mail and began to read; her mouth went dry as soon as she read it. It was from her supervisor, asking her to come into his office for a moment regarding the e-mail she just sent. She grabbed her pen and pad of paper in case she needed to take notes and walked over to his office located at the end of the hallway. When she reached his half opened door, she lightly knocked then let herself in. Morgan, her supervisor, sat at his desk while clacking away on the keyboard and his face half turned away from her. He wore a crisp white Oxford shirt with a muted orange and blue tie and black slacks. His bald head reflected the fluorescent glow of the lights overhead; Monica named him Mr. Clean in her mind the first time she met him. When he saw Monica sit down across from him, he stopped his furious typing then turned fully to face her while placing his arms on his desk, immediately assuming the role of a high school supervisor who had better things to do, but had to be there for the sake of "the kids".

"Monica," he said in a nice voice that held an undercurrent of steel, "I wanted to talk to you about your e-mail from this morning."

"Yes?"

"Well . . . . it's not what I was asking for. I wanted information from the past six weeks. You gave me something completely different."

"Oh, really? Sorry about that."

"Yes, I know you are." He made a steeple with his hands and rested his chin there. His face carried a look of concern tinged with bitterness. "Is everything okay with you? I mean, I know you've been busy and all lately, but I just want to make sure you're okay."

Monica shook her head. "Sure, I'm fine." Yeah, right. "Why wouldn't I be?"

"Well, I'm just concerned because, well, you've let the ball drop on several matters, things that had a certain deadline on them."

"Oh, well, I am really sorry-"

"And," he said without giving her a chance to explain, "I have had to correct mistakes from your work these past two weeks. You've never been like this before in the four years you've been here. That's why I wanted to know if everything was okay with you." Monica wanted to just get up and walk away from this conversation; how could she tell him what was truly going on? How could she even put it into words that the life she currently lived was a boldfaced lie? Her life needed more than a 401K, light conversations at the coffeemaker with people she did not like and work that honestly did not matter to her.

"Sorry, I've had some things on my mind lately, but they should be working themselves out shortly. I do not want to become the weak link in our chain." She smiled, but wanted to retch instead. She did not give a shit what this company did or how much they wanted to protect the concerns of people whom she did not know. What one does in order to keep up the appearance of a cog simply amazed her. However, it must have been the correct thing to say; Morgan's eyes widened with overbearing joy with his wide fake smile. He leaned back in his chair, the sign that he was feeling better and that the meeting was soon over.

"Well, good! I am so happy to hear that. I really do appreciate you and your work and I want you to continue with that good trend. I have faith in you, you know that."

"Well, thank you for the note of concern." Yeah, right. Monica got up and walked out of his office while her stomach growled with hunger and the need for a Jazz Age book.

Anthony Patch was a deeply troubled man, she thought as she finished her book and took another bite of her turkey sandwich, enjoying the myriad of tastes that hit her tongue: the honey baked slices of turkey, the sharp Swiss cheese, the crisp flavor of the lettuce leaf and freshly cut tomatoes. Rather than sit at her desk, she decided to spend her lunch hour outside at Stone Park, located only two minutes away from her office, surrounding herself with the blue sky and slightly warm breezes that still held hints of Summer's lingering caresses competing with Autumn's cold yet still tender embrace. Once she reached the end of *The Beautiful and Damned*, she reread the last paragraph, making sure she read it correctly. She did not expect such an ending and such an action from the main male character. He seemed to be weak and troubled, but she could not help, but feel sorry for him and his tragic wife, Gloria. The Jazz Age obviously had a darker side; shame no one realized it until it was too late. Monica checked her watch as she finished her sandwich and realized that she still had half an hour left. Grinning to herself, she pulled out another book from her messenger bag and began to read, immediately getting lost within the words.

"Hey, Monica, do you mind if I sit here with you?"

Thanking the gods she wore her shades so that no one could see her eyes roll with exasperation, she looked up and saw one of her co-workers, Erica, standing in front of her while holding her lunch bag with baited breath. Of the ten people in Monica's department, Erica was the one that got on her nerves the least; she knew that Monica liked being alone and did not interact too much with the others simply because she had nothing remotely in common with them. As far as Monica was concerned, she worked from 8 to 4:30 and that was that. There was no need for any social interaction with people that would deem her strange anyway, so why bother? Erica knew this to a point and gave Monica her space, but deep inside she wanted to get to know her better. Erica's life consisted of her husband, their five-year-old girl and her job. She reveled in listening to others talk about their lives, secretly wishing to do what they did, but never getting the gumption to do it. She lived because Death was too easy.

Monica was an enigma to Erica; she very rarely talked about herself and what she did for fun outside of work. Aside from *Good Morning* and *Have a Good Night*, Erica never heard Monica utter another word during the day. She talked to others on their floor, casually asking if they knew anything about her, to which they replied no and why ask? It wasn't so much that Erica wanted to be friends with Monica; all she wanted was to know something about her so as to add to her woulda coulda shoulda pile in her life.

Erica stood over Monica, blocking out the sun from her face, smiling and holding her lunch bag while Monica just sat there, trying to find a way to get rid of her.

"Hey Erica," she said in a monotone voice. "What's up?"

"Oh, nothing. Just saw you out here and thought you might want the company." She shook her bag as though snakes were inside. "Trying to brown bag it this week until we get paid. Roger and I decided to cut our overspending for this month and save for our kid's education."

Like I really care about this, thought Monica, but instead she said, "Oh, cool." Erica beamed even more so, as if she received approval of the highest level. "Yeah, well, we're trying!" She stared at the empty spot again and said, "So, do you mind?" while shaking her bag towards the empty spot next to Monica.

"I just began reading this book and-"

"Oh hey, no worries! You won't bother me in the slightest!" Erica then sat down next to her, her slender frame taking up half the space on the bench. Monica groaned inwardly, but picked up her book and continued to read, trying hard not to let this distraction deter her from reading.

"So, what are you reading?" Monica lowered her book and turned to face Erica's smiling face. "Any good?"

"I just started reading it, so I don't know yet." Erica then grabbed the book from her hands and began flipping through it while Monica stared at her in absolute shock.

"Huh," she said while flipping through it, "print's too small for my taste. Do they make it in a larger print?"

"Uh, may I please have my book back? I just bought it." Erica continued flipping through it for a moment then handed it back to Monica with a thoughtful expression on her face.

"Could never get into reading," she said thoughtfully. "Too much time spent on reading something that didn't happen, although I do like those romance books. You like those? I like the ones that are full of smut and stuff; I try to read them when Roger is at work or when he's out with the boys." Monica sat listening to her co-worker prattle on and on, not really caring what she had to say. Her lunch hour was her time to unwind and relax with a good book away from everyone, but today's lunch was not to be.

"Erica, I need to get back to my desk," said Monica in the middle of Erica's prattling while getting up from the bench. "Sorry."

"Oh hey, no worries, I'll walk in with you, okay?" Monica sighed with a tired resignation as Erica led the way back to their building.

The rest of the day proved to not be any better; although she only had two hours left of work time, it seemed to drag on forever. The work that continued to pile up on her desk was the same. The co-workers that chattered on about the latest news of movie stars were the same. Everything was the same with no changes in sight. It was all the same and Monica hated every minute of it. As she drank from her white office coffee mug while reviewing the new slew of e-mails received during her lunch, she felt dead inside. Monica did not feel even a modicum of love or care for what she did; it paid her bills and that was that. When she took the position four years ago, her supervisor stated that he wanted only people who wanted to make their job a career in life and not those who were planning to move on to something else. Monica, while she agreed with Morgan just to get the job, wanted something entirely different inside. The only problem lay in trying to get to that something else. Sometimes at night, she imagined herself in an empty house, staring out of a solitary window to a verdant valley filled with flowers of every colour and majestic trees that seemed to touch the sky. She could smell the air, tasting its flavours of cotton, lemons and honeysuckle and felt the breezes against her dry yet wanting skin. She wanted to be a part of that paradise. It lay on the other side of the window, showing her what she truly desired with no plan in trying to get there. She yearned to be free and alive, awakened to something different than what others felt in their own life.

Monica always knew that she was different, but did not know how or why. People used to comment on her eccentric ways as far back as she could remember; even other kids during her grade and high school years would remark on her strangeness and how there was no label for her.

"I think you're blatantly trying to be different than everyone else," a girl in her high school once told her. Monica remembered how those words stung even though she knew it was not true; how could someone be strange on purpose? "You don't know what you want in life because you refuse to label yourself," said one boyfriend from her past. He wanted her to find a niche and stick with it, but how could one do such an action if they belonged to more than one niche? People like Monica were full of stuff that did not make any sense, not even to them. Some, once they released their inner stuff to the world, became different people almost overnight without any regrets. Others went completely insane, having lost their grip on reality and slipping too fast and far into their true world. Still others, like Monica, buried it deep inside themselves due to not wanting to show how unique they were to the world for fear of rejection, hatred and alienation. Monica was miserable because she wanted to explore her inner world, sampling everything from the buffet, but she did not know how to take the first step. It was truly painful to see others eating from the buffet and all she had was a stale and hard roll that someone threw away. She deserved better than that.

Finally, 4:30pm arrived, a large thumbs up for Monica to leave. She logged off her computer and left, not saying a word to her co-workers who stayed behind to chatter among themselves. It took her only two minutes to get from her building to her car and soon she drove home.

When she reached the front door of her apartment, the tears rolled down her face, spotting her shirt and landing on her hands as she opened the door. Once she closed it behind her, Monica leaned against the door and gave in to her sorrow, frustration and fear for ten minutes. When she had no more tears to cry, she went into her bedroom to change clothes then sat on the couch in her living room with her book and began to read. Her body sagged into the cushions and yet she felt as though there was nothing left inside of her. Something soon had to be done about her situation; crying every day was getting old even for her. There had to be a solution, but what? She could not go to her family; they would only claim that her worries were trivial and that there were worse problems out there and aren't you glad you're still alive and blessed by the Lord? She was not involved with anyone and her small number of friends were scattered all over the country so she couldn't just meet up with someone for tea. It was up to her to figure out a way to get out of this mental mire. But one step at a time; she snuggled deeper into the couch and allowed herself to travel back in time to help Sherlock Holmes solve another mystery.

Three solid hours later, she finished the book and with it, a possible plan for her own quandary. After placing her book back on the shelf, she rummaged through her messenger bag and found her journal. Thumbing through it, she realized that she had only written on two pages; it was still new and barely used. Grabbing a pen from her tea tin that sat on her computer desk, Monica opened to the third page and wrote whatever came out of her head:

Two eyes, one of blue,
See backward like Janus

Except I got a better deal.
Past reflections are seen
Across the orb, milky undertones
Surfacing like an oil slick
That smells of rose petals.
Two eyes, one of blue,
Are used to pour through ancient tomes
That tells of Mankind's history
From hard earned intellect
To widely practiced hedonism. I count myself
Among the less fortunate, those who
See while using their own will.
My frequently worn glasses
Humble me.
Two eyes, one of nothing.

When she finished writing, she read over her words to see if they made a modicum of sense to her; to her satisfaction, they did. Feeling somewhat better, she turned to the next page and poured out more of the putrid black ink that internally corroded her; four hours later, she placed her pen and journal on her coffee table, walked to her bed in a haze and fell into a deep and satisfying sleep once her head hit her pillows.

"This is NPR, National Public Radio."
Monica rolled one eye open to check the time on her clock; 6am glared back at her in red LED lights. She blinked twice then rolled out of bed, feeling better than she had in several weeks. Walking to her kitchen to make a pot of tea, she noticed her journal. For a moment, she wondered if last night even occurred, that her four hours of writing were only in her creatively starving mind. She prepared her pot then walked back to her couch and flipped through her journal. Instantly the words blazed on the page as her eyes made contact with them; poems and flash stories created from ideas and frustrations that had been bottled up for so long. Her release into the journal soothed her and made her feel confident; this was her help, her life preserver in the dark sea of

melancholy and wasted time. Monica grinned and hugged her journal close to her body. Finally, a form of salvation had arrived.

At 8:01am, Monica stared at her computer screens at work, trying to figure out the best way to fix her current snag without it getting too hairy. She fumbled through her stack of papers, wondering if this was some twisted form of déjà vu. Thankfully her supervisor did not need her results until tomorrow yet she wanted to tackle the problem before anything else cropped up. After sorting through more documents, she found what she had been searching for and typed her response in the blank spaces on the electronic form. As she typed, her eyes casually glanced over to her journal lying on the desk, ready and waiting for her next outpouring of words and thoughts. For the first time in quite a while, she could breathe.

That night after finishing off yet another book while tucked in her bed, Monica dreamt of sitting in front of a massive blank canvas that stood in the middle of a warehouse. She wore a pair of baggy green pants with the legs rolled up to her ankles and a paint splattered men's Oxford shirt with the sleeves rolled up. She was barefoot with an ankle bracelet that jingled when she moved. Her hair was pulled back into a messy ponytail while two paintbrushes stuck out from it. A white paint smudge stained her left cheek, but she paid it no attention; her entire focus was on the canvas. She held a thick paintbrush in her left hand that dripped cerulean blue paint; it tingled with anticipation of being used by her. It wanted to convey her thoughts into shapes on the blank canvas. Outside, the sun beamed with pleasure, sending its streams through the many windows of the room, warming it just right. Monica scraped her bare feet along the canvas-covered floor, feeling the roughness against her soft skin and she shivered with pleasure. While John Coltrane performed <u>Blue Train</u> on her CD player, Monica thought and thought and thought some more, then dove into the canvas with a bold strike of her cerulean blue. She stepped back, eyeing her first mark then, with a slow and satisfying smile she dove in again, only letting up to change brushes and colours. First blue followed by viridian green that later complimented a blood red mixed with gold. The myriad of colours made her dizzy, but she continued on; whatever lay behind the blank canvas had to come out. It was up to her to coax it out from its shell.

Her strokes were bold and curvy, uneven and taut, but she refused to stop even if she made a mistake on the canvas. Art was something not to be restrained or held back just to please the masses; Art lived to dazzle and inspire others, inflaming passions and dares into their own creative worlds. What she had to offer was no less than others' attempts. She painted as if her life depended on it, giving up every morsel of herself so the painting could come out. She painted all day and all night, never realizing that the sun had gone down, giving up its reign on the sky to the moon. Her CD was on constant loop so that she would not have to keep walking back and forth to the CD player. She wanted John with her during this time; his playing helped ease the cramps in her hands as she painted. Where there was once a blank canvas now showed a chaotic blend of stripes and lines, zigzags and curves, all made with many colours. The myriad of shapes and designs had a somewhat orderly look to it, as if the chaos was truly planned. There was a method to her madness and Monica was proud of it. When she awoke at 6am the next day, she felt even better than before. She woke up with a plan.

"I still don't understand why you're doing this. I mean, you're making great strides with the company, the department loves you, and you have proven yourself to be one of our better employees. I just don't get it," said Morgan while sitting at his desk and shaking his head in denial. Monica sat across from him with a determined look in her eye. "I just don't get. Was it something we did?"

"No, nothing like that, but I feel that this is right for me," she replied with a calm voice. "I have been unhappy for several months and this was my only option."

"I can look into raising your salary!" protested Morgan as he gripped his empty coffee mug in frustration. "How does $50,000 sound to you? $60,000?"

"I'm sorry, but my two week notice stands. I will begin clearing out my desk today. Thank you for all you've done." Monica got up and walked out the door without a backward glance, leaving Morgan in a state of frustration, anxiety and worry. While staring at the chair once occupied by Monica, he reached into a side drawer and pulled out his trusty bottle of antacid tablets. He popped three large tablets in his mouth and chewed them as if they were pieces of candy. Two-week notice, he thought as he chewed. He never thought that Monica was unhappy with her job, not even in the slightest. He had always prided himself on making sure he took care of his employees; Morgan made sure that they steadily received signs of appreciation. His face drew a blank while his mind replayed Monica's speech over and over.

When Monica reached her desk, she released the breath she had forgotten she held inside of her. At once, all of the stress, confusion and frustrations rolled away from her body, leaving her limp like overcooked pasta. She was free and while her rash action was terrifying, it also liberated her. Monica sat at her desk facing her monitors, but nothing on them made any sense to her. The new e-mail alert sounded through her speakers and, glancing down at the bottom right corner, noticed that Morgan sent an e-mail titled <u>ON A SAD NOTE</u>. She rolled her eyes in exasperation then clicked it open.

IT IS WITH GREAT REGRET, began the e-mail, THAT I MAKE THE FOLLOWING ANNOUNCEMENT; MONICA BURTON JUST TURNED IN HER TWO-WEEK NOTICE. I AM VERY SORRY TO BE LOSING ONE OF MY BEST EMPLOYEES IN THIS DEPARTMENT. THEREFORE, THE ENTIRE DEPARTMENT WILL BE TAKING MS. BURTON OUT TO LUNCH IN TWO WEEKS AS A FOND FAREWELL. PLEASE SCHEDULE ACCORDINGLY. THANK YOU.

Monica read the e-mail then deleted it from her account. She glanced around to her co-workers at their desk, trying to read their faces while they too read the e-mail. Well, it's Sydney or the Bush, she thought, bracing herself for their reactions. Five seconds later, Erica jumped up from her desk and ran over to Monica's with a look of profound sadness on her face.

"I just can't believe it!" she said while wringing her hands in nervous exasperation, "I just can't believe it. Why would you quit your job, Monica? I thought you liked it here!"

"I'm just ready to move on," she replied with a ghost of a smile on her face as she tried to turn back towards her monitors. Of course, that action was now near to impossible, for everyone else had gathered around her desk, each with the same look of sadness on their faces. Monica couldn't believe it; you guys did not care for me when I was an employee and NOW you act as though you care, she thought while a slow smile spread across her face. It was too much and yet humourous at the same time.

"Oh Monica, we are so going to miss you!"

"We always liked working with you, Monica!"

"So, what are your plans?"

"Is your husband going to be the breadwinner now?"

Monica just smiled at their questioning faces. "I just decided to change my life," was all she said, much to the disappointment of her co-workers who persisted in asking more questions. They asked their questions not out of concern, but simply to be nosy and pry whatever information they could gather from her life. Since she was the secretive one in the department, they had to know something about her and what she did after work. Monica, however, would not give them an inch. Much to their disappointment, she turned back to her monitors and resumed working, ignoring them completely. After several minutes passed, they gave up their futile questioning and went back to their own desks, some angry at Monica's attitude towards them. In Monica's mind, work had already become a distant memory of the past. She worked in a mindless state, her thoughts focused on the time to go home and the other half of her "plan".

4:30pm finally arrived just as she lifted her head from reviewing some papers. She yawned and stretched then looked around; everyone else was gone for the day. They did not even say good night to her, but then again, did they ever in the past? She placed her papers in a neat stack then pulled out a pad of paper and one of her purple pens. Thinking for a moment, she placed pen to paper and began to write.

MORGAN,

ALTHOUGH I GAVE MY TWO WEEKS NOTICE TO YOU TODAY, I HAVE DECIDED TO MAKE TODAY MY LAST DAY. PLEASE FIND MY PASS CARD NEXT TO MY PHONE AND ALL PERSONAL ITEMS REMOVED FROM MY DESK. THANK YOU.

MONICA BURTON

She signed her name to the letter, tore it off the pad and reviewed it, placed it in an envelope under Morgan's closed door and then walked back to her desk and cleaned it out. 20 minutes later, the dirty job was over and Monica walked out of the company's doors with box in hand for the last time.

Monica stood in the main hallway of a massive library that held books of every genre and subject; books were also stacked from the floor to the ceiling or in messy piles that one could spend hours sorting through just for the sheer fact of taking on such a task. She closed her eyes and smelled the scents of the place: glue, paper, leather, musty dreams and archaic words, all mingled together that made her head swoon. She wanted to bathe in such tempting scents for she knew that it would only aid her in her search for something greater, something that explained just who and what she was with regards to the rest of the world. After sniffing the main hallway for a time, she opened her eyes and walked while noticing the gigantic windows that revealed a verdant valley that stretched on for miles, mingled with a sky so blue that one would be moved to tears just catching a glimpse of it. Her bare feet made no noise as she walked on the cold marble floor. As far as she could tell, there was no one else in the library, but just her and the thousands of books.

Sunlight beamed through the windows and landed on some of the piles and stacks, giving the books an eerie yet pleasing glow to them. She stopped at one point and ran her hand along a weathered brown leather book with gold letters embossed on top that read *THE HISTORY OF TEA*. She thumbed through the tome, causing a flurry of dust to fly straight into her eyes and nose. She sneezed once then laughed as the sound traveled through the library, echoing through the many cases that she had not even begun to peruse. She looked behind her in curiosity, wondering if anyone had heard her sneeze then remembered that she was the only person there. Satisfied, she continued reading about the history of her favourite beverage. After some time had passed, she pulled the book from the pile and sat down in one of the comfortable wingback chairs to give her legs a rest while reading. She snuggled into the chair, feeling it enfold her, and then opened the book to where her finger held the page and continued to read. The sounds of her turning the pages echoed down the hall, but she did not care for she was in heaven. Unfortunately for her, she woke up.

It took her five days to pack all of her belongings and move them into her car and a U-Haul, while taking off an hour each day to do research towards her next step. She wanted out of her current city, ready to wipe the slate clean and move to a new town. During one day of research, she decided on a small artistic town four hours away that spoke of promise and a chance to really live the life she so desperately wanted. After making a couple of phone calls to inquire about a place to live, she confirmed a two-bedroom apartment near the library, ready and waiting for her to move in. Once everything was done towards the apartment, she contacted her former place of employment and told them of her new home address and to please forward any future mail there. She also discovered a bookstore that was currently looking for an assistant manager in the new town. She faxed off her resume in the morning, spoke with owner in the afternoon and had the job before the sun set. Monica couldn't believe how easy her transition had been, but it was. This was yet another good sign that she was making the right choice.

On the last day, she stood in the middle of her empty living room, looking around at the bare walls with a slight sense of wonder.

"As soon as I move into my new place, I am going to play one of my Frank Sinatra CDs while drinking a glass of raspberry lemonade," she said to herself then walked out of her old life for good.

The trip was amazingly simple; her old and new lives were connected by one reasonably well paved four-lane highway. Monica left at the crack of dawn, hoping to get her new life started on the right foot. When she pulled out of her old parking lot, she took a deep breath and released it through her nose, only looking ahead and never back. She drove by her old place of employment and waved to the menacing building with its tinted windows. The sights and sounds of her old place seemed to lose their colour as she drove by them, but not once did she look back. When she and her car named Pierre hit the highway, Monica began to laugh while tears rolled down her face. It felt good to have the tears come not due to sadness, but because of happiness. After her eyes finished their watery sacrifice and her face felt tight due to the dried tear streaks, she thumbed through her music to see what would begin her one-way trip. She had her CD cases splayed on the passenger seat, ranging from soulful jazz vocals to French chanson to Goth/Industrial to folk to her Vocal Muses, Tori Amos and Kate Bush, as she enjoyed the sunny day with a bottle of iced green tea and mojito mint gum.

Monica's eyes focused on anything that looked interesting on the highway, including a tree with shoes of all shapes and colours tied to the branches. It fascinated her so much that she stopped the car on the side and took several pictures of it with a promise to increase their size once exposed and hang them in her new living room. In her past place, she barely had any art hanging on the walls due to a lack of time. Now she would make the time for art no matter what. Suddenly, she felt lightheaded and began to giggle.

"Time for a little Tori, I think," she said while opening the case with one hand. She popped the CD in her player and gave in to Tori's words that made no sense and yet did at the same time, coloured with images and thoughts too personal to be shared yet shared anyway. While Tori sang, Monica's mind wandered to an incident that occurred several days ago between herself and her mother. While Monica desired to live a life of one's own choosing no matter the cost, Diane, her mother, thought otherwise. Her father, Charles, had died five years ago due to a stroke so Diane did everything she could to fill up the gap left by him. Unfortunately, Diane's life was filled with trying to please others and worrying what others thought of her, even if they mattered or not. She also craved control over anyone as a tactic to fill up her void due to low self-esteem. Creativity, while a cute hobby, did not pay the bills in her mind, so when she received the phone call that her daughter turned in her two-week notice at her high paying employer, she was more than just a little concerned.

"I thought you liked your job, Monica," her mother said with a worried tone on the phone. "I thought everything was going okay."

"It was for a time, but then I realized that it was not for me anymore. It's time for me to move on."

"So, do you have a new job set up?"

"I'll be working in a bookstore."

"So, you mean to tell me," said Diane with rising anger, "that you gave up your $40,000 job just so you can float around with some damn bookstore? Is that what I'm hearing?!"

"No, not float around, but work more on myself, to which I've not been able to do. I want to explore and find out more about myself and-"

"You know, you really disappoint me, Monica. I thought I had raised you better than that. Why in the world would you want to do something that foolish? I kept telling you to save your money just in case if you ever lost your job!"

"And, I did, too." Monica tried hard to keep calm, but found it increasingly hard to do so while listening to her mother prattle on about matters that simply no longer interested her.

"No you didn't! I know you didn't!"

"So, why did you ask me if you already knew the answer?"

"Don't get arrogant with me."

"Not trying to, but I simply wanted to know why you would ask me a question, only to decide that I must be lying. Explain that to me, please."

"I am just so disappointed in you right now. I spent so much money sending you to the right schools, only to watch you fail like this. I . . . just don't know what to say."

"Well, let me put it to you like this," said Monica, relieved that she found her spine again. "My life is my life and no one else's. You, as a parent, did a good job in raising me, even after Dad's death. Am I pregnant? Am I doing drugs? Was I ever disrespectful towards you or Dad? No, I was not. The only problem you have had with me was my spending habits when it came to books and when I forgot to send Dad a birthday card last year when he was out of town even though I called him. Honestly, Mom, if that is all you've been worried about, then consider yourself lucky." Monica went quiet after her speech, satisfied that she had done the right thing even if her mother thought otherwise. "I am only four hours away; you can come by and visit anytime-"

"You never invited me to your current apartment!" Monica sighed; this was not over yet. She tightened her grip on the phone and continued her defense.

"Yes, I did. Many times, in fact. Yet, how many of those times did you accept?"

"Well, there was that one time I came over and you did not want me upstairs because you had company."

"Okay, and what was wrong with that? You weren't even staying long, remember?" Monica took a deep breath, feeling the air whoosh out of her lungs. "Why are you insistent on people not being perfect? Why do you try to measure others according to your scale? People are not going to measure up as long as you do that. We, as humans, are not perfect. Never have been and never will. However, why do you spend time focusing on what people don't do as opposed to what they do? Also, why do you always focus on the past? The past is gone; let it go. The incident you just spoke of happened over a year ago. Why do you do that?"

Diane was quiet; Monica wasn't sure if that was a good or bad thing so she went on. "I am moving to a smaller town. I have already picked up a job as an assistant manager at their bookstore. The pay is less, but it suits me. Anyway, I have no outside bills and I have been saving my money. You always said that everything happens for a reason; I know it is true now." Diane was still quiet on the phone, leaving Monica to wonder if she hung up on her or not. Finally, Monica said, "I love you even if you hate my guts or not-"

"I don't hate your guts, Monica. I just worry about you, that's all."

"I appreciate that very much. It shows you love me. However, I am 35 years old; time for me to strike out on my own. If I fail, then I fail. If I succeed, then I succeed. But the point is that I go on after learning whatever lesson I received."

"I know, I know . . .I just wish you could have told me this sooner."

"It was going to happen sooner or later."

The two met up later that night for a celebratory dinner at Diane's small yet comfortable home. After her husband died, she moved out of her larger home and into something that would give her enough room without it being too much or too cramped. The dinner was light and pleasant and afterwards, the two shared a bottle of wine and talked of the good ol' days when Charles was alive. They laughed, cried a little, and then Monica got up to leave. Her mother opened the door for her then hugged her as if she would never see her only child again. When they pulled away,

Monica saw tears on her mother's face. She wiped them off with her hand, smiled then left. Diane watched her daughter's car drive off until she could no longer see her lights.

Four hours of smooth driving later, Monica saw a red and orange coloured wooden sign welcoming her to Mabon. She smiled as she drove by then her eyes focused on the upcoming scenery: massive trees loomed on either side of the main road, their branches hanging over just enough so as to provide comfortable shade for the pedestrians who walked on the rather wide bricked sidewalks. Stores with colourful awnings and signs faced her on both sides of the street; several people sat under bright blue umbrellas in front of what looked to be a café named **J.A.V.A.** Monica made a mental note to check it out later today if she had time while her new place of employment named Wenchang Books stood next to it. She pulled her car into a close parking spot and got out, stretching her legs and arms as she smiled, feeling the filtered sun's rays on her face. She closed her eyes in a moment of triumph; she was actually here.

"Are you applying for our resident scarecrow position?" Monica opened her eyes and, realizing that her stretched out body was indeed ready for troublesome birds, brought in her arms and legs and turned to find the source of the voice while her face turned redder than a tomato. A man sat at one of the tables in front of the café with a cup of what looked to be tea and a book face down on the table. Monica grinned as she walked up to the commenter.

"Thanks," she said in a jovial mood, "but I have already accepted another position in this town, one that has far better benefits."

"Ah, and that would be-"

"Assistant manager for Wenchang Books." The man's eyes widened for a moment then relaxed as a grin crept on his face as he took a sip of his tea.

"Assistant manager, huh? Well, so you're the one everyone's been talking about. Welcome to Mabon," he said as he took another sip. He placed the cup back on the table and sighed. "Ah, there is nothing better than a good book and a cup of tea, wouldn't you agree?"

"Oh yes, I agree most heartedly. There's nothing like a good cup of tea-"

"Or chai."

Monica grinned. "Or chai."

The man finished off his cup then got up while placing his book in his worn leather satchel. "Well," he said while stretching and yawning, "it's time for me to get back to work. But still, welcome to Mabon." He walked around the table towards her and held out his hand. "My name is Benjamin Algren and I'm the English Literature professor at Janus, the liberal arts college here in town." Monica took his hand and gripped it tightly.

"I'm Monica Burton. Nice to meet you."

"Pleasure is all mine, Monica."

Benjamin released his hand from her grip and walked to his navy blue car, waved again then drove off, leaving Monica still on the sidewalk, still waving, still grinning like a schoolgirl.

"I see our Lit prof has introduced himself to our new resident," said a warm voice behind her. Monica turned without any surprise to face a 50-ish tall and slender woman dressed in black sandals, black yoga pants, purple short sleeve shirt and funky coloured jewelry that accentuated her short and spiky grey hair. The woman pushed her glasses up her crinkled nose. "So, you're Monica, huh," she said with a genuine smile on her face. "Name's Miranda Cole, owner of Wenchang Books and your boss." Miranda walked over to Monica and gave her a big hug, releasing scents of lemon verbena from her clothing. Monica closed her eyes and fell into the hug; it felt just right. When she pulled away, Miranda's eyes sparkled with a fire she had never seen before as she stared at Monica. "I'm so glad you finally made it!" she said. "We've been hit with a rush of orders and lately our shelves had to be restocked several times a day. Don't get me wrong, I'm all for profits and whatnot, but lately it has just been ridiculous!"

"Well, if you want me to start today, I can. Just let me find my apartment, try to unload most of my stuff and then I can come back later, if that's okay?"

Miranda patted her shoulder tenderly then said in a softer tone, "No, you just got here. Take your time in getting moved in. The work will be here whenever you're ready. Go find your new home and relax tonight. In fact, may I suggest a place for dinner? Try Stingrays; it is two streets over by the fountain. They have great food and the prices aren't too bad, plus the servers there are really cool folks. Tell them who you are and perhaps they'll make your first dinner there for free." Miranda patted her shoulder again then walked back to the bookstore. Before she opened the door, she turned around and said to a still standing Monica, "Welcome to Mabon," with a beaming smile then opened the door and let herself in. Monica stared at the storefront for several seconds then got in her car and drove off in search of her new home.

After getting lost twice, Monica finally found her new home named Siren Court Apartments. She grinned; it seemed as though everything in the town had a special name. She turned into the main driveway of the complex and looked around, her head going back and forth in trying to take in as much as possible. Oak trees dotted the landscape of the place while pictures of mermaids were located everywhere and in different medias: paint, mosaic, even brick. A fountain made of blue and green coloured tile with stone mermaid statues holding vases from which the water came from stood in the middle of the complex. Monica drove by and whistled at the master craftsmanship of the statue then drove on to find her place.

She found her building, #36, and pulled into the parking lot with U-Haul in tow. She stretched and yawned as she got out of the car then rubbed her hands together with glee. Monica locked her car then walked to the leasing office located in the garden area across the road. As she walked, she noticed there were several brightly coloured mermaid statues dotted through the area. The leasing office stood by the swimming pool where several people either sat in beach chairs or made use of the pool. She found the front door and let herself in, jingling the front door chimes shaped like mermaids. A young woman with long bright red hair sat at a desk to the right of the front door, typing furiously on her keyboard while staring at her monitor with a serious expression. When she heard the chimes, she glanced up, noticed Monica and then broke into a bright smile.

"Greetings!" she said while getting up from her chair. Monica noticed she wore jeans with thick black sandals, a black shirt that said ARTIST in tie dye colours, and small silver hoop earrings to accommodate the six silver rings on her hands and small silver ring in her left nostril. She walked over to Monica and shook her hand with an almost bone crushing grip, causing Monica to wince slightly. The woman, realizing her strength, released her grip and blushed slightly. "Sorry about that, but I've been taking grip classes in addition to my yoga classes lately; looks like they've paid off." She stared at her hand for a moment then brightened up again. "Sorry about that; I tend to go off on tangents. Anyway, I'm Gina, the leasing manager. Are you a new tenant or just looking?"

Monica decided she liked her already. "I'm Monica Burton. I called several days ago about moving here."

Gina beamed. "Good to finally put a face with a name, Monica."

"Good to finally be here," she said with obvious relief.

"Sure! Anyway, I have your keys and new resident packet ready for you." She walked back to her desk, picked up two silver keys and an ocean blue coloured thick folder, then handed the lot to her. "Inside the folder you'll find the history of the town, maps, coupons to several of the restaurants and cafés here, your lease, and other goodies for you to read whenever. You have two keys with one of them being a spare. Well, shall we go to your place?" Monica nodded and Gina led the way. As they walked through the garden back to Building 36, Gina asked, "So, what brings you to our neck of the woods?"

"Well, it's kind of hard to explain."

"Try me; you would not believe the things I have heard in the past ten years here."

"Well, I came here because . . . I wanted to be around other creative people. Other people who live outside of the box, so to speak. I needed a change in my life and it was not going to happen while I lived in my old city. I hated my job, did not care for my co-workers, and felt my life stifling. I've wanted to explore my creative side, if I had one at all, and see what I had been possibly denying myself for the longest time." Suddenly, Gina stopped just as they reached the door to Monica's apartment. Her face held a solemn look as she turned to Monica and placed a hand on her arm.

"Dear, I know exactly what you're talking about. I came here for those same reasons. It is hard to live around people who can't and won't understand you. My old home sounded just like yours; I felt like an outsider most of my life. Even my own family, although they loved me, never really understood just why I needed to paint at three in the morning while listening to blues music. When I tried to show them my work, they either patted me on the head like I was an obedient dog that did a trick, or they asked me when I was going to give up my little hobby so I could settle down with a man and have kids." Gina unlocked the door to let them in. Monica walked into her new living room with awe; soft blues and greens occupied the room with enough space for her furniture and art while the neutral oatmeal carpet balanced out the colours. The entire apartment had an ocean/beach house feel to it; each of the rooms held either the blue or green colour from the living room with gracious spaces that gave rise to the imagination. Monica walked through the place twice, her wide eyes taking in as much as possible, while Gina remained in the living room with a knowing smile on her face.

When Monica returned to the living room, she said, "This place is amazing, Gina!"

"That's usually the first reaction people give when they move in. Glad you like it, though. That's how I felt when I moved here as well."

"Oh yeah, go on with your story."

"Sure, but how about if we sit on the floor? Do you mind?"

"Hey, it's my place and you're my first guest! Why not?" The two women sat on the floor while the white noise of the air conditioner buzzed over them.

"So where was I? Oh yeah – I had no problems with wanting to get married and all of that, but I wanted my art to be an important part of my life as well. My family and friends could not understand that. So, I did some research and discovered Mabon. After spending the weekend here, I made up my mind to move here. My family was against it yet they still sent me off with their blessing. Ten years later, I'm happy I made the decision to move. Do you know," she said as she scratched her left elbow in an absent minded way, "that not one of my family members has visited me since I moved here? They'll call from time to time, but none have visited."

"Even though they live an hour away?"

"Funny, huh? They would actually enjoy visiting here; everyone is pretty friendly, especially to newcomers."

"Oh yeah, speaking of which, I met this guy while I was parked outside of Wenchang Books. Really nice guy, too."

"Oh really?" said Gina as she moved closer to Monica in anticipation for any secrets. "What did he look like?"

"Taller than me, slender build, brown hair, green eyes. He's a professor at-"

"Janus, right? Yeah, that's Benjamin. Dr. Benjamin Algren. He really is a nice guy. Single too, ya know." Gina stared at Monica for a moment then said, "He has a sister living with him, ya know. Did he mention her?"

"No, we just talked for a brief moment and then he left to go back to school. What's she like?"

"Ophelia? Pretty cool. She'll remind you of a hip and funky librarian, but she's sweet just like him. She does have her 'colourful' moments to say the least, ya know. I've known the two of them for a while now; they've been here for quite some time. She's quite a bookworm, just like Benjamin. If you're into books, you'll get along with them famously."

"Well, I am going to be the new assistant manager for Wenchang Books."

Suddenly, Gina squealed as she hugged Monica like a long lost sister. "Oh, so you're the one Miranda was talking about! Now it makes sense! Dear, you must come and hang with us; we've got a small group of folks that throw literary dinner parties every week. Once you get settled in, let me know and I'll introduce you to the rest of the gang."

"Wow," said Monica in shock, "thanks!" Gina then got up and helped Monica up as well.

"Well, gotta run, but hey, call me if you need anything. In fact, I live in the same building as you so drop by 36-A anytime after five for scones and tea. I make my own, ya know?" With that, she let herself out while humming a song, leaving Monica in better spirits than she had felt in a long time.

Monica spent the remainder of her day unpacking as much as possible, trying to make use of the daylight while she had it. The first thing she unpacked was her CD player; five minutes later, the sounds of Frank Sinatra could be heard through the entire apartment as she walked back and forth between the U-Haul and her place. By the time the sun had set, her clothes and most of the kitchen were unpacked and settled in. She found her tin of instant raspberry lemonade, made a cup of it and drank it down while sitting on the floor. She looked around at her new surroundings and sighed. Already off to a good start, she thought as she got up to take a shower. Afterwards, she unhooked the U-haul from her car then drove off in search of a good first dinner in town. She decided to try Stingrays at the recommendation of Miranda as well as walk around to get a better idea of the town's layout. She parked the car on a side street then got out and began her initial trek through her new home. The streetlights were designed to look like gas lamps from the Victorian period, dotting the streets while giving off enough light for the folks who enjoyed a good nightly stroll. Once Monica found the main street, she felt at home; people were out either with others or by themselves, enjoying the night just like her. The two cafes were busy with patrons either sitting inside or people watching outside while Wenchang Books' front was wide open and well lit. Monica saw Miranda walking to and fro while helping customers yet she looked far from stressed or fatigued; she enjoyed her job knowing it was not a job, but her livelihood. Monica walked on, leaving her new place of employment behind and onward to the next visual delight.

Couples strolled arm in arm all around her and for a moment she felt lonely. Her last boyfriend five years ago proved to be quite a piece of work; after getting off work late one night, he proceeded to get very drunk, take her car keys and drive around in her car before running it straight into the poles that held up a flight of stairs at her old apartment complex. Her car was totaled, but he survived with barely a scratch, a $500 fine and one night in jail. After that fiasco, she swore off men completely, wanting to spend more time in developing herself. Only problem was that she did the opposite; she squelched anything that looked to be remotely interesting inside of her and tried to fit in with the rest of the world, of which proved to be disastrous.

However, she thought as she strolled along, things seemed to be in the process of changing and for the better; her times of self denial of her creative side were over, giving way to a life filled with eccentric ways and likes. She was ready for it. Monica continued to walk down the street, taking in as much as possible with her eyes. The colours seemed to be too bright, too unreal for her to imagine and yet she walked among them while the townsfolk delved into this town with no shame or fear; it was a part of them after all so why hide it? She grinned to herself then hid it for a moment; she did not want people thinking she was crazy or off her rocker. Suddenly she stopped in mid stride in both walking and in thought: why would she want to hide her smiles? Everyone else was engaged in their own colourful lives and smiles were abundant. People here did not have a problem with her smiling. Satisfied, she grinned again and continued on her way till she reached Stingrays on the corner. She peered through the windows to stare at the small wooden tables in the restaurant with a minimal amount of light given by a single white candle on each table. Several single people were either eating their food, reading a book while waiting for their food, or talking to passersby at their own tables. She went in and was immediately greeted by a young man who led the way to a table, produced a menu for her to look over then dashed off to the next new patron.

Monica looked over the menu's choices and began to salivate; everything sounded good to her since she had not eaten all day. The menu held an array of choices minimally priced, followed by a wine list and a dessert listing that was to die for.

"I highly recommend the chicken paprika unless if you don't like poultry or paprika." Monica lowered her menu to reveal Dr. Algren standing at her table with a smirk on his face. "I try to come here at least once a week; the food's just that good."

"Uh, thanks," she stammered, "I wanted to treat myself to a good dinner tonight and my boss said this was the place to do it." She stared at him half wanting to invite him to her table and half wanting him to go to his own. She wanted the peace and serenity, but at the same time wanted to make new friends as well. Mabon seemed to be the kind of place where the norm was to not be the norm, a fact that Monica purely enjoyed. However, she still held onto her loner status that required her to shun people and alienate herself from the rest of the world. It was her protective wall that served as a defense mechanism when things got to be too hot or too weird. Benjamin stood at her table with expectant eyes; she could tell that he wanted to sit at her table, but was unsure if he could just make himself at home at her table or give her room. After all, they had just met today yet she had something that he wanted to get to know on a deeper level. He decided to take the plunge first and see if she would follow.

"Hey, do you mind if I sit with you? I don't really want to be alone tonight for dinner." He made as if to pull the chair from the table while his eyes still focused on her uncertain ones. She struggled inside between saying yes or no to his question, but the sudden light in her eyes gave him his answer.

"Sure, I would love it if you sat with me." Monica did everything she could from coming close to fainting in making that decision; she really wanted to be alone tonight, but knew that if she wanted to truly be a part of this town, she had to swallow her nervousness and take the plunge. Benjamin smiled as she pulled the chair out and sat down. He took the white cloth napkin from the table and placed it in his lap with fluidity, something she had never seen before in a man.

"So, aside from the chicken paprika, what else is good on the menu?" she asked in what seemed to be a logical opening to a possible conversation. She had to start somewhere.

"Hmmm, well, pretty much everything. I think I've tried it all and have had no complaints thus far. Are you allergic to anything?"

"No, not really, at least, I don't think so."

"Well, that settles that, then. Seriously though, try the chicken paprika. You won't be disappointed." At that moment, the waiter came up, talked to Benjamin for a bit (he was one of his students), then took their orders and walked off, leaving the two in silence. Monica fiddled with the napkin in her lap while her eyes focused on everything else, but Benjamin's face. The last time she had dinner with a man was her dad a month before he died. Benjamin, clearly amused and awed by her nervousness, stared right at her face and grinned. She was an attractive woman both inside and out. He wondered, however, if she knew that as well.

"So, how long will you be in Mabon?" he asked just as her eyes focused back on his. "You do realize, however, that once you move here, you're here for good? The townspeople tend to stay here until they become part of the winds that blow through the trees, or something along those lines."

"Well, I don't know how long I'll be here, but I do like it so far. It seems to be what I have been looking for all my life. A place where people can be themselves."

"The eccentricity pours out of Mabon like a waterfall, if you haven't figured that out yet. All of us are quirky in one way or another. Gina over at Siren's Court is an artist, sculptor and violinist, while Arabella, owner of Bergamot Tea, is our resident tealeaf reader and psychic. Have you met her yet?"

"No, not yet, but she seems interesting already."

"Oh yeah she is, but I'll let you make that determination. She moved to Mabon about six years ago after recovering from a serious mental breakdown. She lived in a mental institution for three years before finally channeling her frustrations and problems into growing herbs in their gardens. Soon, she was making homemade teas for the staff and showing signs of improvement. Anyway, go by Bergamot when you have a chance; it's on Changer Street, about five blocks from here. Just follow your nose and you'll find it soon enough."

"Thanks."

"Don't mention it. So anyway, that's her and then there's me. Aside from teaching, I am also a writer. Have one book already out and currently working on my second one." He paused for a moment. "If you'd like, I'd like to give you a copy of my work. Are you a reader?" He slapped his forehead with his hand. "Duh! You'd have to be, seeing as how you're working at Wenchang. Sorry for the dumb question."

"Hey no worries and to answer it; books have been my friends for most of my life. I don't know where I would be without them. Yes, I would be more than delighted to have a copy of your book."

"Cool!" Just then, their food arrived and soon the conversation gave way to eating. From the first bite of her dinner, Monica knew Benjamin was right. The chicken paprika was delicious.

"So, I understand you have a twin sister," she said while they sipped on their coffees after dinner. Stingrays had nearly cleared out except for the two of them and one other couple, but they did not notice anything; after dinner they struck up conversation on different subjects and neither one wanted to go home just yet.

Benjamin took a small sip then gently placed the cup on the saucer without making a sound while his blank face stared at her. Monica, for a moment, thought she had made a mistake in talking about her until Benjamin replied.

"Yes, her name is Ophelia. She's kind of like me; we both like to read voraciously, we are both quite eccentric, and we are both a bit on the shy side."

"Gina told me that she's like a funky librarian."

Benjamin laughed. "Yeah, that's her, all right. She even dresses like one. Hey, if that's what she likes, then who am I to complain or change her ways? She's being herself and that makes me happy."

"You truly do care for her. So, when do I get to meet her?"

"Oh, she drops by your bookstore from time to time. I'll tell her to stop by to make herself known to you."

"Great!" Monica took another sip of her lukewarm coffee then took a look at her watch. Benjamin caught the act and said, "Am I keeping you?"

"No, not at all," she replied while blushing, "but I do need to get back to my place and clean up some more. Thank goodness I don't start work tomorrow."

"Well hey, do you mind if I come over and help you out some? My class is not until 11am tomorrow and I am a bit of a night owl . . ." Monica, although touched by the act of kindness, wanted to be alone tonight. However, the almost pleading look in his eyes made it hard for the words to come out of her mouth. She sighed inwardly then said, "Sure, why not?"

Benjamin grunted as he picked up one of her book filled boxes while Monica opened up a box in her kitchen and took out her purple and black coloured coffee maker and matching toaster. Since he so readily volunteered to assist her, she made sure he worked his ass off just to see him sweat and possibly regret his decision. However, he did not complain and cleaned out every box he touched, opening far many more than Monica, in addition to unloading the couch, loveseat, bed set and a couple of tables. They stopped around midnight even though Benjamin opened two more boxes while she sat on the floor. Several minutes later, Benjamin joined her and stretched his arms.

"Wow, now I'll know why I'll feel so crappy tomorrow morning," he said with a tired grin. "I hope I helped out somewhat."

"You did and thanks. Can I get you something to drink?"

"Nah, I'm good." Monica got up and made her way into the kitchen to grab a cold bottle of water. She turned around and saw Benjamin standing at the doorway with a grin on his face. Monica, not knowing what to do, grinned back. "So," he said as he leaned against the doorframe, "is there anything else I can help you with tonight? Like I said, I tend to be a night owl and my class is not until 11am. I really don't mind helping with any other heavy stuff you might have put off."

"Actually, I'm good with everything; you helped knock out some parts of unpacking that I was not looking forward to. I really appreciate your help; let me take you out to dinner or lunch sometime this week, okay? It's the least I can do."

"I'll take you up on it. How about if I stop by the store later this week and we'll take it from there?"

"Sounds good to me." Monica walked by him and into the living room towards the front door. Benjamin watched her movements and picked up immediately that she was ready for him to leave. However, he planned to go against her mental wishes and instead stick around for a bit, just to watch her squirm and because he was intrigued by her. Ever since they met earlier that day, he could think of nothing else, but her; something about her triggered a desire to know more about her and her reasons for moving to Mabon. He wanted to know if perhaps her reasons were the same as his. He walked back into the living room and sat down on the floor, causing Monica to frown somewhat then quickly recover into a tired smile. She joined him on the floor with distance between them; she did not want to give him any ideas of further actions just because of her sitting next to him. At this point, she wanted to make new friends and nothing more; relationships were out of the question. She wanted to spend more time with herself, discovering what made her tick.

"So, why did you come here?" asked Benjamin, wanting to get right to the point. "Was it because of a breakup, did you lose your job, or was it something deeper than that?" Monica visibly tensed so Benjamin smiled, trying to let her know that whatever she had inside of her, it was okay to bring it out into the open. She had nothing to worry about. Monica, however, felt quite the opposite; at that point, she was not really in a mood to reveal her past to a man she just met. He was a stranger, albeit friendly one, but still a stranger to her.

Her eyes focused on his slightly eager ones and said in a calm voice, "Perhaps another time. Too tired right now." Benjamin's face fell a bit in disappointment so she quickly added, "It's been a long day. I would love to tell you my reasons for coming here, but just not now. Maybe during our lunch or dinner?"

"Sure, I would love that," he said brightening up once more. The two got up from the floor and walked to the front door. Monica opened it for him, revealing the night sky that held a cool whisper of Autumn's arrival to the town.

"Well, thanks again," she said, "and hopefully tomorrow will be a good day for you." Benjamin gave her a hug that lasted longer than necessary then said as he pulled back, "It is tomorrow." He leaned over and kissed her cheek then turned and walked to his car and drove off, leaving Monica still standing by the open door, clearly intrigued by her visitor. A hand went up to her cheek and she rubbed it tenderly, not realizing her actions. She could still feel his lips, causing a tingling sensation on her cheek.

Chapter Two

The day came with oolong tea and sunlight filtering through cotton ball clouds that kept Monica company as she walked to her first day of work at the bookstore. Two nights later after spending time with Benjamin, she was ready to begin her new job. After seeing what her new boss wore at the bookstore the other night, she felt that she could relax and even experiment on some styles she had wanted to wear in the past, but did not have the courage to do so. Even though Miranda told her to begin working after a week, Monica wanted to begin as soon as possible.

When the kettle announced itself with a loud whistle, Monica emerged from her bedroom dressed in a long black shirt, black boots that reached her calves, a bright green short sleeve button down shirt that accentuated her figure, blue and green dangle earrings and a black headband to finish out the look. Monica checked herself in the full-length mirror and smiled as she walked into the kitchen to prepare her tea.

Ten minutes later, she walked down her street, enjoying the slightly cool yet sunny day while taking the occasional sip from her travel mug. The people she encountered sat on the front porch of their homes, walked for leisure and exercise or painted while sitting on the sidewalks. One slender young man dressed in torn jeans, grey shirt, and brown sandals sat cross legged on a street corner, furiously drawing in a beaten up sketchpad with a charcoal stick while other sticks of varying lengths sat next to him. Monica walked by, trying to not to look at his work and yet look at the same time, then stopped all together and stood behind him, fascinated by his bold strokes and lighting-like moves. What initially looked like chaotic lines and blots was instead a young woman dressed in a kimono gazing up at the sun while holding an umbrella. Her eyes tried to follow his stained fingers, but soon gave up and enjoyed watching him.

Suddenly, he stopped and turned around to face his new admirer. He smiled, showing all of his bright white teeth and said, "Greetings, fellow traveler! How long have you been on the ride?"

"Ride?' asked Monica with a note of questioning in her voice.

"Ride; you know, the whole thing we call Life is actually a ride. The ride we take over and over again, whether we like it or not. The purpose of the ride is to learn what you can, appreciate what you can, and love without restraint. Our rides are special to each and every one of us which is why we must be more aware of such ride."

"Ah, I think I see," said Monica in a slow voice, still not too sure of what he was talking about. "I have been on this ride for 35 years."

"Lovely, fellow traveler! My own ride has lasted some 30 years, but I lost count along the way." He scratched his bald head with charcoal stained fingers in a momentary state of a lost thought then continued, "No matter, I am still on the same path so I know I am okay." He glanced at his picture then at Monica's inquisitive face and asked, "Do you like my work, fellow traveler?"

"I do, actually. It's beautiful."

"Then take it as my gift to you," he said as he ripped out the page from his book and handed it to her. Monica took the gift as though it was the first gift she had ever received in her life.

"Thank you, fellow traveler," she said in his 'language', "and now I must be off to work. Take care of yourself and keep to your ride."

"I plan to do such and the same to you as well!" The artist then turned back to his book and immediately began drawing a new picture, instantly forgetting the meeting that took place only seconds ago. Monica stared at him for a moment then continued on her way to work with new artwork in hand. As she turned the corner, she glanced one more time at the artist then frowned; he had disappeared as though he was never there. She looked down at her hand and saw the work. Perhaps his ride made a turn he did not expect, she thought as she walked on.

Monica caught sight of Miranda walking back and forth through the bookstore while filling up empty spots on the bookshelves with multiple copies of titles. When she walked in, Miranda stopped in mid stride and broke into a wide smile.

"Monica!" she said as she placed her latest stack in one of the reading chairs, "Good to see you here! Ready to begin your employment?"

"Yep, sure am. I've gotten most of the moving process taken care of. Besides, you looked like you needed help the other night and I felt bad for not helping."

Miranda held up a hand in protest. "Dearie, this is my life and my love. I love it when people buy books from me, even when it gets to be too much. But still, I'm glad to see you. Ah, what's that you're drinking?"

"Oh, just a cup of oolong, one of my favourite teas." She finished off her mug, placed her art piece on a side shelf, and sighed with satisfaction, giving Miranda a reason to smirk.

"What's so funny?" asked Monica with a ghost of a smile on her face.

"Oh nothing, it's just that you remind me of me whenever I have a cup of tea. I find it to be so soothing during any time of the day so I keep a stash of at least twenty different kinds in the storeroom." Miranda led her to the back and opened the door, revealing a large and comforting room that contained an oatmeal coloured loveseat, two five shelf bookshelves filled to the brim with books and magazines, several pantry drawers, a small table with several chairs and a small stove and refrigerator. Monica walked over to the pantry and opened one of the doors then whistled in appreciation; tea of every kind sat in boxes, tins and bags on the two shelves.

"I have several kinds of oolong too; picked them up when I was last in China."

"When did you go to China?" asked Monica as she reached for a bag labeled Dragon Pearl Jasmine and opened the bag to sniff its contents. Instantly, the image of jasmine flowers and *camellia sinensis* being picked by slender and expert hands along a hidden valley lost by time appeared in her mind. She could feel the sun beaming down from the impossibly blue sky on her head, but she did not pay attention to it, for she was completely lost in the moment. She looked down and saw her hands picking the tea leaves and flowers side by side, not knowing how she got there or really caring at that point. She felt the texture of what she picked and placed in her bags that slung over her shoulder. Her hands picked with dexterity and care, not missing one leaf or flower. The scents permeated her senses, giving her a heady feeling. She blinked once and found herself back in the storeroom. She blinked again and looked down at the bag.

"Are you all right? You look a little flushed." Miranda came over to her and placed a hand on her shoulder. " Do you need to sit down for a moment?"

"Er, no, I'm fine. It's just that, well, never mind."

"What, dearie? Tell me what's on your mind."

"Well, don't laugh, but I could have sworn that I was in some valley picking the tea leaves and jasmine flowers for this blend, like somehow I had transported to China and became a tea picker. Crazy, huh?" Monica laughed then stopped when she realized that Mirada was not sharing her mirth.

"Dearie," she said as she took the bag from her, "happens all the time, especially with that blend. Funniest thing, but I'm used to it by now. Every so often I like to take a quick sniff just to go to 'that place'. I keep telling myself that a hidden sect of Buddhist monks who had found Shangri-La made the tea and placed the magic from that city into their teas. Thank the gods for that." Miranda placed the bag back on the pantry and walked out of the room, leaving Monica to wonder about her new boss.

Townsfolk, students from Janus College and tourists stopped in the bookstore in a steady stream, giving Monica and Miranda more than enough in the way of a "good" day. Monica stocked the shelves and helped out customers who had questions, but she did not hover over anyone; the tone of the place was of relaxation with a book that would hopefully become a good and trusted friend to the customer who picked it up. Miranda sat at the cash register, happy to ring up purchases and help out with any questions that Monica could not answer on her own. Monica was in her element at the bookstore, smiling more than she had ever done so in quite some time. Many of the regular customers introduced themselves to Monica, making her feel right at home. One woman even offered Monica freshly made blueberry muffins still hot from her oven as a welcoming present.

Around 1pm, Miranda went into the backroom to prepare a pot of mandarin orange green tea for the both of them since the traffic slowed down while Monica thumbed through an art magazine as she sat by the cash register. Suddenly, the front door chimes rang as a young woman walked into the bookstore. She wore a long short sleeved and slender black dress with white flower print, clunky black Mary Jane shoes, silver hoop earrings, and her dark brown hair was pulled back into a thick bun. Monica looked up and saw the newcomer and smiled as she got off her stool.

"Hi, welcome to Wenchang Books, can I help you with anything?" The much taller woman walked up to Monica and smiled faintly while pushing her glasses up on her nose just as Miranda came from the storeroom.

"Hey Ophelia, good to see you!" she said as Monica blushed in embarrassment and grinned. "That book you ordered is finally in. I'll be right back."

"Thank you, Miranda," she replied in a soft, but strong voice as Miranda walked back to the storeroom, leaving Monica with her. "You must be Monica, the new assistant manager here. I am Ophelia Algren." She extended a slender hand to Monica and she shook it; Monica noticed that her skin was extremely soft. "My brother told me all about you." Her black frame glasses slipped down again and she pushed them back up.

"It's such a pleasure meeting you too," replied Monica. "He told me you would be coming over sometime. I take it you're a regular here."

"I spend more time among books than people. Books have been my friends for as long as I can remember." Monica wished she could spend the rest of the day talking to her about books and her other passions if she had any; she felt an instant bond with her.

"You sound just like me; that's one of the reasons why I moved here."

"It is good to meet a fellow bibliophile in Mabon. Of course, there are many in this town, as to be expected, but still it is nice to meet new ones." Ophelia beamed a smile at Monica just as Miranda came back out with book in hand. She had several dust bunnies on her shoulders, but she paid them no attention.

"Well, here ya go, dearie! Took me forever to find it, but I found it!" She handed the small red hardback to Ophelia and said, "Getting to know my new assistant? So far, she's done one hell of a job, plus she's 'tried' the dragon pearl," causing Ophelia to chuckle.

"Oh my, I am sure it probably freaked you out, yes? When I had my first cup, I too went to that place. Simply amazing, do you not agree?" Monica nodded mutely while cursing inwardly at her idiotic behaviour while Miranda laughed.

"Yeah, it almost knocked her off her feet, but I'm sure she'll get used to it in time. I can tell you're made of strong stuff," she said as she patted Monica on the arm. Monica walked back to the storeroom to pick up her cup of tea, leaving the two other women in the store.

"I like her," said Ophelia in a thoughtful tone. "I like her a lot."

"So what does Benjamin think of her? He must think of her pretty highly if he told you about her."

"Only that she intrigued him from their first conversation and he kissed her on the cheek the other night at her apartment."

"Oho, she didn't tell me about that," beamed Miranda. "I'll wring the truth from her yet."

"Well, I am sure she will tell you in time, Miranda." Ophelia glanced at her watch. "I am supposed to be at the college now. Tell Monica I look forward to talking to her at another time and that Benjamin will be coming by later for Possible Date #2 plans."

"I will. Take care of yourself and see you soon, okay dearie?" Ophelia held her newly acquired book close to her chest and walked out of the store just as Monica came from the storeroom with two blue and white Chinese cups filled with tea. She handed one to Miranda then took a small sip from her own, savouring the delicate tastes that rolled down her tongue and into her system.

"Oh, did I miss Ophelia?" she asked while blowing on her tea. "I really wanted to talk to her more. She seems-"

"Different, eccentric, quiet, artistic, did I leave anything out?" joked Miranda. "Yeah, she liked you too. Wanted to let you know that her brother will be by shortly to talk about *Possible Date #2*?" Monica rolled her eyes in mock disgust to Miranda's comment. "So, were you going to tell me about your Possible Date #1 with Dr. Algren, or were you going to keep me in eternal suspense?"

"Oh look, I need to help that customer over there."

"Nice try; we're the only two people in here, plus we have two wonderful cups of mandarin orange green tea with a full pot in the back. Spill it."

"What's there to say? I went to Stingrays, like you recommended, and he saw me there. He asked if he could share my table, to which I said sure. We talked for a good bit then he asked if he could help me with moving in. I wasn't sure at first, but I eventually said yes."

"Oho, really now! So, what happened then?"

"He helped me unload some boxes then we sat and talked a bit longer. After a while I got sleepy so I politely told him good night. He wants to go out again and in fact," said Monica while checking her watch, "he should be here sometime this week."

"Yeah, Ophelia said he was coming by later today to talk to you about Possible Date #2. So?! Was that it?"

"Well . . . he did kiss me on the cheek before leaving. Nothing more than that." She took another sip of tea that had cooled somewhat. "I like him, but I'm not ready for anything serious or even remotely serious. Right now, I want to enjoy my life and get to know my creative side, if I even have one."

"You do dearie or else you wouldn't have come here. Trust me on that. You may have had flashes of it, but it is most certainly there." Miranda took a sip of her tea then said, "Ophelia likes you, dearie, just from that one conversation. That's a good thing, especially if you were possibly considering dating Benjamin."

"Are they that close?"

Miranda stared into her teacup, not saying anything for a moment, then replied, "Yes, they are. They are twins after all, dearie. I think Benjamin was born first and then she came seconds later. In any case, if you impress one, the other will be just as impressed. It's like they share one brain or something. Kinda spooky at times."

"There's no weird kinky incest thing going on between them, is there?"

"Monica!"

"Hey, I had to ask since you said they were so close and all. . . . so, are they?"

"Monica! Both are single and no, they are not into each other, to answer your question. Ophelia is very happy being single, but

Benjamin is looking for someone, as I have heard through the grapevine."

"So, has he shown any form of interest in anyone here yet?"

"Aside from you, no. He pretty much knows everyone here and in some weird way, we are all friends or work colleagues or students of his."

"So I'm fresh meat, then?" Monica's response made Miranda sigh with slight frustration. She set her cup on the counter and looked at her assistant square in the eye with a slight smirk on her face.

"Okay, so are you interested in him or not? If not, then this conversation needs to end right now and we can get back to work. Still be in a good mood, but no more talk about Benjamin. If you are, then I will tell you everything you need to know about the eccentric yet really nice lit professor. So, are you interested in him or not?"

When Benjamin showed up later, both Monica and Miranda were once again up to their elbows in customers. The wave came back while they discussed the very man that walked through their door. He spotted Monica talking to a customer and patiently waited for her to finish. When she did, he caught her eye and she waved then walked over to him.

"Hey, how are you?"

"I guess I'm still recovering from when I helped you the other day. Guess my body's not used to that kind of labour."

"Sorry to hear that."

"No worries on that; it's simply amazing what can be accomplished with several cups of coffee and a honey bun. But I digress: it looks as though you've gotten quite acclimated to working here, huh?"

"Yeah; I feel right at home," she replied. "Oh yes, Ophelia came by earlier today. Finally got to meet her. I like her just from the one conversation I had with her." Miranda, while walking towards their general direction, looked up from her notepad, saw the two of them chatting away and then walked to a different location without stopping.

"Glad you guys finally met. So, are you interested in perhaps dinner again tonight, provided that I don't crash your party of one?"

Monica laughed. "I would love it." She looked for Miranda in the store and found her writing in her journal while walking around. "Miranda, when do we close up?" she asked.

"Go ahead and go, dearie. I'll be fine for the rest of the day."

"Are you sure?" Miranda cut her a look that meant *go out and have fun with him, you idiot*! Instead, she replied, "Oh yes, I'll be fine. See you tomorrow at 10." Benjamin walked to the front door and held it open for Monica. As she walked through, she murmured, "Wow, interesting."

"What is?" asked Benjamin after he joined her and the two walked down the street. He casually brushed his hand against hers to "accidentally" hold it, but she held her hands behind her back, destroying any attempts.

"Interesting that you held the door for me. Never had that happen before. For some reason, I thought chivalry was dead."

"It isn't, as far as I am concerned. I wish more men were like that, but unfortunately I am in the minority in that school of thought. Men today, I fear, think that women should be objects to treat any way they deem fit. Treating women like pieces of meat is neither hot nor trendy; it's just downright wrong."

"I'm so glad to hear you say that," Monica replied with a note of relief in her voice. "But the way, I hate to ask you this, but how old are you?"

"Why? Do I sound like I should be your father or something along those lines?"

"No, but I am curious. I like to know more about people who intrigue me." Benjamin stopped walking and stood in front of her, causing her to almost trip over her feet.

"Ah, so I intrigue you, then?" he said with eyes that suddenly looked older than the rest of him. Monica straightened herself up and stared at him, wondering if perhaps she was wrong for showing a modicum of interest towards him. She wanted to enjoy herself and her new life, but at the same time she desired friendship, especially from someone who understood what it was like to be different. She placed her hands on her hips and said in an almost defiant tone, "Yes, you do intrigue me. Now, how old are you?"

"I'm 45 years of age. I have never been married nor do I have any children out of wedlock. I do not smoke cigarettes and the last time I had anything alcoholic to drink was about three weeks ago. I don't do drugs although I did try pot once and it made me so sick that I swore I would never do it again. I did try being a vegetarian for about a month before I began missing hamburgers. Is this enough for you or do you need more?" He placed his hands on his hips, mimicking her, and smiled like the Cheshire Cat. "Have I passed your examinations, Ms. Burton? Can we go to dinner now so I can do what you're doing to me right back at you? Oh yes, I am taking you out on a date, in case if you did not know. I like you, Ms. Burton, I like you very much. I want to get to know you better and I hope you want to get to know me better aside from knowing my age." Monica stared at him in mute shock as he took her hand in his and continued their walk down the street.

He led them to Chrysanthemums, the Chinese restaurant in town. When they reached the front door, Monica smelled egg drop soup and garlic wafting in the breeze. The restaurant's storefront was red with jade symbols dangling from red ropes across the front, while the front door was painted a bright, but not garish red. Benjamin opened the door, allowing Monica to walk in first with him behind her. She blinked several times just to make sure what she saw was real: there were several small tables with red silk tablecloths on them along with small painted bowls that held water and a small flower. Chinese calligraphy written in thick black paint covered the walls in a tasteful manner that also made the place seem bigger on the inside. Benjamin led them to an empty table and pulled out one of the chairs for her to sit in then made his place on the other side. Monica's eyes still wandered around the restaurant, trying to take in as much as possible. Benjamin chuckled at her tourist-like behaviour as the waiter came up with two menus and handed one to both of them. He walked off with an order for a pot of oolong tea just as Benjamin said, "So, I take it I chose well for our second unofficial date?"

"You chose well and thank you. How long has this place been here?"

"As long as I can remember; it was here when Ophelia and I moved here. I try to come here as much as possible, more so than Stingrays. Don't get me wrong; I like Stingrays, but this place feels absolutely delightful." Monica stared at her dinner guest carefully, her mind going a million miles a minute with questions that answered themselves before the questions completed in her mind. How could a guy like this be single? He was charming, intelligent, had a good personality, treated a woman like a woman; what was the catch? Monica stared at him so intensely that she did not realize she had stated her thoughts out loud to him. Benjamin's eyes grew wide with mock surprise then he laughed.

"Why do you think there is this terrible secret about me?" he asked. "Why are you looking for something bad to come out while we eat Chinese food?"

"Because you are too good to be true, that's all. I wonder why you are the way you are. I wonder why you are single-"

"Not for much longer, I hope."

Monica ignored that remark and continued. "I've dealt with men before who sounded like you and yet all they had on their mind was a good toss in bed and nothing more."

Now Benjamin looked truly offended. "I am sorry to hear that," he said just as the waiter returned with a steaming teapot and two blue and white teacups. Benjamin remained silent as the waiter placed the items on the table yet his eyes were focused on her. They opened their menus and placed their order and waited until the waiter left to resume their conversation.

"I want you to know that I am completely serious now. In any case, no, I am not trying to get you into bed. No, this is not a game; I am tired of people playing stupid mind games on others, leading to a general mistrust of others and of themselves. I have been hurt before, Monica, and believe me, it took all I had to pull myself out of that depression."

"What happened?"

"My heart was broken by someone who claimed to love me, but all she wanted was someone to hurt, taunt and mentally destroy. She came very close to succeeding."

"Why did you allow such behaviour?"

"Because I did not know my worth."

"How long did you date her?"

"Four long years. Things got so bad that during one of our fights one night, she pulled out a handful of my rare books, threw them in a metal trashcan and set fire to them. She did that because I was not able to take her shopping; I had classes the next day and I was trying to prepare notes for them. I told her that I would take her out later, but she would not listen. She wanted to go out right then and there and because I placed my job before her that one time, she decided to teach me a lesson. That was when I took a good look at myself in the mirror and wondered just what in the hell I was doing."

"So what did you do?"

"I kicked her out of my home and threw her belongings out right after her. She was so stunned at my rash treatment of her; she called me several times a day, asking for forgiveness and that she loved me. Finally, she gave up and Ophelia and I moved here. I do not want that kind of person in my life; I no longer want to compromise my hobbies and likes. I want someone who is like me: an eccentric freak who enjoys and loves being different. We don't have to be twins like Ophelia and I, but I at least want to meet someone who is not afraid to be different." He poured tea into their cups, releasing the fragrance of the oolong into their senses. Monica closed her eyes and drifted along the perfumed waves, immersing herself into the sensation with no qualms. Benjamin took a deep sip while his eyes watched Monica's pure enjoyment of the tea, knowing at that moment that he was in love with her.

When the food arrived they ate in silence, both enjoying their dishes without the need to express it in words. Benjamin wanted to tell her more about his past so that she would understand his reasons for being the way he was now. Monica, while eating, thought about what he had told her thus far and tried to digest it. When they finished eating, Benjamin asked, "So, has anyone told you about Laurel yet?"

"Laurel, who's Laurel?" Monica scrunched her nose.

"Ah, I see they've not. Huh. Well, I will say this; look for her in two days, okay? She usually hangs out in the library. Yes, definitely check out the library in two days. I think that's a Tuesday."

"Okay, but who is she?"

"That I will leave up to you to find out. I hope you're a fan of poetry."

"Yeah, I love it, but what does that have to do with me meeting some woman named Laurel?" Benjamin smiled in response, a sign that the current conversation was over. Monica took a final small bite of her food then said while chewing slowly, "Thank you for tonight, Benjamin. This was rather sweet of you."

"Well, you're very welcome, but I was going to do this anyway." He checked his watch and sighed. "Well, it's about 7 right now. Where would you like dessert?"

"I don't think I've got room in me for dessert. Maybe some more tea?"

"Tea sounds good to me. We can visit Arabella's place or you can come back to my place. I have quite an assortment of teas, ready to be enjoyed and savoured. Don't worry; if you come back to my place, you'll be in good hands."

"Your place sounds good to me. Let's go." They called the waiter over for the bill and take-out boxes and soon they were out the door and walking once more. The night air held a chill while the sounds of the nightlife enveloped them. Monica's eyes took in everything around her as if she were leaving that very night.

"Take it in slowly, Monica," he said, startling her out of her sight gazing. "You live here now. This is your world." Monica visibly relaxed as they walked on, but her eyes kept darting here and there, wondering at the colours of the town. Everything was bright, almost too bright to take in. The air smelled of excitement, newly discovered passions and sensations beyond her understanding. The townsfolk seemed to have a connection to whatever it was and their lives reflected such connection. People seemed more at ease in Mabon without any worry of failed plans, crushed dreams, or hopes that went awry. There was something here and she wanted to know more about it; perhaps it could help her. She was so wrapped up in her thoughts that she did not realize Benjamin was talking to her until he actually placed a hand on her shoulder, bringing her to a halt. She blinked once slowly then looked up into his eyes and smiled for lack of anything else to say.

"Did you hear one word I just said?" he asked while smiling. "I take it by your grin, however, that you did not. No matter. I was telling you about my neighbourhood and the location of Janus. Would you like to take a walk through the campus for a moment?"

"That would be nice." They reached the corner of Elder and Oak Streets then made a right onto Oak and suddenly the landscaping changed from hip, urban and artistic to older bungalows and larger trees that lined either side of the street like silent guardians that forever watched and protected the humans. Benjamin led the way up the street to the college.

"That's my house on the right," he said while pointing to a bungalow with a Toyota Corolla parked in the driveway next to it. Several of the lights were on in the house, giving off a warm and comforting feeling that made Monica almost jealous. As they walked on, the streetlights turned on all at once, illuminating their way towards the college. They walked in silence, both enjoying the night for different reasons. Monica enjoyed the night because it allowed her to think clearly regarding her plans for a future in the town. She had no idea as to the length of her stay; all she knew was that she was here with a clean slate. She had only been here several days and already it felt like home, more so than her last place of residence.

Benjamin enjoyed the night for a completely different reason; he enjoyed it because it gave him a chance to actually see Monica without any outside interference. She was a natural beauty, one who did not need any superficial trappings or materialistic influences to define who she was and what she was all about. She hid behind a self-created wall, but already he could see cracks, a sign that she was breaking free of what she used to be into what she needed to be. He took a deep breath and caught the scent of jasmine, hibiscus and watercolour paint. In short, he picked up Monica's inner scent. He smiled; she truly belonged here and yet she still not know why. He knew Mabon drew her here for a certain reason; why else would she be here? Why else would he take such an interest in her? She was made of more than blood, bones and skin. She was special, just like everyone else.

They soon reached the college. Benjamin took Monica's hand again and led her through the tree-lined area that had gaslight lamps along the pathways, revealing stone statues on either side.

"Most of the statues you see are of Roman gods; there's Apollo to your right," he said while pointing, "and Neptune along with

Saturn over there." Monica gave each marble statue her full attention; how cool was it that a college had Roman deity statues on their campus? As Benjamin showed her other statues, she tried to remember her two years of high school Latin and failed miserably yet it was still fun. The college kept up with the maintenance of the statues and it showed; each statue seemed to glow with a soft white light that added to the night's natural lights. Benjamin then led her to a smaller, but still impressive statue of a bearded man that stood away from the other statues. They stopped in front of it and Benjamin took a breath.

"This is Silvanus, Roman spirit of woods and fields," he said after exhaling. Although it was smaller than the rest, it definitely stood out; at its feet lay several bunches of wildflowers, cards, tarot cards and other items. Some of the items looked like they had been there for quite some time while others were new.

"Why have people left these items at his feet?" asked Monica.

"Because Silvanus represents the magic of the woods and forests around Mabon. People around here believe in such things and they sometimes feel the need to give small tokens in exchange for enjoying said magic. However, there are always other ways." Before Monica could ask another question, he whisked her off to enjoy the rest of the campus. People were out and about, adding to the general energy of the air that moved on its own. Monica had a secret obsession with colleges and universities; these were the places that truly shaped a person into something formidable for the world when they finally left the hallowed halls. For a time, she used to collect pens and coffee mugs from different universities then soon gave it up because her obsession led to cluttered knickknacks that were soon forgotten. Perhaps it was time to renew the interest with Janus, she thought while grinning.

"I miss being in school," she said as they passed by a small group of students sitting on the steps of the History Department building. They were deep in a discussion concerning Napoleon and why Waterloo was doomed from the start. "My degree was pre-law, but it turned out to be a waste."

"Oh, why? Did you not enjoy practicing law?"

"Actually, I never practiced, but became a paralegal instead. A paralegal, I discovered, is nothing more than a glorified secretary who does all the work while the lawyer gets the credit and the bigger salary. I worked for one law firm and found out within a week that the two attorneys I worked for did not appreciate the fact that their paralegal was smarter than both of them. After six months of working there, I was called in to the office of one of the senior attorneys, who informed me that my services were no longer needed. The two attorneys I worked for were not even in the office during the time of my dismissal."

"That's just messed up. So, what did you do for a job?"

"Did what I knew I could do: went back to working in a bookstore until I landed another corporate job. There's just something about a bookstore that excites me. None of my past relationships were into reading books at all."

"Well, I'll have you know that I adore reading; so much so that I am an actual teacher of Literature!" Monica stopped walking and stared at him with a mock frown while his eyes opened wide in mock innocence. "It's true! I wasn't sure if anyone had told you-" Monica punched him in the arm and walked on while laughing as Benjamin rubbed his now slightly tender shoulder and winced.

"Very funny, *Doctor* Algren," she said. "And yes, I was already informed of your employment. Well, now that we have that out of the way, why don't you show me around your hallowed halls of higher learning?" She batted her eyes at him and he grinned while taking her hand again in his.

"Very droll, Ms. Burton. Now, over there is the English Department." He pointed to a small two-story brick building covered in ivy on her left. A light was on in one of the rooms on the second floor. Benjamin cursed under his breath. "I forgot to turn my light off in my office. Would you mind if we go there for a moment? I can't stand leaving lights on." Monica shrugged yes then the two made a sharp left. Students and other college folk milled around in the night air, clearly enjoying themselves in the comforting cool breezes. When they reached the building, Monica noticed three male students hanging around the steps. When they saw Dr. Algren they walked towards him with notebooks in their hands.

"Dr. Algren, Dr. Algren!" yelled one of the students, a tall lanky young black man with an immense green backpack on his back. He waved his small notebook in the air while grinning crookedly. "Dr. Algren, I'm so glad you came back to campus tonight. We've been talking about your lecture the other day? Regarding Thackeray's Vanity Fair?"

"Yes, Joseph?"

"Well, it's about Becky Sharp, sir," said the second student in the group, an older and shorter white gentleman. "We finished reading it after class and well, we just don't agree with you with regards to her acclaimed status within society. I mean, you're right on several points, but-"

Benjamin held up a hand, silencing him immediately. "Gentlemen," he said softly, "as you've noticed, I am with a guest. A date, in fact." Now, for the first time, the three students glanced next to him and saw Monica, who grinned and waved at them. "I know this is a terribly important subject for you, and I would love to dive right in as I normally do, but can it wait until later? Can you hold off slicing and dicing me for a while?"

"Sure, Dr. Algren."

"Yep, you got it."

"Of course."

"Good," he said as he took Monica's hand again and led her inside, leaving the students who suddenly lost their energy fueled debating streak. As they walked down the main hall, Monica took note of the various framed photos and art pieces that hung on the walls. "So much talent," she said, "and yet the randomness of it all seems to work here."

"It does, doesn't it? I was just thinking that the other day while walking to my office. You have a good eye for art, Monica." He stopped her in front of a watercolour painting of a woman wearing a wine coloured short sleeved dress and seated by an open window that looked out to a garden. The woman's face was hidden, but the tight bun revealed enough to her.

"That's Ophelia, right?" she asked. "When did you do the piece?"

"About a year ago. I was in a watercolour mood for a month and that was all I used when I wanted to paint something. She, at the time, was in a Dickens mood and wanted to dress like his female characters, or at least try to. In any case, I caught her staring outside of her window at home one Sunday morning so I quickly set up shop and painted her as fast as possible. Of course, I found out later that she had hoped I would have painted her and so kept unnaturally still in the hopes that the Watercolour Muse would descend upon me and take over my body."

"You and Ophelia are rather close," she said as they resumed walking. "I know you guys are twins, right? How does that feel to you?"

"Like a part of me was taken from my body when I was a baby and used to create her. We used to finish each other's sentences when we were younger and even created a language for the two of us when we wanted to speak in code in front of our parents." They reached the stairs and went up with Benjamin leading the way. Monica wanted to know more about the eccentric twins, but felt that it was wrong to delve in too deeply, fearing that she might excavate some hidden family secret buried for generations.

When they reached his office, Benjamin unlocked the door and let them in then closed the door after her. His office was exactly as Monica had pictured it; several five tiered shelves packed to the gills with books, pamphlets, yellowing documents, and old plants that should have been thrown out years ago took up most of the room, while his wooden desk free of clutter or debris seemed to be out of place there. He had two framed art nouveau posters on the walls plus a strand of dark wooden Buddhist prayer beads hung from a thumbtack on the right. Monica's eyes found the beads and walked over to them while Benjamin rummaged through his desk. She picked up the beads and instantly the scent of rosewood wafted through her nose. She ran her hands along the beads, her fingers trying to touch them as if each one was different than the rest.

"I picked those up several years ago when I went to Boston for a book convention," said Benjamin right behind her. He was ready to go, but stopped when he saw Monica touching his beads.

"Do you ever use them?"

"Only when I am at my worst, which thankfully does not happen too often. No, I love to show them off, but I need to use them more. They really do help calm the mind when it has become cluttered with inane nonsense." Monica touched the beads once more then let herself out of the office with Benjamin following after turning off the lights.

The walk back to his house was quite different than the walk to the college; Monica, through some feat, decided to make an effort to talk to him. After all, she thought, he did take her out to dinner and invite her to his home for tea. She was no longer in the mood for tea, but wanted to spend more time with him. She wanted to trust again and it had to start with one person. After her last boyfriend, she placed herself behind a brick wall with no chance of any cracks. After moving to Mabon, however, she wanted a change that would hopefully begin with Benjamin.

"So, what do you like to do for fun?" asked Benjamin. He held her hand, refusing to let it go for any reason. He wanted to feel her at this moment with no expectations or planned out thoughts. He wanted to feel her for the first time, caught unawares and vulnerable to not only his emotions and thoughts, but hers as well.

"Me? Well, I read many books for a starter. I want to try my hand at other things, but I'm not sure as to the direction I should take. I've given it some thought, but I just want to make sure I don't screw up."

"There's no way you can, Monica. That's the beauty of being a creative person; you do what just comes to you without any planned thought. Sure, once the groundwork has been laid out a plan to formulate the rest of it is a good thing, but the start off is always the hardest to do. It's very hard especially when you've held yourself back for so long."

"I know that feeling all too well. I had thought about trying my hand at painting or making collages; I made a collage a year ago and showed it to my mother, who proclaimed that I was wasting my time and that I needed to put energy into scrapbooking."

"Scrapbooking? Seriously?"

"Yep. Anyway, she claimed that scrapbooking would last longer than the collage I had made. I, on the other hand, wanted to hear some form of, oh wow, that's really pretty, or, look at all those colours! Something, anything than telling me I needed to go into scrapbooking."

"So, what did you do?"

"I trashed the collage and never did it again."

"That's a shame. I think you might want to pick it up again."

"But, they're dumb and-"

"Is your mother here, Monica? Does she live with you?"

"Well . . . no."

"Then why are you still trying to mold your creativity into what others want? Have you asked yourself what you want? If you make collages on bulletin board paper, then do it! Promise me, though, that you'll frame them and hang them in your apartment, okay?"

"Uh, okay." Monica waited for the other shoe to drop with Benjamin; it still did not come. They finally reached his home and he let them in. The house was moderately decorated with many bookshelves bursting at the seams with documents, pamphlets, and of course, books. The furniture was modest in appearance and held tones of beige and white. No artwork adorned the walls except for one watercolour painting of a woman holding an umbrella outside. The umbrella hid her face, but Monica assumed it was Ophelia again.

"What kind of tea would you like?" asked Benjamin while walking to the kitchen. "I have many different kinds."

"Mind if I come in there and see what you've got?"

"Of course not. Be my guest." Monica walked in behind him and noticed the boxes sitting on the ledge above his sink. Every kind of tea imaginable from oolongs and greens to black, white, and even some red, or rooibos, from Africa sat on the ledge. Benjamin prepared the kettle and pulled out two mugs from another drawer then waited for her choice. After looking over the boxes twice, Monica finally chose a white tea mixed with plum. She handed the box to Benjamin who placed a bag in both their cups.

"That one is one of my favourites," he said as the kettle picked up heat. "You've got good taste." Several minutes later, the two sat on his couch, sipping gingerly at the hot fragrant tea. Monica detected each flavour in the aromatic steam and sighed wistfully.

"I used to hate tea," she said while trying to balance her hot mug between her hands. "I thought tea was for intellectuals only."

"You don't consider yourself to be an intellectual, then?"

"Well, back in the day, I didn't. Benjamin, I was one horrific wallflower, desperate for anyone to look at me yet not knowing my own worth in the world. I was a loner and I wanted it that way. Although I did and still do read a lot, I did not consider myself to be on the level of those who drank tea." She took another sip and continued. "I used to think a lot of things, ideas and thoughts that just don't make a lot of sense to me now."

"You feel as though you've learned your lesson, so to speak?"

"I feel as though I have finally grown up. No more nagging parents who were never satisfied with anything that I did and came down on me for every little mistake I made. No more working for a company that held no interest to me whatsoever and stifled my true self. No more holding back in what I want in life just because it might be different that what others expect."

"Sounds like you want a lot for yourself; something you've never had before, huh? Been there, done that. I swear, you sound just like me sometimes. Two eccentric peas in a pod, huh?" Benjamin chuckled then took a deep sip of his tea.

"So, where's Ophelia tonight?"

"Out with some friends probably. Don't really keep up with her; she's her own person and I respect that. She was one of the few people who helped pull me from my spiraling depression. She understood what it was like to not be able to be yourself and plus, we're twins. We feel things at the same time and understand one another on a level that most would and could not understand. She helped me and I was grateful for it."

"Good to know you can rely on her when things get rough," said Monica. "That's good that you have such a wonderful and supportive rock on your side."

"Trust me; I am grateful for her every day." He finished off his cup then got up to make another. "Do you need anything while I am up?"

"No, but thanks just the same." Monica took another sip of her tea and mused on what he had said earlier. It was an attempt at him trying to get closer to her, understanding just why he was the way he was and that hopefully, she could and would respect him for it.

Several minutes later, Benjamin came back with another steaming cup of tea in his hands. He sat on the floor, sitting next to Monica's legs, took a small sip then said in a low voice, "Am I presumably jumping the gun?"

"Jumping the gun for what?"

"In how I feel about you. Wanting to date you, knowing that it would make me very happy if you wanted to." He raised his eyes to glance at her for a moment then focused once again on his tea mug. "I have been lonely for quite some time."

"I find that hard to believe. Everyone seems to know you or of you; you and Ophelia seem to be quite popular with the people I have met thus far."

"True; we do make quite the pair here in Mabon. Everyone loves us for our eccentric ways, making us fit in quite nicely. However, due to the friendship status, plus the fact that I know just about everyone here, my dating life has been quite nil. There have been slight sparks every once in a while, only to turn out later that the woman was not interested in pursuing said relationship with said professor for whatever reason. I don't know; perhaps I'm just too 'out there' for some," he said while taking another sip of his tea.

"I don't think you're out there as others may claim. I find you to be quite normal, at least by my standards." She finished off her cup then placed it on the floor next to her. Right now, the last thing she needed to hear was a whining session from some guy with regards to his dating life. Although she was glad to spend time with a possible new friend, she did not count on having to become a counselor tonight. Soon, there was a lull in the conversation, giving Monica a chance to focus on her empty tea mug while rolling it around in her hands.

Benjamin noticed her shift in focus and said, "I'm sorry, would you like to go home now? I don't mind driving you there."

"Actually, yes I would love it if you could," she said, much to his surprise. She placed her mug on the coffee table then walked to the front door with him following close behind her. He was crushed; she obviously did not want to spend any more time with him than necessary. Once again, he had blown it with a woman that he really thought he had a shot at. He led them out to his car then soon drove off.

Monica stared out of window, watching the houses pass by like blurred paint. She felt sorry for Benjamin, but at the same time refused to get suckered into the 'bleeding heart guy' routine. She had her own life to live, ready for the new changes since she discarded the old life. She sighed heavily then noticed that Benjamin flinched at the sound. She closed her eyes in silent resignation and waited for when his car stopped at her place. Benjamin gripped the steering wheel tightly, frustrated at how tonight ended. He should have not talked so much about his past, especially to someone who was trying to move beyond her own.

When he heard her sigh, it was just one more nail in the proverbial coffin for him with regards to his dating life.

Soon, they arrived at her apartment complex and he pulled in the driveway in front of her place. When he turned off the car, he remained in his seat, still strapped in. He did not face her. Monica tugged on her seatbelt, making as if she was about to get out of the car, then stopped. Without turning to face him, she said, "I had a nice time tonight, Benjamin. Thank you."

"Sure." He still did not face her, but only tightened his grip on the steering wheel more. Monica sighed again and noticed that he flinched once more. "Look," he said in a slightly annoyed tone, "it's obvious to me that you want out of the car, right? So, why are you trying to be nice about it?"

"What are you talking about?"

Benjamin turned his frustrating eyes towards her. "Oh, come on, Monica! You've been sighing for the past five minutes now and even at my place! Just get out of my car, okay? Sorry to have been such a bother to you, but I really thought-"

"Thought that we would just hit it off? Good lord, I just got here and within the first couple of days, you pounced on me like a cat with a rubber mouse!" She refused to back down on this argument no matter what. "Sorry if I don't return your feelings, but I am new here, fresh with scars from my old home that I am trying to remove. I'm sorry that you can't find someone to spend your life with, but that woman is not me. You might want to stop telling people about your past; it's your past, but let it go. That's what I did with my own. I'm ready to move on with my new life, but for now, I want to do it alone, understand? Look, I'm sorry I don't feel the same way for you as you do for me, but that's Life." Monica unlocked her seatbelt and got out of the car. When she reached her door she heard, "You're right," from behind. She turned and saw Benjamin halfway out of his car. "I'm sorry if I came on too strong for you; you just got here and all I've been doing is trying to get you as my girlfriend."

"I appreciate the honesty," said Monica as she unlocked her door, "but I am still not interested in dating you."

"Fair enough. Can we be friends, then? I wouldn't mind that if you don't." Monica opened her front door and turned on the living room light then faced him and his pleading face and said, "Maybe," then shut the door and called it a night.

"So, I take it by your long face that tonight did not go well?" asked Ophelia as Benjamin walked into the living room and slumped onto the loveseat. She sat on the floor, eating chocolate covered strawberries with an opened book of poems by John Keats on her lap. Benjamin said nothing, but closed his eyes. "Oh dear, it really did not go well, then. Here," she said while lifting up her box to him, "have a strawberry. They make you feel better." Benjamin opened his eyes, looked at the strawberries, and then took one. He stared at it for a moment then popped the whole thing in his mouth and chewed noisily. "So, are you going to tell me just what happened or you going to torture me with endless silence?"

"Ophelia, sometimes-"

"I drive you nuts. I know, brother dear."

"It did not go well at all. She doesn't want to see me anymore." Ophelia sighed.

"Well now. Another strawberry?" Benjamin took another one and popped it in his mouth, not caring if he dribbled or not.

"I like her, very much. She reminds me of me."

Ophelia arched an eyebrow. "Does she now? That would be interesting, now wouldn't it?" Benjamin glared at his sister for a moment then relaxed his face.

"Stranger things have happened in our lives."

"True, but then again…." Benjamin took off his shoes and walked into his room, closing the door behind him. Ophelia watched him until he closed the door, then shrugged and ate another strawberry as she resumed her book. Strange indeed. She placed her book on the ground and walked to his door. She knocked once.

"What do you want?" he said behind the door.

"I think I am going out. Need anything?"

"No." Ophelia wanted to go inside and talk more to him, but knew that he would only crawl further into his shell. When he was ready, he would talk. She went into her room and began getting ready.

After getting out of her bath scented with chamomile bath salts, Monica dressed in her black yoga pants and one of her oversized shirts and relaxed on her couch while classical music played in the background. She wanted to forget this night had ever happened and yet she could not. Benjamin, although a nice guy, was just too much on a second date. She felt only a modicum of regret in being so rude to him, but people like that would not take the hint unless it were just short of brutal. He was nice, however, but not nice enough to make her want to go on another date with him. She stretched and yawned then got up to make a cup of chamomile tea to help her relax and have a good night's rest. It was the least she could do.

Ophelia stood in front of her full length mirror, turning this way and that, making sure that her clothes looked good for tonight. She wanted to go out and have some fun, blow off some steam and momentarily forget the world. After rummaging through her closet for some time, she finally decided on a long black skirt with clunky black shoes and her long sleeved purple sweater since there was a slight chill in the night air. Her hair was pulled back into her signature bun firmly against her head. She slipped on her black clip dangly earrings and finished applying her dark purple lipstick, checked her self one more time then left with a smile on her face. Her hangout of choice for the night was several blocks away, but she wanted to walk rather than take the car. She walked out of her room, took a long look at Benjamin's closed door and then walked out. She strolled down the sidewalk with her black messenger bag on her shoulder, enjoying the crisp Autumn night. Others were out as well with similar thoughts.

Soon, she reached Regina's, a bar and coffee shop that catered to the theatre and literary folk, and walked in. Immediately, several people greeted her with waves and smiles. She smiled back then walked over to an empty table and sat down. Soon, a young waitress dressed in all black with black shoulder length dreadlocks walked up to her with a large grin on her face.

"Hey there, sweetie," chimed the waitress, "good to see you. Something special going on tonight?"

"No, just wanted to get out of the house, plus I have not been here in a while." Ophelia reached in her bag and pulled out her black-rimmed glasses. "May I have a Cape Cod, please?"

"For you, anything." The waitress sauntered off, giving Ophelia a chance to people watch. It was a relatively quiet night, but there was a good crowd in the place. The sounds of laughter could be heard every so often, giving her a reason to smile. She loved coming here when everything else was closed; it gave her a chance to get out for a while and spend some time with friends or by herself. The local theatre troupe spent most of their time here when they were not rehearsing for their latest play or show. Ophelia was friends with several of them and even helped out from time to time with making costumes or helping with the stage decorations and sets. She felt at home in the theatre; she considered it one of her many homes.

Her waitress returned with the drink, placed it on the table then said in a singsong voice, "Don't worry about your tab tonight. That gentleman over there is paying for all of your drinks." She pointed to a man Ophelia had never seen before then walked off while humming a tuneless song. He was ruggedly good looking with short and spiky blonde hair and chiseled features while wearing jeans, hiking boots and a black sweater. He held up his drink in a toast to her and she did the same with a frozen smile on her face. As much as she appreciated the nice gesture, she wanted to spend her time alone. She took a sip of her drink and smiled; Oscar always did well when it came to making Cape Cods. She closed her eyes as she took another sip.

"Excuse me, may I sit down with you?" Ophelia opened her eyes and found her admirer standing in front of her with a cheery grin on his face. "You looked like you needed some company."

"I appreciate your thoughtfulness," she said in her usual soft tone, "but tonight I am enjoying my time alone. Thank you, however, for being so kind as to pay for my Cape Cod."

"Not at all Mrs.-"

"It is Miss." He arched an eyebrow at the correction. Ophelia was not in the mood for such dramatics.

"Miss, you say? Well now, aren't I the lucky one?" He pulled out a chair at her table and sat down, much to Ophelia's inner protesting. "My name is Brad. Brad Tanker." He extended a hand towards her and she shook it in kind then released it quickly. "I'm an attorney in Silver Springs and was traveling back home today from a case in Eddings. People told me about this town so I figured I would spend the night here and get a good night's rest." He swirled his drink in his glass, took a sip and then said, "Looks like I made the right decision."

"Well, Mabon is a nice town full of many things to do for the curious traveler."

"Nice things . . . and nice people as well," he said then took a sip of his drink. "So tell me, Miss whomever you are; are you with anyone?"

"No, not at the moment. In fact, not at all and I like it that way."

"I'm sure you do, but for tonight, would you like a change in that? I promise to be a good Boy Scout." He saluted her then finished off his drink, causing her to groan inwardly. "So, how 'bout it?"

"I am sorry, but I want to be alone tonight. I appreciate your thoughtfulness on my behalf, but not tonight." She finished off her drink then stood up to leave.

"Whoa, whoa, slow down there, little lady," said Brad in a very bad cowboy drawl, "I ain't meanin' ta harm ya. At least let me buy you another drink."

"I am sorry, but no." At this point, several of the theatre troupes caught wind of this exchange and made as if to walk over to "assist" if necessary. Ophelia got up from the table, grabbed her bag and left, leaving a very stunned Brad at the table. She winked at her friends, letting them know it would be okay, then slipped out the door and into the night. Once outside, she breathed a sigh of relief then began her walk back home.

"Hey! No one does that to me!" Ophelia stopped in her tracks and for a moment, refused to turn around, but did so anyway, only to see Brad walking up to her with a determined stride. When he was a foot away from her, he huffed once in frustration then said, "Listen, sweetheart, I don't know what kind of guys you've dealt with before, but I'm the real deal! I don't have time for games-"

"So do not play them, then," she replied in a cool tone.

"I've known women like you before, ya know. They think that just because they've got some education that they're all badass and shit. But this is still a man's world and men ALWAYS get the upper hand!" He walked closer to her, grabbed her arm and pulled her to him. She could smell the whiskey on his breath and feel his very erect cock pressing against her skirt. This was just too much, even for her.

"So, why don't you do us both a favour and take me back to your place, huh? How 'bout it?" Ophelia closed her eyes briefly in tired resignation and then pushed him away with a force that surprised him. He stood there with a stunned look on his face as she now rose up to her full height that made her taller than him by three inches, crossed her arms then said, "It is because of people like you that I live in this town and not some other. I may be an educated person, but I am no piece of meat for you to dangle on your arm." Brad, obviously not taking the hint, walked back up to her, clearly apparent to get his way or else. Once he reached her, he grabbed her arm again then suddenly his face went slack. He stared at her with a puzzled expression on his face, took several steps away from her, then fell like a sack of potatoes while holding onto his crotch. She had given him a swift, but true kick with her three-inch clunky shoes that also had steel toes. Brad groaned like a kitten as he rocked back and forth on the ground while Ophelia walked off, now convinced that it was a good night after all.

The next day came with rain. Monica ran from her car to the bookstore, hoping that she would not look too much like a drowned rat when she got there. Thankfully, her boss was there with several towels ready to be administered to both her and customers. When she raced inside, Monica grabbed a towel and walked to the back room to dry off as much as possible. Thankfully, there were no customers so Monica took her time in toweling off. Ten minutes later, she heard the front door chime. She finished off her drying and made sure she looked decent then walked out to assist whomever had arrived. When she walked out, she saw Ophelia talking with Miranda and Ophelia was bone dry. When she saw Monica, she smiled and walked over to her.

"Hello, my dear," she said in her usual soft tone, "how are you?"
"Good, good, how are you?"

"Doing rather well." Ophelia seemed to tower over Monica today; perhaps it was her shoes, she thought then dismissed it. Ophelia turned to Miranda and said, "Mir, do you mind if we finish that up later? Come over to my house for scones after work, okay?"

"You got it!" Ophelia grinned then took Monica by the arm and led her to a corner of the store, giving Monica a slight reason to worry.

"Monica," began Ophelia, "Benjamin told me about last night. I must say that it did not go well. He was quite crushed."

"Yeah, well, not to talk about him, since he is your brother, but he seems a little too hasty for my taste. I hope you didn't come over here on his behalf, because I'm not interested in him that way."

"No, not at all. I came because Benjamin is my brother and I love him, plus I like you as well. As much as I would love something to occur between the two of you, I refuse to force anyone to do something that they are not completely interested in doing. I came here today as a friend, if that is okay with you."

"That's fine with me. I like you and your brother, but, like I told him last night, I really want to be alone for awhile."

"Of course; it is always good to have some solitude in one's life. It helps us balance emotions and feelings that are currently out of whack." Ophelia extended her hand to which Monica shook while thinking that she had quite a firm grip for an eccentric librarian. When they pulled their hands apart, Ophelia said, "Well, my dear, I must go. So many things to do in such little time. Thank you for talking to me today; I truly do appreciate it." Ophelia gave her a soft smile then turned and left the store into a now sunny day, leaving a slightly confused Monica.

"So, what was that all about?" asked Miranda while carrying a box of books to the front desk.

"To tell you the truth, I really don't know, but I'm not complaining about it. She seems so neat, so refined and yet strange."

"Strange, huh?" said Miranda with a wink. "Yeah, well, she used to get that a lot around here. People just couldn't handle her Ophelia-ness. Benjamin was like that in the beginning; people approached them cautiously and soon got used to their ways.

Although Benjamin has warmed up a lot since they moved here, Ophelia retained her charm and quiet grace."

"I can see why people would not know how to handle her; she is quite different. So, where are they from?"

"Well . . . . " Miranda appeared to not want to answer her question; she suddenly found a notebook more interesting than the conversation at hand. She began to thumb through it for a moment then looked back up at Monica with a strange look on her face. "I think that is something that only they can answer for you. It's their story to tell you, not mine."

"But, what's the big deal about them?"

"Like I said," replied Miranda with a slight edge in her voice, "they'll tell you when they are ready." Monica held up her hands in mock surrender then began to unpack several boxes in the back room that arrived yesterday, giving Miranda the full front of the store. She refused to ask Miranda any other questions regarding the twins; was it really so important, she thought as she removed several copies of a book entitled *Tales From a Goth Librarian* from a box. She stared at the book, liking the Goth chick with the very red lips on the cover who stared intently at a leather journal in her hands. Probably the author, she thought as the placed the copies on a small metal cart then continued with unloading. The job gave her time for her mind to drift off to subjects of her grocery list, places to visit in Mabon, and the twins. Miranda walked up to the cart and sorted through the books.

"Hey, did we get a Goth book in? We've been getting calls for that one; apparently, it just won another award, making it number two or something," she said while she sorted through them. When she found them, she grabbed all of the copies and placed them on a display stand.

"I've never heard of the author," said Monica. "Who is she?"

"Some Southern author who apparently has been doing well with this book; it's her first out of the publishing gate and every one on Amazon has been praising it." She handed a copy of Monica . "Here, check it out for yourself. I've already read it and I loved it, especially the story entitled *Silk*. You'll never look at red ribbons the same way again." Monica thumbed through the book and soon her eyes found a poem about drinking tea with Edgar Allan Poe. She read it through with some chuckles then walked to the storeroom and placed it in her messenger bag. Maybe they could get her to come for a book signing, she thought as she returned to the storefront and began helping a customer who entered the store with a bewildered look on her face.

Chapter Three

"She asked about you and Benjamin after you left, wanting to know where you guys came from," said Miranda after she took a sip of her tea. Ophelia sat on the floor in her living room, holding her empty cup between her hands. She sighed once in slight frustration then said, "Mir, you could have told her. It would have been okay for you to do so."

"As far as I am concerned, no it wouldn't. These are your lives we're talking about, not mine."

"Of course. When the time comes, we shall both let her know."

"Speaking of both, where is he tonight?"

"Probably sulking in the library. I have not seen too much of him since he went out with Monica."

"She must have really crushed him."

"She did and yet I understand why she did it. My brother is so desperate to have someone in his life that the first possible person that comes along is fresh meat for him. Thank goodness I do not have such feelings."

"Well…you do, but you, what was it again?" Ophelia smiled at Miranda's confusion. She took Miranda's hands in her own and stared into her eyes. At once, Miranda's confusion cleared. Ophelia then got up to make another pot of tea.

As Monica walked towards the library, the cool autumn air swirled around her head, making her feel giddy, and then moved on in search of others. Today was Tuesday and according to Benjamin, Laurel would be at the library. She opened her mouth, allowing some of the night to enter; she tasted hints of jasmine, apples and lovingly touched velvet. The houses stood side by side like peacefully sleeping creatures, each filled with lights and different colours. Some of the houses had open blinds, giving her a good look into some of the lives of Mabon's residents; one house showed a group of four adults sitting at a table, playing some sort of card game, while another showed a man and a woman seated on the couch reading books. One other house revealed an elderly couple sharing a tender kiss. Monica felt her cheeks go red as she hurried on.

True, she did miss the touch of another, layered with kisses and soft words spoken to each other. She did not like being alone at times, but for now, that was the only option she had, especially when it came to Benjamin. She did like him, there was no doubt on that, but he was a bit on the desperate side.

Was it so wrong that someone showed you how much they wanted to be with you?, Her inner voice asked her. *He liked you and wanted to be with you. There was no mind game being played, nor was there any misrepresentation. He liked you and that was that.*

"I don't care about that right now," she answered out loud, not caring if anyone heard her or not. "I want to explore more of myself. Love comes later." Soon, she reached the library and with it came a sigh of relief from her. It was a decent sized brick establishment with three columns in the front and the words MABON LIBRARY painted on the top. The library was still open, so she walked up the stairs and let herself in. Instantly, the scents of old books and leather greeted her as she walked along the main aisle. There were shelves filled to the brim with books on either side of her, while posters of various people holding books adorned blank spaces in between the shelves. Monica found the main desk and with it, Benjamin reading a book. For a moment, she wanted to turn heel and run back outside, but chided herself for being such a scaredy cat. She walked right up to Benjamin just as he glanced up from her book.

"Hi," he said in a flat tone. "How are you?"

"Good. You?"

"Oh. Fine." He glanced at his book for a moment then back at her. For a split second, he wanted to reach out and touch her on cheek, but closed his hand into a fist under the counter. Just as he made his fist, Monica absently touched the cheek he kissed on their date, feeling the tingling sensations again. She blushed just as he released his hand and placed them both on the counter. Sighing, he said, "So, what brings you here?"

"I'm here to meet Laurel. Remember, you told me about her and today is Tuesday."

"Oh yeah. That. Well, just go up to the second floor in about thirty minutes and then you can meet her." Monica meandered off to a side table, giving Benjamin a chance to get back to his book and not talk to her. She thumbed through some magazines on the table then sat down and found an article about the history of elderberries, immediately piquing her interest. Benjamin resumed reading while glancing every so often at her over the top of his book. He wanted to talk to her and ask her just who pissed her off so badly as to harden herself against anyone who showed an interest in her. It wasn't fair to people like him who truly wanted to get to know her better. He shook his head and went back to reading his book. The sooner he forgot her, the better off he would be.

Thirty minutes later, Monica glanced at her watch then got up and found the stairs leading to the second floor, leaving Benjamin at the desk. She climbed the carpet covered stairs with a mixture of apprehension and excitement; just why was this person so important? What was she, some sort of Tarot card reader or something along those lines? When she reached the second floor, it was partly dark and no one was around. She walked along the still shelves in search of a table. She found one by one of the open windows and took a seat. Monica folded her arms on the table and looked around, waiting to hear something from anyone and getting a little spooked out in the process. The moon directed some of its light into the room; Monica was in direct contact with the heavenly beam and her fears seemed to ebb away for a moment. She glanced up at the moon and for a brief moment, felt a tug on her heart. She felt tears well up in her eyes and she brushed them aside with her hands. Now was not the time for this, she thought angrily.

"Why are you crying?" Monica jumped out of her seat and looked behind her to find a young woman dressed in a simple dress staring back at her. Monica laughed shakily then sat back down with relief washing over her. Just a woman, that's all.

"You scared me!"

"Happens all the time," she replied warmly. "I take it you were looking for me?" The woman's eyes stared right into Monica, not giving her a chance to lose focus.

"Yeah, I was told to meet you tonight although I don't know why." The woman held a mysterious smile on her face, but said nothing. "So, I take it you're Laurel?"

"Yes, I'm Laurel. Please to make your acquaintance." Monica raised her hand for her to shake, but Laurel quickly moved away from her. Monica, thoroughly confused, retracted her hand then said, "I'm Monica. Would you like to sit down?"

"I can't stay too long tonight. I never do."

Weird chick, Monica thought then quickly dismissed it; weird was the norm in Mabon. She might as well get used to it. "So, who are you? What do you do around here?"

"I'm a poet, or at least, I was. You know, sometimes I can't remember." Laurel laughed and it sounded like bells. "What I mean is that I used to be a poet, but no more."

"Why did you give it up? Not enough time or something?"

"No, I died." For a moment, Monica stared at the now serious looking woman, not hearing her ears. She felt glued to her chair as blood rushed from her face.

"You . . . . died?"

"Yes, I died." Laurel noticed the look of disbelief on her face then said in clarification, "Oh, I guess no one told you. For some reason, no one ever tells new people that I'm dead. Must be some thrill or something." Laurel scratched her chin as Monica sat with her mouth open in shock. A ghost? She wanted to reach out to her and see if perhaps her hand would pass through her body, but knew that would be too corny, even for her. Instead, she took a good look at her own hand under the moonlight.

"So, that's why you wouldn't accept my hand," she murmured to herself then, changing her mind, stood up and walked closer to Laurel, trying to get a good look at her "guest". Laurel's skin was extremely pale, almost shimmering and transparent; Monica could now see several shelves clearly through her "friend".

Laurel grinned then said, "Hey, don't treat me like I'm some damn stage attraction!" Apparently, the demur woman Monica spoke to earlier was now gone, replaced with the fire of a raging poet. "Yeah, I'm a ghost, but sit down and let's talk, okay? You must be new here; I'm sure you've got questions, right?" Monica nodded dumbly then sat back down in her chair as Laurel floated closer to the table. For a moment, neither one said anything, but just stared at each other. Monica had a million questions to ask Laurel, but for some reason, her tongue was stuck to the roof of her mouth. Laurel's tongue, however, was ready to be used. She sighed then said, "I used to live in town until I got stupid."

"Got stupid?"

"I . . . wanted to know answers to some questions. I did things to get those answers." She lifted up the hem of her dress then let it slide out of her hands. "Guess I was right."

"Right about what?"

"I was just right," she said in a hesitant tone. "Let's just leave it like that." She shrugged her transparent shoulders as if that explained it all.

"I was told you show up every two days or something, right?" asked Monica, her tongue finally free from the roof of her mouth. "Why Tuesday?"

"Don't know. Maybe I saw a full moon one Tuesday night and I'm trying to relieve that feeling in death. Who knows? All I know is that I get visits from people on a weird schedule. Some seek my advice while others just want to talk to me about everything under the sun, or moon rather."

"Don't you get bored at times listening to people prattle on and on about stuff that you could care less about?" Laurel grinned, making her look a little less of a ghost and more of a human.

"You'd think I would, huh? Well, to tell you the truth, I'm glad for the company. The other nights I wander around completely invisible to everyone in the library. I try not to make any noises even though everyone in the town knows about me. You ought to see the people that come here, trying to talk to me even though they can't see me! I stand right behind them or up above, laughing away while they're trying to 'communicate' with me." Laurel ran a hand through her hair; Monica felt the cool breeze against her arm and she shivered.

"Are you the only ghost in the library?"

"I . . think so, although I really haven't looked. Of course, being in Mabon, anything is possible, huh?" Monica shrugged her shoulders; Laurel got the feeling that she did not know what she was talking about. She continued on a new topic. "You know what I would love to do sometime?"

"No, what?"

"I've always wanted to leave the library and walk around in the town."

"Wait, I thought you could do that?"

"I can, but honestly, I don't like doing it by myself. Everyone who comes to visit me is so caught up in the arts or my writing or what's it like being dead that, well, no one has ever asked me what *I* wanted." Laurel stopped for a moment and looked at Monica with a searching gaze. "I don't know, but you look like someone that might want to do that with me. Would you?"

"Sure, I'd be delighted!" At that, Laurel floated several feet from the ground and laughed.

Five minutes later, Monica walked downstairs to the lower level while whistling a tune. She saw Benjamin helping a young girl with locating a book. She wanted to wave to him, but decided against it and walked outside. A cool breeze met her and she smiled in kind as she walked along the sidewalk towards downtown.

"Well, that was neat," said a voice behind her. Monica turned around and saw Laurel materialize out of thin air. The ghost twirled around with arms raised then stopped and walked next to her living partner.

"Damn, I wish I could still smoke," said Laurel as she ran a hand through her hair. "I miss being able to do that while writing in my journals. Give me a pot of strong black coffee, my pack of smokes and I was ready to take on the world with my words."

"When did you live here?" asked Monica.

"Back in the 70s, believe it or not," Laurel replied. "Back then, Mabon was still the same artsy place, except, well, it seemed to be a bit more . . . open?"

"Open," said Monica. "Open as in-"

"We were still trying to live the 60s. Of course with this place, that wasn't too hard of a stretch." She let her voice trail off as her eyes now took in the dark and brightly lit houses around her. "I miss being alive, ya know. Well, sometimes I do. Still, at least my questions were answered."

"Again with those questions," said Monica in a frustrated tone. "Are you gonna tell me just what those questions were, or do I have to 'find' them myself?"

"Your questions, as I am sure you have, are your own, just like mine were my own. Back then, I wore all black and wanted to know everything: the world, my life, the people around me, everything. Only problem was that I wanted to know more than what was right before me. Now, well . . ." said Laurel as she trailed off. Monica walked on in silence; there were some times in Life when nothing needed to be said. This was one of them. As the two walked down the street, Monica kept glancing up at the streetlights, noticing how each one's light washed over her in a brief baptism. An owl hooted in the distance and Laurel waved her ghostly arms, trying to mock scare Monica, yet all it got was a snorting laugh.

Laurel lowered her arms and sighed. "Damn." The two then reached Monica's apartment complex. When they reached her apartment, she unlocked the doors, turned on the living room lights and found Laurel already inside looking at her books. She glanced up at Monica and grinned.

"I forgot you can do stuff like that," said Monica as she shook her head in resignation. Laurel floated through her apartment, oohing and aahing at every little thing. She tried to pick up several items, but her slender hand floated right through them. Monica watched her exploration from a distance; she had so many questions to ask her, but kept quiet. This was her time to enjoy being outside of the library. Half an hour later, Laurel returned from the bedroom a third time and found Monica sitting on her couch waiting for her.

"Sorry about taking so long in your place," she said wistfully, "but I wanted to take everything in."

"Don't worry about it." Laurel walked through the front door with Monica right behind her. When she reached outside, she saw Laurel floating over the fountain. Monica waved at Laurel to get her attention and soon, the two were off for another adventure. When they were several blocks from the downtown area, Laurel stopped. Monica stopped as well and looked at her partner quizzically.

"What's wrong?" she asked. Laurel frowned as she gazed at the activity. She ran a hand through her hair then sighed.

"People."

"What about them?"

"I don't know if I want to be around that many people. I mean, I know most of the town knows about me, but no one has ever seen me outside of the library. Kinda weird, ya know?"

"Well, if everyone knows about you, then you should have nothing to worry about, right?" Laurel sighed again and brought her hand up to her mouth as if she had a cigarette dangling between her fingers. She looked down at her ghostly hand then pulled it down in frustration.

"Monica, I appreciate what you've done for me tonight," said Laurel, "but I don't want to go any further. Can we walk back through some of the quieter neighborhoods? I'm . . . just not ready yet. I thought I was, but I guess I still have a way to go." Monica, without thinking, grabbed Laurel's hand and squeezed it. Laurel smiled at Monica then the look changed to shock, matching Monica's look as they both looked down and saw that Laurel's hand was somewhat solid as it held onto Monica's.

"H-how did you do that?" whispered Laurel.

"I thought you did that?"

"I've never been able to do this."

"How does it feel to you?" Laurel lifted up her hand and twisted it back and forth to get a better look at this miracle. It looked more solid than ever. She lowered her hand then focused her eyes on Monica's face. "Is this another answer to a question you've had?"

"Strangely enough, it is. All part of being in Mabon, I guess."

"I guess. Hey, can I ask you a random question?"

"Sure and I'll give you a random answer: banana."

"Cute. No, really, I'd like to know this: where are you buried?" Laurel stopped in her light footsteps and kept her back to her. "Did I say something wrong?"

"No, not at all," said Laurel with back still turned. "I. . . well, I don't have a burial place. I threw myself in Lake Noirae. It's not that far from here. The townspeople left my body there once they discovered it, like I was part of a shrine to depressed poets."

"Then how did you-"

"Show up here? All I remember after jumping into the river was black then a rushing noise in my ears. When I opened my eyes again, I could see the world yet not in colour. When I lifted my hands to my face, I could see right through them. That's when I knew I was dead." Laurel turned to Monica with eyes drenched in sadness and regret. "That's when I knew several of my questions had been answered."

"I'm so sorry."

"Don't be. I made that decision; no one forced me to do it. Anyway, I walked back to the library and saw several people sitting at a table while reading one of my poetry books. They were all crying and talking about how much they wished they could have spent more time with me when I was alive. When I walked up to them, they screamed until I calmed them down and told them of what I did. I thought that perhaps they would then spent more time with me as they had said, but instead all they wanted was to treat me like some sort of poetry goddess to be worshipped and placed on a pedestal. That's how everyone is here more or less. I might get a rare person who gives a damn about me, the real me, yet sometimes even they want something from me. Even in death, I can't escape the bullshit that clouded me before." Laurel raised her hands to her lips again as if she had a cigarette then slowly pulled them down in sadness rather than anger. "Being out tonight means more to me than you'll ever know."

"I think I can understand that." Monica led her friend back towards the library while using a long way for Laurel's benefit after her revelation about her death and the outcome afterwards. To be admired only in death; was that was Life was truly all about for some people? She shook her head to clear the thought and instead showed Laurel the neighbourhood to calm her down. Throughout their hour long walk, Laurel showed pleasure at the houses, foliage, and other items of the quieter streets, leaving the hustle and bustle of downtown far behind. Laurel seemed more at ease among the quiet as well as Monica; soon, the two struck up a conversation of a neutral topic.

"So, how did you come here?" asked Laurel while a chilly breeze wafted through Monica's hair. Laurel glanced over at her friend's dancing hair and smiled. "You have beautiful hair," she murmured. "It moves with the wind like a child."

"T-thanks," stammered Monica and the two walked on. "I got here because I hated my previous city and my job."

"What did you do?"

"I worked for a company that I hated. I felt I needed a change of scenery."

"Oh." Laurel paused for a moment to run her hand through a rose bush, stirring up their heady scent. Laurel breathed in deeply and said, "Their scent is almost too powerful for me. I will say this:

my senses have become stronger since being dead." Her friend touched the roses as well and their scent, while pleasant, was far from overpowering. It was simply a scent and nothing more. The dead woman looked at her hand again and said, "I still can't believe my hand went solid earlier. I had almost forgotten what it was like being solid."

"I would say you're welcome, but I know I had nothing to do with it. I just felt like touching your hand. I wanted to touch a friend." Laurel floated up several inches while her eyes looked down at her new friend.

"You're the first person who has ever said that to me since being dead. Actually, since being dead and alive." The ghost floated back down to Monica's level and floated ahead while Monica caught up with her and the two continued their silent yet enjoyable walk.

When they reached the library again, a clock nearby struck 10pm. Laurel's eyes lit up with passion as the sonorous dolling shook her to the very core. She closed her eyes, stretched out her arms and smiled into the night sky.

"Isn't that a lovely sound?" she whispered to herself, not really aware that Monica watched her with a mix of fascination and envy. "Things like that still make me feel good inside." She turned to Monica. "Sometimes, it's all we have."

"It is all we have," said Monica in agreement. "When I was younger, I used to think I had this small purple ball inside of me, just waiting to come out. Trouble was, I had no idea how to get it out of me."

"What was the purple ball to you?"

"Something important. Something that would free me from whatever I was feeling at the moment. Something that made me smile whenever I thought of it. I don't know, perhaps I was just looking for an excuse."

"Seems to me you've still got that purple ball inside of you," said Laurel. "Seems to me that your purple ball is more than just a purple ball, know what I mean?"

"Not really." Laurel turned to face her friend and traced a finger down her cheek. Her finger felt like a dry and cold piece of soft fabric.

"Take care not to ask questions that have answers like me," said Laurel in a cryptic tone. "I like you, Monica. I really do. Promise me that you'll visit me when you get your ball out, okay?" Monica nodded yes, although deep inside she was laughing at her current situation. Here she was, talking to a dead woman who was also a friend. Here was a ghost of a woman who lived more passionately than her. Monica felt her purple ball quiver inside of her and she placed her hands on her stomach to feel its warmth. Laurel looked down at her friend's stomach then placed a faint hand on top to feel whatever she felt.

"It feels good," Laurel whispered. "So this is your ball, huh?"

"Yeah, I guess it is." The two friends looked into each other's eyes. Suddenly, Monica thought of Benjamin and Ophelia and laughed, jarring Laurel out of her newly created bond with her.

"Okay, you're scaring the dead woman," said Laurel with a smirk on her face. "What's so funny?"

"Nothing and yet everything," she said while calming down. "Thank you for a lovely evening, Laurel." Monica took both of Laurel's hands in her own, ignoring the chill that came from the now solid hands, and smiled. "Thank you for showing me, Laurel. I really do appreciate it."

"No problem, my dear. I don't know what I did, but I am glad just the same." Laurel released her hands then said, "Well, I guess this is where I get off. Thanks again, Monica. Remember to come visit me when the ball is out." Laurel walked up to the doors, passed a hand through one of them, then smiled and waved at Monica as the rest of her slid through. Monica took several steps back and watched a small light dance from window to window, finally lighting a small window on the second floor to the right. Monica, not knowing if she could see it or not, waved once more at her new friend, as the light slowly dimmed then went out all together. Monica placed her hands on her stomach again, enjoying the warmth that lingered deliciously.

Miranda sat behind the cash register with a cup of hot Earl Grey tea in her hands as she listened to Monica eagerly tell her story of her adventure with Laurel last night. Miranda listened and nodded her head every so often, then smiled when she told her of watching Laurel's light dance around the library then fade out. She placed her mug on the counter and said, "Glad you were finally able to meet her. It seems as though she really liked you. No one has ever taken her out of the library for a night stroll, let alone take her back to their apartment."

"According to her, no one had ever asked her what she wanted to do. Most people were too busy asking her their own questions."

"You know, I brought her food the first time I met her. I didn't want to know the secrets of the universe; all I wanted was to share what I had with her. She didn't eat it, of course, but she did take its essence. Still, I'm glad you took her out for a walk; seems to me like she needed it."

"Well, I think we'll be doing more of that in the future. I never thought I'd be calling a dead woman a friend of mine." Just then, the front door chimes rang. Both women looked up and saw Benjamin walking into the store with a shy grin on his face.

"Hello ladies," he said while walking up to them. "How's it going?"

"Fine, fine," said Miranda while glancing at Monica, searching for any sign of emotion on her face. As Miranda talked and Benjamin replied with light banter, Monica kept a pleasant expression on her face, but inside was screaming with joy at the sight of him. She wanted to apologize for being so rude to him and take him out for tea and dinner or anything else. Not now, she thought while trying to calm her inner self down. Benjamin, while conversing with Miranda, occasionally glanced at Monica. After seeing her in the library last night, he thought about what she had told him, realizing later that she was right. He needed to let go of the past and move on, even though he thought he had done just that. The day that you no longer think about your past girlfriend or bring her up in mild conversation is the day that you are finally rid of your past, he told himself one night. He wanted to try again, but under a different beginning. She was worth it to him.

"So, how are your classes so far?" asked Miranda, jarring both Monica and Benjamin to the present.

Benjamin blinked owlishly several times then replied, "So far, no one has wanted their money back, if that's what you mean." Monica laughed at his joke and he blushed in kind. "I think the kids are really getting into what the esteemed Dr. Algren is trying to ram into their brains. Who knows, maybe one of them will want to become a professor too."

"Passing on the legacy, so to speak?" asked Monica, trying to join in the conversation. This time, Benjamin placed his full attention on her and smiled warmly, the blushing a distant memory. He had been waiting for her to say something to him or just to join in the conversation.

"Yes, something like that," he replied. Monica wanted to look away from his gaze, but found it hard to do so.

Miranda, noticing the two of them staring at each other a long longer than needed, piped up with, "Well, Monica, isn't it time for your break?"

"I just got here," said Monica, not getting the very obvious hint. Miranda grumbled well naturedly then walked off with her mug, leaving the two to figure it out. Monica watched her walk off just as the thinly veiled hint came crashing down. She looked back at Benjamin and blushed.

"So, it's your break, huh?" asked Benjamin.

"Looks like it is," she replied as he took her hand in his and the two walked out of the bookstore. Miranda bent over some boxes behind a couple of shelves. When she heard them talk then the door chimes, she chuckled to herself and resumed unpacking.

The day proved to be excellent walking weather; people walked along the streets of downtown enjoying cups of coffee, tea and even roasted chestnuts purchased from a young man who stood on one of the street corners with a red painted chestnut wagon. He dressed like a character from a Charles Dickens' novel and even spoke with a British accent to passersby who were interested in purchasing a bag.

"So, what's with the change of attitude about me?" he asked. "I am curious. You do realize that I wasn't too fond of you last night."

"I know and I wanted to apologize. I had no right to talk to you like that. Besides, I met up with Laurel," Monica replied. Benjamin started to say something, but Monica held up her hand and stopped walking. "In case if you're wondering; I was scared for a couple of minutes, but then I got over it. We actually walked outside for a while."

"Outside? That's never happened before! I saw you leave by yourself."

"She can turn invisible, ya know. She walked right behind me as I left. We went back to my apartment so she could have a look around then we walked though the neighbourhood and finally back to the library."

"Crazy. So, what does meeting up with her have to do with us?"

"Well, she made me realize that I want to be happy. I want to be happy with no obstacles and doubt. That and-" She glanced around as they walked and found that no one walked near them, "her hands became solid."

Benjamin stopped in shock. "How in the hell-"

"I don't know, but it happened twice." On impulse, Benjamin took Monica's hand and placed it against his lips. He sniffed it then lowered it then pulled her closer to him and kissed her fully on the lips, much to the surprise of everyone who suddenly appeared around them. Several people clapped and even the chestnut boy pulled out his small accordion and began to play a romantic tune. When they pulled away, even more people began to clap. Monica, being a good sport, curtsied then led him out of the throng to a quieter place.

"Thanks for getting us out of there," he said. "It seemed like a good idea at the time. Actually, I've wanted to do that ever since I first laid eyes on you."

"I know you did." The two then set off towards Arabella's Teashop, hoping for a quiet place to talk.

When they reached the building, Monica instantly fell in love with it; the large purple door with different coloured flowers painted all over gave off a warm and eccentric feeling. There was no sign, but everyone who lived in Mabon knew of Arabella's. Benjamin opened the door for her and Monica walked in, immediately greeted with the scents of cinnamon, coriander and vanilla. Tea from around the world sat in bags and jars on shelves all over the store, while the front counter held several steaming teapots going on all at once. There were several high back chairs and tables in the shop and half of them were occupied. They walked up to the counter and read the chalk written menu that hung overhead.

"Well, if it isn't Dr. Algren!" boomed a high-pitched voice from behind. They both turned around to see a short and slender woman with flaming red hair that stuck out all over her head with a thick black cloth headband to hold it down while dressed in a black short sleeved floor length dress and many silver bangles on either arm. She wore black-framed glasses, completing her eccentric look. "Dr. Algren-"

"Benjamin, please Arabella. You know we go through this every time," he gently chided her. "We've been friends for how long?"

"Too long!" she beamed then focused her attention to Monica. She looked her up and down once then said to her, "You're a tall one!" Monica tried hard not to laugh and instead coughed into her fist. Arabella blinked once then said, "So, who's your friend, Benjamin?"

"This is Monica, Arabella. She just moved here. I've told her about your tea shop and that she had to come here." Arabella's face lit up at the compliment. She waved her hands frantically while saying in a singsong voice, "Find a spot, find a spot, both of you, and I'll take care of the rest!" Benjamin guided Monica out of Arabella's way and led her to an empty spot.

Once they sat down, Monica said, "Wow. So that's her, huh?" She saw the short fiery woman muttering to herself and pacing while grabbing and replacing things on shelves in what looked to be preparation of tea. Benjamin glanced back at Arabella then gently laughed.

"So, how much have you heard about her?"

"Only what you told me." Just then, Arabella walked up to their table with a black teapot and two black mugs. Monica watched as the woman placed the items on the table with such precision and ease with no words; was this even the same woman she saw a minute ago she wondered? Once done, Arabella looked at both of them with a grave look and said in a low tone, "Go to Lake Noirae tonight, as the moon shines its best." She then walked off; once she reached the counter, she was back to her manic self, leaving both Benjamin and Monica with questions.

"What was that all about?" she asked as she poured a cup of tea for Benjamin. While she poured, the scents of several berries from the teapot permeated her nose, leaving her slightly woozy, but quite energetic at the same time. She then poured her own cup as Benjamin blew on his to cool it down. When he took his first sip, he leaned back into his chair and closed his eyes in satisfaction. Monica sniffed hers then she too took a sip…. and found herself sitting in the middle of a forest clearing. Monica looked down and noticed that she still held the cup in her hand. She placed the cup on the ground next to her then took a good view of her surroundings. The tall and wide oak trees made a wade circle around her while their branches blocked out part of the blue sky and sun. She heard the sounds of rushing water from all around and birds somewhere off in the distance. A brown squirrel darted from tree to tree, unaware that it had a visitor in its realm. She looked around once again and found herself to be alone.

"Well, now what?" she asked herself in a slightly frustrated tone, not even worried that she was no longer in the store, or Mabon for that matter.

"What do you mean, well now what?" Monica jumped and searched for the source of the mocking voice. Her fear turned to relief; it was Benjamin leaning against one of the tree trunks. Monica picked up her mug and sniffed it again then placed it back on the ground.

"Do I even want to know?' she asked as Benjamin laughed, increasing her frustrations regarding her current situation. "What's so funny?" she asked.

"Nothing really, but it's just that this is the second time this has happened to me when I drank that blend of tea from her."

"So . . . where are we?"

"Well, it's hard to say, but, let me ask you this; are you open minded?"

"Considering that I took a ghost out for a night on the town, plus the fact that this town is not exactly 'normal', I would answer . . . yes."

"Good and yes, I picked up on the sarcasm." Monica stuck out her tongue. "Anyway, thanks to Arabella and her tea, we're on the other side."

"Other side." Monica clearly had no idea what he was talking about.

"Other side as in Otherworld, other side." Suddenly, there was a low hum, low enough to be considered a slight vibration in the ground, but it was there. Monica held up a hand to silence Benjamin then lay down on the grassy floor and placed her ear to the ground. The sound of humming wafted through her body like a gentle wave, guiding her mind and soul to another place in another time. She closed her eyes and was able to see those that made the noise; they ranged in size and shape, but they were all transparent and willowy in movements. They floated all around her, some even passing through her body, giving of scents of burning wood and pine trees. She wanted to spend the rest of her life with them, fully ready to give up everything in the mortal world. They beckoned her with slender long arms and hands, wanting her to be a part of their world as well. She could feel herself sinking into the ground, ever closer to their world filled with lights and beautiful music. The Others had chosen her because she could see them.

Meanwhile, Benjamin watched as Monica's body began to slowly sink into the ground. He raced to her body and grabbed her free arm and pulled with all of his might. For a moment, her body would not give an inch in his direction. The Others wanted her because she was special. Benjamin, however, wanted her more. He pulled again and soon, her body appeared on top of the grass again. He continued to pull until she was safely in his arms then he moved her far away from the spot. He propped her up against one of the trees and removed dirt and grass from her body. Her eyes were still closed and there was a faint smile on her lips. Once she was pretty much clean, he took her face in his hands and kissed her on the lips, freeing her from the spell. At once, her eyes fluttered open then closed half way as she fell into his kiss with an equal passion as the birds sang their hearts out and the waters rushed with passion and grace.

"The first time I came here, I didn't fall under their Spell," said Benjamin as they sat under the tree. "I was already prepared, so to speak."

"So to speak?"

"So to speak, as you can see."

"So I see." She rubbed on the arm that Benjamin had pulled on and winced a little.

"Still hurt?"

"Yeah, but you did what you had to do. I appreciate it."

"No problem. So, what else do you want to know?"

"Well, for starters; we're in the Otherworld, right?"

"Right."

"And we're not in Mabon anymore, right?"

"Well . . .yes and no. We are definitely on the Other side, but we are still in Mabon. In fact, our physical bodies are still in the teashop, although to the average person, it looks like we've gone to sleep. Regular customers of Arabella's know the signs. Anyone who has had Elder Tea takes a trip over here. Can't help it, actually; elderberries are, shall we say, a little touched with extra goodness, especially for those who are more than what they appear to be?"

"Huh. And how do you know this?"

"When you live in Mabon, it pays to know things." Monica looked at the crown of trees overhead. "We're all kind of 'touched' in this town," he continued. "That is what draws us here; our eccentricities and our extra tendencies. Ophelia and I fit right in, as do you, correct?"

"Correct, I think." She looked around at the beautiful trees and listened to the humming under them. "I can hear that," she said like a defiant child.

"I know you can. Tell me, have you always noticed things that just made no sense to you? Ever had things happen to you or by you with no explanation?"

"Yes, I have. I tried telling people about the things I could see and do, but no one would believe me. My parents wanted to send me away to a hospital at one time, but I convinced them otherwise. They always told their friends I was different than other girls and young women; I was just weird." Benjamin shook his head in sympathy; how many times did he hear this from his students, friends and others in the town?

"You came to Mabon because of your differences; almost everyone here is like you at one level or another. They come to this town and other cities around the globe, seeking to be around others like them who will not hate them for being who and what they are." Monica ran her hand through the grass, sighing as it tickled her skin. Everything around her felt alive and too bright for her eyes. She placed a hand over her eyes to block it out, but it did not help. She wanted to cry, but not out of sadness; finally, what she was looking for was on the other side of the door. Did she, however, have the strength to open it and walk through, no matter the consequence? Suddenly, her world turned upside down and inside out and she received no instruction manual for it.

Benjamin reached for her hand and placed it on his leg just as Monica closed her eyes. She opened her eyes again and found herself back in the teashop, just as Benjamin was about to pour another cup.

"Uh, are we about to go back?" she asked with trepidation.

Benjamin laughed. "Dear, it's only in the first cup. The others cups are mundane, but still delicious tea. Trust me." He handed a fresh mug of the tea to her. She took one sip . . . and remained in the chair. With a sigh of relief, she drained the cup in one sitting, allowing the taste of the slightly hot elderberries to flow down her throat and into her system. Benjamin watched her with eager eyes. Monica glanced around the shop nervously.

"How long have we been gone?" she asked.

"Probably several seconds. Time in the Otherworld is different than over here."

"So, did you enjoy the Elder Tea?" asked Arabella who suddenly appeared next to Monica. She turned to face her hostess and tried to smile, but it came out shaky.

"Um, it was . . . . . interesting." Arabella turned towards Benjamin and grinned as if she harboured a secret.

"I take it you two went to the Grove, huh?"

"Yes, you know we did," said Benjamin. "Why else would you have made that tea for us and especially her?" Arabella made a shooing noise at Benjamin, but kept her grin.

"Because she belongs here in Mabon. You'll be taking her to Lake Noirae tonight, I take it?"

"Of course,, but you never said why."

"My dear," said Arabella in a surprisingly somber tone, "you already know the answer to that." She turned and walked off, leaving the two with more questions than answers.

"Arabella arrived in Mabon two years ago on a warm Saturday night," said Benjamin as they walked back to the bookstore. "When she arrived, she could barely hold her head up as she walked into the downtown area, dressed in a worn dress. Her condition caught the attention of several of the townsfolk and they took her to Jacqueline's home for food and some rest."

"Who's Jacqueline?" asked Monica.

"She's the owner of the flower shop on the east side of the town. She's also one of the Goths in town." Monica stopped walking.

"Goth? There's a Goth scene here?" She slapped her forehead. "Of course there would be," she said with a sigh and resumed walking. "So, do they get together and do things here?"

"As far as I know, yes. It's about twenty of them or so and I think they do something called 'black collar lunch' every so often. They head to the cemetery and set up a nice picnic and just enjoy their day among the dead. I've been once and, although I'm not into the scene, I am a sympathizer."

"So, what's the name of Jacqueline's flower shop?"

"Les Violettes Riantes. The Laughing Violets." Monica tried hard not to laugh, but it came out anyway.

"That's brilliant!" she cried as they reached the bookstore. Miranda saw the two walking up and opened the door for them with a deep bow that bordered on the ridiculous.

"Lady and Gentleman," she said as they walked in. "Good to see you again! You've only been gone for twenty minutes with thirty more to spare." Her eyes sparkled a bit as she said this. Monica and Benjamin looked at each other and smiled in kind.

"I think we're gonna be okay," said Monica as she kissed Benjamin on the cheek then helped a customer who looked lost. Miranda turned to Benjamin, expecting an answer. All she got instead was a shrug and a wave good-bye as he walked out of the store.

Four hours later, just before closing time, Benjamin walked back into the bookstore and waited patiently on Monica who helped a young woman search for vegetarian cookbooks. When she saw Benjamin, she smiled and waved, causing him to blush. He waved back then began looking through a magazine.

"Hey, that's my professor Dr. Algren!" she exclaimed. "He's one of the coolest teachers ever." She then looked at Monica's face and continued with a sly grin, "So . . . you and Dr. Algren, huh? Wow, that's pretty cool! So, what's he like outside of the classroom? I mean, he's cool in the classroom, but is he just as cool outside of it?"

"Yeah, I guess you could say he's pretty cool outside of the classroom," said Monica. She continued showing cookbooks to the young woman; once she picked out two that seemed pretty good, she led her over to the front counter and checked her out. When she left, after waving good-bye to Dr. Algren, Miranda turned the OPEN sign to CLOSED and locked the door. Benjamin walked over to Monica at the front counter and took her hand in his.

"So glad to see you again," she said as he nodded in kind.

"Whew, I am so glad today is over," said Miranda, completely ignoring them both as she flopped herself in one of the reading chairs and took off her shoes. She wiggled her toes in their thick black wool socks and sighed. "So, what do you two have planned tonight?"

"Arabella mentioned that we should go to Lake Noirae tonight."

Miranda sat up at the mention of the lake. "Does she know yet?" she asked in a low tone. Benjamin walked over to another chair and sat down. He crossed his arms and sighed.

"We had the Elder Tea today on her break, so it's safe to say that she knows."

Miranda arched an eyebrow in surprise. "You need to tell her, Benjamin. Tell her all of it before you go." Monica stared back and forth at the exchange and wondered just what in the hell they were talking about. She always hated it when people talked about her while she stood right in the middle of them. If there was something that needed to be said, then it needed to be said without any flouncing around.

"Okay, you do realize I'm here?" she said while waving her hands around. "So, is someone going to tell me or do I need to guess it myself?"

Benjamin looked at Monica and said, "Of course. That is rude to talk about someone when that person is right there. Miranda and I were talking about Mabon, or rather, the stuff that makes Mabon. Mabon is a special town and there are other places like it all over the world, as I told you earlier." He glanced at Miranda's face, searching for some sort of sign that he was on the right track. Miranda made a rolling motion with her fingers as if to say *go on*. "These towns and cities in this world have certain 'contracts' with the Otherworld."

"Contracts?" asked Monica dubiously. Benjamin cleared his throat and thought, *all right, let's go all the way with this. She has a right to know after all.*

"Long ago, Mankind and the Otherworld were close, so close that our kind and their kind freely walked through what was and still is known as the Veil. The creatures of now myth and legend were and are still real. Vampires, werewolves, ghosts, fairies, you name it. Every legend, every creature of myth from around the globe comes from the Otherworld. Well, as humankind advanced with science and modern technology, they wanted less and less from the Otherworld, claiming them to be evil and unnatural along the guidelines of science. As humankind progressed, the Veil became thicker and thicker till for 100 years, no one could travel back and froth. Hence these cities and towns like Mabon began to appear. There were still humans who wanted to keep the friendship with the Otherworld alive, for if they forgot like the rest of the world, no one would remember what it was like. So, through these contracts and pacts, this world kept in contact with the Otherworld and, well, Mabon is like a signpost for all who feel out of place in the modern world. People like you, Miranda and others in this town came here either by free will or something inside of them drew them here. You've had something inside of you stirring for a while now, haven't you?" Monica nodded yes and suddenly, the large purple ball inside of her began to jump. She held her stomach, knowing deep down that she was not truly experiencing such a sensation, but it still felt real. She nodded again as she felt the warmth spreading in her stomach.

"All my life I have felt just . . . wrong, like I was a mutant or something. I wanted to make use of my creative juices, if I even had any, but I never knew how to go about doing that."

"You felt angry, alone and ashamed for what you felt, right? Frustrated at wanting more yet not knowing how to get more," asked Miranda, now joining in the conversation. "Dearie, we've all felt that way. That's why we are here in Mabon. Others have felt it too and they went to their closest places, seeking refuge or otherwise."

"So, what was the forest grove that Benjamin and I went to today?" asked Monica.

"That's one of the go-betweens of Mabon and the Otherworld," said Benjamin. "We could have gone to the other side if we wanted to, but the tea only lasted ten minutes and we would have just disappeared if we walked on. Tonight, however, we'll be going to

Lake Noirae. The lake is another go-between worlds, but tonight we're going to the Arcanum."

"Arcanum?"

"The Arcanum is the oldest library in both this world and the Otherworld," said Miranda. "The collection of books is quite astounding as well as the place itself. Seeing as how you're a bibliophile, don't get too lost among the shelves. You'll see what I mean once you get there." Miranda glanced at Benjamin briefly then continued, "The Arcanum is one of the middle points for those who live in this world and in the Otherworld. It is also a neutral zone. People with grudges against someone or something maintain a sense of peace in the Arcanum. It's just better that way. It's also good to keep the peace because if they do not then Master Assam will."

"Who's Master Assam or do I need to find that out for myself?" asked Monica.

"He's the Archivist and Guardian of The Arcanum. He is the keeper of records and books, imparting all forms of knowledge to anyone and everyone who seeks it. Most people who request his assistance have never seen him; only a rare few have."

"So, what does he look like?"

Miranda smiled enigmatically. "I'll leave that up to you. If he wants to be seen by you, trust me, you'll know it." Outside, the sky darkened as the day gave way to the night. Soon the moon would be out and Benjamin and Monica had to be at the lake during that time for them to do whatever the hell they were supposed to do. Miranda glanced at Benjamin again and this time let her eyes linger on him longer than necessary with a thoughtful glance. Benjamin noticed Miranda's stare and chose not to acknowledge it. He knew what she was thinking and for him, now was not the right time. He would tell Monica when he was ready. Miranda, however, had other plans. She needed to know if this was going to go further than planned.

"Benjamin, where's Ophelia tonight?" Benjamin turned to face Miranda full on and glared.

"I am here," said Ophelia, materializing out of nowhere right next to Miranda. Monica jumped at seeing Ophelia then glanced at everyone's faces, checking for any signs as to what the fuck was going on. She sighed, catching the attention of Benjamin; he grinned as if to say *you'll know soon enough.* "I take it you two are telling Monica everything?" said Ophelia in her usual calm tone.

"But of course," said Benjamin. "She's Awake now." Ophelia walked to Benjamin's chair and took his hand in hers as the two smiled at each other. Miranda glanced at them then at Monica who was now completely lost with this situation. Was someone going to eventually tell her or should she wait for the DVD?

"Monica," said Ophelia while still holding Benjamin's hand, "it would appear that we owe you an explanation and fast."

"Well," said Monica with false bravado, "I'm ready. What is it?" Benjamin looked at Monica with a sad expression on his face then closed his eyes just as Ophelia released his hand and closed hers. Suddenly, a bright white light covered their bodies, momentarily blinding Monica while Miranda just stood and watched; their transformation still amazed her even though she was used to it by now. The light disappeared, revealing two tall and slender beings with sea foam green skin and small gills on their necks. Thick and straight hair the colour of night lay past their shoulders in one long braid, accenting their large blue eyes and very pointed ears. Monica couldn't believe it. She rubbed her eyes, hoping that this was not a dream or a nightmare. The one that was Ophelia walked up to Monica and caressed her cheek. Her skin felt cool and rubbery, but not unpleasant.

"We are ambassadors of Lineal, our city in the Otherworld," said the Ophelia creature in a voice that made Monica want to cry with happiness. It sounded pure, like spring water running over crystal. It was almost too much for her to handle and it took all of her willpower to keep from running out of the store with tears running down her face. Ophelia, feeling her discomfort, lightly touched her on the forehead to clear her discomfort.

Monica blinked twice then looked up at Ophelia and smiled. "Thank you," she said in a shaky voice. "Your voice…bothered me."

"You are welcome." Benjamin walked up to Monica and took her hands in his while his large eyes stared deeply at her and inside of her. She looked back into those eyes and felt a stirring inside of her. Those eyes, she thought, remind me of something-

"From long ago and deep within you," he said in the same musical voice. "I need to speak with you in private." He looked up at Ophelia and Miranda and said, "Please give us five minutes." The two left, giving them privacy that was desperately needed. Monica, although excited with this revelation, also felt numb inside. Her mind felt split in two; finally, she had her answers and yet she felt as though it were all a dream. Benjamin squeezed Monica's hand, breaking her clouds of thought and into the present once more.

"Are you afraid of me?" he asked. Monica shook her head no then yes while her eyes never left his. "I do not want you to be afraid of me; we have a journey to the lake tonight, if you're still up for it."

"What is your real name?" she asked.

The ambassador smiled, revealing impossibly white teeth. "I am known as Shevrahaplentia, but please call me Shevra. It is easier to say." Monica tried saying his name, which came out funny and far from the correct pronunciation. She scrunched her nose in frustration then just said, "Shevra." Shevra pulled her closer to him. She smelled hints of ocean water and warm sand from his body and leaned into him while half of her face was in his tunic as she inhaled his body scent. Part of her thought that this was all a dream, that she would wake up and find herself back at her old home, waking up to another day of working at her old company while being surrounded by the negative forces she tried to escape from. The other half knew it was not a dream, that finally her questions about herself and the world around her could be answered. She had always known that there was more than what circled around her like vultures. She knew there was more to life than just waking up, going to work at a boring job, then returning home to do it all over again. The purple ball inside of her felt larger than ever as it bounced inside of her while giving off even more warmth. She couldn't wait to see Laurel again. She hugged Shevra tightly, not wanting to let him go. He returned the hug with an equal amount of passion and relief then pulled away as he placed a hand on her warm stomach and closed his eyes.

"I hate to be the bearer of bad news," said Ophelia to them, "but the moon is almost out. You two need to go to the lake if you are to be there when the door appears." Shevra nodded gravely to his sister while Miranda pulled Monica to the side. When they were alone, Miranda said, "Look, I know you're probably overwhelmed right now with what was just revealed to you, but you needed to know this if you were going to live in this town and especially since you and Benjamin are together. Remember, the town knows about them as well as the contract; you are not alone on this at all. We've all gone to the Arcanum at one point in time as well as visited the rest of the Otherworld."

"I appreciate your concern for me," said Monica, "but actually, I'm quite all right. I do feel shaky, but other than that, I'm good." She looked up to see the twins discussing something in earnest then glanced back at Miranda. "I appreciate what you've told me," she said while placing her hand on her arm. "Thanks for doing that."

"Hey, what are bosses for?" said Miranda while shrugging her shoulders then walked back to the twins with Monica behind her. When they reached the two, they immediately stopped talking and stared at both women with a blank look.

"Did we interrupt anything serious?" asked Miranda. "We can give you two more time, if need be."

"No, that is quite all right," said Ophelia. "We were only discussing Shevra's plans for he and Monica once they arrive at the Arcanum. Perhaps Master Assam might grant them an audience for a moment, if he can take the time to actually stop doing research and shelving books to interact."

"It will be good to visit the Arcanum again," said Shevra wistfully. "I have not been there in about five years." Monica left the group and walked over to the window to look at the night sky and the twinkling stars and planets. For a brief moment, everything she had ever cared about seemed to diminish in size and concern; all of the petty matters that had occupied her mind in the past were now futile. Nothing that mattered in the past matters now, she thought as Ophelia walked up to her and placed a hand on her shoulder.

"I am so glad you are taking this news well," she said in her usual calm voice. "Shevra is especially glad, considering what was forced upon you in such a small amount of time."

"I just realized how small our lives truly are," said Monica, more to herself than to Ophelia. "I have always known that there was more than just what was in front of me. Now, I am beyond convinced and I am glad for it. Everything that I had doubts or questions about suddenly make sense in some weird but understandable way." She turned to Ophelia and smiled. "What is your true name, by the way?"

"My name is truly Ophelia," said Ophelia with a large grin that revealed all of her slightly pointed teeth. "I refused to change my name once we came over as ambassadors."

"So you two are ambassadors for your home city? Has there been anyone else that came over?" Ophelia glanced away for a moment, obviously not wanting to answer the question just as Shevra walked up to the two and said, "Monica, it is time. We must go." Something crossed Ophelia's face close to relief as Miranda unlocked the door, hugged both Shevra and Monica and then let them out into the night. Ophelia stood by one of the windows, watching her brother walk down the street while holding Monica's hand with such certainty.

"Are you concerned for them?" asked Miranda while holding two mugs of tea. Ophelia turned and graciously accepted the steaming cup of Silver Needle White tea.

"Somewhat, but I trust Shevra highly. He is of my blood, after all, and I know he cares deeply for Monica." Miranda took a deep sip of her tea, not caring if she burned herself or not. For some reason, she needed to feel that sensation at that moment. "He would not allow anything to harm her, not when he finally has a chance to feel love again." Ophelia glanced outside again and took a sip of her tea then looked down into the cup. "I have never had this blend before," she murmured. "It is quite good." Miranda said nothing, but sipped again.

As they walked along downtown, Monica's eyes glanced from side to side as they passed by townspeople; she waited for someone to scream bloody murder at seeing a seven foot mythological creature walking through downtown Mabon. No one screamed, yelled or even pointed fingers at them. In fact, several people walked up to Shevra and said hello or asked him about upcoming class, leaving Monica with more questions than answers. After talking to the fifth person, Monica said with a laugh, "Okay, okay, so I get it." Shevra stopped walking and turned his head to the side in a questioning manner.

"I do not understand, Monica."

Monica flayed her arms around her. "All of this! I get the fact that people here know of your true nature. I get it, I get it!" She crossed her arms in front of her chest and huffed, giving Shevra an opportunity to laugh as he led her along to the lake. The two fell silent when they reached the beginnings of the grove; Monica could no longer hear the sounds of Mabon as crickets chirping, owls, bats and other nocturnal animals now replaced them. Monica looked behind her and noticed that their previous path was now covered in thick verdant bushes. Shevra stopped at the beginning of a stone laid path and looked up at the moon as if waiting for something. Monica looked up as well and noticed that the moon looked a bit fuller than normal, but then she never really paid attention to such matters. Shevra stared at the sky for several seconds then said, "Follow me," and continued walking with Monica close in tow.

The stone path looked to be recently laid out to Monica, but she knew deep down that it had been here for years, decades, probably centuries. From time to time, the moon sent several beams of light down to guide their way, assisting them towards a very important goal. The two kept quiet as they walked along, but Monica's mind burned with many questions. She wanted to know more about Shevra and his kind, why he and Ophelia came from their city as ambassadors, and why Ophelia had that strange look on her face before they left. She looked at his darkened back and thought about Benjamin, his human side. She felt a slight tugging on her heart; even though she cared deeply for Benjamin, she also felt the same for this creature, for they were one in the same. Nothing would ever be the same, she thought just as Shevra stopped walking and she almost bumped into him.

"Lake Noirae," was all he said as she walked around him to get a better view of the clearing and of the lake itself. The lake was a standard sized lake, but that was where it ended its resemblance with other lakes. While other lakes would have an inky look to them at night, this lake was brightly lit and sparkled like a crystal ball. Monica's eyes grew wide at this beautiful body of water.

"It's so beautiful," she whispered then fell silent as she thought of Laurel. Suddenly, she felt Shevra's body against hers.

"This is, but one way to get to the Otherworld. There are many others, some beautiful like this and some as bad as your worst nightmare. Since we are going to the Arcanum, there is no danger.

However, stick close to me, for some of the creatures in the Otherworld are not friendly towards your kind." Monica swallowed nervously and nodded just as Shevra walked from behind her and, taking her hand, led her closer and closer to the lake's surface. For a moment, she thought they were going to swim in the lake, until an immense wooden door covered in the same sparkly substance materialized in the middle of the lake. She looked down and saw that Shevra's feet, when they reached the lake, did not sink, but instead stayed well on top of the water. Before she had a chance to let that register in her mind, she too was walking on top of the water. At first, she wanted to cry if for no other reason than because she was doing the impossible, but then held it in and just focused on the door. When they reached it, Shevra turned the knob and suddenly, Monica felt her whole body sucked into blackness. She closed her eyes.

Time passed. Monica wanted to throw up, but the feeling quickly left. Her eyes were closed, or at least that what she thought. She felt something cool on her cheek and her back. She groaned for a second then stirred as she felt sturdy hands take hold of her arms and lift her up.

"Are you okay? Did you suffer any bruising?" asked Shevra. Monica twisted and turned her body, wincing only once when her right leg turned to the left. She looked down, expecting missing body parts on the ground, but saw none. She patted herself once then grinned like a child.

"My leg hurts a bit, but other than that, I'm fine, " she said. She turned to look at her companion under the dimly lighted hall, watching him brush off dirt and debris from his robe. "Are you okay?"

"Yes, I am fine," Shevra said then paused. "Thank you for asking." Monica blushed before she realized it; she held a hand up to her warming face and gave a ghost of a smile to Shevra who bowed in return. "I should have warned you about our little trip," he said. "Sorry about that."

"No problem." She shook her head to clear out the lingering cobwebs then looked around her and smiled widely. They stood in the middle of a hallway with white marble floors and wooden walls.

The floors were covered in a thin film of dust and leaves while spider webs occupied some of the cracks and corners in the walls. To the left of them was the door that led to Mabon, while the hallway continued on to the right.

"Shevra, did we make it?" she asked.

"We did indeed; this is one of many hallways leading to the Arcanum." He straightened his robe a final time then said, "Follow me and do not walk in a rush." The two then set off towards the Arcanum, leaving Mabon behind. Monica walked next to Shevra as they walked along the massive hallway lit by large wooden torches that burned with an eerie bluish flame. As they walked, Monica glanced from left to right at her surroundings with interest. The walls appeared to be made of a dark cherry wood with strange symbols and designs carved into the wood. Some appeared to be faintly glowing while others were not. She stopped at one symbol that looked like ripples in a pond and stared at the faint red glow it produced. She stared at the glow for a moment then realized that Shevra was far along the hallway so she scurried to catch up with him. Shevra continued to walk down the hall, his long robe making faint whooshing sounds against the debris-laden floor. Monica peered over his shoulder and saw more of the hallway ahead. She sighed and continued walking in silence, her mind spinning its wheels.

"I've seen this place before," she said in a soft voice while her eyes darted all around. I've been here before in my dreams."

"Dreams are another way to travel to the Otherworld," said Shevra as they walked along. "The only problem is that people think they just had a wonderful dream or a terrible nightmare, when instead they actually came here. Imagine having to tell people that they have the ability to travel in their dreams."

"They wouldn't believe it."

"Precisely why the cities and towns like Mabon are not that well known to mundanes. People like you are drawn to them for unknown reasons until it is made clear to them. Their whole world is turned upside down and once they open that proverbial door, they can never go back." Shevra fell silent, giving Monica time to process what he just told her. Were her dreams in the past signals of what was to come for her? She glanced around the hallway and knew she truly had been here before. Perhaps they were, she thought as understanding finally dawned on her. Mabon proved to be more than just a small artistic town, she thought. She had hoped to find her true self while being a resident of the safe and secure town. However, all of that changed when the true side of the town revealed itself as a waypoint for those from the Otherworld, a place that had been in the shadows of Earth for as long as possible. She thought about the many myths and legends she read when she was younger and smiled; now, it appeared that the myths were not myths, but historical facts. Finally, the questions that burned through her mind after reading books would finally be answered. No longer would she have to wonder if her mother was going to call a priest to exorcize her daughter of the "demons" that permeated her mind. The world shifted into focus and for the first time, she could see.

Chapter Four

The hallway stretched for miles then suddenly it changed into blue skies with fluffy clouds while leg high monkey grass became the new floor. Birds of every colour flew around while small winged creatures of the no longer imagination darted here and there.

"Welcome to the Arcanum," said Shevra with the first smile he'd worn since they arrived. Monica looked around with awe and slight confusion.

"Where *is* the Arcanum?" she asked.

Suddenly, shelves as high as the sky began to appear all around them, filled to the brim with books of every shape and size. As soon as the shelves appeared, all sorts of beings winked into existence. Humanoids, dwarves, elves, faeries and other creatures walked around the two in their own searches for documents and tomes while Monica stood gawking like a child in the middle of it all. Shevra held a hand up to his face to cover his smile.

"By Puhera, can it be you?" Monica turned and saw an older version of Shevra walking towards them with a wide grin on its face. Shevra's face broke into a wide smile as he embraced the newcomer. Monica smiled at the welcoming attitude between the two and for a moment felt sad because she wished her mother could be here with her. She watched as the two embraced then pulled apart while they still held on to each other's arms.

"Verthe, it is good to see you!" cried Shevra. "It has been a while, has it not?"

"Indeed, it has!" replied Verthe who turned and saw Monica standing there. Verte looked at her then back at Shevra with a questioning look. Shevra pulled away from Verthe and said, "Teacher, may I present to you Monica Burton from Mabon, human side. I am her guide for her initial visit to the Arcanum." Shevra then bowed low to Verthe, but he did not notice for he stared at Monica with an intent gaze. Monica wanted to hide under a rock to avoid that gaze; she felt as though she was being judged for crimes she may or may not have committed.

"I am Verthe, member of the Darjeel Order and I bid you welcome to the Arcanum," Verthe said in a deep voice, bowing low to Monica then rising up gracefully. "Shevra used to be a student of mine many years ago, studying to become a scholar of my order. Now that he is a guide for you here, it fills my hearts with happiness and pride for him, praise Puhera." Verthe bowed low once more then rose with a warm smile on his strangely beautiful face. "Are you a student as well, Monica of Mabon?"

Monica blushed. "No, well, I mean, that is-"

"She was told by someone in Mabon to come here," replied Shevra, sparing Monica. "She walks the Path."

"I see. Well, enjoy your time here, Monica of Mabon. Shevra," he said as he took Shevra's hands into his own, "I can not tell you how good it is to see you again. I wish I would stay longer, but I am needed elsewhere. I came here to locate several documents concerning our local flora and fauna for a conference and so I must be on my way." Verthe tightened his grip on Shevra's hand briefly and for a moment, Monica thought she saw tears in his eyes. "May your days be full of warmth."

"And may your cup never dry," replied Shevra with the farewell greeting of the Lin . . . . . and tears as well.

"Verthe took Ophelia and I in after our parents died in the Lin War," said Shevra as they walked through the Arcanum once Verthe had left them. "We were both very young at the time. Verthe was both our mother and father and later my teacher."

"So, are all Lin like you and your sister? Shape shifters, I mean." Shevra chuckled briefly, causing several fox demon scholars who sat at a large red mushroom table to glance in his direction, temporarily breaking their intense research. Shevra bowed low to them, showing his respect and they nodded their heads in kind then went back to their studies.

"Yes they are, but the Darjeel Order combine both male and female magicks, making us very dangerous to others. We were used as weapons in the Lin War. Although I am a member of the order, I did not agree with the war. We use our powers for good, building a more stable world for our kind and I intend to see such an event occur in my lifetime."

"You mentioned the Lin War," she said in a flat tone. "What was that all about?"

"A scar upon my people's history that will never be forgotten," said Shevra with a note of venom in his voice. "The Otherworld spoke of the war for quite a time afterwards and even now, we are reminded of such when the right or wrong time occurs." Shevra led them to a random section of shelves and began reading the titles.

"What are you looking for?" she asked.

"A book that will explain the war for you, but I think I might have the wrong spot."

"You do, Member of the Darjeel," said a calm voice that seemed to come from all around them. Monica looked around anxiously, trying to locate the source of the voice, while Shevra just smiled.

"Ah, Master Assam," he said as he led Monica to a table, "thank you for pointing that out to me. I did not want to spend most of time conducting a fruitless search."

"It is my job," the voice replied with a soft chuckle at the end. Monica, while seated, still looked around for the source of the voice, but found none. Suddenly, she heard a soft whirring sound like a ticking clock behind her and to the left. She turned towards a small cluster of shelves, but saw nothing.

"I see the young human is confused," said the voice again, this time much closer along with the whirring and clicking sounds. "My child, do not fret. I am no monster, only a humble guardian of this sacred place." The voice died for a moment, but the clicking and whirring sounds continued on. "Now," it said in a thoughtful tone, "where on earth are those books . . . . . I had placed them by the Mermaids and Sirens section, but perhaps someone moved them . . . . ah, here we are. Darjeel Master, I have found a book that I think will explain the war to the human, if you do not mind. It has been quite some time since I researched such a subject."

"Not at all, Master Assam." The whirring and clicking noises grew louder and louder. Monica looked around at the other patrons, wondering if the noise was bothering them. They were in their own worlds with their books and documents and appeared to not notice.

Just then, something light brushed against Monica's right shoulder. She turned and gasped. Hovering over her was a giant brass mantis staring at her with an inquisitive look while it clutched a very thick book in one of its claws. Monica trembled just as Shevra placed a hand on her arm.

"This is Master Assam," said Shevra in a reverent voice. Monica stopped shaking and took a good look at the mantis; it was a large construct made of perpetually moving and visible brass gears while brass plates covered part of its body. Its eyes rolled around in their sockets, making a clicking sound, while its antennae moved here and there as if constantly searching for something. It continued to stare at Monica for a moment with its strange eyes then placed the book gently on the table between her and Shevra. Monica glanced at the title; the large blue leather-bound book read **THE LIN WAR** in gold letters across the top of the book.

"I am so sorry that I could not locate it earlier," said Master Assam in a voice so gentle that Monica did a double take. The mantis then moved back from the two and folded its arms in waiting. Monica could not believe it and yet she could at the same time.

"You . . . were the voice I just heard all around me?" she whispered, unsure of her voice.

Assam chuckled, causing several gears to whir even faster in its 'stomach'. "Yes, child, I was that same voice. Now, tell me, why are you looking up books on such a subject, Darjeel Master?"

"I told her of my past and my background. She has a right to know."

"Ah yes, the Lin War," replied Assam while its eyes rolled around. "I was not there yet I do remember hearing of it through others that passed through here. A terrible time it was; from what I was told, blue Lin blood covered the fields of your home for months due to the loss of so many."

"By Puhera's tears, it was a terrible time," said Shevra. "My parents were caught up in the war and were killed because of it. Had I been older during that time, I do not think I would have been a part of it. Thank the gods I was too young then."

"You would not have had a choice," said Master Assam. "They forced many of your order to join against their will, although some did join voluntarily."

"What was the war about?" asked Monica, fully caught up in this discussion.

"Long ago," began Master Assam as his voice took on a deep storyteller tone, "the Otherworld came into existence. A world of magic, danger, good versus evil and wonders beyond description. For a time, we Other folk were happy for our world had neither boundaries nor any limitations. We simply were and still are." Several beings sitting near them noticed Master Assam talking to the two and moved closer to hear what he had to say; it was a rare treat to hear a tale told by the Guardian and Archivist of the Library of the Otherworld. Master Assam's voice was rich and powerful yet calm and comforting as it passed through the many hallways and areas of the Arcanum. He possessed the power of knowledge, academia and older magics; he was one of the few creatures of the Otherworld whom all respected.

"My child," said Assam when Monica stared at him with a questioning face, "you must understand that the Lin War began not when the actual battles took places, but during the beginnings of the Lin race. That is key to this tale. To continue, in one corner of the world lay an area now almost forgotten. However, the inhabitants of that area were powerful magicians and weavers of the Path. Unfortunately, they used their magic for evil; they could have done wonderful things with what they knew. Due to the misuse of their knowledge, they inadvertently struck up bad chords between themselves and other races. Fights and battles broke out here and there, causing a slow decimation of their kind. There were some who wanted to change their ways to good, finding a place among the rest of the Other folk, while others wanted to continue in their evil ways. Even more fights occurred and soon, the one became two. Those that desired good fled to another part of the world while those that remained evil, thanks to their own devices, fled the world altogether and searched for a new world to occupy and control."

Assam stopped speaking for a moment and lifted its head towards the sky blue ceiling. The gears in its eyes whirred and clicked and for a moment, Monica wondered if it was about to shut down. However, he lowered his head once more towards the steadily growing group and continued on.

"Those that stayed to become good in their ways were soon known as Lin while those who fled eventually discovered a new plane and named it Earth." Shevra glanced at Monica's intense face. "They became known as Humans." Monica's eyes went wide with an incredulous look as she looked around the area and noticed that everyone was now looking at her. She looked away from them in a form of shame then looked into Master Assam's brass eyes.

"We came from the Otherworld?" she whispered. Assam nodded yes, causing some of the gears to whirr. She shook her head in disbelief. "But I thought we were the product of evolution or God?"

"Neither, it would seem," said Master Assam in a tender voice. "Humans and Lin came from the same line, but when the Humans left the Otherworld for Earth, they lost their ability to perform magic. They also lost their memory over time of ever being able to do so. Once tales of the humans reached the Otherworld with regards to their loss of memory, attempts were made to rekindle a sort of peace with them. Since they no longer knew where they truly came from, it was seen as wiping the slate clean. However, there were some folk from the Otherworld who came to Earth and discovered that some of the humans still retained a sliver of their knowledge yet without the evil intent. It was then that contracts were formed with cities, making sure that those who retained the Gift or the Path would remember the Otherworld.

"With that in mind, let us now turn to the Lin War. About 300 years ago, several male Lin decided to travel to Earth for their studies; traveling to and from was commonplace. In any case, these scholars landed in London or Aurwen, one of the many towns and cities that held a peace bond with the Otherworld. Humans of the Path welcomed them as their studies went underway. After a time, they fell in love with human women and several even married them. When it was time to return, they took their wives with them back to their city. While some greeted the scholars and their human wives with happiness and acceptance, others did not. They remembered all too well of the humans' past and found themselves distrustful of any humans.

"Those that protested were, at first, silenced in a peaceful attempt, but they later refused to lay down and accept; they felt that they were the better of humans and wanted to keep their race pure from such taints of long ago." Assam whirred and clicked for several seconds. "I guess you know the rest. Fights broke out everywhere, the scholars were executed while their wives and children were tortured in the worst possible way. Fights became battles, battles became wars, and soon there was blood."

"My parents were on the side of accepting and treating humans as equals," said Shevra. "We came from the same source, albeit evil, but that was in the past. They paid for their beliefs with their lives, something I will never forget."

"None of the Lin have forgotten, Master Darjeel," said Assam, "for it was because of that war that your order was used as weapons rather than healers and priests. Since they both carried the magic of both male and female, their power towards evil was unsettling."

"If you knew the history of your people with regards to this war," asked Monica, "then why did you want to become a Master Darjeel?"

"Because, like my parents, I believed in the ability to do good with my combined magic. I wanted to help remove the wound of the past to create a new beginning for my people." Master Assam nodded his giant head in agreement then looked down at the book he had located for them.

"It would appear that my tale has taken the place of you reading the book," he said with a metallic chuckle. " I do have a rather nasty habit of going on and on with my words." The crowd dispersed and went back whatever they were doing before yet glad that they were able to listen to one of his 'lectures'.

"Well, I for one am glad that you did," said Monica while handing the book back to Assam. "I never knew this history, but I feel better for knowing it. Would it do me any good for me to tell others about it?"

"Although there are towns and cities in your world that know of us and what I just told you, trying to tell the blind ones would do you no good."

"The blind ones?"

"They are those who continue to forget their past and that magic exists," said Shevra. "They are blind to the world around them, focusing only on their daily limited lives. They are born, they live and they die. Sometimes, there is a spark of something hidden, something longing, but it usually squashed out. On Earth, technology is the ruler and magic is nothing more than fairy tales parents tell their children at night. You, however, are aware of your

inner spark or else you would not have been drawn to Mabon."
Master Assam listened to the exchange with interest. Shevra turned
to Assam and bowed low with Assam repeating the action in kind,
and then Monica cried out when he suddenly turned and skittered
off to the shelves in the blink of an eye.

"You are most welcome here at any time," floated Assam's voice
from all around. "May your Path be strong." There were more
clicks and whirrs and soon the Arcanum was quiet.

Shevra turned to Monica and said, "I think it's time we went
back." Monica said nothing, but offered her hand and let Shevra
lead the way back to Mabon. She had much to think about.

The trip back to Mabon took less time for the two. When they
returned to the forest grove, it was still nighttime and Shevra had
turned back into Benjamin. He checked his watch; only 30
minutes had passed since they left. Monica shivered and crossed her
arms as cool air blew through the trees.

"How far is it back to town?" she asked while watching her
breath come out in steam.

"It's about a ten minute walk, but I can get you home faster,"
replied Benjamin. "Hold on my coat." Monica grabbed his thick
wool coat and suddenly the grove around them trembled and
shook. She closed her eyes, fearing she would get sick as the sound
of rushing waves came to her ears. "Okay, we're here," he said in her
ear. Monica opened her eyes and found them standing in front of
her apartment.

She released his coat and said in wonder, "Thanks, but what did
you do?"

"We Lin are also known for teleportation; it helps greatly in
certain situations." Benjamin brushed off his coat for a moment
then continued, "Get some rest tonight." He turned as if to walk
away until Monica said, "Would you like some tea or something?"
Benjamin turned with a smile and followed Monica inside.

"It felt good being back in the Otherworld," he said as he blew
on his steaming cup of Earl Grey. He took a small sip then sighed.

"Why don't you go back to your home more often?" asked Monica who sat on the floor by his feet with her own cup in hand. "How is it there?"

"It's okay, but to tell you the truth, I like it here in Mabon. The humans have been welcoming to me and not once have I had any problems, although Ophelia feels differently. She loves Mabon as well, trying to learn everything she can for future studies and the like, but she misses home more than I. I guess you would say she is more of a Lin than I." Benjamin chuckled then took a deep sip of his tea and exhaled, watching the steam come out of his mouth.

"I bet," said Monica, taking another sip of her tea. "So, I gotta know; did you really have a girlfriend who hated your geeky ways, or was that something you made up for my benefit?"

"Actually, I did have a girlfriend, but that was before we moved to Mabon. We did try other cities before coming here, some connected and some not. Our last city was not and it was torturous not being able to shift into my true self outside. During that time, I stayed as Benjamin." Monica stole a glance at him as he talked then back at her mug. So much in so little time. Although Benjamin looked like a typical human, she knew that he was not. She felt a tug at her heart.

"Benjamin?"

"Hmmm?"

"Would you mind changing back into your true self?" Monica's eyes glanced away for a moment then focused back on his shocked face. "I appreciate you being honest with me. So," she said while placing a hand on his arm, "would you? I would feel comfortable if you did. For a moment, I want to cry and I don't know why." Benjamin stared at her in shock, almost dropping his mug on the floor. He placed the mug on the coffee table and moved down to the floor to sit next to her. He took her hands in his own and asked, "Are you sure?" Monica's smile was her answer and he smiled in kind; he suddenly glowed with a soft white light and soon, Shevra sat next to Monica while still holding her hands.

Shevra looked down at her hands and said in a soft voice, "Thank you for understanding, Monica." Monica felt tears brimming in her eyes, but she refused to let them fall. Instead, she leaned over to the Lin Ambassador and kissed him on his soft and cool cheek. When she pulled away, Shevra grabbed her face with his hands and kissed her fully on the lips. At once, Monica felt lightheaded and happy as she shared this touching moment with the ambassador. As they kissed, she felt his hands leave her face and move slowly down her body that caused ripples through her skin. She thought she heard a sea gull crying in the distance, but blocked everything out, but Shevra and his soft hands.

They kissed for several minutes then Shevra pulled away from her and said, "I wish to open the clam with you," in a sincere tone. Monica shrugged her shoulders, not knowing what he meant, causing Shevra to chuckle. "I forgot that you are not familiar with our terms," he said. "Open the clam means making love." Monica blushed and nodded yes. "Open the clam is a sacred ritual in Lin. It is the ultimate form of emotion shown between two individuals." Monica nodded again, showing that she understood the situation. "First, I must undress you." He got up from the floor and helped Monica to the couch then slowly removed her clothing and placed each layer carefully on the floor by their feet. Shevra's eyes focused on her own while searching for any signs of uncertainty or fear. The last thing he wanted to do was scare or force Monica into something that she did not reciprocate in kind. Monica's eyes were, thankfully, clearing enjoying her current situation. Shevra let out a small sigh of relief and continued to undress her.

When she was completely naked, she instinctively crossed her arms over her chest as a knee jerk reaction until Shevra tenderly pulled her arms away. "Do not hide yourself from me," he said with a smile in his voice. "You are a beautiful woman." Monica allowed him to pull her arms away. Once done, Shevra then said, "Now, you must undress me." With trembling hands, she reached up to his shimmering robe, noticing that it felt like silk, and then slowly removed it from his body and placed it reverently by his feet. She noticed that his was completely naked under the robe and solid white shift. His chest was smooth and muscular while his lower half revealed a very large and throbbing member that quivered. When she finished, Shevra then got up and led her to her dark bedroom.

"Do I need to turn on the lights?" she asked.

"No, please do not. You will not need it," said Shevra in a cryptic tone. He led her to the bed and sat her down next to her. Her eyes adjusted to the darkness and she could quickly make out his dimly glowing skin. Shevra could see her perfectly in the dark and he smiled as he saw her hesitation on her face. He cupped her face in his hand and murmured, "Qualan ule mathala," then brushed his lips against hers. She shivered when his cold and soft lips met her own, wanting him to take her right then and there. Shevra then laid her down on the bed while he lay next to her on his side.

"Close your eyes," he said and Monica did so. Suddenly, she felt something warm and thick seep over her body. She wanted to cry out at the shock of it yet kept her mouth shut. The thick liquid traveled down her body, between her breasts and just at the tip of her warm sex. She shivered then cried out as part of the thick liquid seeped into her sex, pulsating as it did so.

"Qualan ule mathala," she heard whispered in her ear as the liquid now solidified inside of her and began a slow thrust. The rest of her chest remained covered with the liquid until it too began to solidify and caress her. It felt as though there were ten hands all over her, touching and pleasing her in a way she had never felt before. She heard Shevra's words over and over in her body as the liquid pulsating inside and on top of her. She reached up with her hands and felt Shevra's semi liquid body hovering over her. She felt kisses lighter than a butterfly's wings caress her neck and forehead and she ached with every one of them. Monica opened her eyes and saw Shevra's glowing and slightly liquid form pulsating over her while his eyes focused on her. The two then closed their eyes at the same time just as his body turned completely into liquid and enveloped her.

For a moment, she panicked, thinking that she would not be able to breathe, but soon relaxed when she found out that she could. The liquid slowly covered her body while his thrusts increased with speed; Monica moaned with every thrust and at times heard Shevra moaning as well. She felt the pressure inside of her wanting to be released, but it felt too good to stop. She could tell that Shevra was about to have an orgasm; she wondered deep down just how it would show within the Lin ambassador. She found out soon because just as she came and opened her eyes, she saw Shevra pull up from her body and, with a scream sounding like several seagulls in flight, turned solid once more as his chest morphed and blossomed like a deep green flower while the smell of salt water hit her senses. His eyes were wide open and focused on the ceiling, but he could not see for he was lost in the experience. Monica stared wide-eyed at this eerily beautiful display while the smell overpowered her. Her eyes fluttered and soon she fell asleep with Shevra soon after.

Shevra laid next to his sleeping partner, watching Monica's body slowly rise and fall. During his life, he had only two lovers, one female Lin and his last human girlfriend before he moved to Mabon. The Lin female was his first love while the human girlfriend was barely tolerable when she was not drunk or drugged out of her mind. Monica was different. She exhibited a desire that he had not experienced before, a desire to understand and know more now that the faucet of her inner self had been turned on. Monica's past seemed to be a shell of herself; she never had a chance because she refused to allow herself to have said chance. Now that she lived in Mabon and finally understood just why she was brought here, the floodgates opened and nothing was held back. Her orgasm was proof enough. Shevra calmed his mind down for the moment and turned his attention to his sleeping partner. He watched beads of sweat trickle down her face; one landed on her lip and he reached over to brush it off. When his fingers touched her lips, Monica's eyes fluttered open. When his eyes met her sleepy ones, he smiled then placed a cold hand on her cheek. Shevra's body provided just enough of a glow so that Monica could see him in the dark bedroom.

"That was wonderful," he said. "I hope it was wonderful for you as well."

"I . . . I've never seen anything like that before," she stammered as images came flooding back into her mind, dissolving any cobwebs of sleep. "It was beautiful."

"Thank you. Were you afraid at all?"

"For a brief moment yes, but I knew that you wouldn't do anything to hurt me, although I will admit that your body turning your liquid was quite, um, well-"

"Unsettling?" replied Shevra with a smile.

"I couldn't have said it better myself."

"I will not harm you and you are free to tell me if something does not please you." He shifted a bit on the bed then lay on his back. "Since we have experienced this particular ritual, we are now bonded together. What we did is not for casual reasons. When the Lin mate with someone, it is for life unless death, treachery or a mutual consent to dissolve the union occurs. My Lin mate, my first love, died."

"What happened?" Monica snuggled closer to her Lin partner and draped an arm over his hairless chest. She smelled a faint yet still detectable salt-water scent. Suddenly, she noticed her arm vibrating on Shevra's chest. She looked up and saw tears in his eyes.

"Yasmin died due to being poisoned," said Shevra as tears rolled down his face. "She was out swimming by some of the coral areas of the ocean by our city; it was one of her favourite pastimes aside from reading and making her own blends of tea."

"She sounds like me," said Monica, trying to lighten up the situation. Shevra glanced over at her and gave her a ghost of a smile then focused on the ceiling again.

"She went out after spending some time with me, promising to return to my home later that night. According to one of our healers, she must have stepped on a violet fish while out swimming. Violet fish, although very beautiful, are one of the more dangerous sea life creatures. As soon as she stepped on it, the fish stung her with its toxic fin, immediately sending the poison into her system. Within a minute of receiving the poison, one begins to feel dizzy and nauseous. Yasmin, being a strong Lin, barely swam back to town then dragged herself to the Darjeel temple. She knocked on the door once and fell into a coma just as the door opened.

"The healers brought her in and, once identifying her, sent for me. I raced there as fast as I could, but I was too late. She was dead when I reached the temple. Verthe was there; in fact, he was the one who opened the door and brought her in."

"That must have been truly hard for you," said Monica, trying to offer sympathetic words to a horrible situation too late.

Shevra patted her hand. "She meant the world to me; she was a student in the temple when I met her. She had not received her Final Training in which she would accept the male aspect into her life. We started as friends and fellow followers of Darjeel then soon our mutual feelings for each other developed."

"So, was Yasmin not able to heal herself because she did not have the male side of your magick yet?" asked Monica in confusion.

"Sadly yes. I could have even given her a part of my male magick to help her remove the poison from her system, but it was too late." Monica rolled over to her night table and turned on the lamp. Shevra could tell from the look in her eyes that she had more questions and was not prepared to go back to bed.

"So, with me having my own Path," she began in a thoughtful tone, "is what I have male or female?"

"Your magick is female," answered Shevra. "Only a member of my Order can have both. Even though your race and mine stemmed from the same root, you are not able to do what I can do."

"Not even if I want to become a member of your Order?"

"I am sorry, but the Darjeel Order is only for my race." Monica lowered her head in silence as Shevra took her in his arms and held her tightly. "You can only do so much with what you have, but don't worry, I will assist you in your training, if you'd like." He felt Monica nod her head yes.

"The fact that humans came from the same creature in the Otherworld as the Lin did is still a concept I'm trying to swallow," she mumbled in his arms. She looked up and lovingly stared into his eyes. "Not that I am complaining, mind you, but it's still an interesting theory. It makes me sad, though."

"Why?"

"Well, because of our stubbornness, the humans lost most of their magical side when they reached Earth. I wish we still had more of it."

"In your own way, you have some of it left in you. Through coming to Mabon and entering into the Otherworld, your internal blocks have been removed. So, rather than a trickle, you now have a flood." Monica removed herself from his embrace and laid on her back to let what Shevra said digest. It was truly a shame that she could not tell her family about her new gift; they would immediately come for her and lock her up in the nearest mental hospital for 'her own good'. She knew she was not insane, nor did she need any help from a doctor or little red pills to take away the pain. The Otherworld was real; there was no more room for doubt in its existence or her own difference in the world. There were others out there who were in the same position and suddenly, she no longer felt alone. She turned off the light and closed her eyes just as Shevra laid down next to her and soon, the two were asleep again.

She dreamt that night of an immense forest grove with trees dressed in eternal autumn leaves while the air smelled of fresh apple blossoms.

When Monica awoke again, she was alone. She yawned and stretched then got up to put on a pair of black yoga pants with an oversized shirt. She brushed her hair to control the tangles then walked through the apartment looking for Shevra although she knew he was already gone. As she searched each room, her smile increased as thoughts of last night came back to her. It seemed so far away that she visited a major place in the Otherworld and yet it was only yesterday. A blush came to her cheeks when her thoughts replayed opening the clam with Shevra; being with an Otherworlder sexually was quite . . . . interesting. She laughed then clapped a hand over her mouth then let her hand fall. She beamed a smile while standing in her living room; she had every right to be happy.

She found the note when she reached her kitchen. She took it back to the living room and sat down on the couch. Her eyes glanced over to Shevra's empty mug still on the coffee table then at the note left by him.

Monica,

Thank you very much for last night. I appreciated our time together. I am also glad we opened the clam. Perhaps this is a fresh start in a good direction for us both. I look forward to such and I hope you do as well. In any case, I will be teaching today while Ophelia will be at the theatre rehearsing tonight. Please come by my home after 7 tonight and spend the night with me. I will make us breakfast tomorrow, if you wish.

Qualan ule mathala,

Benjamin

Monica skipped through her apartment getting herself ready for work, already wanting the day to hurry up and finish so that she could go to his home.

Thirty minutes later, Monica walked out of her apartment fresh and ready for the new day, only to later realize that she left her car at the parking lot by her store. At that moment, a gull screamed from overhead and suddenly, her petty concerns dissolved and replaced with something brighter. A smile appeared on her face as she began her ten-minute walk to work, fully intent on enjoying the sunny yet chilly autumn day.

As she walked along, she noticed a black clad person bent over something in someone's yard. The person seemed to be intently focused on whatever they were doing at the moment. Monica stopped walking to stare at the back of the person, wondering what they were doing. Several seconds later, the figure sat up and turned around with a bunch of herbs in her hand. She was dressed in a long sleeved black velvet dress with a black and purple corset over it. Her skin was white as milk that stood out in the dress, accentuated by her black bobbed hair with black lipstick and dark eye shadow. The woman saw Monica staring at her and smiled as she walked towards her.

"Greetings and salutations," said the woman in a slightly smoky voice. "Who might you be?"

"I'm Monica Burton. I work at the bookstore downtown." The woman's eyes lit up in recognition.

"Ah, you work with Miranda, yes? Very nice." She looked down at the bunch of herbs in her hand then back at Monica. "Gathering a bunch of herbs from my friend Tom; lets me take some of his stuff every now and then. Trying to get stuff ready for our black collar lunch tomorrow. He's a Faerie, ya know. Good with plants. Great green thumb." In another time, Monica would have been freaked out by the Goth woman's conversation, but since last night, things had taken quite a turn for the better.

"Ah, you must be the one who owns the floral shop that I've heard about," said Monica, causing the woman to smile a black-lipped smile. She pulled her shoulder bag around to the front, dropped the herbs in and then extended her hand for Monica to shake.

"Name's Jacqueline. Jacqueline du Mauvais. Anyone tell you about our Goth scene here? You look like a sympathizer." Jacqueline pulled her hand away and took a good long look at her clothing; Monica wore one of her long black skirts with black opaque tights, a black long sleeved shirt with black clunky shoes and silver hoop earrings to complete the outfit. She adjusted her shoulder bag on her shoulder then grinned.

"I guess I'm more of a Goth than just a sympathizer," Monica replied, earning a nod from Jacqueline.

"Stop by the store sometime. Would love to see you. We do black collar lunch once a week at the cemetery. Goth Night in the basement of my store. Created it myself. Good speaker system, that." Jacqueline beamed with pride. Monica couldn't help, but chuckle at Jacqueline's confidence and her staccato speech.

"How many Goths are in the town?"

"'Bout thirty of us here. Like family, ya know. Anyway, gotta push off. Stop by sometime. Later!" Jacqueline pulled up her skirt, revealing very large black combat platform boots and then headed off in the other direction with a confident and yet creepy walk. Monica shook her head in wonder; this town had more than its share of wonders and surprises, she thought as she continued her walk to work, more than ready for a day of selling books with Miranda.

Several weeks passed. Since her time in the Arcanum, Monica's world turned promptly upside down; she had been blind to the supernatural charm of Mabon while still able to feel a tingle. Now that she had visited the other side of the Veil plus began an intimate and deep relationship with a person from the Otherworld, the true side of Mabon came out in full force. Ghosts from every age floated by, each whispering their own tales of loves lost and won, sorrows and joys and repeated moments of history long lost except in books. The mermaid statues at her apartment complex winked at her a couple of times, almost causing her to run into a telephone pole. When she told Gina about it, Gina just smiled then stated that they must have been having a slow week since they normally jumped from their base and swam around in the pool. Of course, it didn't help when Monica caught Gina swimming with the statues in the pool one night. When she saw Gina's shimmering tailfin wave at her, she stripped naked and joined them for a night of cold swimming.

Certain trees and other greenery sighed and sang songs in their language, floating their words along the breezes of the eternal autumn town. From time to time, an Otherworlder would suddenly pop into existence somewhere in the town while the human inhabitants went on with their day. Occasionally, a visitor to the town would catch sight of something out of the ordinary and would either run screaming in the opposite direction or try to ask someone if they too just saw a creature made of leaves and twigs only a foot high suddenly walk in front of them and begin dancing a jig. Of course, the townspeople would only laugh at that person, stating that perhaps they needed a cup of tea or a sit down on a bench to regain their senses followed with recommendations of where to do said activities.

Monica enjoyed her newfound sense of the mortal and Otherworld worlds around her, giving her a new outlook on life. She no longer thought about her miserable time back at her old home for it had dissolved into the past, never to be reborn again. She found that she could send invisible lines to various people to find out what they were thinking as well as "tap" someone on the shoulder to get their attention. When she visited Laurel again at the library, she was able to made her dead friend become solid for over an hour with barely a thought. Laurel patted her shoulder and told her that it was good to see her purple ball out in full force.

Her friends steadily increased, each blessed with the Sight of the Otherworld or touched by its magick. With every friend she learned more of her own Path as well as the magick that surrounded their town and their lives. Of all of her friends, Shevra proved to be the most influential of her life. During their time spent together, Shevra told her more of life in the Otherworld along with projected images created by Shevra's magic. Each time they 'opened the clam', Monica discovered something different about her lover that proved to be quite intoxicating yet scary at times. The bond between the two was strong; at times, she could hear Benjamin lecturing to his classes while he could hear her thoughts that sprinted along like graceful gazelles in a valley. Ophelia, noticing the change in Benjamin's attitude, welcomed it greatly. She knew Monica was good for him and he was good for her. Benjamin could feel Monica's every emotion and could also send her pleasant thoughts whenever she felt down or angry. She usually sent him jokes at the wrong times, causing him to break out in laughter while teaching class.

Ophelia spent much time with Monica, trying to further her knowledge of the Lin and how they and humans used to be one and the same. She also taught her their language, wondering if the knowledge buried deep inside of her would come up just by listening to her speak it. After a day of listening non-stop, Monica was able to ask both Benjamin and Ophelia basic questions in their language. A week later, she could hold her own during conversations between the twins without asking them to slow down. Her Lin side was waking up and it was hungry for knowledge.

One day, while Monica set up a display of cookbooks, Jacqueline walked in with a tall and very pale man who dressed in similar style to her, complete with long red hair pulled back with an indigo coloured ribbon. Jacqueline caught sight of Monica and walked over to her just as Monica got up from the floor.

"Monica, good to see you," said Jacqueline as she beamed a smile laced with deep purple lipstick. "Having black collar lunch in about an hour. Can you come? Would love to have you." She turned to her friend and said, "My husband Timothy. Professor of Ancient Roman and Greek Studies at Janus." Timothy grinned as he pushed his round glasses up his nose.

"Good to see you again and good to meet you, Timothy," said Monica. "Let me ask Miranda to see if I can get off work, okay?" She left the two and walked to the storeroom. She found Miranda opening several boxes of horror paperbacks with her back turned to her. Before Monica could get a word out, Miranda said with a chuckle, "Yes, you can go, just as long as you are back in an hour. I'm leaving early so I need you to close up shop later on today."

"How did you know I was going to-"

"I have extra sensitive ears, dearie," said Miranda as she now stood up and faced her assistant. "Plus, I could smell Jacqueline's perfume before she even walked in. Have a good time and let me know what the black collar lunch is like!" She turned back to her boxes with a satisfied grin on her face as Monica walked out with the same grin.

Monica walked to Phoenix Cemetery with Jacqueline and Timothy while receiving a bit of background information about the group. The day was chilly with a clear blue sky overhead, but when they reached the cemetery, the sky suddenly turned to a misty grey that only appeared over the cemetery and nowhere else. Monica looked up at the sky and the distinct line between the two skies then walked on. Such things were normal for Mabon.

"So glad you came with us today," said Jacqueline. "Always good to have new blood, ha!" Timothy grinned at the bad joke and even Monica smiled at the corniness of it. As they neared the group, Monica could hear someone softly playing the violin as they walked through the cemetery. She adored the fact that most Goth people danced to their own beat and followed their own path, although many who did not understand them labeled them as freaks of a bad kind and worshippers of Satan. She only saw them as lovers of the creepy and misunderstood, breathing life back into classic horror and the Gothic story. They understood that everything had a light and dark side; respecting and acknowledging the dark side was too important to ignore. She looked forward to meeting everyone.

There were twenty or so other black clad people sitting on black and grey blankets scattered throughout the tombstones of the cemetery. Some were enjoying glasses of wine while others munched on various fruits and vegetables. The violin player sat to the far right of the group on a large weathered rock. His head was lowered while he played a sad yet beautiful song on his red violin. He wore clothing of a Victorian gentleman: a long black coat that seemed to reach his knees with a crisp white shirt and black pants. His boots, however, spoke of modern times – thick platform boots with silver buckles. All of the attendees listened to him with rapt fascination; some of the women had tears in their eyes. When the violinist finished playing, everyone clapped politely. The man stood up and bowed low with violin and bow in hand.

"Thank you, one and all for your ears," said the man in a mellow voice. "I truly do appreciate it." Monica could not keep her eyes off him; he was tall and slender as his clothes fit him like a glove. His skin was a dusty grey while his short and spiky red hair stuck out in all directions, enhancing his pierced pointed ears. His golden eyes flashed like bolts of lightning while his red lips spoke dripped with seduction, hedonism and predatory fascination. He turned to the recently arrived trio and said with open arms, "Jacqueline! Timothy! And . . . who might this be?" he said with a grin. Monica walked over to the violinist and extended her hand.

"I'm Monica Burton," she said while shaking his slender hand. "I was invited by Jacqueline and Timothy today. Beautiful music." The violinist smiled back, showing all of his teeth.

"Monica, welcome to our black collar lunch," he said with a hint of an accent that Monica could not place. "I'm Auberon and I'm pleased you enjoyed my music so." Auberon continued to shake her hand while his eyes never left her face. Those eyes, she thought; how can they be so golden? Auberon released her hand then walked over to an Asian woman who only had eyes for him. He caressed her cheek and she audibly sighed.

"Brought a blanket," said Jacqueline as they walked around trying to find a spot for themselves, "unless if you enjoy sitting on cemetery grass."

"No, I think I'll enjoy the blanket more." The trio spread out the grey and black striped blanket on the ground then sat down. Instantly, twin women dressed in all black with white blonde hair walked up to them with plates covered in food.

"Please, won't you have some?" said the twin on the left at Monica while the twin on the right held out her plate. Monica accepted it and noticed that it was an assortment of cheeses and crackers plus three rather large strawberries. She took the plate and nibbled on a piece of cheese while Jacqueline and Timothy received the same. The cheese melted in her mouth with a slight smoky aftertaste and soon, she had gobbled down half of her plate.

"What kind of cheese is this?" she asked once the twins moved on to the others. "It's incredible!"

"It's from the Otherworld," said Timothy around a mouthful of cheese and crackers. He swallowed then continued, "Auberon brings it to our black collar lunches since he has so much of it. He is a trader of goods on both sides and is able to pick this up at a decent rate." Monica's eyes glanced over to Auberon who was still entertaining his Asian friend. He whispered something in her ear and she giggled while holding a gloved hand to her mouth. "He was known as the Bone King," said Timothy in Monica's ear, startling her. "He used to steal the bones of the dead from cemeteries and graveyards all over the Otherworld and on Earth as well and then used them in his magics and for other reasons. It was said he could also steal the bones from a living person as well, reducing them to a quivering mass of flesh and blood. He was very high up in the Unseelie Court until one day, he stole the bones of an important member of the Court during a heated argument-"

"Of which the bastard had it coming," said Auberon who had suddenly materialized between Timothy and Monica, causing them both to jump. He winked at Monica then laughed, a rich sound laced with the smoky fog of the cemetery. He glanced at Timothy, who shifted over to the side to give him room, as he settled himself next to Monica. Monica could feel his body heat and almost fainted; he smelled so strangely . . . Jacqueline couldn't help, but laugh out loud as she sipped from her glass of apple juice. "Yes, I stole the bones from one of the lovers of the Unseelie Queen when he insulted me and my heritage, of which I am sensitive about. The Viril are proud, even though we are undead." Monica caught a whiff of his scent, but could not figure out the contents. Strangely enough, the mixture was somewhat pleasant and fitting for their current circumstances.

"I stole his bones in the middle of the night; each one smelled of his ridiculous perfume that he wore in order to continue his favour with the Queen." Auberon's eyes glazed over for a moment, revealing a flash of black malevolence that Monica had not thought possible with him. He blinked once and it was replaced with his usual sparkling gold. "I placed him in a deep sleep so that he would not wake up while I did my work. When it was all over, I released him from the spell just as I was about to leave. Unfortunately, I underestimated him; apparently, he wore a charm warding all harm come to him. Although he no longer had any bones, he still leapt from his bed with a dagger covered in deadly nightshade, aiming it straight for my heart." He touched his chest briefly.

"I barely made it out, but not before he nicked my chest with the blade. Even though I am undead, the poison still affected me. I threw myself out of his window and flew off as fast as I could." Monica cocked her head with a questioning look on her face; Auberon laughed as he stood up and arched his back, gaining everyone's attention. They watched in fascination as immense skeletal wings erupted from his back. They creaked as he flapped them once then, with a small salute, flew straight up into the eternal grey sky. Everyone watched as the Bone King flew with grace and style; he dipped and turned with precision and not once did he lose footing. Several minutes later, he glided back down towards the group and landed in the same spot he took off. The wings folded upon themselves and soon disappeared in his clothing. Several of the group clapped politely as he did a light bow then joined Monica back on the blanket.

"That is what saved me from true death," he said in a calm tone. "I flew to my town to find a healer who could remove the poison from my system. When it was removed, I went to my home and rested for a while. Some time later, I heard rumours that the person whose bones I stole had died; seems his charm did not work at all. I knew that I could no longer go back to the Court. However, everyone knew me as the Bone King, so I came to Earth through one of our portals and landed in London.

"The year was 1910. I had never been to Earth, but had heard stories of the different cities here. I knew of some of my kind who had traveled here and remained on Earth so I went looking for them. I found them living by one of the cemeteries; they opened the door before I could knock on it, welcoming me in and allowing me to stay with them for a while. I could not go back to Merden, my home city, for some time, so I had to make do with living in London. I found that the folk I stayed with worked as gravediggers for the churches in their area. I also took up a job working in familiar territory and soon, I began trading items among the humans and Otherworld folk in London. I gained a reputation as a trader and it stuck with me.

"Ten human years passed before I set foot in the Otherworld again; when I did, I realized that no one recognized me. There were no warnings from the Unseelie Court or bounties placed on my head. It felt good to return home, but it still felt different since I rejected my title. When I traveled to Merden, I learned that there was a new Bone King and my name had 'disappeared' from the records, thanks to my family who tried to help me. I gave them my eternal gratitude and left after a while. Now I am Auberon, Trader and Bard of the Darkness. I've spent the past month here in Mabon and so far, it has been good to me." Auberon yawned and stretched, giving off more of his unusual odor. "What's great is that I have been able to travel more since becoming a Bard and Trader than when I was the Bone King. I still steal bones from time to time, but I no longer use them for any personal magical purposes. Have you ever visited the Arcanum?"

"Yes, I was there not too long ago," said Monica while both Timothy and Jacqueline stared at her in shock.

"Ah, then you must have either heard or seen Master Assam, then. He and I came to a rather interesting agreement many years ago. Although he is Archivist and Guardian for the Arcanum, he does not get to leave the place. Fortunately for him, there are many who bring him the information he requests and needs in order to add to the stock. I provide bones for him and he reads the history that emanates from them." Now it was Monica's turn to stare with shock. Auberon waved his hands in a placating gesture. "Bones are records of history long ago and of the people who lived during those times. In a way, reading bones is like reading the rings of a tree to determine its age. It's quite simple, really: Master Assam tells me where to go and I go there to collect the bones. Sometimes, the bones are still, how shall we say, fresh?" Monica rolled her eyes at the lame attempt in black humour. "I make no apologies for what I am and what I do," he said in a suddenly stern voice. "I am proud to be what I am, much to the hatred of those who are living. Some see my kind as a blemish upon their fair Otherworld, even though it has its share of malevolence and deception. I do not think of myself as an evil being, just one that is sinister." This time, he flashed a grin so wide and toothy that Monica wondered if perhaps now was a good time to leave and yet she felt herself lingering for more of his words and unusual scent. Auberon's eyes flashed once more as he stared at her while grinning his grin that would have made the Cheshire Cat quite jealous.

Timothy, thankfully, checked his watch then said, "Monica, we need to get you back to work. Miranda needs to leave early, right?" Monica nodded and soon, the trio made their goodbyes and plans for next time with the others. Monica felt somewhat bad that she did not get a chance to converse with the other Goths, but knew that she would see them again soon. As they got up to fold their blanket and clean up their plates, Auberon walked over to Monica and said in a low voice, "Thank you for listening to me and my long winded tale. For some reason, it felt good to speak of it."

"You are quite welcome," she replied. "I'm glad you were willing to tell me." Monica stared into his eyes and felt a slight tug, just as Auberon's eyes flashed. She could smell his scent even more so along with a desire to touch his skin. Suddenly, Auberon winked then, in a flash, leapt across the rest of the seated group to his rock. Once there, he whipped out his violin from behind him and began to play once more, but this time, the song was lighter than the previous song. The group waved good-bye at the leaving trio as they made their way back to the town. When Monica reached the cemetery gate, she could no longer hear Auberon's violin. She looked up and noticed that the sun was high in the robin's egg blue sky; the dividing line of the skies could still be seen from far away.

When the trio reached the bookstore, both Jacqueline and Timothy hugged their new friend then gave her information regarding their Goth Night, which was to occur in three days. Auberon would be there as the guest DJ; he had developed a love for music, especially Goth music and had an amazing CD collection from his travels.

"Best there is, ya know," said Jacqueline as she ran a hand through her hair. "Pretty neat that an undead faerie is our DJ."

"Did you catch his scent?" asked Timothy, to which Monica nodded yes. "It's his own special blend. Tried like hell to buy some of it from him, but he won't sell." Miranda knocked on the window and waved at the black clad trio. Monica hugged them once more with a promise that she would attend Goth Night, and then walked into the store, ready to resume her bookselling duties.

As Miranda watched the couple walk off, she asked, "Okay, so I gotta know, dearie; how was it? I've never really understood the whole Goth thing, but I still respect them for being themselves underneath all that black."

"Well, I have to admit; they were a great bunch of folks, plus I got to meet Auberon."

"Oh yeah, he used to come in here from time to time. How is he?"

"For an undead faerie, pretty cool."

After Miranda left an hour later, Monica prepared a pot of tea then walked back out to the store, patiently waiting for closing time which would occur in three hours. Every so often, someone came into the store looking for a book, to which Monica would locate for them and send them on their merry way. She then returned to her never empty cup of tea to sip and enjoy while watching people walk by. Occasionally, an Otherworlder would walk, crawl, or fly by, but it no longer raised any anxiety with her; she simply sipped her tea and enjoyed the beautiful afternoon.

30 minutes before closing time, Benjamin walked into the store, receiving a thorough hug from Monica. She could smell his saltwater scent as she pulled him closer to her, not wanting to let him go. He returned the embrace with the same amount of passion. When they finally parted, he sat down in one of the chairs while Monica told him about her lunchtime. When she finished, Benjamin sat back in his chair and stroked his chin in a thoughtful manner.

"I haven't seen Auberon in about 20 years," he said. "The last time I saw him was during a bazaar in my home city. He was haggling with a tea seller over the price of a rare tea made with scales of sea dragons. From what I've heard of him, he no longer has any alliance to anyone and tries to keep his personal life to himself unless if the person asking is worthy enough to listen," he said while casting a sidelong glance at Monica.

Monica chewed her bottom lip in silent deep thought for several minutes then said, "He told me that he gives bones to Master Assam, claiming that they possess the history of the Otherworld." She looked at him point blank. "Is that true?" Benjamin steepled his hands in front of his face and sighed as he tried to come up with a plausible answer then realized that the truth was the only answer for this question.

"Yes, it's true, but not in the way that you are thinking. The bones that are given to Master Assam are from very, very old souls who decide to become one with the Otherworld and keep it going as part of its eternal soul. Auberon used to steal the bones from others, but he has now taken a different path from his former cursed title of Bone King."

"So, if he still takes bones, then is there a current Bone King?"

"Oh yes there is. A woman, I am told. When Auberon fled his title, his kind replaced him with a mere figurehead, for they still consider him to be the rightful owner." Monica closed her eyes for a moment, trying to still remember Auberon's scent and his sad tale. Benjamin watched her with interest then got up from his chair and embraced her from behind. She opened her eyes once his hands found her waist.

"Let's go out for dinner tonight," he murmured in her hair. "Does Stingrays sound good?"

"That sounds great," she replied as her mind continued to ponder about Auberon. He was quite the enigma and rightfully so.

Stingrays proved to be quite busy that night; almost every table was full. After waiting for five minutes, they were finally seated to a small table in the back, providing some solitude for the couple. After they received their menus and their waiter took off with their drink orders, Benjamin said, "Do you mind if I shift to my true self?" Monica looked around with wide eyes.

"Is it safe to do that?' she asked while looking around. "Are there any . . . . you know . . . . normal-" Benjamin laughed while holding up his hand to stop her.

"It's quite all right," he said while chuckling. "I chose this place tonight because it is a haven for Otherworld kind and the citizens of the town. I will be quite safe." He closed his eyes while his body began to glow. Monica watched with fascination as her lover changed with liquid grace from a human male to a Lin Master of the Darjeel before her eyes. At times, the shifting still took her by surprise, but she refrained from completely freaking out. Within seconds, Shevra now sat across from her dressed in pale green pants and long sleeved cream shirt that shimmered when he moved.

"Wow," she said before realizing it, "when you do that, it still catches my breath."

"I hope in a good way?" asked Shevra with a small wink just as their waiter walked up to their table with their drinks. The waiter took their dinner orders then walked off again, leaving the two in peace once more.

"I wanted to continue our talk about Auberon, if you don't mind," said Shevra as Monica waved him to continue while taking a sip of her water. Shevra coughed once then went on. "I figured since you are still new to the area that you would not mind this impromptu history lesson. It makes living here somewhat better, I find." Monica silently nodded in agreement. "Auberon belongs to a race of faeries that must die when they are born. A local priest or priestess kills them and then they are awakened to their new life as one of the Viril. Their allegiance, if one could call it that, is with the Unseelie Court of Faerie, although the Court does not care for them too much. Call it a terse covenant between the two; the Court provides status while the Viril provides protection and strength from those who try to do the Court harm. From what I learned, the Viril are one of the oldest races in the Otherworld; no one really knows where they came from, but when they arrived, they made their presence known."

"So, they have to die when they are born so as to become a true Viril?" asked Monica. Shevra nodded sagely. Monica took another sip of her water while giving Auberon more credit than she had before. Shevra took a small sip of tea to whet his throat then continued.

"The Viril are fierce faeries, almost savage at times, but they also are involved in the arts and culture. Their kind produces more literature than any other and yet they are hated and feared for what they are by the other races of Faerie. When one thinks of faeries, one thinks of beauty and grace, a perfect and immortal being. Even the Unseelie Court has their version of beauty and perfection tainted with darkness. The Viril are disliked because of their undead nature, as though someone spit upon the faeries with a curse to last all time. However, as with the customs of the Unseelie Court, they must respect and honour the Bone King for he, and now she, is royalty no matter what. When Auberon was chosen to be the Bone King, I was told that the ceremony was beyond all ceremonies of Faerie. Even members of the Seelie Court made an appearance to catch a glance of the Viril's new king. When he arrived dressed in his withery grey cloak and bone crown, the room literally gasped as one. True, the Viril are not known to be of beauty, but Auberon was different; he was truly a beautiful creature, as you no doubt can agree with me." Monica's eyes flashed over briefly as she pictured the fiddler speaking to her earlier in the cemetery. He was a beautiful creature with just a hint of something morbid in her mind. She blinked once and the image went away. "When he arrived in the Unseelie Court to be crowned king, it was quite an event."

"So he had to leave it all behind just for the sake of killing one of the lovers of the Unseelie Queen," murmured Monica while Shevra nodded. "It was wrong what he did, but at the same time, I feel sorry for him."

"I do as well," said Shevra just as their food arrived. They ate in silence, giving Monica a chance to ponder over what Shevra told her. Now that she met Auberon, she wanted to meet other Viril, ones that were more of their true form than he. What was their city like, she thought. Would it be a typical city or would it be a necropolis? Monica glanced at her lover who ate his meal in silence and sighed. She had learned so much since moving to the small artistic town with still more to come. Meeting the townsfolk here was great thus far, but knowing that there was a whole other world beyond the Veil was something else entirely. I wonder what my mother would say if I told her that I was currently dating a shape shifter from another world, she thought then began to laugh, breaking the silence that enveloped Shevra. He looked up, blinked once, and then said, "What's so funny?" Monica placed her fork along the plate.

"Just had a thought about my mother and what she would say if she knew I was dating you."

"Well, if it ever came to me meeting her, she would meet Benjamin and not Shevra. Not everyone is awake and from what you told me, she most certainly is not awake and probably never will be." A ghost of a smile appeared on Shevra's face while a frown occupied hers as the wheels in her head began to turn again.

"So, a person that is not awake yet will not be able to see the Otherworld?" she asked.

"All they would see is mist before them," said Shevra while eating. "Not all humans have it inside of them. For some, it was burned out of them due to general ignorance, hatred, and more importantly, fear of the unknown. Some have been taught all their lives that certain things in the world cannot and do not exist; therefore, the inquisitive nature is killed. However, those who opened their minds in various ways wake up that dormant part of their makeup. They begin to question more and more and soon, they are drawn to a town or city like Mabon where they will be embraced for 'coming home'. Some leave their families behind; a terrible shame, but the Call is much stronger than any other bond out there."

"How long has this been going on?"

"Since the dawn of humankind. When humans arrived on Earth from the Otherworld, some struggled to remember their magical side while others were blissfully wiped clean. It was a dangerous time especially for those who slightly remembered what it was like to exist in the Otherworld. To go from magical to non-magical probably caused some to go insane or to end their lives right then and there. However, as I have stated before, some maintained what they remembered and kept it from those who did not. But, of course, as Time wore on, those who were awake were seen as envoys of the Devil, carrying out his foul deeds to the good humans on Earth. I am sure you have heard of the Salem Witch Trials." Monica nodded, feeling a cold stone form in her stomach. "Case and point." Shevra finished off his meal then wiped his lips with a napkin.

"So, am I a faerie or something?" she asked, causing Shevra to laugh.

"No you are not, but you do have traits of the Otherworld inside of you. When we first met, I talked to you because you were an attractive woman, but I also talked to you because I could smell your essence immediately."

"What do I smell like?" asked Monica with a grin. Shevra closed his eyes and inhaled deeply.

"Apples and burning leaves, for now," replied Shevra as he opened his eyes again. "Apples are a sacred fruit to the Otherworld. Have you ever eaten an apple and, for a moment, got a mental whiff of *something else out there*?" Before Monica could answer, Shevra continued. "There are those who awaken with help from others, both human and from the Otherworld. There are also those who awaken and have no idea what to do. They plunge right into it without proper guidance and are therefore immersed into the Otherworld. Many of those people end up in human mental institutions."

"Like Arabella?"

"Exactly. She awakened without anyone helping her and it literally drove her insane. Thankfully though, she did meet someone while committed who could help her during that process. Once that happened, her mind became clear and to her doctor's relief, was deemed sane within six months, never knowing that they did not do anything to help her. She was released, arrived here in a tattered dress, and the rest is history. Her friend, however, went completely to the Otherworld and has not looked back. From what Arabella told me, they still keep in contact with each other and her friend brings in exotic tea blends from her travels from time to time." Monica, realizing she had been sitting on the edge of her chair, leaned back to give comfort to her aching back. The waiter came up to clear their dishes and asked if they wanted any dessert, to which both replied no. After he left again with dirty plates in hand, Monica fell into a silence while thinking about what Shevra had told her. All of the fairy tales are true, she thought, causing her to shiver a little. Creatures of myth and legend were no longer just ideas placed on paper; they were real. Suddenly, the magnitude of what she had learned so far hit her like a ton of bricks.

"So, the fairy tales everyone grew up on are real?," she asked. Shevra nodded. Monica fell into silence again while the mental wheels spun even faster. It was so much, too much actually. What does one say to all of this, especially one who is awakened? Everything in her life was turned upside down. Were her parents even her true parents? It was one thing to acknowledge that she was different than others, but this . . . . well . . . .

Shevra noted the look of concern on her face and wondered if perhaps he had told her too much. He reached out with his hand and took hers while his eyes never left her face. For a moment, Monica looked down at the pale green hand, wondering whom it belonged to, then blinked several times and realized it was Shevra's.

"So much," she murmured to herself, but Shevra heard it anyway. She tightened her grip on Shevra's hand then said while looking at him squarely in the face, "What of the sci-fi and fantasy authors out there? Are their books actually journals of what they have seen or experienced in the Otherworld? Is fiction actually true?"

"Some of them, yes. Others heard their tales from someone else who traveled through the Otherworld. Still, others travel to the

Otherworld through their dreams and they write down their experiences, not realizing that they were actually there." Monica had always loved reading fantasy novels, enjoying the escapism they provided for several hours. In thinking back, however, she thought about her emotions while reading them. Did she feel excited to be reading a new book, or was it a deep connection between the magic of the book and the magic within her? Some of the books provided so much detail that one wondered if they truly had visited their fictional land. Now Monica knew otherwise. The waiter brought their check and Shevra pulled out some bills to pay for dinner along with a generous tip for the waiter, who blushed as he received it then thanked them both. Monica barely heard him; her mind was already far away in the Otherworld.

Chapter Five

The two left the restaurant to enjoy the Autumn night while strolling back to Monica's apartment. Shevra refrained from talking, only providing a warm body to walk next to Monica who was still lost in thought. She felt her hands slowly losing their grip on this current world yet she struggled to hold on although now she wondered why. Why remain in this world when there was another that had been calling to her mostly all of her life? She finally found what she needed and yet so much more.

They reached her apartment in silence. Monica looked up and, realizing that she was home, searched for her keys absentmindedly while he watched her with careful and hooded eyes. She found her keys after a while and let herself in, then turned to him and kissed him on the lips.

"I know I've been quiet," she said in a clear voice, much to his surprise, "but you've given me a lot to think about. More than I could ever hope to think about. Right now, I need to be alone. No offense to you and no, I am not angry with you for telling me all of this. In fact, I truly do appreciate it. I love you. Good night." She cupped his face tenderly then walked into her apartment and closed the door, leaving a surprised, but relieved Lin Ambassador. He placed a hand on his chest and soon transported to his home, where he quickly realized he was not alone.

There, standing in the middle of his living room, were two Lin, one male and one female, dressed in the common robes of their people. Ophelia sat in a chair by the female Lin while tightly holding her hand. When Shevra saw them, he smiled widely and extended his arms in a welcoming gesture.

"Ana! Nedai! How wonderful it is to see you," exclaimed Shevra as the other Lin smiled as well then embraced as Ophelia watched. "I have missed you, brother and sister."

"We have missed you two as well, Shevra," said Ana as the three continued to hug. When they all pulled away from each other, no one had dry eyes. Ana wiped her eyes on the sleeve of her robe while Nedai allowed his to fall down his face without any concern as they sat down on the couch while Shevra sat on the floor near them.

"Would you care for anything?" asked Shevra. Ana shook her head no while Nedai began to speak.

"Shevra, we come to you because we need you. We have already spoken with Ophelia and now it is your turn. Trouble has been brewing in our city and some feel it is the beginning of another war." Shevra's smile instantly fell and was replaced with a grim frown as he glanced in Ophelia's direction. "It comes to this: some of the Lin are becoming agitated that more and more humans are coming to our city. Normally, there would be no problems with that, but now it is different. Humans and Lin are marrying each other with the result of half-breed children. For some Lin, they see this as our blood being thinned out to the point of nothing."

"But that is ridiculous!" cried Shevra. "Humans and Lin were once the same race. Our magic is still strong, even with marrying humans."

"Brother, please," said Ophelia in a calm voice, trying to calm him down. Ana glanced at Ophelia and smiled tersely, knowing that this was not going to be an easy topic.

"Some will agree with you, Shevra," said Ana, now joining in the conversation, "but there have been threats on mixed families and especially their children, claiming them to drag the Lin towards a more human lifestyle. They see humans as animals, mere things that desecrated their world and deserve only death."

"More and more fights have occurred among humans and Lin and now, our streets run with both human and Lin blood." Shevra stood up and paced the floor. Another war, he thought, would not be good for my people. We are still cleaning up the mess from the last one. Such a shame that while there are those Otherworld races that have accepted awakened humans, others like the Lin still refuse to do so. Ana and Nedai watched their older brother pace with furtive glances at each other.

"Brother, they came to us because they needed help," said Ophelia. "Surely, you must understand this." Suddenly, Shevra stopped pacing and fixed them both with a direct glance.

"So, what is the Order of the Darjeel's role in all of this?" he asked, ignoring Ophelia. Nedai looked at his hands while Ana answered.

"To be used in cleansing the Lin from the human stench," she said in a calm voice. Shevra began to shake with anger while his skin glowed with a dark green glow.

"How dare they?" he said in a low and tight voice. "How dare they use the Order for that?" Ana got up and walked over to her angry sibling and placed a cool hand on his shoulder. "Please, calm yourself down." Shevra noticed the tears forming in her eyes and soon he calmed himself down, but only for her sake. Nedai watched without a word, but moved closer to Ophelia.

"So, are there others of the Order who are against this war?"

"Most are for it, while those who are not are quickly . . . made to see the truth."

Shevra looked at Nedai in horror. "Torture?"

"No. They are placed under a spell that makes them only see their side of the war."

"I see." Shevra closed its eyes and thought of Monica. Qualan ule mathala, my love. "I am sorry, brother and sister, but I can not be a part of this war." Ana and Nedai walked over to their sibling with shocked looks on their faces.

"B-but why not?" asked Nedai. "You are one of the stronger Darjeel. This war needs you."

"Although I feel strongly about this, I can not be a part of this. Besides, I am with someone here." Suddenly, both Ana and Nedai's eyes lit up with happiness.

"Shevra, what wonderful news!" exclaimed Ana. "Ah, and how long have you known this Lin female?" Shevra looked shocked.

"Lin female? No, I am with a human female, one who is awakened." Ana gasped in shock as Nedai cursed under his breath. Shevra lowered his eyes, now knowing his siblings' side of this war. Ophelia gasped in shock as well. She had thought they were on the side of unity, not war. How wrong she was.

"You told me you were for those who wanted to marry humans," she said in a stunned voice. Nedai turned to her with a cold expression on his face. Shevra walked up to him and placed a steel grip on his shoulder.

"You are with those who want pure Lin blood," he said in a low voice.

"It is better to be with your own kind, Shevra, rather than the human animals," spat Nedai with a sneer. "Remember who you are."

"I remember who I am, brother, but perhaps you need to be reminded of the same?"

"You reek of fish guts!" cried Ana, using one of the Lin's more heinous insults at her own sibling just as Ophelia rushed up to Ana. She tried to reach for her younger sister's arms, but Ana was too quick for her; in a second, Ana flipped around and, with a dagger she had hidden in the folds of her clothing, struck her older sister with precision and without any remorse. Shevra's mind almost fell apart when he saw his beloved Ophelia slump to the floor, her blue blood steadily pumping out of the fatal wound. He knew that she was dead, even if he tried all of his healing magick on her. He turned to the treacherous two and glared at them.

"I will not join a war that I do not believe in, nor will I leave Monica," said Shevra in a calm, but threatening voice.

"Monica! Hah! Is that the dog's name?" said Ana as she wiped her blade clean on her robe without a second thought. "You will join this war!"

"Never." Suddenly, Nedai, in a display of unnatural Lin speed, ran behind Shevra and placed his hand around his neck. Before Shevra could figure out what he had done, everything went black. Before he completely gave in to the black, he heard Ana say, "Burn the body."

A flash of green. Shevra's face in pain then oblivion.

Monica sat up in bed, soaking wet with sweat. Her heart beat frantically as she tried to sort out the fuzzy details of her nightmare, but the more she thought about it the fuzzier it became. Finally the nightmare left her mind, leaving her freezing in her sweat soaked sheets. She ran a hand through her hair then wiped her face with the sheet. Why did she see Shevra's face in pain like that? Rolling over to her nightstand, she turned on the lamp and reached for her phone to call him. It rang three times then picked up on voice mail. When the machine beeped, Monica left a message for him to call her back as soon as possible then hung up. She tried laying down and going back to sleep under the white noise of her fan, but after thirty minutes of tossing and turning, finally gave in and got up. She had only been asleep for thirty minutes before the nightmare woke her up. She tried to read again, but found that she could not. She thought about calling Shevra again, but decided against it. He's probably deep in sleep like I should be, she thought. She tried to read her book a second time and this time was able to get into the story. Soon, she felt her eyes go heavy so she walked into the bedroom with book in hand and continued to read until she passed out with the book laying on top of her. She had no more dreams that night.

Three days passed without a word from either Benjamin or Ophelia. Monica asked almost everyone in Mabon if they had heard from either one, to which everyone said no. She even walked to their house and knocked on the door. When no one answered, she scribbled a note and stuck it under the door then walked off, her mind now lost within a maze of conflicting thoughts. On her lunch break the next day, she went into Arabella's teashop and ordered a pot of Earl Grey. Minutes later, Arabella came over with pot and mug in hand and placed them on the table.

She noticed Monica's sad face and asked, "What's wrong, dearie? You look like Hades pulled your frown all the way to the Underworld." Monica smiled at the eccentric woman and invited her to sit with her. Arabella looked around her shop, making sure no one needed her, then sat down and poured Monica a cup of tea then pulled out her own purple and black mug and poured a cup as well. Monica smelled her steaming cup then sipped; the bergamot hit her senses like a tidal wave. She placed her cup on the table and grabbed her head.

"Arabella," she said while chuckling, "do you have any tea that is not super powered?"

"Only for the normal folks, dearie. Now, what's on your mind?"

"Well, I've not heard from Benjamin in quite some time. Three days to be exact. Have you heard from him?" Arabella thought about it for a while then sighed.

"Nope, sorry. Tell me, have you had any dreams?"

"Yes, I did have one the last night I saw him. A flash of green, then Benjamin's face in pain and then black." She took another sip of her tea. "Does that mean anything to you?"

"Not really, dearie, but then again, it might. Tell you what, come by the store when you're done with work and I'll read the leaves for you." Monica took the older woman's hand in her own and tightened her grip just as tears fell down her face. Nothing needed to be said.

Black, turning slowly into grey.

"Shevra's awakened now. Go and tell Stoke." Shuffling of feet then a door closing. Shevra blinked several times as his eyes felt like sand bags. He tried to look around, but his head felt heavy and dense and so he let it drop to his chest. He had no idea where he was, but he did know that the person talking was a Lin based on the accent. He also knew that while one had left, the other that gave the order stayed. Suddenly, Shevra felt cool hands under his chin as they lifted his head up to face them. He blinked again as he looked into the face of a Lin male he did not recognize.

"W-who are you?" Shevra croaked as the Lin held a cup of cold water to his lips. When his lips touched the cup, he drank the water down immediately. The Lin said nothing, but placed the cup on a side table and continued to hold Shevra's face in his hand. Shevra shook the hand away from him, feeling much better, then looked down and noticed that he was not bound.

"Did you really think we were going to gag and bound one of our own?" said the Lin with a calm voice. "We are Lin, no matter what path we choose."

"If that is the case then why even have this war?" said Shevra, still confused by all of this. The Lin male said nothing, but sat down in a chair next to Shevra. He glanced around, taking in his meager surroundings; they were in a small wooden room with a small window to the left, revealing his home city within reach. Shevra was home.

"A bittersweet moment, is it not?" said the Lin male. "You are home and yet you came here not of your own free will. I hate that, but it was necessary."

"Necessary that my own brother and sister kidnap me and drag me home, only to help out in a war? That my twin sister should die at the hands of her own flesh and blood?"

"I said it was bittersweet, did I not?" The Lin male tilted his head to the side with a questioning look. "However you, as with the rest of the Darjeel Order, are needed during this time. You will either fight for us willingly or not, but you will fight for what is right for our people." The Lin smiled while Shevra glared at him. "Oh yes, I heard about your human female lover on Earth. I still don't understand why there are some Lin who wish to mate with those traitors, those . . . . animals."

"My lover is no traitor. She is awakened and loves everything about the Otherworld. She does not wish to hurt anyone, let alone the Lin. She is a person on the Path!"

"She may be, but she is still a human." Just then, the door opened and in walked an older Lin male with two younger male Lin following close behind. The Lin who had spoken to him saluted the older Lin then walked out without a glance at Shevra and closed the door behind him. The trio stood before Shevra, who only stared back with a blank look. He was still unsure as to what his people were going to do with him and to make any rash move would be.....unwise. After several minutes of silence, the older Lin cleared his throat then said in a deep voice, "Let me apologize for your unnecessary means of getting here. That was not the intention. Although you are not for this war, you were meant to come here peacefully."

"Sending my own brother and sister to my home in Mabon for war was not what I had in mind," said Shevra with a weary tone in his voice. "My twin sister is dead now, all because of this." He looked the Lin up and down, searching for anything familiar. "I do not know you; who are you?"

"I am Tyranil Stoke, leader of the Free Lin and soon to be your general," said the older Lin with a smile on his face as he leaned closer to Shevra. Shevra could smell hints of peppermint on his breath and immediately thought of Monica drinking a cup of her night tea before going to bed. Before he knew it, he smiled at the image, sending the wrong signal to Tyranil, who smiled back. "It would appear that you are pleased at what we are about to accomplish," he said in a smug tone, snapping Shevra back to reality. He shook his head then stared at Tyranil with a glare on his face.

"I was thinking of my lover, Monica."

"Yes, of course you are." Tyranil stepped away from his prisoner and paced slowly around the room. The two other Lin that came in with him stepped to the side, giving him room. He appeared to be wrapped up in his thoughts and for a moment, Shevra wanted to delve deep into his mind and find out just what he was planning to do with regards to the war and Shevra himself. Why were the Lin about to engage in another war? Didn't they learn from their mistakes in the past? So many died and for what? A peace that came wrapped with thin strings, a peace that was uneasy and not trusted by both sides. Shevra sighed, catching the attention of the general, who stopped and faced Shevra once more.

"You sigh," said Tyranil in a gentle voice. "Why?"

"I see no point in this war. According to our history, the Lin and humans came from one race and although the humans have forgotten their ways, I see no reason to create another war based on the fear of a few Lin who refuse to accept change. In Mabon, I met a wonderful human woman who has awakened to her true nature and accepts it for what it is. I, along with many others including my dead sister, have been helping her in discovering her true self for the first time and I see nothing wrong with that at all. Plus, she loves me dearly as do I and this war or whatever you want to call it will not change my mind from that simple fact." Shevra closed his eyes for a moment then opened them again and focused them completely on Tyranil. "You will have to kill me first before I will accept any part in this war." Tyranil stared at the member of the Darjeel Order in silence; deep down, he was fearful of this Lin and what power he truly possessed. When he was younger, he had seen the Darjeel accomplish many feats that no ordinary Lin could accomplish, magick even beyond their own understanding. Since they occupied both male and female magicks, they were almost invincible....and a great weapon against those who vowed to destroy their way of life. Tyranil snapped his fingers to his soldiers and one of them grabbed a chair for him to sit in. He took the chair and sat down within a foot of Shevra, still in silence. He ran his slender hands through his hair and said in a quiet voice, "We shall see."

Monica arrived at the teashop just as the door opened for her to come in. Arabella locked the door behind her and led her to a small table where a teapot and two cups sat. Monica sat down while Arabella sat across from her and poured both cups then added the appropriate amount of sugar without saying a word. Monica watched the little woman work with such precision that for a moment, it was hard for her to believe that this was the same manic teashop owner she met earlier. Both cups were now filled with hot and fragrant tea; Monica leaned over to take a whiff of her cup then crinkled her nose.

"What is that?" she asked as she leaned back in her chair. "Spearmint? Peppermint?"

"To tell you the truth, my dear, I'm not quite sure. A friend brought it over from the Otherworld and I've learned not to ask too many questions about what I get from time to time." Arabella pushed her glasses back up her nose then lifted the top of teapot and took a whiff. "Huh, it looks to be about right. Monica, grab me a bowl from the counter, would you?" Monica did what she was asked then sat back down just as she handed the bowl to her. Arabella emptied the teapot's contents into the bowl, leaves and all and then stared at the bowl for a moment before placing a finger into the hot liquid. Suddenly, the liquid disappeared, leaving only the leaves and remnants of the tea. Monica stared in silence, not taking the risk in asking her a bunch of dumb questions and screwing up her concentration.

Arabella stared at the bowl once more then exhaled over the bowl; a thin stream of blue smoke flew from her mouth and into the bowl, stirring up the contents while causing them to hover slightly above the bowl. Arabella removed her finger and shook her head as she gazed at the spiraling mixture.

"Hmmm, this doesn't look too good, dearie," she said in a sorrowful tone. "I can't see him at all. He's not here, but of course you already knew that."

"He must be in the Otherworld, then, right? I mean, that's the only other place he could have gone to, right?" Arabella only stared at her and shook her head again, causing the floating matter to fall gently back into the bowl.

Two weeks passed. Monica was near the emotional cracking point. She now knew beyond a doubt that Benjamin and Ophelia were missing. She had wondered if perhaps she had done something to him to make him angry with her, but then quickly dismissed it; they were very much in love and she knew that her fears of him leaving her were asinine. No one had seen or heard from them at the college and the theatre and all of their friends were just as worried as she. Some even visited their home and found it to be completely locked and dark inside. Notes were left, along with voice mail, e-mails and even flowers left on their doorstep. Monica blinked, trying hard to keep the tears from falling down her face, but they did so on their own accord. She did not want Miranda to see her so upset, but it was, frankly, too much. While unpacking her second box of journals, a sob escaped her throat and soon, she laid crumpled on the floor, sobbing into her sleeve. She wept with pain, anger, frustration and love, of which none helped her feel any better. She just wanted to cry.

"Monica, please, get up and go to the backroom," said Miranda in a tender voice. She helped her up and brushed lint from her clothes then walked her to the back room and sat her down while she fixed a cup of strong Earl Grey. Monica smelled the warm bergamot drifting through the room and wanted to feel better, but it was useless. Benjamin was missing and there was nothing she could do about it. Miranda handed her a cup of steaming hot tea then sat down across from her. She placed a wrinkled hand on Monica's arm and said, "Perhaps he's gone to the Otherworld for a serious matter, dearie."

"B-but he would tell me if were going somewhere," said Monica through hiccups while holding the cup in her trembling hands. "He would tell me."

"But, dearie, maybe he left for an emergency. Maybe he couldn't tell you where he was going because he knew it would upset you." Monica sniffed once then stared at her cup of tea. The steam rose in swirls from the cup and caressed her face lovingly, giving her somewhat of a reassurance that things really would get better for her and hopefully for Benjamin too. She sighed again and took a quick sip then fanned her burning tongue.

"He's gone to the Otherworld," said a steady voice behind them, startling the two women. Monica turned around and saw Arabella standing in the doorway. Her pupils seemed to be larger than normal and she was dressed all in red, something Monica had never seen her do before. She stared right at Monica and continued to speak in that same tone. "He's gone to the Otherworld because there will soon be a war among his people."

"How do you know this?" asked Miranda.

"I went there with my Elderberry tea and asked some of my friends. They heard through the grapevine that the Lin are becoming restless again due to the human problem. It is split between those who want to continue their relations with humans and those who want to keep the Lin blood pure."

"Sounds like the Nazis," said Monica after she took another sip of the tea, feeling slightly better. Arabella shook her head in agreement.

"When the last war occurred, there was much blood spilled in their land. Lin blood. Now, I fear it might be more than Lin blood; there were grumblings of removing themselves from the connected human cities and making an example of them to everyone else in the Otherworld. I don't know what part Benjamin will play, but I can guarantee that it will probably be against his will." Arabella suddenly turned around and left the store, leaving the two women with more questions than answers.

"Arabella has always done that," said Miranda, shaking her head in wonder. "Leaves you more confused than ever." Monica finished off her still hot tea, not caring if it scalded her throat, and got up from her chair with determination.

"Benjamin needs me," she said in a surprisingly strong voice, "and I am going to help him. I have to go to the Otherworld and find his home city."

"And then what?" said Miranda. "You, a human woman, are not the sight that some of the Lin want to see right now. I understand why you want to do this, but understand that it will be rough getting there. His land is on the edge of the Otherworld overlooking a major body of water, plus you have to deal with the mer creatures that live in the water as well. Some of them are not friendly towards humans, but they are not friendly in general. That is just their nature."

"Miranda, I appreciate you wanting to keep me safe, but I know Benjamin needs me now. I don't know what's going on, but I am going to find out." The younger woman looked at the older women with that same determination; she knew what she was doing was right. It would be easy to just hide in Mabon, but given the circumstances, it was a waste of time. Miranda continued to stare at her in silence for several minutes then said in a heavy voice, "Go, then. I care about you, dearie, and I don't want you getting hurt or worse. However, promise me that you will return, no matter what happens to you. Promise that for me."

"Why would you think that I wouldn't come back? This is my home."

"I know, but take it from someone who has traveled to the Otherworld several times; there are things there that will entice you to stay, things that will try to cloud your judgment and although you are a strong woman, you need to be on your guard." Monica smiled then left the store, leaving a woman who suddenly aged five years within a second.

Monica walked through downtown, trying to remember the location of Jacqueline's flower shop. She needed a favour and she was the only person who could possibly help her. Although it was a beautiful day and everyone was out in full form, she paid no attention to it. She needed Jacqueline. After making two wrong turns, she found the flower shop and walked in to the smell of rose petals and the sounds of a woman singing a mournful song. Jacqueline, dressed in her usual Gothic attire, stood behind her counter thumbing through receipts with her black frame glasses perched on her nose. When she heard the door chime, she looked up and smiled and walked around the counter to greet her new customer and friend. The two hugged for a moment then released each other.

"Monica, good to see you. Been busy. Missed you at Goth Night. Most fun. What's up?"

Monica's slight smile fell to a frown. "Jacqueline, I need to find Auberon."

Jacqueline looked shocked. "Auberon? Why him? Something wrong? Nothing good comes from him."

"Have you heard of any disturbances in the Lin area? I was told that there was talk of a possible war among them and that it might spread to some of the human cities."

"Whoa, not good. Why him?"

"I need to go through the Otherworld and find Benjamin; he's been gone for some time and he might be with his people. I need someone to help me navigate my way through to his home city. If he is caught up in this possible war, I want to get him back before it escalates into something greater."

"Understand, but why Auberon? Not the most upstanding person of the Otherworld."

"I know that, but he may be the only hope I've got. He's got a foot firmly in both worlds and I don't want to go on my own. For some reason, I trust him for this matter." Jacqueline nodded once then moved away from Monica and closed her eyes. While Monica watched the very still Goth woman stand before her, Jacqueline reached out with her mind to Auberon, trying to locate him. Who knew where he-

"Jacqueline," said a velvet voice in her mind, *"why are you here? Do you know where I am?"* Jacqueline snorted as she heard sounds of women laughing seductively around him while the image of Auberon lounging naked in a bed large enough for five people flashed through her mind. She snorted again while he tried to cover himself from her mental prying eyes. *"So, you now have my attention. What do you need from me? It must be important."*

"Auberon, Monica needs you. The woman I introduced you? Cemetery?"

"Ah yes, she was quite lovely. Why does she need me?"

"Her Lin lover is in his home city. Possible war. She's going to find him. Needs your help to get there."

"And she thought I was the person to help her? Hmmm, I don't know."

"Please, Auberon. I like her. Help her."

Suddenly, Auberon stood fully dressed in the flower shop without a word. Monica gasped while Jacqueline only opened her eyes and smiled.

It hurt. That was the only thought in Shevra's mind as Tyranil worked on the Darjeel, forcing him to join or else. At first, the mind meld felt like an itch in the back of his mind, enticing him with the future glory of the Lin people. However, Shevra was stronger than that and the initial meld quickly disappeared followed by something that now caused him pain. It was magic of a darker nature, one reserved for enemies of the Lin. This magic consisted of actually going into the person's body and becoming that person, doing their will no matter what. Shevra closed his eyes in pain, trying hard to remember Monica's face and Mabon, but they were blotted out by images of battle, images of glory and Tyranil's mental voice booming through his mind. Even a member of the Darjeel Order could not withstand such pressure; it was the Darjeel who created such magic in order to keep their people safe from any threat. Sad now that the magic created for safety would now be used as a weapon of coercion. Shevra could feel sweat running down his face in rivulets, but paid it no mind. All he had at this point was Monica. Shevra shook as another wave of pain ran through his body.

"So, shall we do this my way or *my* way?" asked Auberon with a hint of sarcasm in his voice, making Monica wonder if she did the right thing in asking for his assistance. The two had left Jacqueline and were now walking down the main street in order to get their plan set in motion. "I know we are doing this for your lover's sake, but I wonder just how much of my input you want or if I will be the smiling yet quiet Otherworld ambassador to the lovely female human."

"Look, if you don't want to help me, then I will do it on my own," said Monica in a stern voice. She cared not for his charm at this point; she needed him to be serious no matter the cost. "I figured you were my best hope in trying to find out what happened to Shevra."

"Sadly enough, I am, but let's remember one thing: if we do this my way, then we will do it *my* way. No questions asked during certain events, understand?" Monica almost swooned at his 'scent'; it seemed to get stronger when he was emotional about something.

She blinked once then said in a clear voice, "No questions. I understand. Your way."

Auberon smirked at her response. "Now you sound like Jacqueline."

"Before we go, can we go by his house?" Monica, still wondering if perhaps this was a good idea, led Auberon to Shevra and Ophelia's house. Monica wanted to run there yet kept her calm. When they reached the house, it looked empty. Auberon sniffed the air.

"There has been a death here," he said as Monica raced up to the front door, knocking away all of the notes and flowers from the front porch and pounded on it. Auberon then reached in his coat pocket, pulled out a key made from bone and used it to open the door. The door opened without a sound. Monica glanced at Auberon then walked in. Everything looked in its place throughout the house until they reached the living room. There, on the floor, was a dark spot that smelled faintly of burnt seashells. Auberon reached down to touch it then stiffened and coiled back like a snake.

"What's wrong?" she said as he stuck his fingers in his mouth.

"Female Lin. Dead. Magical fire." He turned to face her. "Did you know of a female here?" Monica's legs felt weak as she found a place to sit. She buried her hands in her hair and began to cry. Auberon remained silent; nothing needed be said.

After Monica cried for several minutes, she lifted up her head, revealing her red-rimmed eyes to Auberon. Auberon knew now that she was even more determined to find her Lin lover. They left the house without looking back and made way to the forest grove in silence. Auberon wanted to ask her questions, but felt that if she wanted to talk, she would on her own time. They soon reached the beginning of the forest grove that led to the lake. Auberon looked down at Monica then took her hand in his and the two shuffled through the thick grove. Once they entered the grove, all sounds from the outside world were cut off, leaving them in complete silence. Monica shivered just as Auberon tightened his grip on her hand. His hand feels colder than ice, she thought. The Hand of Death. Auberon walked through the grove without a second glance at the limbs that stuck out in all directions or the dry and dead leaves that stuck here and there on the skeletal limbs. Monica followed closely behind, not really knowing what to expect yet she placed her trust in Auberon completely.

Soon, they reached the lake. The water was a weird shade of blue, as if the colour was suddenly struck with an illness. Auberon released his grip on Monica's hand and walked up to the lake then dipped a hand into it. He sniffed it, poured it back into the lake and then turned to face Monica.

"They have already changed the lake," he said in a dead voice. "We can still get to the Otherworld, but I don't know where we shall end up." He took her hand again and then closed his eyes. Monica looked around and noticed that everything looked hazy, as if covered in a thin fog, then looked back towards the lake and now noticed a door hovering over it. Auberon pulled on her hand and the two walked towards it just as the door began to open, revealing a dark forest. When the reached the water, they walked several inches over it. Monica could hear strange sounds coming from the forest, sounds of animals and other creatures not known by Man. She wanted to turn tail and run in fear, but Auberon, feeling her discomfort, squeezed her hand.

"I'm here," was all he said as they walked through the door and into the Otherworld. When they reached the forest, the door closed behind them and disappeared, giving Monica no other option than to follow her undead guide. The forest, at first, appeared to be shrouded under a blanket of nightfall, but Monica quickly realized that the forest itself was dark. The trees were dark blue and purple while the grass looked to be stained with elderberry juice. There was, however, enough light from the sun peeking through the trees for the two to walk on the cobblestone path.

"Auberon, where are we?" she asked in a small voice.

"We are in the Forest of Sadness; this is where the lost souls reside."

"Ghosts?"

"No, these souls were born as souls and nothing more. They were never accepted in any other place except here. Be warned; if you stray from the path, you will be tempted to follow their melancholy voices into an eternity of nothingness and desolation." Auberon resumed their walk down the wide path with Monica following closely behind while looking at her surroundings. The air smelled of cinnamon and rotting apples while eerie sounds could be heard from all around. Something the size of a Great Dane covered in violet feathers flew over their heads, missing them by several inches. Before Monica could ask what it was, Auberon turned around and covered her ears with his hands just as the creature made a sound that would have sent her to her knees with bloody tears streaming down her face. Monica stared in shock at the creature flying over them, knowing that her guide would explain later. Auberon stared at the flying creature circle them once then fly off to the east. When he thought the creature was truly gone, he removed his hands from her ears then placed them on her shoulders in some form of comfort. He could tell she was shaken up by what just happened, considering that she had no prior knowledge or warning of it.

"They are very dangerous to anyone who is not dead; their cries cause even the strongest person to weep blood from every pore on their body. Sometimes, the person will go further than that and kill themselves because their cry is too strong against their own lives."

"It was beautiful," sighed Monica.

"They get their victims through their beauty." Without another word, Auberon grabbed Monica's hand and continued down the forest path. Eyes of green, gold, and other colours stared out from bushes and behind trees at the two travelers through their area.

"So, how far are we from Lineal?" asked Monica as they walked.

"Several days." Auberon was not in a talkative mood; all he wanted to do was get them away from this forest. It had such a strange feeling to it, one that even an undead Faerie thought was most unnatural. The air still smelled of cinnamon and rotting apples to Monica; she tried to not breathe it in as much for her head began to hurt.

After an hour of walking, Auberon exclaimed, "The end of the forest is near. Let's go!" He tightened his grip on her hand and ran. Monica looked around and noticed that there were several wispy forms following them with long arms out towards them. They want us to stay, she thought as she began to run faster than Auberon. He glanced at her then behind them and soon, he too quickened his pace.

"They're trying to trap us; they can tell we're almost at the end of their realm!" Monica ran with as much energy as she could muster just as she felt a soft hand brush against her arm. She screamed and continued to run. The end of the forest was almost a yard away; with a scream, she leapt into the full day with Auberon following right behind her. Both landed in knee high grass and they turned to see that now every lost soul and creature of the forest stood at the edge, screaming in vain at their escape.

"They can't do anything to us now," said Auberon in a calm voice. "We are safe.....for now." He helped Monica up and dusted her off then made sure he was free from debris. She looked around her new surroundings and gasped; they now stood in the middle of a vast verdant valley with massive oak trees dotting the area. A dragon the size of a football field flew far off in the distance, but Monica could still see the gleam of its bright yellow scales as it reflected light from one of the two suns in the sky. The other sun, a smaller red orb, was lower in the sky than the other yet it radiated enough warmth that Monica took off her long sleeved shirt, revealing a short sleeved white shirt underneath. Auberon glanced away, trying hard not to notice her very nice form. This Lin was a very lucky person indeed, he thought then removed that idea from his mind. He was here for a reason.

After Monica tied her shirt around her waist, the two set off towards the suns for there was no path for them to follow. Auberon wanted to cover as much ground as possible before the suns set; even though this area was not as bad as the previous one, they were still in the Otherworld and Monica was still not used to its ways. She might be awakened, but she was still a virgin as far as he was concerned. Auberon's mind wandered as they walked through the grass that moved on its own without wind while Monica's head turned this way and that as she tried to catch the constant wonders of this world. This was where her beloved was from, she thought as she stared at the beauty of this place and the occasional habitant that passed by. Some, knowing Auberon for what he used to be, bowed in reverence or scampered off in fear that he would steal their bones. Monica watched as a traveling band of humans (or at least she thought they were) dressed in swirling colourful clothing from several yards away recognized Auberon and waved frantically at him.

"Auberon," she said while tugging on his arm, "I think they want to talk to you." Auberon looked up and over at the group then continued to walk on.

"They want nothing from me now, only what I was before. They are gypsies and scoundrels, nothing more." Auberon continued to walk with Monica behind him yet she kept glancing in their direction, watching them with slight pity trying to flag the former Bone King down. Finally, one of their male members ran towards them with lightening speed. As he approached, she noticed that his clothing kept changing colours while his long red hair streamed from his head. Auberon continued to walk knowing that this young man was fast approaching them. When the man reached them, Auberon finally stopped to face him with a sneer on his face. The man dropped to his knees and bowed to Auberon while whispering in a language Monica did not understand.

"He is calling me by my old name, the Bone King," said Auberon in a voice devoid of any emotion. "They think me to be a god."

"Well, you are still in some ways," said Monica, "but don't you need to do something? Talk to him at least. See why his group wanted to talk to you." After grimacing at Monica for her logic, he helped the man up from the ground, dusted him off and said in his language, *"Well met, traveler. How can I be of service to you?"*

"Bone King, it is good to see you in these parts. We have missed you terribly." The man's eyes shone with a zealot's fervor as he gazed upon Auberon. Although she had no idea what they were saying, Monica still noted the gleam of worship in the young man's eyes. Auberon was disgusted.

"So.....what can I do for you?"

The man's face fell somewhat. *"Bone King, one of our members is sick; she suffers from a broken leg. We need you to change her bones-"* Auberon grabbed Monica's arm and stormed away from the man as fast as possible.

"Auberon," Monica cried, "why are leaving him? What did he say-"

Auberon turned around so quickly that Monica almost fell over backwards. His eyes were completely black while his skin turned as black as a burned corpse. He leaned over so that his nose touched hers. Monica smelled his scent even more so than ever. She took a step back, but still held her ground.

"I am no longer the Bone King," he growled in a deep and grating voice, like two stones rubbing together. "What I do in this or your world is for my own sake. In fact, I'm only doing this as a favour to Jacqueline and nothing more." He glanced at the young man who still stood then back at Monica. "I am tired of that title, my dear," he said in a calmer, but still dangerous voice. "I am simply Auberon now. Leave it." His skin returned to its former dusty grey colour as he turned to face the young man once more, sighed and then led Monica on, leaving the man in a desolate state. Several minutes passed before Monica looked back again; the young man was gone as well as the group.

The two walked through the valley for some time in silence, although Monica's mind still buzzed with how Auberon had acted towards the young man. He still should have helped, she thought. Title or no title, he still should have helped. As they walked, she found herself staring at her partner and guide, an undead faerie. How much did she want to know of his past? True, he told her his story, but she felt he left much more out. Question was, did she really want to know more about him? She shook her head no then realized that she did the action. All she wanted was to find her beloved and get him back to Mabon. Of course, it was going to be hard considering that his people were about to have another war, unless if the war had already started. Add to the mix that she was a human who loved a Lin and, well.....

Auberon wanted to help that young man, but he could not. When he walked away from his title, he did so in order to free himself from the wrath of the Unseelie Court, which was almost impossible since faeries never forgot anything unless if they grew bored with it. He was forever grateful that they had grown bored with trying to capture him, even though he had even run into some of the court members from time to time and they did not even recognize him. Faeries, he thought with a snort, are so unpredictable. Including him. He had the power still to do what was needed to that woman's leg and yet....and yet. He watched several sprites fly over their heads, their laughter sounding like twinkling crystal bells, and hated himself even more. He glanced back at Monica and saw her gazing at the sprites with a mixture of fascination and wonder on her face. He smiled briefly as they continued walking.

Monica felt as though she was going mad and yet she kept herself in check while following Auberon through the grassy area. This place seemed too unreal to exist and yet here she was, walking along with an undead Faerie in the search to find her Lin lover. In her world, people walked through their lives with dulled or glassy eyed expressions, going through the motions of a dismal life that held no prospects. In this world, however, everything had a place, a function and it was well known. She could feel the energy rising through this place, coursing through her body and pounding with a beat that she had heard all of her life and yet never knew of its source. The game had changed now that she was a willing and coherent player and she was glad of it. Her thoughts drifted to Shevra and what he was doing. Why were the Lin so engrossed in starting another war? Although humans and Lin came from a single race, she did not know why the Lin hated and feared her kind. Was it anger because the human brothers and sisters negligently forgot their ways and went at full speed towards their own destruction? Why couldn't the Lin just teach them their old ways to possibly change the current state of affairs? Wouldn't that be a better option?

"No, because humankind, or at least most of them, would go mad if the knowledge they used to posses suddenly fully came back to them. They would not know what to do with such power," said Auberon in a flat voice, jolting Monica out of her mind fog.

She shook her head and said, "Sorry, I did not know-"

"You said your thoughts in your mind. You are one of the humans who is both awake and aware; you are coming back to your old roots so to speak, plus you are in the Otherworld now; consider yourself to be quite drenched."

"Thanks for the attempt at humour," said Monica with a wry grin on her face, "but I still think that if the Lin were to come to the human world, then quite possibly both their lives and ours would benefit greatly from it. Humankind has been going through a downward spiral since the dawn of time. Sure, we've had some major events happen to us, but if we were equipped with our old knowledge....well, imagine the possibilities." Auberon stopped walking and turned to face her. He placed his cold hands on her shoulders while smiling a sad smile.

"My dear Monica, how much you have to realize," he said in a soft tone. "Humans are damaged goods; to give them back their previous potential would eventually be their undoing. It is better if a few retain what knowledge they know, or become awake and aware like you, but never go back to being what they used to be. The majority of humans only know war, pain, suffering and death. True, the Otherworld knows of suffering, pain, war, and death, but we also have ways of handling such matters without it spilling over into your world. Humans see those things as reasons to do things in life. We see it as last options and even then, we still find a better solution." He leaned in closer to her and it took Monica all her strength to keep from fainting from his overpowering scent. "You are one of the luckier ones, my dear, plus you are loved by one from here. Humans have given you a gift that is more powerful than any bomb or nuclear device created. Remember that." Auberon removed his hands from her shoulders and walked on, not caring if Monica was right behind him although he knew she was. He could feel her desire to know and want more growing; she understood.

Shevra pressed his face against the window of his new home, watching Lin walk by in preparation for war against another beautiful sunny day. He wanted to be out there with them, but knew that that time would come. He sighed with happiness; he was grateful that the general showed him the error of his ways in not wanting to support the war. As a Lin and as a member of the Darjeel Order, he had a job to do. Preserving his race was first, outweighing everything else. The waters of the ocean sparkled under the sun and for a moment, he wanted to run outside and take a swim like he used to do before leaving for-

A sharp pain entered his head, causing him to reel away from the window. He groaned as he held his head while trying to find something to sit on. Immediately, he found a chair and sat down while massaging his temples. He could not remember why the pain came only that it did and whatever thoughts caused it to occur was now dead in his mind. He massaged until the pain finally left him, leaving him just as happy as before. He got up and walked into the kitchen to prepare a cup of tea before his meeting with his order, wondering what strategies they would discuss in order to defeat those that opposed them.

Somewhere, deep in his mind, was a name hidden far enough to not be erased. He placed it there before......something. He felt a gentle tickle from that name, but when he tried to remember it, it hid from him. He shook his head and made his tea.

The grassy valley soon turned into a fairly large city that looked like it was stuck in the turn of the 20th century on Monica's side of the Veil. While Auberon walked on, she turned to give herself one last look at the grassy plains they just came from then turned back and continued on. She came here for a reason; hopefully, she and Shevra would come back together so that she could have more time to explore this world, but not yet. Not yet. The noises of the city jostled her thoughts, snapping her to attention as she followed Auberon through the city. People of every race, colour, size, and even species walked by her, fueled with their own daily events and chores while not caring about the human woman and Viril Faerie that walked through their streets. They wore clothing appropriate for that time period, but in brighter and flashier colours. A blue skinned man dressed in a bright yellow pantsuit and bowler hat passed by them while riding his bike and it took Monica everything not to turn around and stare. Although she was getting used to the sights and inhabitants of the Otherworld, it was still quite an eye opener. Auberon, as usual, did not pay attention to this city; every city was the same, human or Otherworld. Each one held their mysteries and wonders, but to him, it was all the same. Being undead had its advantages, he thought then chuckled. Although they were surrounded by the city's noises, Monica heard him chuckle. She tugged on his arm and said in a loud voice, "What's so funny?"

"Nothing," he said without turning around, "except for a small reminder of my Life and how I got cheated."

"You're not making any sense."

"Sorry, was I supposed to?" He felt her eyes staring daggers in his back as they walked along.

"Auberon, can we please stop for a moment and get something to eat?"

"We need to move along," said Auberon in a flat voice.

"I know, but-" she tugged on his arm again with more force, stopping him in his tracks as people still continue to move by them. He turned to face his partner with a smirk in his eye while crossing his arms over his chest. "I want to stop, Auberon. Look, I know this place is nothing to you, but it means something to me, plus I'm hungry. Can we find a place to just rest for a bit? We've been going at it pretty hard and my feet and starting to hurt." Auberon continued to stare at her in silence then grabbed her arm and turned to the right down a side street. Before Monica could protest, they arrived at a small café nestled between buildings and went in, finding a table by one of the windows. A humanoid server told them of their specials and, after taking their orders, left the two in somewhat solitude.

"Now, my dear," said Auberon after taking a sip of water, "have a grand time looking into one of the major cities of the Otherworld." Monica watched the inhabitants of the city carry on with their lives without a care in the world while the buildings and other structures sat like silent golems, forever waiting for an event that would never take place. She placed a finger on her cheek and realized she was crying. She blotted her face with her napkin then realized she was also sweaty from the walking. She blotted her arms, face, and neck with the napkin then placed it back in her lap while Auberon stared at her in silence.

"You humans still fascinate me," he said in a soft voice. Monica sipped from her water as a response; what else could say to that? "So predictable at times and yet not in others. You call yourselves masters of your destinies and yet will turn into little children when faced with something higher up on the food chain. You spread like a virus in your own world and yet can take hours trying to describe a flower to a blind person." He shook his head. "You could have turned around and walked back at any time, even though your love for this Lin is strong. I could have even helped you get back home with use of a portal or my wings and yet I did not and yet you did not ask me." He leaned in more towards her while she took another sip of her water, still not sure of what to say or do at this moment. Although they had been walking for some time, he still remained fresh and clean as before while his scent remained the same. "Why are you doing this?" he asked simply as his eyes took in every inch of her.

"Because my lover needs me."

"How do you know that?"

"Because I just know, that's all. Look, why should I have to defend myself to you? You didn't have to take this job."

"I know, but this is fascinating to me. Being undead is boring sometimes so every once in a while, I like to do things just out of a dare, see where they lead, and go on from there. The thrill of the unknown is so seductive, wouldn't you agree?" He sat back and crossed his arms over his chest, leaving Monica with more questions than answers. Was she doing the right thing? What if she arrived in the Lin city, only to find that Shevra did not want her? She began to tremble yet kept herself firm; she did not know what to expect other than what her heart told her. Shevra was alive and there against his will. She had to get to him.

"This is something I have to do," she said with a note of resolute in her voice. "I have to."

"Ah my dear, no one is denying that; you are quite a resilient human. But, I want to know just why you are doing this. The real reason." He smirked when she creased her brow in frustration. "You know the answer, or do you? Is finding Shevra your only reason for doing this?"

"Of course," she retorted, "why wouldn't it be?" He held up his palms in mock surrender just as their food arrived, giving Monica enough time to allow his thought seed to take root in her mind. While they ate, Monica glanced at him periodically, of which Auberon found it to be amusing. He knew she was thinking of his question and was trying to formulate an answer that would sound somewhat coherent. Truth be told, however, was that the real answer was not coherent at all. He knew that from being around her thus far and he still praised her internally for sticking to this rather than wanting to go home and just wait. Not doing anything, however, was worse than actually doing something about it.

Just as Auberon reached for a piece of bread, Monica said, "So why are you really here? I mean, you don't know Shevra and we are not exactly the closest of friends. So, why?"

"I told you, I am doing this for Jacqueline," he said then took a bite of his bread. He chewed for several seconds, swallowed, then added, "What, were you expecting something malicious from me just because I am a Viril? Not all of us are evil, especially me."

"So, what are you then?"

"I am myself and that is all you need to know about me."

"But you're the one leading this trek. How do I know you're not just leading me to my own death? Seductive you may be, but still.... I want to know everything."

Auberon laughed as he took a bite of his grilled fish. "Ah, so now the little human wants to know everything, hmmm? My dear, if I were to tell you everything right now, you would be a drooling vegetable, no matter how aware you may be of this world. Be careful of your request, my dear. Let me lead this trek and that is that. It will not be over quickly in time for tea, nor will it be easy. There might be times when I may have to do what I used to be known for and no, you will not like it."

"So, why didn't you help that young woman in the caravan? Was it because of your pride or the fact that you couldn't reveal you had a tender side?"

"Good parry and thrust, but the game is still mine. Yes, you're right. I should have helped, but I did not. Now, eat. We need to leave soon." Monica stared at the Viril digging into his fish for a moment then she too began to eat with relish. This was not over yet, she thought as she chewed while it began to rain outside, dabbling the city with a touch of grey. What she did not know was that Auberon held the same thought at the same time. True, this was not over yet. He had barely begun to play his hand.

Shevra awoke with a start and looked around his room with wide eyes. The room was still in the cool night and everything was in its place. He could hear several male Lin laughing and talking about something of no consequence to him. He wiped his forehead with a corner of his blanket and it came back sweaty. He tried to fully remember what it was that woke him up, but all he could remember was a human woman with a tear running down her face. Why would that bother him, he thought while sinking back into bed. He closed his eyes and the face entered his mind once more. Who is she? Do I know her? Suddenly, he felt a tear roll down his cheek. He wiped it off with a finger, licked it and then settled into sleep. He thought no more of the human woman.

The walk through the city proved to be quite fast, for soon they entered a meadow filled with immense trees made of golden bark and teal leaves. The leaves swayed in the gentle breezes that accompanied the two while the trees' fruit, a large swollen purple coloured apple, gave off a heady scent. Auberon stopped by one of the trees and began plucking some of the fruit from its branches while Monica stood back and watched. When he had at least five of the strange fruit, he handed one to her and said, "If you eat one of these, it will help with your stamina during this trip." He bit down into one and juice spilled from it and down his chin. He licked his lips while chewing then swallowed and grinned a purple stained smile. Monica looked at the fruit and almost gagged for its flesh looked diseased and slightly mauled, but she took a bite anyway. Instantly, her mind reeled with the tastes of coconut, apples, and lime all blended into one while her chin dribbled with its juice.

"This is wonderful!" she said while munching, not caring if the juice now stained her shirt. Auberon quickly glanced away then back at her face. "What do you call these things?"

"You know, I never really knew its name, only that it was quite the delicacy." He stuffed the rest of his piece in his mouth then continued walking with Monica next to him. She took some of the fruit from his arms to help him lighten the load while trying to wipe her now sticky chin clean with her shirt.

"This stains will never come out of your shirt," smirked Auberon, "so you might as well get some new clothes when we reach the next town."

"I don't have any money so this will just have to do, unless if I can just wash off."

"You're with me, so money is not a question. Remember, I live here as well as Mabon so I have us both covered." The two soon fell into silence as they walked along while the sounds of the meadow gave them somewhat comfort while their minds were not.

"Auberon?" said Monica after a half hour of silence.

"Hmmm?"

"What is Lineal like? Shevra told me a little of it, but not enough for what I am planning to do. Have you ever been there?"

"Once and sadly enough, I never went back until now. Never had a reason to since the Otherworld is so vast. Well, the city is located by one of the major oceans of this world so the city gets both the beauty and the destruction of Nature. The ocean is occupied by not only marine animals, but merfolk as well."

"Like mermaids and all that?" Auberon smirked at her and for a moment, Monica felt a slight tingle in her stomach.

"Yes, mermaids and all that. However, although humans have turned merfolk into seductive beings with a penchant for fish/human sex, real merfolk are quite the opposite. While some of them can be seductive, there is a coldness there that will never be warmed. They seduce with the intent to kill."

"Are they beautiful?"

"Yes they are. Almost too hard to look at because of their beauty. Even I was temped once upon a time with a female merfolk. Thankfully, I am already dead so I proved to not be a tasty specimen for her." Monica stopped walking and stared at Auberon with wide eyes.

"When you say tasty-"

"I mean tasty. Yes, they eat their victims." Monica stared at him in horror then picked up her walking. Suddenly, the meadow lost some of his beauty in her eyes. Suddenly, everything did.

"What am I doing?" she murmured causing Auberon to now stop and look at his partner.

"I beg your pardon?"

"What am I doing? Is this the right thing to do? I mean, merfolk that eat their victims? I never knew that. Humans don't know that. They made merfolk into sex idols. Are the Lin any better? Wait, they hate humans, right? What if I'm too late for all of this?"

"You don't know so don't start playing yourself like that. We don't know except that a war is brewing there. Shevra, from what you have told me, loves you. If you truly want to know, think of him and see for yourself." Monica walked over to one of the trees and sat down by it while placing the fruit in her lap. She braced her back against the cool smooth bark and closed her eyes. Immediately Shevra's face appeared in her mind and with it came pain so great that she screamed and rolled over on her side while clutching her stomach. Auberon raced over to her and sat down next to her while wondering just what in the hell happened. Her forehead was cold and clammy as he placed a hand there while she shivered. He said her name several times then, when he received no response, took the human in his arms and raced off to find a healer. There had to be one nearby, he thought as he ran with unnatural speed and arched his back out to release his massive skeletal wings. Soon, they were in the air high above the meadow as he searched for a nearby town that would be somewhat caring for a human woman. Monica barely stirred in his arms, but she was still breathing. At least she was still alive, he thought as he spied a small town to the northwest of the meadow. He circled once then swooped down through the trees and landed with grace in the middle of the town. The people of the town, wood elves, stopped what they were doing to face their new arrivals.

Auberon gently placed Monica on the ground then said in a loud voice, "This human needs medical attention. Do you have a healer here?" He flapped his wings in impatience. Several male elves walked up to Monica in silence and took her in their arms then led her to one of the simple houses in the town with Auberon behind them.

They brought her into the house filled with all kinds of drying herbs and books and laid her on a soft thick bed and began to remove her clothing. Auberon raced in behind them and, folding his wings back inside, ran up to the bed, but was held back by one of the elves. He held up a slender brown hand and said in a tender voice, "You have no place inside here, Bone King. We will take care of her now. Please, go outside. We will come for you when we are done here." He turned back to the human and continued to strip her. Auberon tried to peek through them, but found it to be almost impossible, so he walked outside then looked for an inn of some sort to possible drink away his frustrations. As he walked, several of the elves watched him with wary eyes; they knew of his kind and the power he possessed. One young female bowed low as he walked by, calling him by his old title of Bone King. Auberon stopped to look at the elf then reached out a pale hand to touch her cheek. When his hand touched her cheek, she closed her eyes and sighed, giving Auberon satisfaction. He removed his hand and walked on, leaving the elf with memories of contact with him burning in her mind.

He found the inn after getting lost twice and stepped in. The smells of baked bread, cheese and herbs permeated his nose and he was glad for it. Although they had only been on the road for a short time since the city, the reasons for him coming here sapped enough of his energy. What was wrong with Monica, he thought after he gave one of the serving women an order for a tall flask of something, anything. She seemed fine until he told her to think of her beloved Lin. Was that simply it or was it more? Was he pushing her too hard? The woman came with a very large metal container of something smelling of honey and cinnamon that foamed on top. He paid the woman then took a deep sip, hoping that all would be well. He would hate to have to take her bones.

"It has been quite some time since I last saw this."

"Truly, Master?"

A chuckle. "Although I have been alive these past 500 years, the last time this occurred was when I was your age."

"A miracle, then."

"Quite and yet....you have heard of the war going on in their city, have you not?"

"Indeed I have, Master. She is probably going there or coming from there."

"What she is right now is one of the reasons why they are coming to war again. It should not have to be that way. Other kind here have fully embraced relations with humans; the Lin should be the most accepting-"

"Given the fact that humans and Lin came from the same race, right Master?"

Another chuckle. "Correct." A few moments of silence while working, then:

"Master?"

"Yes?"

"Was that the Bone King who brought her here?"

Now, a deep sigh. "Yes, you are correct, although I do not think he goes by that any more. Too much pain inside and out, plus the Viril have chosen a new queen to take over."

"The books claimed that he was their most influential and that the current Bone Queen will willingly step down whenever he is ready to take the throne again."

"My, my, someone has spent quite some time in the Library."

Blushing. "T-thank you, Master. I enjoy spending my free afternoons there. It is so quiet and peaceful."

"Hand me that towel, please. Thank you. Now, apply that compress here."

"Yes Master.....wait! She's fluttering her eyes."

Monica heard two heavily accented voices speaking over her. She blinked twice, moved to sit up then saw that she was not alone. Two elves stood by her bed with a small table covered with dried herbs, a bowl of water, towels and other items of healing. Both elves were tall and slender with black hair twisted into thin braids that fell down their back and across their chest. The male on the left was slightly taller and more muscular than the female yet they looked to be twins. Their extremely violet eyes stared back at their patient with mirth and humour, glad that she finally woke up and that she appeared to be okay.

"Where am I?" she asked just as the male reached over and handed her a cup filled with cold and delicious water. She greedily drank it down then handed the cup back to him.

"You are in the town of Aedya," said the male with a smooth deep voice. "I am Hensal and this is my student, Aeria." The female bowed low. "You were brought to us by Auberon several hours ago. It seemed you had quite an experience."

"Yes," mused Monica as she tried to remember the details. "I remembered we were walking along and that I was asking him questions of the Lin city. Then.....I think, I went to sit under a tree and the next thing I remember was waking up just now."

"Yes, you have had quite a shock to your system," said Aeria as she applied another cool and wet towel smelling of peppermint on Monica's forehead. "But, you seem to be fine now."

"What happened to me? Was I poisoned?" The two elves laughed, sounding like sparkling crystals.

"My dear, far from it," said Hensal then turned to Aeria and nodded. Aeria nodded back and ran out of the room, leaving the two. "Aeria has gone to fetch Auberon for me. What I have to tell is for both of you."

"How did you know Auberon?"

"He was the Bone King, was he not? True, I do not understand the Viril, but they are a part of this world and yours too. Auberon was and still is quite a figure with enough to destroy or cure. A blessing and a curse; such is the way of the Viril. They are the most misunderstood race here." Just then, Aeria came back with Auberon quickly following behind her. He raced over to Monica's bed and took her hand in his then smiled.

"Glad to know you're doing better," he said. "For a moment, I thought I had lost you."

"You know you're not getting rid of me, no matter what. Even after this mission." She stared into his eyes and he stared back; no words needed to be said. He tightened his grip on her hand just as Monica felt a lump in her throat. The two elves stood to the side and watched the play unfold between them. Neither one said anything, but they already knew. Auberon finally pulled back from her to turn to Hental. Now he wanted some answers.

"So, was she poisoned? Did I do something to her? Trust me, I had no intention of-" Hental raised his hand then gestured for him to take a seat. Auberon found a chair and sat down with anticipation. Hental then turned to face Monica while Aeria held her hands.

"It would appear, my dear, that you are pregnant." Monica's jaw dropped in disbelief as she touched her stomach.

Chapter Six

"How long?"

"Several weeks." Aeria smoothed Monica's hair away from her face while Monica rubbed her stomach. Auberon could not believe it; how could she be pregnant? He stifled a chuckle at that asinine question then sauntered over to her and placed a cold hand on her brow.

"Do you still want to go to the city, now that you know of your condition?"

"Yes. I have to find Shevra and let him know that he will have a child. Perhaps that will bring him back, unless if it's too late." She struggled to get up, but all three gently laid her back down.

"Rest now," said Hental, "and be our guest. You are not far from their city, but for now you must rest." Monica slipped under the warm covers and was soon fast asleep. Hental turned to Auberon and motioned for him to walk outside.

When the two were completely out of the house, Auberon said, "I am forever grateful for your help with her." He glanced back at the house then at Hental again. "You have my thanks." Hental held up a hand to silence him as a smile spread across his face.

"No thanks are needed, Bone King-"

"I am no longer the Bone King!" snapped Auberon as Hental smiled a little wider.

"To many of the Otherworld, you will always be the Bone King. You have done more for others than the previous kings, proving that the Viril are more than just the undead of the Fae. You bringing her here was proof enough for me as well as the rest of this town."

"I had to do what was right and nothing more."

Hental arched an eyebrow. "But of course, there is always more, isn't there?" Hental then walked away, leaving Auberon standing in the middle of town. He glanced at the home where Monica lay asleep then walked towards it again. He had to check on her one more time. When he reached her room, he found Aeria reading while sitting by her bed. Their eyes met and for a second, Aeria smiled then went back to her book, giving him the okay that he could approach the bed. He crept up to Monica and placed a hand on her cheek.

"Her breathing is regular and the baby is fine," said Aeria without lifting her eyes from the book. "I know you care for her, more than you will admit, dear Bone King." Auberon's eyes flashed for a moment then refocused on Monica. Dear Monica, he thought, why you? He turned and left the two to their solitude while he needed to find quite the opposite.

Monica slept. The bed was perfect in firmness, the sheets and blankets were perfect in temperature, everything was perfect. So why did she feel sadness? She imagined a picture of Shevra's face followed by Benjamin's then took a deep breath to keep the tears from flowing down her face. She loved him and as far as she knew, he still loved her. She wanted to tell him of their child, but at this point she did not know if he was even still alive. All she had was hope and even that held by a single strand of thread. She dreamt of her mother and how she would react if she ever met Shevra or even visited Mabon. Would she be able to fully appreciate the makings of the town, or would she reject it in favour of saving her soul? Would she be able to understand the relationship between this world and the Otherworld? Would she deem her daughter insane?

Her mother drifted away and soon a new face came into her mind: Auberon. He may be an undead Faerie, but he helped me when I needed it, she thought as he winked at her. To her, he was the ultimate rogue: no cares nor worries, a life of constant travel and the power to do whatever the bloody hell he felt like doing at that time with the choice of doing something completely else at the last minute. Was he capable of loving someone? Was there a heart underneath the rake? She mentally shook her head, thinking that she sounded like a trashy romance novel. She was quite happy with someone else and there was no room for anyone else. Those questioning thoughts of Auberon did not need to invade her mind at all. Suddenly, she felt something cold and yet tender on her cheek. It felt good, whatever it was, and she wanted to open her eyes for a moment, but soon drifted into deep slumber.

During their time of being in Aedya, both Auberon and Monica enjoyed the hospitality of the elves. They never lacked food or sweet water, nor were they ever bored. Monica was glad to get out of bed and enjoy the town of the wood elves, posing questions to anyone who looked her way. This was her first time to truly interact with beings in the Otherworld; it was one thing to speak to Auberon, Master Assam, or even Shevra and Ophelia, but it was something completely different to be inundated with people from the Otherworld. She was delighted.

"So, how long do your people live?" she asked a small group of female elves who had playfully kidnapped her once they received news that was awake and doing well. They offered freshly picked and cut fruit from the groves by their town with sweet and cool water and a loaf of dark bread with a crumbly and delicious pale yellow cheese. Monica ate everything, sampling the new foods with sheer pleasure. Once she finished eating, she began her questions and inquiries of her caretakers. She knew this was a possible once in a lifetime moment and the best thing to do was dive right in.

"Some of us live to be several hundred years old," answered a young female elf that sat on Monica's right. "Others do live longer than that."

"So, you are immortal?" Several of the elves laughed, but not in mockery.

"No, hardly not," said another elf across from her. "We simply live with Nature around us. We grow when it does and sadly, we die when it dies as well. We are like blades of grass, slender and fertile yet strong against the winds and the harsh rain. We thrive and we grow for that is our nature. We take our energy from all around us and we give back with thanks." Monica nodded her head at the response and for a moment wondered what would happen if she decided to stop looking for Shevra and lived among these people. They lived simply without any desire for anything that they could not handle. They did not walk around with expensive clothing, cell phones, iPods, and anything else that humans used to fill the Void in their lives. Rather than adapt to their world, some humans wielded it like an unknowing child with a gun.

"And now, we have questions for you," said the elf on her right. "What is Mabon and other human cities like?"

"Well, as you know, Mabon is one of the humans cities that have a pact with the Otherworld, standing as gates between the worlds. Mabon is twice the size of your town and yet everyone knows everyone there. Both humans and people from this world live there. Other cities are way larger and smaller than Mabon and each one is unique. While some do not have the pact, they are still just as wonderful and interesting to discover and explore."

"We have read the stories of humankind," said another elf in a somber tone, "and we know of your kind's past. Humans and the Lin used to be of one race until the humans left and discovered the world you live in now. How does it feel for someone like yourself to be in the Otherworld now?" Monica was quiet with reflection. Since arriving in the Otherworld, she used all of her energy trying to get to the Lin city with hopes of finding Shevra, but now that she had some time to rest, she could finally enjoy her new surroundings.

"Beautiful, amazing, frightening, everything beyond what my mind could possibly understand and yet I do understand it all," she said in a wistful tone. "I wonder if humans have gone mad while visiting your world." Several of the elves shook their heads in sadness.

"Some have done just that," said the elf on her right, "for some of your kind no longer have the magick inside of them to fully comprehend what they see here. Some come here by means of drugs or other intoxicating methods. Others unlock something deep inside of them and when they arrive, they think they are hallucinating. Still, others like yourself have had the calling inside of you, never lost in Time or through dead ends in their Path. The call to be awakened once more came to you, dear sister, and you answered it well." She placed a hand on Monica's stomach and instantly, Monica felt small but firm stirrings of life within. She placed her own hand over the elf's and smiled.

"Why did you choose the company of the Bone King?" asked another elf. "Surely, you know of his past and his power."

"Why do people still call him the Bone King? Auberon gave up his title many, many years ago due to an incident at the Unseelie Court," said Monica, causing many of the elves to gasp.

"You know of this?" said several in unison.

"Of course. He told me one day although I have seen quite the opposite since we have arrived here. People still bow to him while asking for his help."

"He has the power to kill or cure, making him one of the most dangerous creatures in our world," said the elf on her right. Monica turned to her and smiled while taking her hand.

"Before we go any further, what is your name? I'm not that great in remembering names, but I promise I will remember everyone's here." The elf smiled and placed a hand over her chest.

"I am Tuathae and I am one of the teachers here. Forgive me and my many questions, but we do not get too many humans in our town."

"No, the pleasure is all mine," said Monica with a goofy grin on her face. She turned to face the rest of the elves and asked them their names as well.

"Yumani."

"Alesa."

"Jaela."

"Korrin."

"Finally, Gaelin." Monica nodded after each elf gave her name to her.

"Now I feel better. To continue, Tuathae?"

"Ah yes, you are quite the eager student. Auberon has the power to give life and take it away. He is one with Nature here and that makes him perfect in such a flawed way."

"I live in darkness, and yet one can find pure tenderness there," chimed in Auberon from behind Monica, startling her. He sat down next to her and placed a hand on hers while staring at her intently. "I am glad to see you're feeling better," he said with that same tenderness that he spoke of.

"How can someone like yourself know and be able to express such kindness and tenderness to me when you live with such darkness within you?"

"Ah, such the philosopher," he joked. "In my world, there are no added emotions used to confuse and torment the mind. When I love, I love purely without any added intent. When I kill, I kill without any added intent. I am purely in the moment and within that single thought. I like to call it unity of purpose. Too many humans are so caught up in adding their own garbage to whatever emotion or act they are feeling at the time. It cheapens it, makes it less than worthy to anyone who receives it. I, on the other hand, can take that single thought and focus all of my intent into that thought, thereby making it pure. Do you understand?"

"Strangely enough, I do. You're the kind of person that is rare and dangerous in both worlds," said Monica. "You have no distractions, no deficit in your attention span. You accomplish what you set out to do, correct?"

"Absolutely." He turned to face the rest of the group. "And now, I will take my leave so that you can enjoy the rest of your time here without me breathing down your neck." He swiftly got up and walked towards a group singing songs around a small bonfire. Monica watched him walk off then turned back to face slightly surprised faces.

"What?"

"Sister, why did you choose him to accompany you? Surely you could have made this trip with someone else? Why him?"

"Because I needed someone who has spent a lot of time here. Someone who was good with direction."

"How long have you know the Bone King?" asked Tuathae.

"I've only met him once. Why?" The elf smiled a smile that hid more than reveal while others began to ask her other questions.

"I have never been to your world," said Alesa. "Tell me of the flying mechanical machines your people use to go from one place to another."

"Can humans still talk to trees?"

"Can you get us books from your world?"

And on it went for several hours, giving Monica the time of her life. Auberon glanced back at her and the group several times while drinking elderberry wine.

After several hours passed, Tuathae pointed towards something in the sky. Monica looked up and saw a being in a brilliant white chariot flying through the black velvet night. All chatter stopped as faces glanced upward to witness this moment. A spray of stars showered from the chariot and hung for a moment in the sky then disappeared.

"That is the goddess of the night," said Tuathae with reverence in the voice. "We honour her every thirty days with gifts and songs. Human sister, would you care to join us?" Monica blushed furiously as she nodded yes. The elves helped her up then led her towards the bonfire where Auberon sat. When he saw her approaching, he stood up and raised his cup to her.

"So, they talked you into singing the songs for the goddess?" he said. His breath smelled of freshly turned earth and something slightly sweet, giving her a woozy feeling. While the elves prepared their nightly ritual, Monica glanced down at the cup. Auberon followed her eyes and smirked.

"I take it you've never had elderberry wine before?" he asked. Monica shook her head no. He offered his cup to her and she took it in both her hands and took a small sip. As soon as the dark liquid made contact with her tongue, she began to tremble. Auberon, now thoroughly enjoying himself, took the cup from her trembling hands then took a step back to watch her unfold. Although Monica was trembling, her eyes were wide open and she could not believe what was revealed before her eyes; everything had a pale yet noticeable glow and the elves were taller and thinner than before. Some wore antlers on their heads while others had bright green leaves growing from their body. She looked up to the goddess of the night and her eyes zoomed onto her face. Her pale skin mirrored by long flowing waves of ebony hair brought tears to Monica's eyes. She wore a simple white toga and silver jewelry. The goddess saw Monica and waved to her as a welcome. Before Monica could wave back, Tuathae walked up to her and placed a warm hand on her shoulder, cutting off her connection.

"Drinking elderberry wine in the Otherworld, especially a person such as yourself, gives you heightened sight. You see another aspect of ourselves and a full glimpse of the goddess; we are here should you find yourself about to become unraveled." Just then, a male elf pulled her away from Monica, letting her know that they were ready for the ceremony. Tuathae nodded to him then, with a smile at Monica, walked off to begin. Auberon finished off his wine then took Monica's hand and led her closer to the group. Monica's eyes sought everything around her, trying to take in as much as she could of her heightened sight. When they reached the group, Auberon slid an arm around her waist and moved behind her, allowing no space between them. Monica could feel his cold body seeping into her own while his scent permeated her senses. She wanted to faint, but could not thanks to his strong arms.

Tuathae broke from the group and walked towards the fire, instantly silencing all conversations. She raised her arms to the sky and said in a voice that seemed to echo, "We, the Children of the Green, come together this night to give praise and honour to the goddess of the night, Nyx. May your chariot bring peaceful dreams to those who desire it. May you bring security to those who need it. May you bring comfort in the shadows to those who crave it." She lowered her arms just as she began to glow with a soft white light that came directly from the goddess' chariot. Monica looked up and saw the beam connect the two and was in speechless awe.

"You have stopped trembling," whispered Auberon in her ear while tightening his grip on her body. Monica felt something stirring inside of her, something warm and not unpleasant. Just then the elves began to sing; it started off low, like humming with complex harmonies. Monica joined the humming as did Auberon. She could feel his body trembling with the powerful melody and she responded in kind. The elves began to sway back and forth while still humming the melody. Auberon removed one arm from Monica's waist and caressed her cheek with his fingers as she continued humming the melody. Suddenly, there was a great flash of light revealing the goddess in all her glory floating several feet above the bonfire. The glow formed a circle around her as she gazed upon the elves. Her eyes finally found Monica's and her smile grew.

"*An Awakened Human,*" she said in Monica's mind. Monica nodded as her eyes focused on the goddess. "*So much inside of you and yet you are just beginning to understand it all.*"

"*I go in search of my Lin lover,*" replied Monica in her mind.

"*You carry his child. Keep strong to the night for that is where you shall find what you are looking for. In the darkness is pure emotion, satisfaction to your inner questions. You hunger for light, but your nature is of darkness. Be well.*" Nyx cut off her connection with Monica then held up her palms and said in a deep voice, "My children, sing for me and for my journey across the velvet sky. May this night be what you seek." She clapped her hands once, causing a thunderous sound, and then disappeared back into the night. All eyes looked up to find her riding her chariot onward to her next destination. The elves stopped their humming and broke their circle. Auberon released Monica from his embrace, turned her to face him then lifted up her chin and kissed her on the lips. His scent took hold of her senses and soon her arms wrapped around him, pulling him closer. Some of the elves noticed the embrace, but said nothing for they already knew.

After several minutes passed, Auberon pulled away from her then led her to the inn while Monica remained silent. When they reached the inn, he led them upstairs to his rented room and locked the door behind them. The room was small, clean and smelled of dried roses. After he locked the door, he sat Monica down on the bed then sat next to her. For a moment, neither said anything, but stared into each other's eyes. Auberon then placed a hand on her cheek and stroked it tenderly. Monica closed her eyes and shuddered under his touch.

"This is pure tenderness," he whispered. "Free from distractions and lies. This is my gift to you." He then removed his hand and kissed her once more on the lips, now gently prying her lips open with his pointed tongue. Monica opened her mouth slightly and allowed his entrance while tasting elderberry wine on his tongue. Auberon placed his hands on her shoulder and pulled her closer to him while their lips stayed locked. Deep down, Monica knew it was wrong; Shevra truly loved her and she carried his child. But this…..this was different. Auberon gave without any added intent and for right now, she needed it. Auberon moaned a little as they kissed then gently pushed her down on the bed. Soon, hands began to wander around each other's bodies, exploring and touching with nimble and sensation heightened fingers.

Monica released herself from his kiss then began to remove his clothing layer by layer. Auberon sighed with every touch of her fingers, patiently waiting for her to finish so he could do the same to her. When she reached his bare chest, she traced a line down his flat stomach with her tongue, causing him to arch his back.

"No one has ever done that to me before, sadly enough," he sighed. Monica made a circle around his bellybutton with her tongue then unbuttoned his pants. She slid them down to his ankles then got on the floor to remove his boots. Once he was completely naked, she stood up and traced lines on his body with her fingers. Auberon, reaching the end of his patience, grabbed her arm and threw her on the bed then removed her clothing. Her eyes were wide and focused on Auberon's face while his eyes were closed. She could feel the tenderness oozing slowly from his fingers as he undid each button and clip. When she was completely naked, he moved her towards the head of the bed and lay next to her. He draped a hand on her hip and said, "There is no wrong or right. We simply are."

"Yes."

"Do you give yourself to me completely without any other emotion? Do you understand just what you are about to do with me?"

"Yes." Auberon smiled; she was serious. He leaned forward and kissed her and all talking ceased. He stroked her body, feeling each tingle that emanated from her. She was more than willing, he thought as their tongues interlocked. Monica ran her fingers through his short hair and wanted to tug on it, but thought better of it. Thankfully, Auberon felt her need do such an action and pulled away from her for a moment to let her know it was okay. She smiled as the two resumed their kiss while her fingers grabbed locks of his hair. He moaned , but did not stop while she removed one hand and trailed down his chest to find his very erect member. She squeezed it gently, causing him to sigh, then began to stroke it. Auberon opened his eyes then moved his lips down her neck while giving it little bites every so often. He wanted to savour every moment of this feeling while wanting to give her as much of it as she possibly could take. Monica's hand slid faster around his member, feeling it jump in her hands, then rolled away from him and moved him on top of her.

Without thinking, he slid himself inside her and thrust as hard as he could. Monica's eyes flew wide open as his member filled her to almost splitting her apart. She raked his chest with her fingernails and allowed herself to move with his movements. This was beyond anything she had ever felt in her life. Although she had experienced sex only a small number of times, they all paled in comparison to what she was going through right now. This was beyond sex, beyond fucking, beyond everything. Auberon's thrusts were erratic, fast and slow all at once, and she loved every minute of it. She placed her hands on his shoulders and pulled him towards her, wanting another kiss from him. When their lips touched, she felt sparks coming from his mouth and tasted ashes. She opened her eyes and gasped; Auberon had changed. His hair had grown longer and stringier while his eyes turned a bright blood red that glowed with every thrust. His hands now had long and sharp bone claws that creaked with every moment and his back had a large hump that wriggled on its own.

"You wanted all of it," he whispered in a raspy voice that smelled of the dead, "and now you see me for what I truly am." He arched his back while still thrusting inside of her and out sprouted his skeletal wings. Monica's eyes were wide open yet she did not falter; she pulled him towards her again and kissed his cold dead lips as he thrust even faster. She could feel his member growing larger inside of her and yet the pain only intensified her hunger for him. Auberon flapped his wings then lifted her off the bed by several inches while he was still inside of her, never losing stride. Monica's head lolled back, but she still kept her eyes somewhat on the monster that was ravaging her. She wanted to know it all, wanted to know the ultimate pain that came with the ultimate pleasure. Monica simply wanted more. He lowered her to the bed and folded his wings into his back, then rolled over on his back and pulled Monica on top of him. She giggled for a moment then said, "Sorry, but I always get this wrong."

"Here," he said while raising a bony hand, "Let me help you. Take your time." He lifted her up and held his member just so it brushed her lips, then she slid down on it completely. She buckled for a moment, wanting more of him inside of her, then slowed down to a nice rhythm while arching herself over him. He sighed in pleasure while stroking her back with his cold bony claws. She rode him for several minutes, trying hard not to go too fast, but it felt too good for her to be slow. She increased her speed and soon bucked hard enough that the bed frame began to knock against the wall. Auberon closed his eyes, allowing her to take from him what she needed while he took some of her essence as his own. She is mine, he thought, and she knows.

Sweat poured down her neck while making a trail down between her breasts, dripping on his chest, but she not care. Soon, however, her legs began to tremble with exhaustion and she slipped off him. She crawled to the side of the bed and placed her hands over her ears to stop the trembling, but it did not help.

"I'm not done with you yet," he growled as he grabbed her legs and pulled over to the other side of the bed. Her lower half was against the side of the bed while her upper half was still on the bed as Auberon spread her legs open with his knees then slid himself inside her again. She arched her back in pain for he was even larger than before while he grabbed her arms and pinned her down to the bed.

"No, my sweet, you still have so much to learn from me," he said in his raspy voice as he continued to thrust. Monica wanted to cry for the pain was unbearable, but it still felt too good to release herself from him. She moaned his name over and over while she felt her essence being drained from him and replaced with his own. She could smell rotting apples and elderberry wine in the room and knew that it came from him. She closed her eyes and saw the entire Otherworld in its entirety: good, bad, and neutral. She even saw Lineal and the war that had begun, but she could not see Shevra. The image changed to the two of them in a graveyard with the lost souls of the dead floating around, moaning their cries and curses all around them. They refused to move on, only wanting to remain by their rotting bodies and fading memories. For a moment, Monica felt sorry for them, but soon the sounds of Auberon grunting returned her to the present. With a lurch, she pulled herself away from him and crawled once more to her side of the bed, leaving Auberon standing with a still erect member.

"Have you had enough for now?" he said in his normal voice.

"P-please.....no more," she whispered as she began to tremble again. Auberon got into bed with her and snuggled up behind her while placing a slender hand across her hip. He smoothed her hair away from her face and kissed the back of her neck and between her shoulders.

"Are you okay?" he asked.

"Y-yes."

"Do you regret what you did with me?" The shaking stopped.

"No, not at all." He nuzzled her neck again with his nose and sighed in her hair, filling her nose with elderberries. She felt safe with him even though she knew what he was and what he could do to her.

"I gave you a chance to experience that with me. Were you afraid of me?"

"No, I was not," she replied in a slightly defiant tone, causing him to chuckle. He pulled her legs between his and sighed again.

"You amuse me. Most human women would have run screaming once they saw the bone claws and wings. You did not."

"I was curious."

"You know I can take your life at any moment now or I can be tender to you. The ultimate in pain comes with the ultimate in pleasure. That is what Tuathae told you, yes?" Monica nodded. He smiled then snuggled deeper against her. Soon, she felt his breathing become regular and she knew that he was asleep. She closed her eyes and fell asleep as well. There were no doubts.

Something was wrong. Shevra grabbed his head in pain; it was excruciating. He shook his head from side to side, trying to remove the pain, but it only made it worse. He got out of bed and found himself kneeling on the floor with his head between his hands, wanting to scream. It felt as though someone or something was trying to rip his brain from his skull. He did not know when or how it happened, only that he was in excruciating pain. He stumbled to his feet and ran out of the room to see if one of his fellow Darjeel members could help him. By the time he reached someone, he grabbed their robe then fell over on the floor. Thin trickles of blood seeped from his nose and mouth.

Auberon opened one eye and looked down at Monica's sleeping head. He smiled then nuzzled her hair with his nose, causing her to moan quietly. He nuzzled a little harder, waking her up.

"Why did you wake me up?" she said in sleepy tone. Auberon did not respond, but slipped his hand between her legs, finding her sore yet still willing spot. She arched her back and pushed her butt into him, letting him know she was ready again. Taking the cue, he slid two fingers inside of her, feeling her raw skin, but only wanting to give her more of what she wanted and needed. Monica reached back to play with his hair then her hand went down to his erect member, stroking it softly knowing that the pain would come soon. Auberon pulled his fingers from her and laid her flat on her back then crawled on top of her and picked up where they left off hours ago. Her insides felt on fire, but the warmth pleased her. Auberon's eyes flashed red again as he took a little more of her essence while refilling the void with his own.

"I think it's time you reached a new level in your learning," he said then flexed his left bony hand with skeletal claws. Without a word, he began to stroke her leg then traced a line down her leg with a single claw. She saw a thin trickle of blood, but she did not care. Suddenly, he slipped that same claw into her leg, piercing the skin. Monica shot straight up in bed, but Auberon placed a hand on her chest and lowered her back down while still inside of her in both places.

"Now you will feel what I truly am. Seeing is not enough," he said then slipped all five claws into her leg. The pain sent a shot of adrenaline through her system just as Auberon pinned her down with his chest. She could feel his claws digging deeper in her leg, through muscle tendons, until he reached her bone. He began to rake a claw up and down it, sending shivers down her spine while warm blood flowed from the wound and spilled on the bed. His claws scraped against her bone over and over, creating a sensation that was a cross between tickling and being set on fire. Auberon placed his lips on hers, resuming their initial kiss that started all of this and she responded in kind. As they kissed, she could feel his hand sink deeper in her leg as his claws now grasped her leg bone and began to pull it upwards. Monica pulled from his kiss and gasped in pain while Auberon only smirked.

"Relax," he said soothingly, "I'm not going to do that to you. You still need your bones." He chuckled as he lifted his hand from her leg then showed her the blood stained appendages. He sniffed his bloody finger then began to lick them clean. Monica wanted to throw up. Auberon chuckled at her gagging sounds as he rolled over to his side of the bed then began to lick her wound. With every lick of his tongue, the pain lessened till it was only a slight throb. He then sat up on the bed cross-legged while Monica too sat up and examined her leg. There was only a faint scar where his hand violated her, but nothing more. The blood was gone as well. She looked at Auberon, searching for an explanation while he only smirked.

"My dear, how did you feel when it felt as though I was going to take your bone? Terrified? Scared? Curious even? Or, maybe you wanted more?" Monica folded her arms across her shoulders, causing him to laugh out loud. "So, now we must assume the defensive pose. Arms crossed over a chest I just licked and sucked on for hours. Trying to hide yourself from me does not work anymore. Remember," he said as he wiggled his regular fingers at her, "I now know what you taste like. I know your thoughts, probably better than you."

"So, are you happy now that you got what you wanted?"

"Are you?"

Monica stared at him in disbelief. "I-I-"

He held up a hand to silence her. "Truthfully, we both knew this was going to happen, correct? Although you truly love your Lin male, you've been wondering about me, the former Bone King and a Viril. I showed you something you've never experienced before and deep down, you are grateful. And relieved, I might add."

"So, what happens now?" she asked. "Will you still help me find Shevra?"

"Of course I will but remember, we are now a partnership."

"Partnership?"

"Of course. We both took and received from each other, and may I add that it was most enjoyed on my end. This was not something to take lightly. I do care about you, but I also realize you have a lover." He crossed his arms. "So, how do you feel about me?" Monica glanced away from him for a moment; so many ideas ran through her head within those few seconds and yet were any of them truthful?

She glanced back at his expecting face, sighed and said, "I care for you, but I do not love you." Auberon smiled.

"Fair enough." He held out his hand. "Understand that what you need will always be there for you, now or later. All you have to do is ask." Monica looked down at his hand and shook it with her own trembling hand.

Epilogue

Tuathae stared at the beginning of the new day yet her mind was somewhere else. Decisions were made and choices were no longer regrets, she thought as she sipped from her cup of tea. The story has just begun to unfold and with it comes new endings and quite possibly a new beginning. She sipped her tea once more then went back inside her home, ready to begin her day. They had much to do.

Pomegranate

Pomegranate

These things were never supposed to happen:
Snow falling. A child crying.
Leaves falling gently to a pile raked and forgotten.
I remember when dancing was forbidden
And laughter saved the world.
Terrible that the memories of long ago
Have become the saving grace of mankind.
Ashes fill my mouth, giving me a taste
Of what it meant to be human.
Forever, never, immediate gratification
Are within reach, yet I am dead
And locked in a house to provide
Floating chairs and phantom sighs.
I never had a chance; all I had were burned out candles
And dreams discarded by the masses like tissues.
I shall never make apologies for my crimes, but I am a better
person for them;
The coins weigh heavily in my threadbare pockets.
The noose grows tighter and I know what is going on.
Indeed, share some of the tenderness
You planned to waste and my suffering
Shall me nevermore indeed.

Charon's Lament

NOW

I still can't believe I made that decision. After he kissed me long and hard, we got up and proceeded to get dressed. My mind was going a million miles a minute and it took everything inside of me to keep from screaming bloody murder. I still can't believe I made that decision. Once dressed, I went downstairs. I still love him, even though I know what he is. I walked around the kitchen, looking for nothing in particular, when he entered the room, dressed in khaki pants, white shirt and loafers with no socks. His hair looked a little windblown while his normal eyes looked at me. He then walked over to me and embraced me. I felt his now warm skin against my own and I sighed. I loved him so much. When we pulled apart, he produced a small pomegranate from behind his back and I took it. Rather than the usual reddish coloured skin, this one was mottled grey with bluish spots. I looked at it for some time then up at him with a questioning look. What was I supposed to do with this, I thought.

"Eat this pomegranate," he said in a somber tone, "and you shall be saved from a Final Death. You must eat it all, including the skin." I sniffed it for a moment (it smelled like wet socks) and then I took a slow bite. It tasted foul and sickly sweet as the mushy skin gave in to my teeth yet I swallowed my first bite. I felt it go down my throat, burning and cooling at the same time. He just stood there, watching me eat, making sure I did not back down or out of what I had promised to him. However, he did not need to worry for I was not going to change my mind. All I had to do was look at him and my reasons for eating the pomegranate tripled. I closed my eyes and took another bite and noticed that this one was sweeter and less foul. When I opened my eyes, I noticed that everything looked hazy. I felt slightly dizzy but I still stood on my feet. He did nothing to support me; this was my decision, after all. My teeth tore into the skin while juice dripped down my chin and down the front of my clothing. I ate and ate, not caring how the fruit got in my mouth only that it did. Every bite got sweeter and sweeter and my eyes felt like lead weights in their sockets.

When I took the final bite, I chewed once then swallowed it all and wiped my sticky hands on my clothing. I looked up at him and felt like fainting. He was so blurry that I could barely make him out amongst everything else in the kitchen. He stood there, arms crossed, watching me still. I wanted to sleep, to fall down on the floor and sleep for hours, days, whatever. My eyelids grew heavy. I wanted to throw up but I had to keep the pomegranate in my mouth. The last thing I remembered here was him walking up to me and, while placing a hand on my now trembling shoulder, said, "This will not hurt at all." I heard the sound of coins falling and then everything went black.

BEFORE

Alexandra sat shivering in her car as her heater ran on full power while she waited for her husband to hurry up and arrive. Once again, in rushing from their home to open the bookstore on time, she had forgotten her keys, which meant that her husband would have to drive from his work and drop off his set.

"Alex, my darling wife, can't you ever remember to bring your keys?" he said in a joking manner when she called him on her cell phone. "Why don't you call Phillip to see if he can come by early?"

"Because, my darling husband, I want to see you one more time before we both get too busy with our lives." He chuckled and said he would be on the way. She was not careless but forgetful. In fact, she was so forgetful that she had made at least five copies of the main store key since the store opened two years ago. Too much on the brain, she thought as she put in a music CD and let the windows down a bit to light up a cigarette. The freezing air hit her nostrils with a swift kick but she did not care; she had to have that morning cig. The day looked gloomy with a wonderful forecast of thick grey clouds overhead; a perfect day for going to a bookstore and planning to stay for several hours. This was the kind of weather Alex enjoyed for it meant a good flow of customers unless it rained. As one of her many Goth/Industrial mix CDs began to play, starting with the classic

Bauhaus' "Bela Lugosi's Dead" to get her in the mood to open the bookstore, she looked at her storefront with pride.

When she finished law school and passed the bar exam with unheard of ease, her whole family was ecstatic. Graduating in the top three of her class with honors, law firms already wanting her as an associate, it seemed as though she really hit the big time…until she told her family she had other plans with her life. She wanted to open a bookstore instead.

"A bookstore?" squealed her mother when she told her parents on that awfully long night. Her father just shook his head in slow denial. "B-but you've spent so much time and energy on law school! Why in the world would you throw it all away for this 'thing' you want to open?"

"Because you know me. I've always enjoyed reading," said Alex in a calm and controlled voice. "Books have always been my passion." She gave her parents a level look; this was a fight she wanted to win.

"And that's wonderful," said her father, now finally joining in the conversation. "But you've got to look towards your future. Owning a bookstore makes a great hobby, but not as a career move."

"We have always been proud of you, Alex," said her mother as she reached for her Kleenex and blew her nose in a slightly melodramatic way. "We love you so very much."

"So, let me do this, then, Mom. I know I can do it."

"But what happens if you flop?" said her dad who was not a prolific man. "Then what?"

"Well, then I become that wonderful corporate lawyer you've always dreamt of," said Alex with a little arrogance in her voice that her mother picked up right away.

"Don't get an attitude, Alex. You may be 35, but you'll always respect us in our house."

"Sorry, Mom."

"That's better." She blew her nose again and wiped lightly at her flawless makeup. "Well, what about money?"

"What about it?"

"Well, you need money to open up a business, right?"

"Which is why my husband is going to be my silent financial partner." Both mother and father now looked at the quiet man who sat at the other end of the kitchen table. He folded his arms across the top of the table while intently watching the parlay of words. He never really talked too much, but when he did, it was always important.

This was one of those times.

"Joan, Daniel," said Julian in a quiet voice as he leaned forward a bit, "your daughter and I have talked about this for a while now. I fully support her in whatever she does and the money part is not a problem." Julian owned an art gallery in town that always sold more art than they could carry. It seemed that everyone who had money to burn had to purchase art from him for only he knew what was good and what was a futile attempt. Alex's parents were not too thrilled about their only daughter marrying a art gallery owner who dabbled in painting and sculpting as side hobbies, but they later saw the light when they realized just how much he was worth, not only from his art gallery but from his own family that owned several oil rigs in Texas.

Alex watched as he smoothed out his short and neatly styled brown hair, a clear sign that he was getting ready to win them over. Touching his hair in a calm yet confident manner was his signature move in winning the game lay before him, no matter the subject or the prize. "Your daughter has always been the model child, if I may say so," he stated, "and she has never once disrespected you, aside from the typical things that kids do when they think they know better." Both mother and father nodded in agreement. Alex knew he almost had them. "Well, it's not like she's dealing in crack or prostituting herself on the corner just to make ends meet. This is her dream in life, her big, big dream." He leaned back in the chair and let his body relax into the chair. He smiled a smile that was only reserved for sealing contracts for purchasing art. "Haven't you ever had a dream in your life? Something that made you smile every time you thought of it?"

"Well, sure," said her father, trying to frown but failing miserably, "Who doesn't?"

"So, why is this such a hard thing for you to understand? If the bookstore goes belly up, she'll become an attorney like she just said, plus she has my unwavering support both financially and emotionally. Besides, and I don't mean to be blunt, but she IS 35, after all." Joan and Daniel looked at each other, their eyes stating the obvious: *Julian is right. She's no longer a child.* They then looked back at their wonderful daughter and smiled. The bookstore was hers. Julian lightly touched her knee under the table, a sign that he had done it again.

Months later, both she and her husband moved store stock into a small opening located in the midtown area of the city, right in the middle of a heavy populated shopping area that would give them an advantage in sales. Her parents came by from time to time, making sure that their daughter was really going to become an entrepreneur and not some long and elaborate practical joke being played on them. After the store had been opened for a month and her bookstore had already turned a profit, their smiles were no longer forced whenever they came by to see her.

Just as the next song began to play, Alex saw a black Lexus pull up behind her. She got out of her car to embrace her husband who was visibly freezing as he got out of his vehicle.

"Baby," he said while laughing as he got out of his car, his breath coming out of his mouth like steam, "you better be glad I'm in a good mood, or else-"

"Yeah, yeah, I know, or else you would have let me freeze my ass off, right?" She took a step back from him to admire his pick of clothes today: he wore an all black suit with a light purple shirt and a deep purple tie that accentuated his long and heavy black overcoat that she always loved. "Well, you look good today. What's the occasion?"

"Can we finish this inside?" said Julian, his lips now quivering with cold. Alex punched him in the arm in jest as the two walked up to the front door of Wilde Bookstore and unlocked the door. As they walked in, the scent of Nag Champa incense wafted through the air. Julian held his nose and almost gagged as he turned on the lights.

"Sorry," said Alex sheepishly as she turned on the cash register, "didn't realize how much of that stuff I was burning yesterday."

"Yeah, well, at least you're not burning clove cigarettes in here, of which I hate."

"Yes, yes, I know, my dear. It makes you break out in little bumps." Alex walked over to the store CD player and popped in the newest CD from Blackmore's Night and began to open the store little by little.

"So, can I go back to work now?" he asked. "I've got that new exhibit from Tokyo coming in today and I want to make sure that it is ready for the public by next week-"

"Which means that I'll be at home alone tonight," said Alex, finishing the sentence for him. He walked over to her and hugged her tightly while kissing her ear. "No," he whispered, "I want you to come by tonight when everyone else is gone. I want you to look at what we were able to get from that new artist I was telling you about. She is truly a genius when it comes to acrylics. Oh yeah, remember that black leather couch I just bought? We still haven't christened it yet."

"OK," she said as she disentangled herself from him, "what time?"

"I'm thinking 8pm. I'll have take out for us when you get there, plus Absolut." He then kissed her on the cheek, dropped his set of keys in her hand, then with a small wave, left the store to get back to work, leaving Alex surrounded by a thin haze of incense smoke. She watched him leave then returned to her opening duties. She moved through the store quickly, turning on switches, pulling on plugs, stocking up on the newest received magazines and so on. Her purple and black velvet dress swirled on the floor as she ran everywhere to prepare for another hopefully busy day.

Within 30 minutes, the store was ready, which was good because she already had a couple of people standing outside waiting to get in. She checked her clothes and hair for the millionth time in the full-length mirror in the back of the store, then walked back out and opened the door. A pale young woman dressed in black jeans, black lipstick and a black t-shirt with a flaming pentagram on the front with a black long sleeve shirt underneath it and a long black duster coat walked in first. Her long blue-black hair was pulled back from her face, making her look even more macabre. She ran over to Alex and hugged her tightly.

"Lex! I got in at the University of Memphis!" she squealed which made Alex scream in happiness as she hugged the young girl.

"I knew you could do it! I just knew it!"

"Thanks, Alex. I can't wait to begin working on my Masters degree."

"What are you getting it in again?"

"English with a focus on Creative Writing."

"Well, think of me when you become a professor, 'cause I know you'll be thinking of PhD's next. Congrats, Regina!" She beamed with black lipstick in full as she walked around the store, trying to decide what would be a fitting treat for her in being admitted into graduate school. Alex continued putting out new issues of magazines she had received yesterday, knowing that people had called about them. Just as she put out the new *Gothic Beauty*, a periodical devoted to the Gothic sub-culture lifestyle, two customers smiled with evil glee as they grabbed their copies.

"Thank the gods for your store," said an older man dressed in Steampunk attire with a black top hat as he tipped it towards Alex and began looking around the rest of the place.

Wilde Bookstore was not just a bookstore; this was a bookstore for the Alternative Reader. This was for the reader whom every other bookstore pushed out because they were too weird or asked for things that they did not obviously carry. Her bookstore carried subjects from the Marquis de Sade to Lovecraft to Emily Dickinson and so on. She even laid claim to one of the best-stocked and well-researched Shakespearean sections in the city. Her bookstore also celebrated birthdays of famous writers, giving discounts to people who bought their books on that day or who dressed up as that particular writer. She even had a Bad Goth Poetry Night complete with refreshments and prizes awarded at the end followed by Goth/Industrial Night at the local club down the street.

Alex was a highly intelligent woman who was a freak as well and this place was her second home. In her lifetime, she blossomed from a wallflower to a flower with different coloured petals, thorns and even wings, much to the despair of her parents who lived in one of the suburban areas of the city with affluence and culture. They were proud of their daughter even though they still slightly cringed whenever she came by to visit them, dressed in one of her "creative splurges". On some days, she would dress as if attending a Victorian funeral, complete with black lace parasol, black opera gloves and even a little hat that sat sideways on her head. On other days, she would dress in vibrant purples, blues, and greens, presenting herself as a drunk faerie. Still, other times she dressed in khaki pants, Oxford shirt, and her trusty black clogs. After a long discussion with Alex, her parents realized that she really was a good daughter, even if she looked a little odd sometimes and loved the colour black more than normal. The corporate world would not have been able to handle her because she refused to be molded by what they considered to be "normal."

Many people in her past and present thought that black women, especially intelligent black women, did not need to waste their money and time doing things that only "white" people would do, like become a part of the Gothic sub-culture, attend Renaissance festivals, believe in faeries, or own over 500 books in her home, ¾ of them already read by her, sometimes twice. She was not supposed be interested in folk music, existential French cinema, or other such stimulating things for she was trying to be "uppity" and forget her roots, or something like that. She refused to follow what other black people were doing simply for the sake of similar skin color. She had been insulted and made fun of by other black kids in her life, and later adults, because she was a freak. She only saw herself as a woman who wanted to live fully by her own rules and it drove them mad for some reason. A friend once told her of the ancient art of DILLIGAS – do I look like I give a shit – and it worked perfectly in her life for it was exactly what she thought of them and their limiting thoughts.

Alex busied herself with restocking merchandise and ringing up customer's purchases, with the occasional customer letting her know that her bookstore was a place they would definitely come back to. Other customers sat in chairs with a book or magazine, reading the time away. As lunchtime rolled around two hours later, her associate Phillip walked in. He was, as always, dressed like a rogue from a medieval fantasy novel. On this day, however, he chose to wear all black, even down to his newly dyed shoulder length black hair to contrast his pale skin and his high cavalier boots that even Alex was envious of. He walked into the store with his usual air of confidence and arrogance, bowed low to her and said, "Good morrow, my dear Lady. I am here for thine amusement," with a very exaggerated British nasal accent that made her gag.

"Uh, right," she said with a smirk on her face as she grabbed her coat. "I'll be back in an hour now that you're here." Phillip ran his fingers through his jet-black shoulder length hair and waved her off like a bored British lord. Just before she walked out she said, "So the look was all black today, huh? Right down to the hair?"

"I got bored with the brown," he replied in his normal voice that was not full of B.S. "Plus, today looked so gloomy that I felt the need to be in black." Alex shook her head in exasperation as she walked out to her car.

As she drove down the street, she noticed that the clouds seemed to be breaking up, allowing the sun to shine through somewhat.

"It's still cold as fuck outside," she mumbled as she turned the heater to full blast. She drove into the drive thru of Wendy's, ordered her lunch and something for Phillip with chattering teeth then quickly drove back. No telling what kind of condition Phillip had the store in while she had left, she thought in amusement. When she pulled up to the store, the sight within made her shake her head in mock frustration while laughing. There was Phillip, dancing some new dance he learned recently while a group of customers stood around him forming a circle. As she walked in, her Blackmore's Night CD was almost at full blast as Phillip danced nimbly within the circle. Alex, holding their lunches, looked over at him once then walked to the office in the back and locked the door. Some things were better left not seen and covered up with thoughts of a Wendy's Spicy Chicken sandwich.

As she ate in the peace of her office, she heard the music continue on with the crowd clapping to the beat. Several minutes later, she heard shouts and clapping, signaling the end of Phillip's dance. The music went back down to normal level followed by a knock on her door. She opened the door, revealing a very sweaty and happy Phillip as he grabbed his French fries and began to munch away.

"Great moves," she said as she took a sip of her Coke. "New SCA thing or something?"

"Learned it last week during fighter practice. All the ladies loved it when I finally got it right. I think it was used as a love charm in the 1400s or something."

"Great. Don't try and flirt with the customers to buy more of our stuff, OK?"

"You're the boss." He stuffed three French fries in his mouth and closed the door again, leaving Alex alone once more. She finished her lunch then tossed her trash in the garbage can as she walked out and into the store while smoothing out imaginary wrinkles in her perfect gothic dress.

"Hey, which would you rather hear today?" said Phillip as she began creating a candle display by their sitting area, "some more Blackmore's Night or some Garmarna?"

"Actually, I'm in a Mediaeval Baebes mood, if you don't mind."

"No problem." Phillip searched through the store's CD collection, found one of their CD's then popped it in. As the haunting music began, Alex completed the display then began unloading some boxes of books that were shipped to the store yesterday. A couple of people walked by trying to see what new stuff they received then continued their search through the store. Phillip began dusting the Science Fiction & Fantasy section while occasionally looking through an interesting book or pausing to thumb through one of the gaming magazines they carried.

For the remainder of the day, Alex and Phillip worked and had fun, which was every day. They did not have to worry about meeting the demands of some big corporate office headquarters.

The hours flew by like the wind; customers sailed in and out of their place with many sales taking place. Soon, it was 7:40PM, only 20 minutes away from their closing time. As the last customer walked out with a brand new copy of *Sci-Fi Magazine*, Alex took off her black combat boots and sat down on the floor, crushing her all day perfect dress, while Phillip smoked a cigarette while standing in the front doorway.

"Want one?" he asked.

"Sure, why not? We'll be closed soon." Alex walked over to Phillip and graciously took one as he lit it for her. They stood side by side, smoking in cold silence, watching the winter clouds drift by. She looked across the street to see people walking by in a hurried fashion; always places to go and things to do, she thought. Just then, she saw a dark figure quickly walking across the street towards her bookstore.

Phillip snorted, "Oh please! Why is it always one person who has to come in right when we're closing up shop?"

"Yeah, but it would be good to squeeze in one more sale," she said as she flicked her half smoked cigarette out into the cold air as the figure loomed closer. Alex could see that he wore a long and heavy black coat that fell to his knees with a black cowboy style hat on his head. His face was down and half hidden under the coat in trying to keep their face warm. He walked with a determined stride, almost arrogant with nothing to fear. She walked over to the candle display to freshen it up a bit for their last customer. Phillip held the door open for the man once he arrived at the door with a mock salute while saying, "You're our last customer of the day. You'll get the royal treatment." He dropped his butt into a cup by the door then let the door slam behind the customer as he sauntered off, not caring if he was offended by his remark or not. Alex stood by the candle display, still shoeless; she was so tired that she couldn't have cared less if the guy tripped over her boots while walking around. He looked around the bookstore for a moment then took both his hat and coat off, revealing a most unusual man.

He wore all black as well; pants, turtleneck, and boots that looked to have steel toes in them. His hair, black with some grey, was lanky with some of the locks falling over his eyes like an

English schoolboy. His face was sharp, its main features his hawk like nose and startlingly green eyes as his skin looked like a white peach. As he checked his clothing, Alex glanced at him then noticed his hands. His hands made her own hands look like a construction worker's and yet they carried some sense of strength in them. Alex shook the thought out of her head and continued working on her candle display. The man looked at Phillip, who tried to sneer at him but it came out all wrong, and then looked over at Alex. His heart almost stopped beating when he saw her. He was so stunned by how beautiful she was that he almost forgot where he was as he quickly composed himself and walked over to this stunning creature. He had to speak to her.

"I'm sorry if I came at a time when you are about to close," he said in a quiet accented tone, "but I had just heard about your store from a friend. I wanted to see the legendary Wilde Bookstore for myself."

"Well, thank you for coming in," she said, blushing like a schoolgirl, "but unfortunately, we are about to close. You're more than welcome to look around, though, for the next-"

"Five minutes," snarled Phillip standing by the door, impatient and ready to go home. He had a Fantasy Book Club meeting tonight and it was his turn to have it at his apartment. The stranger did not even register what Phillip had said to him; all he could focus on was the lovely purple and black vision before him.

"Well, I guess I'll be quick about it won't I?" Alex smiled at him but inside was fuming. I want to see my husband tonight, and this guy is going to make me late. Why me? The man then walked straight to the Mythology section and looked through a couple of titles. Phillip, now completely pissed off, kept playing with his set of store keys, jingling them loud enough so that the guy would get the hint and just leave. After a couple of seconds, the man pulled out a book entitled Pagan Myths Of Ireland and walked over to the check out area with the book in hand. He handed the book to her, his eyes never leaving her face, then pulled out his wallet and began thumbing through the many bills he carried.

"How much?" he asked with a smile in his voice.

"For you, the low price of $12," said Alex, trying to be nice but still holding back her impatience. "Anything else you need tonight?" Phillip slapped his head with his hand in frustration; just give the guy a wide-open chance to keep them open later than usual, he thought.

"No. I think your friend is getting rather angry with me. I've kept you open too late, haven't I?"

"Well, sorry, but...it's just been a long day for both of us, that's all. Isn't that right, Phillip?" she said over the customer's shoulder, focusing on her now very irritated co-worker.

"Yeah, sure, whatever," he mumbled as he jingled the keys again as a reminder. Alex handed the man his purchase. For a brief second, their hands touched each other. His hands, she thought; they felt so warm and soft like silk. The man glanced at his hands for a moment then back at her.

"Nice place you have here," he said. "Maybe I'll come back sometime." He then put on his coat and hat and walked to the door. When he passed by Phillip, Phillip muttered, "Wanker," behind his back as he opened the door for him. The man stopped once, almost turned around then decided it was not worth it as he walked back across the street into a small crowd of people, disappearing immediately in the cold and bitter night like a ghost in the land of the dead.

"Well, I'm glad he's gone," said Phillip as he locked the door then checked the locks again just to make sure. "What a weirdo."

"Yeah." She looked down at her hands, still feeling the warmth from the man's hands.

"Hey, you OK?"

"Yeah, sure, I'm fine. He just creeped me out, that's all." Alex looked at her watch and sighed. "Shit. I'm sorry, Phillip. You can head out, if you want."

"You sure you don't need me?"

"Sure I'm sure. Have fun at your book club meeting tonight. Tell them I'm sorry I could not make it this time around."

"Sure. Well, take care. I'll see you tomorrow." Phillip grabbed his cloak from the coat peg by the door and with a flourish, let himself out and into the winter night, leaving Alex alone to close out the store. She stared at the door for a while, her mind drifting away with fatigue, then began the closing procedures for the night. As the register tallied up the figures, she quickly called her husband to let him know that she would be late.

"Sorry, some guy came in at the last minute and I'm just now closing everything down."

"Hey, no problem. Besides, I haven't even ordered for us. What do you want? Chinese, I'm thinking."

"Some rice noodles with chicken, dim sum, and an egg roll for me."

"Cool. It'll be here when you get here."

"And the Absolut?"

"And the Absolut."

"OK, love you."

"Love you too." The register finished its closing procedures for the night just as she turned the lights off. She put her coat on and wrapped it tightly on her body then opened the door. Once the cold air hit her, she almost froze as she locked the store then ran for her car. She jumped in and set off for her husband's gallery.

20 minutes later brought Alex to her husband's gallery known as The' Noir. It was located in the university area and catered to anyone who just liked art. On the front window was a large black hole painted on with the words *The' Noir* painted in white around it. Alex pulled up and knocked on the doors. There were no lights on but soon a back door opened, spilling light into the main room of the gallery and revealing a figure walking briskly towards the front. She sighed in frozen relief; it was Julian.

"Hey babe, glad you could make it," he said as he let her in and locked the doors behind them. "So, how was work?"

"Busy as always. You?"

"We put in that new work I was telling you about today, plus made a killing on those vases I told you about the other day." They hugged each other then kissed for a long time. When Alex pulled away, she said, "I can smell my noodles. Food's here, right?"

"But of course." Alex slipped out of her coat then walked with him to the back office where dinner was about to be served.

Several Chinese dishes, six shots of Absolut vodka, and two hours of wonderful sex later, the couple lay on the purple plush carpet floor, naked. Alex propped her head up with her arm and lay on her side while staring off while he sat cross-legged on the floor.

"I love these moments," he said in a slightly slurred manner. "And I love being with you during these moments."

"Me too." She sat up to get another shot of the vodka, quickly lying back down again, feeling the effects of the past two shots.

"Tell me again why I should never drink," she groaned as she held her dizzy head.

"Because it turns your body into putty." Alex lay on her back, staring up at the ceiling. Neither said anything, staring off in whatever direction they faced and allowed the silence to be their music.

The next day brought some sun into the city, which was better than none at all. The weather forecasters claimed that the city would be entering spring very, very soon and that everyone needed to get those bathing suits out. Alex stared off into the beautiful day while sipping on a cup of Silver Needle white tea while Phillip helped a young woman dressed in an a deep purple Victorian cut dress with long platinum white hair find a book on dragons. She knew that he had been trying to ask this woman out in a non-direct way, but so far, she was either too smart for his own good or too dumb to notice his obvious flirtation. She chuckled as she glanced over at the two of them then out into the busy street.

Suddenly, her heart skipped a beat as she watched a man in a black coat cross the street and walk up to her store: it was the man from last night. Alex walked over to the cash register in nervousness, almost dropping her cup of tea in the process, and pretended to look up some prices when he walked in. Phillip looked up, saw that it was the man from last night, then looked back down again quickly, wondering if he had returned to kick his ass for making that wanker comment. The man saw Alex walk from the register to the music display in a deliberate nonchalant way and walked up to her. She turned around unexpectedly and gasped when she realized how close he was to her. He smelled like fresh linen.

"Well, it seems we have a repeat customer," she said, trying not to sound so nervous.

The man flashed an all teeth smile at her. "I wanted to have more time to enjoy your store since I came at such a bad time last night." Alex felt her cheeks go warm; damn it, she thought, I'm married!

"Well, take a look around then." The man bowed low in front of her then removed his coat, revealing the same outfit as before, and hung it on his arm and was about to walk off when she tapped him on the shoulder and asked in a meek voice, "Excuse me, but where are you from?"

"My accent, huh?" His eyes seemed to dance with electricity.

"Yeah. I can't really place it."

"It's a smattering of several places but for now, think of it as just a world traveler."

"Sorry," she stammered in embarrassment, "I'm sure you get that a lot around here. Well, enjoy your visit."

"Oh no, I'm not visiting. I live here now."

"Oh, well, welcome then." The man looked into her eyes for a moment, causing Alex to feel like she was drowning in something thick and not entirely unpleasant.

"My name is Dune Planton."

"Alexandra Winthrop." He gently took her hand and kissed it, making her blush even more so. She felt her body move closer to his, could feel warmth radiating from him, his eyes, she thought-

"Uh, Lexie?" asked a now very concerned Phillip who had suddenly appeared next to her, "did you ever get those books from that publishing company in New Orleans?" Alex looked at him in a daze then shook her head, letting her hand fall as she came to her senses.

"Yes, we got that box in last week," she said to her friend in a now businesslike tone. She turned to Dune and said, "I'm sorry, but I'm needed. Look around as long as you want." With that, she walked off with Phillip to the back room. Once they got there, she leaned against the door and began gulping for air as her stern façade quickly slipped away. Phillip looked at her with concern.

"Lex, you OK? I'm sorry, but that guy just seems a little too weird for me. Coming from me, that should mean something." Alex waved him off then sat down in her chair and laid her head down on the desk. Only one kiss on her hand and it caused her to almost faint from exhaustion. Phillip got a cup of water for her and set it in front of her head then closed the door to her office. She lifted her head for a moment then drank the water in one gulp. I'm happily married, she thought, and I swoon over some guy who is flirting with me. Ridiculous. She stood up, smoothed her deep red velvet dress down then walked back outside to face the store as the owner and not some silly schoolgirl. She scanned the area for Dune, finding him sitting in the reading area with a book in his lap, then walked over to their CD player and popped in a CD by Siouxsie & The Banshees and let their music overtake her. She hummed along with the music as she rang up customers then helped a young man find some books on the Italian Renaissance, soon forgetting that Dune sat in the chair reading ever so calmly.

Even Phillip lost his black mood and decided to dance another medieval dance for the customers; it was becoming quite a regular thing now. The people in the store formed a wide circle with Phillip as the center. He bowed to everyone just they began to clap in rhythm but just as he was about to begin, a hand touched his shoulder. He whirled around to find Dune standing right next to him.

"If you don't mind, I'd like to have a go at this one," he said.

"By all means," said Phillip with a sarcastic bow, "the floor is yours." He stood a little to the side as he waited for this freak to begin and finish what could only be a failure. Dune changed the music to a Corvus Corax CD he had in his coat pocket and moved to the center of the circle. Once the music began to play, a rhythmic combination of jungle beats and bagpipes, the center of attention began to dance, his movements like liquid mercury. Once he began his dance, he blocked everyone out of his sight and hearing, listening only to the music, and his eyes never left Alex's face. All of the women (and some of the men) in the circle watched him with hungry eyes, their minds replaying sexual positions between themselves and the center of attention, but Dune was in another world. Finally, he did a small flip in the air and landed solidly on his feet, causing the customers to applaud wildly. He bowed to everyone then grabbed his coat and hung it over his arm. His breathing was regular and there was no sweat on his brow. It was as if he had just spent the last five minutes talking to an old friend. He turned off the CD player and pocketed his CD.

"I must admit," said Alex as she walked up to him while slowly clapping, "that was great to watch." He bowed low before her then rose up, his eyes never leaving her face.

"I am especially glad that you found my dancing to be wonderful." He moved closer to her body. She could feel his body heat radiating from him again while the scent of fresh linen permeated her senses. His sweet breath surrounded her body like a fog. She frowned in light of the wonderful feeling. Time to end this, she thought

"Listen, sir-"

"Please, call me Dune."

"OK, Dune. You seem like a really great guy. However, I am married." A slight frown crept on his face then quickly left again, leaving a slightly concerned look.

"I'm sorry, I didn't mean to cause any problems."

"No problems at all, but I just wanted to let you know." She extended her hand out to him, which he shook as platonic as possible. "Well, I need to get back to actually managing this place. Stay as long as you want." She turned and walked over to Phillip and began putting in some new music CDs they received. A young woman walked up to him and lightly tapped him on the shoulder. When he turned to face her, she almost fainted.

"I liked your dancing," she said nervously.

"Thank you." He flashed an all teeth grin at her.

"I was wondering, if you're not busy tonight, would you like to maybe go out for some coffee?"

"I appreciate that kind offer, but unfortunately, I cannot."

"Yeah, maybe some other time." She looked absolutely crestfallen as he walked away and began looking through some magazines.

The hours flew by with the bookstore being completely busy in purchases. Dune stayed around for a bit then left for a while to grab some coffee, asking if Phillip or Alex wanted any.

"I'll have a vanilla latte, heavy on the vanilla," said Alex.

"Get me a triple shot mocha," said Phillip with a dangerous twinkle in his eye.

"Oh great, once you get that shit in your system, you'll be bouncing off the walls," she groaned. Dune wrote the orders down then quickly walked out and down the street to one of the local coffeehouses in the area.

"So, I hope you told him you were married," said Phillip once he left. "From the moment he first walked in here, he's had nothing but goo goo eyes for you."

"Well, perhaps his weakness is black bohemian women," she joked.

"Ha. Ha. You did tell him, right?"

"Of course I did. I would never cheat on my husband. You know how much I love Julian."

"Just checking, that's all."

"Well, thanks for being such a good friend."

"Who has yet to hook me up with a wonderful gamer girl?"

"Ha. Ha."

Once again, the closing hour came soon. This time, Phillip volunteered to close down the bookstore while Alex left early.

"You deserve it, so go, OK?"

"OK. I owe you one." Alex grabbed her coat and waved goodbye to Phillip as she walked out and into her car. She sped all the way home, hoping to find her husband waiting for her.

When she arrived, however, the house was dark with no sign of his car. Alex quickly got inside and turned on the central heat then plopped down on their couch and turned on the TV.

When they purchased their house many years ago, they decided to split the decorating. So, the house was half decorated like a contemporary art/writing gallery for Julian, and half bohemian and Gothic for Alex. The couch in the living room, however, was a bright fluorescent blue that neither one wanted but kept it anyway since they received it as a wedding present from a good friend of theirs who had very, very tacky taste in everything.

She got up after a while to get a glass of red wine then sat back down and nursed it, not tasting it at all. When she finally finished the glass, the clock read 10 PM with no sign of Julian. Was he okay, she wondered then decided to call him just to make sure. He could take of himself, but hey, one never knew.

"The' Noir Gallery," yawned Julian.

"Babe, it's me. I'm at home."

"Hey! I'm sorry but I have been working like crazy trying to get this new exhibit into our place. Remember when I told you about the exhibit from France that we would be getting in the not too distant future?"

"Yeah."

"Well, it came. Today. I'm sorry, I should have called earlier."

"Well, will you be home later tonight?"

"I'll try but I can't promise anything."

"Well be careful, OK?"

"I will. Get some rest. I love you."

"I love you too." Alex turned off the mindless TV and went upstairs to bed. She slept hard and did not dream.

Alex awoke to her husband snoring loudly next to her. She smiled as she looked down at his handsomely rugged face then quietly got out of bed and got ready for another day. Today proved to be a little warmer than yesterday, but still cool enough to wear long sleeves or pants. Her look was of a dark librarian:

long black skirt with black sweater and white oxford shirt peeking through with a blood red tie to "brighten" the outfit, and her black clunky loafers. The sun shone brightly and not a cloud could be seen in the sky. When she arrived, she noticed that Phillip had beaten her there.

"Hey you," she said as she shrugged off her coat, "What's with the early morning get up and go attitude?"

"Well, I figured that you needed a break today. So, I woke my lazy ass up and got myself here, complete with fresh coffee and pastries." He opened a large white box in front of her, revealing many assorted cream and jellied filled pastries that Alex could feel already on her hips and thighs. She grabbed an almond croissant and a hot cup of coffee then popped in a Sunshine Blind CD to begin the day anew. An hour after they opened the doors, Dune walked in while drinking a large cup of something hot.

"Good morning all," he said as he walked in. Alex smiled while eating on her stool. Phillip actually smiled at Dune.

"What brings you here today?" asked Alex.

"Just nothing to do today and I thought I would stop by."

"Looking for anything in particular?"

"No, just browsing." Alex and Phillip let him browse in peace, answering his questions about certain things from time to time. After two hours of laughing, talking, and looking, Dune finally walked up to the counter with an armload full of books.

"Wow, will you have time to read all of this?" joked Phillip.

"I have plenty of time on my hands," said Dune. "I don't have a job."

"So how-"

"Let's just say that I have money. Old money and time to burn it with."

"Ah, sorry, didn't mean to intrude."

"No fault on you, Phillip." Dune then paid for his purchases, said goodbye and left. The store only had two other people, so Phillip sauntered over to Alex and said, "Did you hear? Old money. Whatever."

"So?"

"SO?!?! Don't you know that men like that are either good catches for a young woman like yourself, or an assassin that kills for money."

"Give me a break, and a bear claw."

"Lexie, I'm serious!"

"You know, you might want to stop watching *Law & Order* so damn much. That's what I tell Mom all the time. She used to tell me every night 'don't get raped'." Phillip almost threw her bear claw at her.

Several hours later, the phone rang.

"Hello, Wilde Bookstore, how many I help you?"

"Alex? Julian here."

"Hay babe!"

"Hey back. I'm sorry I got in so late last night, but I'll have to do it again tonight. I might be staying at the gallery."

"Damn. What kind of exhibit is this?"

"An exhibit that'll make us so much money that we will never have to work again."

"Ah yes, that kind." A sigh. "Fine. Do you want me to have dinner waiting for you or something?"

"Nah, don't worry about me. I'll be fine."

"OK, well, I gotta run. Take care and I love you."

"I love you too babe."

Alex hung up the phone and sighed again; another night of no husband. She finished off her tea then poured another cup. It was going to be a long night.

15 minutes to closing arrived with no warning. Phillip had a blind date with a friend of a friend later that night.

"It's about time too," he said, "I've been going nuts at my place. I even starting looking at my cat in a different way."

"You bastard," said Alex while laughing.

"Yeah, well, do you mind if-"

"Go. Get lucky tonight, OK? I want to hear every little detail about it tomorrow." With a grin, Phillip threw on his cloak and dashed out to his car. Seconds later, he was off while she finished up the reports then walked outside to lock the door.

"Hi, Alexandra."

She almost jumped out of her skin then relaxed when she saw that it was Dune walking up to her from the side.

"You freakin' scared me." Alex lit up a cigarette and began to puff on it nervously. "What's up?"

"Well, I was wondering; I know that you are married and I respect that, but would you mind going out with me to get a drink tonight? I promise I will be a Boy Scout." Alex stared at him for a long time while smoking her cigarette then flicked the butt into the street.

"Sure, I have nothing to do tonight. I trust you enough." Dune grinned as the two walked down the street to one of the local bars. When they walked in, heat hit them instantly. They found a table in the back and quickly ordered beer from a waitress with blazing red dreadlocks. When she left, they began talking.

"So how long will you be here?"

"As long as I want until my feet become itchy on the soles."

"Phillip told me about you having old money and that I should be careful around you, that you were either a lonely man who needed a wife, or a serial killer who killed for money."

Dune laughed. "Oh please. I'm just a harmless man who likes to go out and buy lots and lots of books and music. I'm actually quite boring." The waitress brought their drinks then left again.

"So, when was the last time you went home?"

"Actually," said Dune as he sipped his beer, "it's been years. I wanted to see the rest of the world before I settled back home as an old man who talks to his stuffed dogs or something."

"One can get their education through travel, I find. I went to Phoenix last year and it was amazing how much I learned amid the tourist traps and stuffing myself with Southwestern food. I still have plans to visit London as well as Tokyo, Paris, wherever. I just want to see as much as I can before my husband and I get too feeble to move around."

Dune smiled at her response; her intelligence was nearly off the chart as he far as he could tell. Her husband was one lucky man. Alex took a long sip of her Pete's Strawberry Ale then asked, "So, are you an only child?"

"Sadly, no. I have siblings. One of my brothers claims to be quite a ladies' man, but I'm always getting him out of more scraps than anything. I remember when he got this one woman pregnant and was actually happy about it, until it was found out later during an exam that the child would be horribly deformed."

"My god. What did he do?"

"Called me up, asking for my help." Dune stared at her for a moment in silence, leaving Alex hanging. She looked around the place for a moment then said, "Well, what did you do?"

"You don't want to know." Alex cleared her throat, wondering for a brief moment just why she decided to have a drink with him. She took another sip from her bottle then said, "So, you don't have a girlfriend, huh? You would be quite the catch given your obvious intelligence and worldliness."

"I am attracted to brainy women, not bimbos with barely any clothes on who can't count beyond three. It's hard when you've got many women surrounding you with these vapid expressions on their faces, being impressed with you when you open a can of soup with a can opener. I want a woman who can stand on her own feet, be proud of who and what she is, and never accept normal as a standard in life." He went silent for a moment then continued. "I was married once, but she proved to be too much for me. I thought that perhaps, she would see me as a partner and lover in time but I found she was too godly for me. I divorced her after many years of being with her and for the first time, I feel like my old self again. The divorce caused some to be upset and others to be quite happy with the decision, but I no longer cared what anyone else wanted from me. I live my life my own way. I'm ready to see the world again, learn as much as I can, and just enjoy the life I have."

"Here, here, well said," she said as she swung her beer bottle in appreciation.

"So, how long have you been married?"

"About five years. It feels longer than that but not in a bad way," she said as the waitress came by to check on them. Alex drained her beer and ordered another as did Dune then she continued. "My parents used to wonder if I would ever get married, since I was so against it in my college years. Yes, I was a card carrying, bra burning feminist with a touch of sisterhood forever, or so I thought."

"Oh no!" said Dune while holding up his hand in mock horror, causing her to snort.

"Yeah, well, after several failed attempts to follow the crowd, I just gave up. I did not want a man in my life; all I wanted was to be myself and to be alone while doing it. Funny how when you don't want something, that's usually when it falls in your lap. I met Julian through Phillip and we just hit it off like that." She snapped her fingers for emphasis. "A year later, we were married. No children, though. We're quite selfish with our free time and children would just suck that all up. So, we play rather well as the urban hip couple who are also quite well off." The waitress brought their beers and Alex took a sip of it, enjoying the cold liquid running down her throat.

Dune took a sip of his beer while staring at her, wondering more and more about her. He slipped his hand in his pocket and felt the tiny wrapped package snugly inside. He smiled; just touching the package made him feel better at times. It was a constant reminder for him. He then pulled out the tiny package and unwrapped it on the table.

"What's that?" she said, peering over her bottle. Dune said nothing but placed a small reddish seed in his mouth and took a deep sip of his beer, washing it down. Alex watched in mute fascination as he did this then wrapped up the remainder of the seeds and placed them in his pocket without a word. Alex waited for him to say something to explain his strange behaviour; when he didn't, she decided she wouldn't as well. If he wanted her to know, he would have told her. He then struck up a conversation regarding small talk and soon, the thoughts of the seeds were long gone from Alex's mind.

Several beers later, the two walked back into the cold towards their cars.

"Will you be all right?" he asked as she was about to get in her car.

"Fine. I'll be fine. Good night and thank you again." She got in her car and sped off, leaving Dune who drove off several seconds later. When she got home, she noticed that the house was dark again. Julian was still at the art gallery. She got in her home and immediately turned on the heat, went upstairs to take a warm bath then prepared herself for bed. Within an hour, she fell fast asleep.

This time, she did dream.

She stands by a dark river that flows ever so slowly. She looks up and sees only dark, not a sky but just dark. The air smells funny, like something.....she looks at the river again and now there are small seeds floating around in the river. Without thinking, she reaches down to pluck one from the water. When her fingers touch the river, she screams in pain.

"Good Morning, this is NPR. The time is 8am."

Alex opened her eyes to the sound of her alarm clock. She rubbed her eyes a little then felt her husband next to her, snoring loudly. She kissed his cheek and got herself ready for another day. Today was the first day of spring, warm and inviting for a sunny day. This was Ostara, a day of rejoicing for all Nature loving folk. Rather than get dressed, she gathered all of her ritual items and brought them downstairs to the living room. She carefully set up her altar then removed the clock that hung on their wall, thereby removing any trace of any modern sound that would distract her from her work.

She removed her clothing and knelt before her altar while facing west. Closing her eyes, she took in three deep breaths, releasing them with the intention of removing any negative thoughts or any distracting ideas from her mind. Suddenly, a slightly cold breeze ran across her back, almost causing her to open her eyes but she held firm to her mood, quickly dismissing the breeze. After several seconds had passed, another breeze caressed her exposed breasts, causing her nipples to quickly harden. She wanted to open her eyes and see if a window had been left open, but she still held fast in welcoming Spring.

Somewhere, some place, a figure sat in a room devoid of anything, eyes closed, breathing regularly, focusing their attention on her. Each chilly breath that it exhaled caressed her body like a tender yet cruel lover. Alex opened her eyes with a gasp as she reached for her robe. Her lips were actually turning blue while her body shivered and shook as if she had been sitting on an iceberg for hours. She looked down at her nipples and saw that they were very hard and slightly pale. She raced upstairs to get dressed, her husband still asleep and oblivious. She wanted to leave her home as fast as possible. Her ritual did not feel right.

Once she arrived at the bookstore, her mood brightened. She noticed that Phillip was not there as she let herself in and began the day's opening procedures. Five minutes before the bookstore opened, Phillip walked in with a dreamy look on his face while holding two steaming Styrofoam cups of Earl Grey tea. He wore his frilly white poet's shirt, black tight pants and cavalier boots. His hair fell loosely around his face.

"Let me guess," said Alex with a smirk as he handed a cup to her, "I'm in for a story, right?"

Phillip took a sip of his own tea then replied, "My bad luck is over." She sat on her stool with her steaming cup and listened with eager interest.

"Well, I told you that this woman was a friend of a friend? I'm surprised I had never met her before at Goth Night or any SCA event. Seems she just moved here not too long ago and was looking to make some new friends. She's into gaming, SCA, all things dark & spooky, reads anything under the sun, in college working on her Master's degree in Ancient Egyptian History, and the best lay I have ever had. We have a date again tonight."

"So you think she's the one?"

"Let me put it to you this way. After last night's talking and sex fest, she has a toothbrush at my place now."

"So romantic." They both laughed as their first customers began walking in. Soon, they were busy with their daily chores and duties of the place. Just before Phillip stepped out to grab lunch for them several hours later, he asked, "So, what did you do last night?"

"Went out with Dune for a beer."

He almost dropped his second cup of tea on the floor. "You're shitting me?"

"I shit you not."

"Damn. So, did you sleep with him?"

"Phillip!"

"Hey, hey, I gotta ask, you know? So, what's he like?"

"Very nice, obviously intelligent, although a bit sad. Told me he was married once but that did not turn out well."

"That's it?"

"I'm afraid so. Sorry to disappoint you." Phillip took a quick sip of his tea then glanced over at Alex, who was holding her tea but staring out at the window with a lost expression on her face. "OK," he said while placing his cup down on the counter, "whenever I see that look on your face, I always know that many thoughts are running through your mind, clashing and clanging. So, what're you thinking?"

"It's just that, well, when we talked last night, I . . . . . I-"

"Yes?" Alex took a deep sip of her Earl Grey tea then looked sincerely at her friend.

"I like him, Phillip. I never thought I would 'like' anyone aside from my husband, but I do. He has so much knowledge up there, so confident and everything, but on the other side, he appears to be a wallflower that needs someone to guide him from his lonely corner. I don't know, Phillip, I just feel like I need to help him, that's all."

"That's all?!", said Phillip in an incredulous tone. "Well, my dear, let me tell you that you don't need to help him. That is not your concern. Be a friend to him, yes, but don't go in any deeper." He took her hands in his own and gazed at her intently. "I love you like a sister, and I don't want you to fuck up your wonderful marriage to a wonderful guy like Julian." Alex looked up at Phillip, who had a grave and serious expression on his face.

"What do I do?"

"You be a friend and nothing more." They both took another sip of their tea, not really knowing what to say in this moment. It was too much.

"So," said Alex in trying to lighten the now deep grey mood both had now fallen in, "I am glad I was able to spend some time with him; you know, make him feel welcome here."

"I can't believe I thought he was a possible serial killer."

"Yeah, I told him that."

Phillip popped a rubber band at her head. "Great, now he's gonna think I'm a freak."

"More so than usual?"

Dune showed up later that day, to the delight of Alex and the embarrassment of Phillip, who mumbled a 'hello' then quickly found something to do.

"I just wanted to tell you that I had a really good time last night," he said.

"Well, good. Me too."

"We need to do it again very soon."

"Yeah." Dune then walked over to the music area. He saw Phillip adding some new CDs to the area. Phillip looked up, saw Dune then smiled nervously.

"Don't worry, I didn't try to kill her," he said with a wink. "Only beer and conversation last night."

"I-I-I-"

"It's OK. I know you're only trying to protect her, as a good friend should."

"Well, I care for her deeply, like a sister. Wouldn't want anyone or anything to harm her," he said with a smile that did not quite reach his eyes as he shook Dune's hand.

"That means a lot to me, Phillip. And," he replied as he let go of his hand, "I would not want anyone or anything to harm Alex either. Her husband is one lucky bastard. I hope he realizes it." Phillip smiled, his tension now completely gone. This guy was OK after all.

"So, I know this might be a stretch, but tonight is Enslaved, Goth night at Club Frazen down the street, and Lex and I were going," said Phillip, trying to be conversational, "and being a possible Goth sympathizer, would you like to go?" Dune glanced over at Alex, who was busy helping some customers trying to decide which Wicca books to purchase, then turned back to him and grinned.

"Count me in."

Later that night, as Alex closed the store, Dune and Phillip stood outside, making small talk while she worked. Once Dune agreed to go out with them, he went home to dress in something more appropriate for the night: black pants, a tight short sleeved black shirt that accentuated his lean and slightly muscular frame, and his thick black boots. Ten minutes later, the three walked down the street to the club, where the music could be heard even from outside. Dune paid for all three and the trio walked into the club. Most of the patrons were customers of Alex's and soon many hellos could be heard as they walked through the main room. The entire place was painted blood red with pictures of people in various black and white BDSM photographs on the walls, giving the effect of an eerie dungeon. Lit candles were all over the place, creating flickering shadows along the blood coloured walls.

"Cool place," yelled Dune over the thump of the music.

"Yeah, well, it helps to relieve our stress," yelled Alex in response. People unashamedly dressed in black clothing of ages past and future stood around, drinking or talking with their fellow freaks, while clove scented smoke permeated the area. The bar led into the main dance floor, where several people were dancing to a song by the Industrial music group Front Line Assembly.

"Ooh, this is my favourite song!" yelled Alex as she handed her belongings to Phillip and joined the other dancers on the floor with lit cigarette in hand. Soon, she began to dance aggressively to the hard metallic beats while Dune watched her as he ordered a beer. Phillip tossed their belongings to the side and looked for his new girlfriend.

While Alex danced, she felt someone touch her shoulder. She turned to find Dune standing before her with a beer in his hand

and a somewhat lost expression on his face. She said nothing but lit a cigarette and continued dancing, not caring if he joined in or not. He quickly finished his beer and began to dance with her and the rest of the 'children of the night'. She was in her own world as she danced yet knew that Dune was dancing close to her. She took another drag from her cigarette as she danced, letting the smoke trail from her lips as her body moved with the music. Phillip stood by the bar, engrossed in a conversation with his girlfriend who had just showed up while still keeping an eye on the two out on the floor. Soon, the song changed to another hard hitting Industrial song by the group Skinny Puppy but the two did not stop to take a breath. Dune was lost within the music as his body made even the most devout Rivet Head ashamed.

After three songs in a row, Alex finally walked off the floor and met up with Phillip and his girlfriend at the bar, leaving Dune on the floor.

"Water," she croaked to the heavily tattooed woman behind the bar as she lit another cigarette. She looked out at the dance floor, saw Dune's still moving body and felt her face go warm.

"So," said Phillip, trying his best to keep her attentions steered away from making a possibly bad choice, "I want you to meet Lyria. Lyria, this is my boss and dear friend Alexandra." Alex extended her hand to the woman, who shook it heartily.

"I love your outfit," she said, still trying to catch her breath. The woman grinned and nodded her head; she was dressed in a sleeveless black patent leather dress that fell to the floor with a dramatic flourish. Her hair was coiled atop her head and dyed a bright and vibrant purple, complimenting her very pale skin decorated with deep purple eye shadow and lipstick, giving her the appearance of a beautiful corpse.

"Phillip has told me so much about you," yelled Lyria over the music. "He says that you and I are way too much alike! By the way, I like your store! I haven't been in there as much as I need to, but I need to change that! I'm glad you guys are around; it gives me a chance to dress like this more than just for Enslaved!" The two grinned to the compliment then Alex took a deep sip of her water and glanced back at the dance floor. The Shroud, a more traditional Goth music group, was now playing and Dune continued to dance, even when most of the other dancers had left to grab something to drink or take a break.

"Like a machine," she murmured, her eyes watching his every move. Phillip, realizing that her attentions were now locked again on Dune, placed his arm around her waist, pulling her close to him, and said in her ear, "Look but don't touch," then walked back to Lyria. Alex glanced at the happy couple while wishing that Julian was there with her. He was not into the Goth scene yet still found it cool enough to hang out with them every now and then. She finished off her water and walked back to the dance floor to join Dune. Once he saw her walking up to him, he grabbed her in an embrace without a word and soon the two were dancing again. He held her in his arms, his eyes locked on hers, as the two swayed to the dark music. She stared back, not really knowing what to do but just go with the flow, although it was becoming harder and harder to think rationally whenever he was around. He slid a hand down her back, just above her buttocks, and began to massage in a tender manner while pulling her even closer to him. His scent of fresh linen overpowered her but she did not care; at that moment, she wanted him desperately. She even felt his erection pressed against her in the one spot that drove her to no longer think but only act. She moved a hand down the front of his pants and began to caress him, not caring if anyone saw her do it or not. Dune's eyes widened for a brief second as her hand made contact then relaxed again as her hand began to slide up and down against him. She closed her eyes and let her body move on its own in pleasure. Phillip looked out at the floor, saw the two dancing rather close, then muttered to himself, "Into the fucking lion's den."

Alex wrapped her arms around his neck and pulled him closer to her; they were within inches of each other's lips. Dune, in testing the waters, slid the tip of his tongue out from his lips and lightly brushed her lips. She closed her eyes in wanting and pulled him closer to her.

He then brushed his lips against hers, wanting to taste them for the first time, but the song ended and everyone left the floor as a really crappy song came on. Alex shook her head as if she came out of a dream and pulled away from him while staring at him as if she had never met him before.

"Alexandra," was all he said as he tried to take her hand but she moved further away, shook her head once more to complete clearing it out and then walked back to Phillip and Lyria. He watched her go back to the bar, his hand still in midair, ready to take her into his arms again.

"Nice dancing," said Phillip with a smirk as she lit up a cigarette and puffed on it nervously. She ignored him and looked back out to the dance floor, then looked away again when she saw Dune now dancing aggressively to a hard song by the group Numb. His eyes were closed and shut tightly, as if trying to remove images from his mind. She did not dance for the remainder of the night.

When they finally left, it was 3 a.m. The four walked back to the bookstore to grab their cars and go their separate ways. All were sweaty, slightly tired and drunk but very happy. Alex hugged Lyria, both happy that they had made a new friend in each other, kissed Phillip on the cheek, hugged Dune lightly then drove off. Soon, Lyria left but not without giving Phillip a deep kiss on the lips. Dune politely turned his head so as to give the couple a modicum of privacy.

"I'll be waiting for you at your place," she said coyly then drove off, leaving Phillip very flustered and with a slight erection. Dune grinned for the happy couple then noticed Phillip's mood had changed once she left.

"Listen, Dune," said Phillip in a very deadpan voice as he lit a cigarette and leaned against his car in a nonchalant way, "I like you. Alex likes you as well, but I worry about her. She's falling for you and I don't want that to happen."

"And why not?" asked Dune casually, although he knew the answer.

"Because she's fucking married, that's why! Look, I love her like a sister, like I told you before, but she is off limits to you. Please, for your sake and hers, be a friend and nothing more." He took another drag from his cigarette then exhaled the smoke in a steady stream from his lips. "I saw how you guys were dancing out there tonight. Don't fucking tell me that did not happen. I don't know what you did to her, but please stop. Don't fuck her, touch her, or even try to hold her hand in a more than friend way." He threw his half smoked cigarette to the street then got in his car and drove off without waiting for him to answer. If he had stayed, thought Dune as he got in his car slowly, he would not understand.

The next day brought much business in the store and gossip within the Gothic sub-culture of the city.

"So, did you see who Alex was dancing with last night?"

"That guy that's always hanging out at her store?"

"Yeah. You DO realize that she's married, right?"

"I'm sure they're just friends, that's all."

"Yeah, well, that may be true, but I don't think so. Did you see HOW they were dancing last night?!"

"Don't you have anything better to do than gossip? So, what else happened??"

Alex heard the rumors, the gossip, and tried her best to ignore it. But, it was next to impossible to drown out since it was all around her. Almost every customer that walked into the store gave her a look that said enough. One person even asked her if she and Dune were willing to perform sex acts for a private party next month for $500. She quickly threw them out, much to their disappointment. Phillip tried his best to protect his friend, but even he had to step in and say something.

"Lexie," he said in a controlled tone once most of the gossiping customers had left, "you know I love you dearly-"

"Listen," she said, holding up a hand to silence him, "I know what I did last night and I did nothing wrong. All I did was dance with a friend, that's all."

"Yeah, but, everyone saw HOW you guys were dancing. At one point, it looked like he was trying to fuck you right then and there."

"No, it didn't."

"Alexandra," he said in a tone that he rarely used with her unless he was absolutely furious with her or anyone else, "I don't want this guy coming around here anymore, okay? What if this shit gets back to Julian, huh? Did you ever think about that? You know he would divorce you right then and there. He's crazy about you and I don't want you screwing up a good thing." She stared at him in silence; deep down, she knew he made sense. On the surface, however, she saw nothing wrong with last night. We were only dancing, she kept telling herself in her mind. Just dancing. Besides, where was Julian when she needed him? He spent more time at that damn gallery than at home with his beautiful and intelligent wife.

Just then, Dune walked into the store, causing the remainder of customers to stop whatever they were doing and watch with hungry eyes to see how this little scene was about to be played out. He wore jeans, Doc Martens and a long sleeved maroon shirt not tucked in with the sleeves rolled up, looking quite refreshed and relaxed.

"Hi, guys," he said in a nonchalant tone. "What's up?" Before she could say anything, Phillip walked up to him, faces within inches of each other, and said in a low voice, "As of today, I'm speaking for my boss and dear friend. I would really appreciate it if you did not come around here so much. In fact, why don't you just leave and not come back for good, hmm?" He glanced at Alex, who found a sudden interest in her clothing and focused all of her attention on it. "I know you understand, right?" Dune looked at her, wanting to make eye contact with her, then looked back at Phillip.

"I only came in here to say that I'm sorry." This perked Alex's attention and her gaze now sought his face. "I don't want to be the cause of any problems, so I wanted to say that I would not be coming around any more." He placed a hand on Phillip, who did not shrug it off, and continued, "You really care for her and I can appreciate that." He then walked over to Alex and, taking her hands in his own, said in a soft voice, "I hope your husband realizes just how lucky he is." Then, to the delight of the customers and the shock of Phillip, he raised her face to his own and kissed her tenderly on the lips for a brief second then walked away without saying a word and left the store. For a second, no one said anything, and soon all hell broke loose.

"Oh. My. God. Did you see that?!"

"So chivalrous."

"I'd give anything to be in her head right now." Alex looked down at her hands with no thought in her mind. She licked her lips, tasting his vanilla lip balm. Phillip looked around at everyone with a look that meant death then walked off without saying a word. Soon, the whispers died and the customers went back to whatever they were doing before. At that moment, Alex felt very, very alone. She wanted that kiss to go further.

The day wore on with no more mentions of what had happened earlier and even Phillip had gone back to a jovial mood, trying to break Alex of the funk she was now in. It felt good to be wanted, she thought as she mechanically stocked items throughout the place. Dune showed more of an interest in her than her husband lately and that was kind of pathetic. All she wanted right now was to do her job as bookstore owner and go home to a hot bath and a solitary meal. Her husband would be, no doubt, at the gallery. She did not even acknowledge her friend trying to cheer her up. Finally, Phillip gave up and pulled her to a corner of the store without a word. She immediately began opening several boxes of magazines that had arrived earlier in the day, trying to block him out of her vision and mind. All she could think of, however, was Dune's vanilla lip balm.

"Lexie," said Phillip in a concerned tone, "I had to do it. Julian is your husband and he does love you, although he's not shown it as much lately. I know how he can be. Once all of these major exhibits are completed, then you'll see just how much he cares. I know he's been trying to make some sort of an effort, right? I love you too much to see you like this. Just remember that I'll always be there for you, no matter what." He squeezed her arm tightly, causing her to look up at his goofy grin. "No matter what," he repeated then turned to walk off. She stopped in mid-motion of placing some magazines in a display stand, not really knowing what to say, but instead dropped her pile on the floor and embraced him tightly.

"Thank you for caring," she whispered then released him to continue working in a normal manner. She was back to herself, he thought.

This time, it was Phillip's turn to close down the store.

"You sure you're going to be OK?" asked Phillip. "I know that Julian has been working all night at the art gallery for a couple of days now." Although she had gone back to acting normally, he was still concerned for her.

"I can take care of myself." She kissed him on the cheek and walked out, getting in her car and driving home. Phillip finished up the closing procedures then locked up the doors. He drove in silence while his mind thought of his girlfriend and when they were going to see each other again. He pulled into his apartment complex driveway, got out of his car and locked it and then walked up to his front door. As Phillip put the key in his front door, he felt a light breeze against his neck just as he heard the sound of coins falling to the ground. He turned around.

Alex drove home. She hoped that Julian would be there, waiting for her. Her hope transformed into sullen anger as she drove up to her dark home. Once again, he was at work. She let herself into her home, sat on the couch in the dark and began to cry.

She was soon asleep on the couch, still dressed in her clothes. She dreamt.

Alex found herself at the dark river again. She looked around at the cavern that allowed no noise to filter in and disrupt this area and yet she could still see due to an eerie glow emanating from the river. She looked down and saw the seeds floating in the water. Remembering what happened last time, she refrained from touching the water and instead began to walk alongside it. The river chugged by her, creating quite an unnatural walking partner. The slightly rocky/sandy trail felt weird under her bare feet (she just realized she did not have any shoes on) while being slightly warm. She looked at her feet again and noticed that she did not have a shadow. Not knowing what to do, she laughed.

"Such a sound that sounds of tears rushing, rushing," said a melodious voice behind her. Alex screamed and turned around to face a young pale woman dressed in a long shapeless grey dress. The woman's eyes felt like hot pokers on Alex's skin as she stared at her without any intent while Alex stared back. After a moment of silence, Alex asked, "Where am I?"

"You are where the Sleeper sleeps," said the woman in the same tone as before. "The Sleeper sleeps carefully, down, down, down."

"Who is the Sleeper?"

"The Sleeper sleeps to escape, escape that which is forever gone." Alex shook her head while trying to make sense of the woman's answers then remembered that she was dreaming. Whatever was supposed to happen would happen in time, she thought.

"What are those things in the river? Seeds?" Alex asked, continuing the conversation.

"They remind the Sleeper of his place, his place among those that can not help themselves. They are the seeds to eat, crunch, tear, remember time flowing backward, onward, ever forever. Nothing. The Sleeper needs them, a reminder of what she did."

"She? Who's she?" Alex felt she was catching on to what she was saying but the same time did not. Now I know how Alice felt, she thought just as the woman reached behind her and grabbed something then pulled out her closed hand towards Alex. She shook the fist twice then opened it, revealing-

She awoke.

Alex looked around sleepily for her husband but he was gone. As the dream came back to her, she cursed under her breath.

"What did she have in her bloody hand?" she mumbled as she got up and looked through the entire home searching for Julian, then returned to the bedroom and realized that he had not even come home. His side of the bed was still made up. She sat on her side of the bed and held her head in her hands, wanting to cry but too angry to do so. What the hell, she thought as images of both

Julian and the strange woman flickered in and out of her mind. What the hell, indeed. Rather than put more energy into matters that she obviously had no control over, she got ready and mentally prepared herself for another day at the bookstore with Phillip. She knew not to hope that Dune would show up. When she drove up to the store, she noticed that Phillip was not there. Probably another great night with his girlfriend, she thought. She opened the store but he still hadn't arrived. After an hour had passed and he had yet to make his usual dramatic appearance, she picked up the phone to call him to see if there was anything wrong. She heard someone coming into the store. She dialed his number and let it ring, hoping that maybe he was out cold from a long night of lovemaking.

"Hello, Alexandra."

She quickly turned around and felt her heart flutter uncontrollably. It was Dune with a very large grin on his face. She hung up the phone, her eyes never leaving his. He wore khaki pants with his infamous black boots and a maroon coloured short sleeve polo shirt. His hair was, as usual, windblown and very flattering to his face.

"What are you doing here?" she asked then regretting it immediately. What else could she say to him? She tried to smile, then frown, then smile again, much to Dune's amusement. Time to save her from a drowning situation, he thought.

"I wanted to stop by and tell you again how sorry I am for causing such a potential mess in your life." He took a step closer as the scent of freshly turned earth filled her nose. "I feel terrible. And…I know that Phillip was doing what a good friend should; keeping you on the straight and narrow. I'll admit, I'm very attracted to you and for a while, wanted to pursue you no matter the cost. However, I needed to be reminded that I can only have you as a friend and nothing more. So," he said while extending his hand for her to shake, "can I have at least that?" She stared at his hand, not really knowing what to do for a brief moment.

"I…Dune, listen, I like you and I want to be friends with you. But-"

Suddenly, a police officer walked in with a stern look on his face. He saw Alex and walked up to her while quickly taking off his hat.

"Are you Alexandra Winthrop?" he asked.

"Yes," she said, not knowing what was going on. Dune stood behind her. "What's going on?"

"I'm afraid I have some bad news to tell you." She took an involuntary step back from him and bumped into Dune. "We found your friend Phillip dead this morning in front of his apartment door." Alex swayed a little then stared at the floor. This cannot be happening, she repeated in her mind over and over again. Dune immediately wrapped his arms around her, as if he could protect her from the words already spoken. She did not even realize he had touched her.

"How.... did he die, officer?" asked Dune with barely concealed grief.

"It looked as though he had a heart attack but we're taking him to the morgue for further research. I'm sorry. I have been telling everyone who was close to him the news today." He touched her arm lightly then walked out of the store and into the bright sunny day. Dune hugged her tighter, knowing that she would crack at any moment.

"Alex, I'm so sorry," he whispered in her ear. Alex nodded in a dazed way then twisted out of his arms. She took a couple of steps then fainted.

When she awoke, she found a very concerned Dune and several customers staring down at her.

"Good, she's come to," said one person.

"How do you feel?" asked Dune as he helped her up.

"Like crap." She then looked around at everyone and knew that he had told them the news.

"I had to tell them," he said, looking worried. Alex patted his arm then sat on her stool.

"If I can everyone's attention for a minute?" she said loudly to the customers as Dune turned off the music as everyone gathered around her. "Dune told me that he told everyone here. I know that many of you knew Phillip, and that he was a great and wonderful person." Her voice cracked yet she continued on. "So, we will be open all day today but tomorrow I will be closed. Also, all the money I make today will be given to Phillip's family for the funeral." She then slid off her stool and walked to her office, closing the door quietly. Dune wanted to console her but knew that for now, she needed to be alone.

Inside, Alex cried and cried until she began to dry heave and cough. Her closest friend was gone and there was nothing she could do about it. She wiped her eyes on her shirtsleeve then walked back outside to face everyone there in the bookstore. Dune stood by the cash register area, trying to help out as much as he could. When he saw her come back out, he rushed over to her but did not touch her. The look on her face was enough.

"Are you OK to finish out today?" he asked.

"Not really." Several customers walked up to her and asked if she was going to be OK. She tried to smile for them but it was obviously forced.

"Guys, I think I will shut down early today. I'm sorry." But there was no need to be sorry. Everyone knew and loved Phillip.

When the last customer left 30 minutes later, Dune closed and locked the door while Alex closed down the register.

"What will you do now?" he asked as he began to straighten up the store.

"Well, I think my husband will be out all night tonight. I don't want to tell him what happened to Phillip. The two of them were good friends. I'll probably go home, get drunk, smoke some cigarettes then go to bed while watching Sleepy Hollow. That was Phillip's favorite movie." She began to tear up again.

"No, I don't think you need to be by yourself." Alex stared at him for a moment then relaxed and even smiled.

"You're right. So, what do you suggest we do tonight, then?"

"We?"

"Of course. Listen," she said while laying a hand on his arm, "Right now, I need a friend. My husband is too busy with his work and I don't want to bother him-"

"This is not some bothersome thing, you know. This is a serious matter."

"I know that. But I want to tell him later, when we are face to face. But still, let's just go out for a drink, OK? I don't want to go home just yet." Dune gave her shoulder a light squeeze then the two left the bookstore for the day and walked down to the same bar they went to before.

"When I first met him, it was at an SCA event," said Alex as she sipped from her Cape Cod. "I thought he was such a puffed up jerk, but when I actually started talking to him, I found a great friend."

"He seemed like he really cared about you," Dune replied. "Not everyone is blessed to have good tight friends in their life."

"Every day he would come into the store, telling me his 'tales of woe', as he put it."

"Tales of woe?"

"His many failed relationships with women. He and I actually went out on a date, but we ended up becoming good friends. Then I met Julian and the rest was history."

"What's your husband like?"

She stared into her glass for a moment before replying. "Well...you remind me of him a little, except your hair is black with some grey. That, and the fact that he mainly wears business suits."

"In other words, I am nothing like him." Alex smiled as she took another sip. He finished his ale and sat in silence for a while. Alex, having nothing else to say, lit a cigarette.

"Those things'll kill you."

"I know," she said in a cloud of smoke. "But so will standing in front of a microwave for too long."

Dune chuckled. "OK, you got me there." She waggled her cigarette at him menacingly then grinned and called the waitress over to take another drink order as she finished off her Cape Cod. When she left, Alex said, "Thanks for being here with me tonight. Like I said, I really don't want to tell Julian about Phillip's death, but I have to. He'll want to hear it from me rather than hear it from someone else."

"True."

"But right now, I just want to sit here with you, drink and talk about Phillip." Their waitress arrived with her order then left again. Dune noticed with some concern that she now had straight vodka; although she was sad about losing her friend, getting plastered was not the way to do it. He placed a hand over her glass, trying to stop her from taking a sip.

"Dune, please," was all she said as she took the glass from him and took a deep sip. After the sip, she looked him straight in the eye and stammered, "Dune, I..." She looked away for a moment then back at him again. "I...shit, I can't do this."

"Do what?" he asked with genuine concern. "Do you want me to do something for you?" Alex's hands trembled as she tried to bring the glass to her lips but failed miserably, causing him to place his hand over hers and help her lower the glass. "Alexandra, what is it?"

"I can't tell you, Dune. Please," she said as she removed his hand from hers, "don't ask me again." He placed his hand back in his lap. Alex drained her glass, lit another cigarette since her last one had died a while ago in the ashtray, then said quickly, "I really, really, like you, and I wish I was not married because I would be with you and only you but I'm not but I wanted you to know this and I can't believe I'm telling you all this when I should be sad that my best friend is dead!" She ended her ramble with a loud sob, causing several people nearby to turn around and wonder what was going on that at particular table. She covered her eyes with her hands, trying to hold back her tears but felt them coursing down her cheeks regardless. She grabbed a napkin without looking at him and wiped her eyes furiously, trying to regain some form of composure but failed miserably since the vodka hit her system. Dune sat fully composed and slightly amused. Funny how people will admit the strangest things during the strangest time, he thought.

"I like you as well, Alexandra." The way he said her name made her shiver involuntarily as she looked up at him with red eyes. "Trouble is, what do we do about it? I know what I want. I'll be honest with you; I want, right now, to take you back to my place, make passionate love to you for hours, have you spend the night with me then wake up to my wonderful homemade cinnamon rolls and freshly squeezed orange juice, go to work, go home, clear out your belongings and move in with me. That's what I have wanted since I first met you." Alex took a long drag from her cigarette then blew a perfect ring into the air as if trying to hide her thoughts from the frank honesty he presented.

"But, we can't," said Alex as she took another drag. She did not like the way this conversation was going, not at all.

"Why do you say that?"

"Because, I happen to be married. I shouldn't have said what I said to you. Just chalk it up to me being drunk and sad because of Phillip's death."

"I don't think so. Don't blame what you just said on booze and sadness. You said what needed to be said to me and now you're trying to cover it up with shit. Don't dumb yourself down, Alexandra. I like the fact that you were honest with me right now, alcohol or no," said Dune as he now placed some money on the table, got up and helped Alex up from her chair.

"Why did you just pay like that?" she asked in a slightly slurred tone as he led her out of the restaurant and into the slightly warm night. He led her back to the bookstore, took the keys from her without a word, much to her tipsy protesting, opened the door and closed it behind them, led her to the door of her office then wrapped his arms around her and kissed her fully on the lips while pushing her against the door. He did not care for the taste of vodka but that was now a moot point. Alex tried to free her from his embrace but soon gave up and melted into his arms and lips. His mouth opened and his slender and long tongue pushed its way into her mouth, twisting itself with hers that was all too willing.

Several minutes passed before he finally pulled away from her. Alex heard his slightly ragged yet even breathing then looked out into the night of the area.

"So, now what," she whispered. Dune said nothing but lifted up her skirt with one of his hands while turning her head with the other to resume their kiss. His fingers found her wetness and slowly slid themselves in, causing her to gasp loudly and almost fall to her knees. He tightened his grip on the back of her head to keep her from falling down while his fingers still moved inside of her. Her lips found solace in his as she wrapped her arms around him, pulling him closer to her; this felt right to her, she thought. Her husband was far away in her mind. Dune kissed her forehead as his fingers increased in speed although he wanted to replace his fingers for something bigger. She deserved what he was willing to offer her. He knew that all along.

Her eyes were shut tight as she leaned against him, thinking of possibly furthering this moment. She knew how he felt for her; would one night be so terrible? Soon, he added another finger; moving it to another level was no longer a problem. She wanted desperately to feel his naked skin against hers, even if it was a quickie, but in a moment of sobering clarity she pushed him away from her and walked to the front door, hugging herself tightly while wishing she did not push him away. He looked down at his wet fingers then began to suck on them, closing his eyes in ecstasy. She tasted of salty overripe mangoes; not his favourite fruit but it still pleased him. Once he cleaned his fingers he walked up to her and tried to hold and kiss her again but she pushed him away, her mind full of shame for what had just occurred and how much she wanted more of it.

"This is not right, Dune. You know I can't do this and yet I want to." He looked at her for several minutes without saying a word. Suddenly, she reached forward and touched his lips with her fingers, remembering that her lips were just there. His lips felt smooth and damp from sucking on his fingers.

"This feels so real," she whispered as she continued to touch his lips. "I just don't know." Then, without warning, she grabbed the back of his head and pulled him towards her. When their lips met again, she felt lightheaded and yet more confident in what she was doing. She wanted more of what he had. Dune embraced her, glad that she made this choice. Right and wrong were, for the moment, thrown out of the window. All she had left was what felt good to her and that was her kissing him.

Suddenly, she felt something push against her from Dune's chest. She pulled away from him in shock.

"What was that?" she asked.

Dune smoothed out his shirt and smiled. "Nothing. You probably felt my shirt bunch up against you, that's all." Alex, now completely sober, turned away from him and said, "I need to go. Now. Come on, give me the keys." Without a word, he handed the keys to her and she let them out into the warm night. She did not say a word to him as she got in her car and drove off. While Dune watched her drive off, he smoothed down his shirt another time, ignoring the slight discomfort in his chest.

She drove home later that night fully sober and numb while her mind still replayed the evening's events in her head. She soon forced them to the back of her mind and re-focused on Phillip. A part of her still did not think that Phillip was dead, but she knew it to be the truth. Phillip was dead. Possible heart attack. She pulled into her dark home and went inside without looking around, not caring that yet again, Julian was still at work. Once she got in, she locked all the doors, checked every room and closet in the house and then took a long and extremely hot bath. She let herself drift off for a moment, allowing the warm water to sedate her. Her body still tingled with memories of Dune fingering her and how much he enjoyed tasting her natural wetness. She closed her eyes, savouring the moment, then released it from her mind and focused on Phillip's death. After some time had passed and her skin began to wrinkle, she got out of the tub, toweled herself dry then went downstairs for a bite to eat. There was still some food left from the other night, so she heated it all up and took it upstairs to the bedroom. She plopped herself on the bed and began to eat, not really caring how it tasted.

When she finished, she decided to call Julian about Phillip. Within the first ring, he picked up, yawning into the phone.

"Hello?"

"Hey babe."

"Lexie! I'm glad you called me. I miss you, baby."

"I miss you too. Listen, I have to tell you something."

"OK, shoot."

"Phillip...Phillip's dead." There was silence on the line for quite some time, then:

"O my god. Lexie."

"Yeah, yeah."

"How did he-"

"Possible heart attack. He was just about to go inside his apartment last night when it happened."

"Damn it. Oh Lexie. I'm coming home. Fuck the gallery." He hung up before she could tell him good-bye and that she would see him soon.

10 minutes later, she heard him fumbling with his keys as he walked in. She calmly walked downstairs and saw that he sat on the floor silently crying. Alex walked over to him, sat down and held him tight, while the thoughts of Dune permeated her mind.

The next several days went by like a blur. Julian finally finished his last major exhibit for the quarter and it took off with success. Alex still operated her bookstore, but the fun brought in by Phillip was gone. Dune still came by occasionally to check in on her. After that night, he acted nice but completely platonic around her, as if to let her know that things would be okay between them. She silently agreed to his new attitude around her, but deep down wanted him even more. Sometimes, while running around and trying to manage the store by herself, she caught him looking at her from the corner of her eye. She pretended that she never saw him do it yet was completely torn.

The funeral was short, with only his family and friends at the local cemetery. Once the official Death Certificate came in and ruled his death as a heart attack, there was nothing else to do but prepare for the funeral. It was Phillip's wish to be buried at the small and quaint cemetery in town; he and Alex used to go on Goth picnics at the place with several of their friends. The caretakers knew all of them and always welcomed them, even if they thought the small group of black clad people was a little strange. Even Lyria showed up for the funeral, dressed in one of her finer black dresses and her purple hair braided into one long braid draped down her back. Julian and Alex were of course there, along with Dune by himself. He stood by her side the entire time but never touched her. Once it was over, Alex introduced the husband to the friend, which was slightly strained but good.

"I did not know Phillip as long as you and Alex did," said Dune in a somber tone, "but I did like him."

"Just you being here means a lot," said Julian, trying to keep his voice even. After Alex told him that Phillip died, he shut himself in their bedroom for several hours while she sat on the other side of the door, listening to him sob. Julian and Alex left in his car once the ceremony was over, while Dune drove off in his own car. It rained on that day, but the temperature was warm. Almost too warm.

One day much later, a day when Alex finally felt like her old self again, Dune dropped in. She still enjoyed it whenever he came by, as did some of the customers. He was not goofy fun like Phillip, but he still held a spark of excitement.

"Hello, Alex," he said while waving a bag in front of her.

"Geez, what's with you men? You seriously want women to get fat, don't you?"

"Oh lighten up. I only brought regular croissants with some homemade pomegranate jam." He set the bag in front of her. "Come on, one little piece, for me?" Alex grabbed a warm croissant out of the bag along with the jam, smeared a piece of it with the jam and bit deeply.

"Oh man," she said through chewing, "how in the world do you make this stuff? It's incredible. I've never had pomegranate jam before; it's tart and sweet at the same time."

"Just an old family recipe but I'm glad you like it," he said, eyes sparkling.

Alex brushed the crumbs from her black silk shirt and said, "Listen, I have a question for you."

"What?"

"Well, I really like it that you come here to visit-"

"Oh, you want me to stop dropping by?"

"No, nothing like that. Would you like to work here? Not to replace Phillip, but just to be here? The regulars like it when you show up, as do I, and even though I know you don't need the money-"

"I'll do it." Alex beamed a smile as she hugged him. She could feel his very firm chest against the shirt along with his muscular arms. She backed away quickly, her mind already replaying their first kiss so long ago.

"Well," she said, trying hard not to sound nervous, "here's how you open the register."

She showed him how to work inventory, ordering new supplies and which donuts and pastries she liked better. When the day ended, both were happier than they had been in quite some time.

"Well, it's been a long day, but I'm glad to be helping you," said Dune as he walked her to her car.

"Well, I'm glad to have you there with me too." They stared at each other for a minute too long then Dune mumbled a see ya later then jogged back to his car and took off. Alex drove home a while later.

When she arrived home, she saw that Julian was home. She walked into the living room and was attacked with hugs and kisses.

"Damn you!" she yelled while laughing. "I need to pee." Julian continued tickling her until the two began rolling around on the floor. He then stopped and kissed the top of her nose.

"Love you," was all he said.

Dune became more and more of a well-liked figure around the bookstore. Women asked if he was single, to which he always replied that he was not interested. Gay men would ask him if he was interested, to which he always replied no. He had his eyes set on one person, the one person he had for only a brief moment. Alex began to think more and more about Dune. She loved it when he laughed, or when he looked at her. His accent made every word he said like a flower, especially her name. Sometimes, when he touched her or brushed against her in a tight spot, she tried to shut out her thoughts of him and his lips.

Everyone liked him. He was just a nice guy that no one could ever date.

Julian, after riding the waves of the French exhibit, started staying late again at the gallery because of a Greek exhibit he recently acquired. Alex, knowing that this was his work, deep down did not like it at all. She got tired of going to an empty home every night then waking up with her husband deeply asleep next to her. Was this what marriage was all about: never seeing the one you love due to work and progress?

"Dune," she said one night as they wrapped up a relatively good day at the bookstore, "got any plans tonight?"

"None at all. You know me. Why? Want to go out for a drink like we used to?"

"I was just going to ask you that." Within minutes, they locked up the place and walked down to their bar. Only ten people were in the whole place, which was fine to them. Once they ordered their drinks, Alex said, "OK, I have to ask. Every woman who sees you wants to go out with you and you refuse. Why?"

"Well, you know I am not gay," he said with a chuckle, "and in terms of women, there is only one woman I want."

Alex almost choked on her drink. "After all of this time, you still are trying to pursue me?" she asked, deep down hoping that he was. "I thought that after our kiss you would have given up on me."

"I still want you. What we did in the store was wonderful, something I had wanted to do for a long time with you. I know you have a husband, but that is how I feel. You can rest assured that I will not make any more advances. But, you are one of the most intelligent women I have ever known. Plus, you're very attractive. Allow me to have my fantasies of you." Alex finished off the rest of her drink in one gulp and asked for another.

"Dune, don't do this to me," she mumbled while looking around, trying to avoid his eyes. It was no use; she faced him once again and felt herself being drawn back into those eyes that sparkled and flashed only for her. Deep down, she loved this. It was nice to have someone pay attention to you. It was nice when someone loved being around you, and it was sad when that person was not your spouse. He placed a hand on top of hers while staring into her eyes. Alex quickly removed her hands as the waitress came up with her drink. She finished off half of it then began rummaging through her black messenger bag.

"What are you doing?" asked Dune.

"I'm giving you my part of the bill so I can go home."

"Why?"

She stopped in mid motion and said, "I don't want to repeat what we did before." Dune knew he had her hooked.

"Would it be so wrong for you to be with me, for one night at least? One night with me would not be such a crack in your marriage." She began weighing the pros and cons of the matter then shook her head in denial.

"No matter what, I am loyal to one person only and that person is my husband. Now, if you don't mind, I'll be leaving." She found some money at the bottom of her purse and placed it on the table. As she stood to go, she said, " I still like you Dune, but right now, I have to go home." She walked out of the bar quickly, leaving him to nurse his drink for a long, long time.

Alex smoked like a chimneystack as she drove along. She decided to drive to her husband's art gallery rather than go home. It would be good to be with the one thing she almost threw away for one night of great sex. When she pulled up to the front door, she saw that only one light was on. She got out of her car and let herself in.

"Babe? Are you in there?" she yelled. No answer. She walked through the gallery and into the back office, where she screamed bloody murder.

There was her husband, lying on the floor, pants around his ankles and his spent cock hanging outside of his boxers. A dribble of sperm hung off his cock. He was handcuffed to a half naked young Asian woman who lay next to him with a slit throat. Blood covered them both. In Julian's free hand he held a bloody knife. Alex bent down to feel any sign of breath from her husband. The woman was obviously dead but Julian wasn't. She then noticed some empty clear pill bottles and a crack pipe lying next to Julian. She stood back up, now in blind fury, and began to kick her husband in the butt with her steel-toed boot.

"Wake the fuck up!" she yelled over and over until he at last woke up. He looked around for a moment then saw the dead woman and began to scream.

"What the fuck?!" he said as he lifted his hand to see the handcuffs. He then saw Alex standing over him and began to cry. "Lexie! What in the hell is this?"

"I don't know," said Alex in a cold voice. "Why don't you tell me?" She then picked up the crack pipe for him to see. His eyes went wide with horror.

"Babe, I don't know where that came from! I swear, I don't!" But, Alex was beyond listening to anything from him.

"You bastard! Every night, you worked here late then came home! And now I find out what you've really been doing: fucking whores and getting back into drugs!"

"Babe, I haven't touched the stuff in years! You know that! You know I went clean for you!" Alex's eyes filled with tears as she listened to these lies.

"All of this time..." she said then walked out of the room to call the police. She could hear him screaming over and over "Lexie! Lexie! LEXIE!!!!"

The police came by and picked her husband up to take him to jail. The woman was identified as a known crack addict and prostitute. Her husband's fingerprints were all over the woman and on the crack pipe. His semen was in the dead woman's body as well. They even found some of the drug in him when he took a drug test. It was likely that he would get life for the murder, said the police, but Alex could not hear them. All she could hear were ocean waves in her ears.

The trial went by smoothly; Alex testified against him with a stone cold face. Julian's pleading eyes could not pierce the thick veil that now surrounded his ex wife. While on the witness stand, he claimed he had no knowledge of what had happened; all he remembered was working late at the gallery, then he blacked out and woke up with Alex screaming in his ear. Although he seemed sincere, the jury did not buy it. They sentence him to life in prison with no possible parole. Alex watched the bailiffs lead him away once the sentence was pronounced, no longer caring what happened to him. As far as she was concerned, he was dead.

The initial week of prison life was terrible for Julian. As soon as he arrived, the other inmates taunted and teased him, whistling out at him and calling him *fresh meat*. He wanted to kill himself but knew he could not. He could not go through with it no matter how hard he wanted to. He was a coward deep down and wondered just what in the hell happened to him. The days passed by like dead leaves falling from a tree and soon, he, too felt the coldness enter his heart. Although he still loved Alex, it still felt foreign to him to feel such an emotion. One night, countless days after his trial, he sat on his bed, staring at the ceiling while his cellmate snored on. Sleep was impossible for him, no matter how hard he tried.

Suddenly, he heard the sound of coins falling to the ground. He rolled over on his side, thinking it was his cellmate, then stopped. Everything went black.

The gallery soon closed; no one wanted to buy from a former crack addict who had gone back to the pipe and killed a prostitute. Alex did not worry about money, however; she sold her home and moved into an apartment in the midtown area. Her lifestyle was still the same with more time to herself. Her bookstore was all she had left. Dune helped her through it all: the selling of the home, the divorce proceedings, the criminal trial of her husband and conviction. Alex looked more and more to Dune for her happiness, of which he was too glad to give. But she was never the same again. However, when she received the news that her husband died of a heart attack, she actually cried. Dune held her as she cradled the dead phone against her chest like a sick child.

One night, as the two closed up the store, Dune said, "Hey, let's go for some Mexican. What do you think?"

"I dunno. I just want to go home and go to bed."

"It's been two months since you last went out. All you do is work now. Come on, just a margarita and some dinner since you never eat, and some conversation." Since her situation with her husband and his death, she had lost over 20 pounds and barely ate anything.

"Actually, dinner does sound good. Let's go."

"Great! How about you drive home with me following you and then we can take my car." She nodded in agreement and soon they were off to her apartment.

"Come on in," she said as they got out of their cars. "I don't have anyone over, but I love showing off my place." Dune followed her upstairs to her place. The building had been built in 1930 and it still retained some of its charm. When they walked in, he whistled in surprise.

"Alex! This place is gorgeous!" The first room was the living room with hardwood floors, followed by the massive kitchen on the right and one of the two bedrooms on the left. Further down the hallway was the other bedroom with the bathroom. At the very end was the den with the great view of a park. The entire place had the feel of a dark and gothic fantasy painting; the main colors were black, violet, white, and silver. Fairies hung from the ceiling while posters and pictures of different gothic and fantasy scenes graced her walls. As Dune walked around, she said with pride, "The decorating is my stuff from my home before." He soon found her leaning by the great window in the back. He wanted to touch her so badly, to feel her skin touch his. He took a deep breath to steady himself then walked up to her. He wrapped his arms around her waist and held her to him, feeling her body give off little shakes. It wasn't until he heard her sobbing that he'd realized she was crying.

"Why are you crying?" he whispered.

"I guess I'm just tired of hiding, that's all." She leaned back into him and watched the street below. People were out, enjoying the Spring night air, fresh and fragrant. It was warm and safe enough for people to walk about on the streets, throwing caution to the wind.

"I'm tired of being alone," he murmured, breaking her focused attention on the street. "It is not a good feeling to dwell in, so I understand what you are going through. When I was married, I thought my life was better off since I had the object of my desire. Turned out, she was cold and hated me. I tried to make it better for her but she refused to work it out. All she wanted was to go home and be with her mother. After years of trying, I finally gave in and released her from the marriage. My brothers hated what I had done but I was beyond caring. I felt I could no longer care about anything again until I met you, Alexandra." He then turned her around so that she faced him. She tried to hide her face but Dune touched her chin gently. He wiped her wet face with his hands then kissed each cheek. She wanted to push away from him, this situation, everything. Ever since Phillip died and Julian went to prison and later died, she lived a hollow existence. The bookstore, her passion and love, failed to make her as happy as before. Dune, however, had been in her life as a good friend, one that stood by her when the worst possible situations came to face her. All he wanted in return was her in one way or another. At first, she could not give more to him, but now . . .was it possible?

He held her face in his hands and kissed her lips. Alex fell towards him and welcomed that kiss. His lips felt warm and it felt good to have those lips connected to hers once again.

When he pulled back several minutes later, he said, "Why do you hide yourself away from everyone? Do you think so little of yourself? You have no reason to feel this way. I am truly sorry for what Julian did to you but remember that you are a strong woman. In the time that I have known you, I have been constantly amazed, enlightened, and attracted to you and. . ." He turned away from her for one brief moment, not sure if he wanted to continue speaking his thoughts to her. Right now, she was vulnerable and the last thing he wanted to do was destroy what they had for the sake of speaking his mind. She stared at him, not knowing what he was about to tell her, but deep inside, she had a slight guess. He took her in his arms and pulled her close to him, saying nothing even though the words were on his tongue, ready to be said and handled in the most appropriate manner.

"Dune, what were you going to say to me?" He did not respond but held her tighter, allowing the silence to be his answer.

Once she cleaned herself up, they left for Kokopelli's Dance, one of the Mexican restaurants nearby. They found a booth by a window and placed their orders. Once their waiter left, Alex lit up a cigarette.

"I thought you had quit smoking?" he asked jokingly.

"I did, but since we're out tonight, I felt like having one." She exhaled a cloud of smoke. Their drinks soon arrived followed by chips and dip. Then, for no reason at all, Alex put out her cigarette then threw away the whole pack. "You know," she said while dipping a chip in some salsa, "I hate cigarette smoke." Dune laughed as he took a sip of his drink.

"I left my home after my marriage ended," said Dune as he ate his spinach and mushroom burrito. "I wanted to see the world, as it were. I felt that I spent so much time on my marriage that I refused to actually enjoy my life. All of that changed when my marriage was over. Now, I am like everyone else and I am glad for it. All I want to do is live again."

"You sound like the typical only child who suddenly got bored with their current life, wanting to trade it in for a newer model," said Alex. "People accused me of that all the time. I was just headstrong, that's all. I refused to be labeled by others. I wanted my own life defined by me alone. My parents and I still have slight arguments as to how I run my life, but in the end they realize that since I have not died of any horrible disease or run off with someone that I must be doing something right."

"But of course," he said while dipping a chip in salsa.

"So, how old are you?" she asked, changing the subject.

"Old enough to know better," said Dune with a wink.

"Come on. I'm 35. Seriously, you look to be about 38, 42 at the oldest."

"Thank you my dear. I'll take that as a compliment."

"Really, how old are you?"

Dune sighed playfully and said, "I am in my 40s and that is all I am going to say." He grinned like a little boy then took another bite of his food.

She sipped her water glass then said, "Why?"

"Why what?"

"Why are you such a nice guy?"

"I don't know, really. I had always thought that nice guys finished last. I was never the popular sort. People always seemed to fear me or something along those lines. I could never imagine why."

"Well, nice guys and girls do finish last. I should know." Dune touched her hand.

"You are a bright, intelligent and attractive woman. You, in all of the time I have known you, have never finished last." She smiled a genuine smile in response, the first in a long time.

"That means the world to me." For a moment, neither one said anything but just held each other's hand. Alex looked down at their hands and said in a quiet voice, "We seem to be having this problem of not keeping our hands off each other, huh?"

"I don't have a problem with it if you don't." She then removed her hand from his then took a long sip of her margarita. "Dune," she said as she set the near empty glass down, "I like you. I'm not going to deny that. But, please, give me time. I know you've been unnaturally patient with me-"

"Which is why I'll wait forever," said Dune then made a grimace. "God, I sound like one of those trashy romance novel beefcake hunks."

"Well, I wasn't going to say anything about that," she joked as she finished off her drink.

When they finished with their dinner they ordered another pitcher of margaritas and continued with their conversation.

"So, how many people have you dated?" he asked as he swirled his straw in his drink.

"Actually, not too many. I dated one woman-" she cut her eyes at Dune, trying to see how he responded to it. His eyebrows raised up slightly and a small smile crept on his face. "Does that bother you?"

"Actually, no. No one can resist you, you know. You're too damn beautiful. So, how long did you two date?"

"For a year until she left the country for two years abroad in Italy." Alex's glance fell towards the table as her voice turned to a little more than a whisper. "She died. Boating accident. Her roommate wrote to me, letting me know of the accident. I cried for a week. She and I loved to do everything together."

"Was she into the Gothic as well?"

"Not so much. She was more into faeries, although we both shared a love for science fiction and fantasy novels. As soon as I finished reading a book I would hand it to her and she would begin reading it or vice versa. We would stay up late at night reading to each other, watching movies, playing role playing games with Phillip, or just hanging out at any coffee bar." Alex fell quiet for a moment, although Dune could tell she had many thoughts on her mind. Suddenly, she continued. "I loved her. I would have married her if I had the chance. After she died, I refused to look at anyone else until Phillip introduced me to Julian at a book signing party. We hit it off completely and soon afterwards we were married." She took a long sip from her glass to wet her throat while trying not to cry in talking about Julian or Phillip.

"How did your parents feel about you being with another woman?"

"Well, they hated it for the longest time, thinking I was going to hell. I remember one long night in which we stayed up talking about the whole situation. My parents had invited Susan and I over to talk to us about our relationship and for them to better understand as to why we were together. So, we talked and they listened, pausing every now and then to ask questions. Finally, at seven o'clock in the morning, my parents hugged both of us and from then on, I was no longer a freak, well, a freak in the sexual sense. They loved Susan just as much as I loved her and when they found out that she had died, they were crushed. I remember my mother actually saying that she would have wanted her to be their daughter-in-law." She crinkled her nose for a moment, causing Dune to laugh and tickle her nose. "She had these great green eyes that seemed to sparkle every time we looked at each other."

"How did you two meet?"

"Well, I was at a coffeehouse, reading Virginia Woolf or something like that. She walked in wearing, get this, purple butterfly wings and a long purple dress. Her hair fell all around her face and shoulders. I looked up, she looked at me and the rest was history." She finished off her glass and began to pour another. "So, what about you?"

"Well, you already know about my one marriage. I was never a dabbler in the fields of womanly delight." He took her hand again and stared deeply into her eyes, wanting her to feel exactly what he was feeling at that very moment. "Alexandra, I love you." Suddenly, her world began to twist and spin, making her feel lightheaded and drunk. She looked at him and realized that he was blushing furiously. She then looked down at their hands touching each other.

"I-"

"Don't say anything. Let what I have said soak in. I want you, Alexandra, and only you. No one has ever made me feel so alive like you. Your presence makes me smile every time and I truly do appreciate it. I know you have gone through some horrible moments in your life but I promise you that those times are over. I love you and I will never let you go." He then pulled his hand away from hers and said, "Now, with that being said, I will wait for you, my dearest. I will not rush you into loving me, but I can safely say that you feel a modicum of what I feel for you, right?" Alex turned away from his truthful eyes and nodded, her hair covering her eyes that now held tears.

"Wait for me, please," was all she said. Dune took a long sip from his glass; that was all he needed. Besides, he had his own ways of speeding up the process if need be.

Once the tension died down, they were soon their former selves but with the added touch of being slightly drunk. Dune wanted to hold her hand and sit next to her so that he could hold kiss her neck tenderly. He wanted to let the world know that he was in love but at the same time, did not want to scare her away after getting this far. He pulled back and stepped into the role of good friend once again.

Two dinners, two pitchers of margaritas, several baskets and bowls of chip and dip and much conversation later, Dune and Alex reached their limit.

"I'm tired and a bit tipsy," she said while yawning. "I need to go to bed. But, I still want to talk to you." Actually, she was stone cold sober and trembling inside from what he had told her but she did not want to let him know it. She loved him just as much as he loved her but she held herself back. She knew it was right and yet she was afraid of losing him just like Julian. But that was a different situation ages ago. She also wanted to be near him.

"Well, I can drop you off at your place, or you can come by my place to finish up our conversation, just two friends hanging out. You can trust me that I will not lay a hand on you. I'm really not in the mood to be alone." Alex thought about this for a while.

"Well, I don't know-"

"Ok, well then, how about you spend the night with me? You can stay in one of the guest rooms. I promise, I'll be good. Besides, I'll be drinking a lot more when I get home so that I'll be completely passed out after we talk."

Alex laughed as he pulled a goofy face. "Are you sure? Do you mind?"

"I don't mind. I'll fix us a great breakfast tomorrow and we can lounge around since the bookstore is closed for the next two days."

Alex grinned. " Isn't it great to create our own holidays? OK, sure. Hey, do you mind if I stop by my place to pick up a change of clothing and some toiletries?"

"Don't worry about that. I have some pajamas that will fit you plus toiletries. I also have a shirt that you'll like and will go well with your skirt. Deal?"

"Deal."

He paid the tab and they left. He drove down several streets then arrived at his home nestled deep among several oak trees.

"This is where you live?" she asked. "These houses are lovely!"

"They are nice, but it's a bitch to keep warm or cold. My utility bill is a nightmare." He turned down one of the side streets and into his driveway. Alex could only stare in amazement at the mansion that loomed before them. It held an old charm with luxurious purple rose bushes all around the home. The mansion was a two story that seemed to extend a block. Most of the home was constructed with deep red brick while the rest was deep blue painted wood.

"You live in this place all by yourself?" she asked.

"Unfortunately, yes. Just me and my many books." As they walked up the winding driveway to the front door, he added, "The house was built in 1890, stayed in the same family all that time until the recent son went bankrupt. I bought it for a steal." He pulled out his keys, opened the door and let her walk in. The sight from the outside was wonderful. The sight on the inside could never be described in words. A winding staircase made of solid oak stood in the middle of the room. Every room, as far as she could tell, had hardwood floors with the occasional colourful Oriental rug lying around. The dining room lay on the right while a parlor and billiard room lay on the left. Straight in the back was the kitchen. A crystal chandelier hung in the very center of the ceiling.

"The bedrooms, all five of them, are upstairs," said Dune while she looked around like a child in a candy store.

"This is absolutely beautiful," she whispered. "I feel like I have stepped back in time." He led her upstairs to the main hallway.

"My bedroom is at the end, while you are more than welcome to pick out any room you wish. However, I will warn you, I am kind of an insomniac, so if you hear someone walking around and reading aloud while drinking don't worry, it's just me." Alex walked up and down the carpeted hallway, looking at every room. She finally chose the room that was closest to the bathroom dressed in violet and white.

"I like this one," she said. "Simple and yet really nice."

"Then it is yours for the night, my dear. Now, how about we get a drink and finish talking?" She took off her shoes and laid them in her room then followed him back downstairs to the den. The den looked like something from Masterpiece Theater, complete with the great deep red leather chair, wall to wall books and plush carpet. Alex sat on the floor and crossed her legs while Dune walked over to the bar to get their follow up drinks.

"What can I get for you?"

"Actually, I would love a glass of water, please." He got up and walked into the kitchen to get her water, giving her time to look around the den, wondering just how many books he owned.

"Don't drink it until I get mine," he said as he walked back to the bar and prepared a whiskey on the rocks. He then sat down in the chair next to her, held up his glass and said in a sage voice, "To the forgotten gods and goddesses of old." Alex held her glass up high then took a big sip.

She wiped her mouth with the back of her hand and said, "Some toast, huh?"

"Well, I have always had a feel for archaic knowledge. The gods and goddesses of old have been forgotten due to modern times and modern ways, but I shall never forget them."

"I used to be the kid who loved reading mythology books just for the sake of doing it; sometimes, I used to wonder if they were ever real or not." He glanced at her for a quick second then raised his glass for another sip.

When he lowered his glass, he said, "What makes you think they were or are real?"

"I have always held to the belief that the legends and myths of the world held some sort of truth to them; that somehow, humankind walked with gods and monsters without a care. Now, all we are concerned with are our iPods, wearing the hottest clothing and getting super abs."

Dune listened to her with great interest; what were the odds he would find someone like her in this day and age? It was too good to be true and yet he felt like he needed to take that plunge. He looked at her as she drank her water then reached in his pocket for his tiny package. Pulling it out, he placed it on his lap and unwrapped it.

Alex saw the package and asked, "Okay, I have got to ask; what are those things?" Dune took one in his fingers and held it up for her to see.

"You don't know? They're dried pomegranate seeds." Now, she was intrigued.

"Ah, trying to seduce ol' Persephone, huh?" At once, Dune glanced at her with a strange look, causing her to feel uncomfortable.

"Now, why would you say something like that?" he asked in a mild tone that did not sit right with her.

"I just remembered my myths; you know, the story of Hades stealing Persephone away to make her his queen of the Underworld," she said nervously. His eyes bore into her like she was on trial. She coughed then went on. "When she arrived there, she refused to eat anything except for several pomegranate seeds. That is why we have seasons; thanks to her eating the seeds, she had to stay in the Underworld with Hades for several months, giving us fall and winter. When she returns to her mother, Demeter, we have spring and summer." Alex let her voice die out as he continued to stare at her in an eerie way. What did she do wrong?

Dune took one of the seeds and popped it in his mouth and began to chew. He closed his eyes and sighed. "Such a tiny seed and yet there is so much behind it, wouldn't you agree?" Alex only nodded, not really sure where this was going. "One feels the tartness of the fruit, yet there is a delicate sweetness that is almost to fragile to understand or comprehend." He popped several more in his mouth and chewed on them thoughtfully.

"May I have one, Dune?" Dune opened his eyes to find her searching ones staring back at him. Without a word, he pushed his pile towards her while his eyes watched her every move. Alex took one, hesitated and then took three more in her hand. She sniffed them, only catching a whiff of something very old and earthy. She glanced at Dune then popped them all in her mouth. Instantly, the tart and sweetness of them exploded in her mouth, causing her body to tremble in a pleasurable way. She had eaten pomegranate seeds before but never like this. Although they were dried, they still held the juices from the fruit and were still quite good. She swallowed them then reached for more but Dune grabbed her hand.

"Are you sure you want more?" he asked in a slightly mocking tone. Alex shook his hand off and grabbed several more and popped them in her mouth. She felt a thin line of drool sliding down her mouth but she did not care. She had to have more.

"I never knew they could be like this," she said as she reached for more. Dune watched her with heightened interest now; he did not expect this at all and yet it was pleasing to see. She took two more then popped them in her mouth and sighed as she chewed and wiped the drool from her mouth. When she pulled her hand away, it was stained red. She looked up at Dune, who still watched her carefully, then licked her hand clean.

"Listen, I'm really tired so good night." Alex yawned and stretched then got up and walked out of the den, leaving Dune still on the floor. When she reached the bedroom, she found a simple pair of pajamas lying on the bed. She picked them up, took one look at them, and then decided to sleep in her underwear.

He stared at the seeds then wrapped them back up in the napkin and placed them in his pocket. He finished off his drink then got up as well and walked into the kitchen to the refrigerator. He opened it, revealing nothing but pomegranates, and took one. He cradled the fruit as he walked back to the den then sat down on the floor while placing the fruit in front of him. With quick precision, he stabbed the fruit with his fingers and opened it to reveal the juicy seeds inside. He grabbed a handful and shoved them in his mouth, savouring the fresh taste while the juice dribbled down his chin. Without wiping his face, he got up and walked up the main stairs to his bedroom and walked in. He removed all of his clothing then sat on the floor in a lotus position and waited.

Alex could not sleep. She tossed and turned in the large bed but refused to open her eyes. Something was trying to keep her awake but all she wanted was to just sleep.

Dune sat on the floor, eyes closed, waiting.

Alex now began to thrash about, trying hard to overcome whatever it was but failing miserably.

Dune remained on the floor. His red stained chin felt sticky but he refused to clean up.

Alex woke up.

"Fuck this," she mumbled as she grabbed a robe from the closet and let herself out to the hallway. The lights were still on in the house but she could not hear anything. She then turned towards Dune's room and saw light underneath the door. She walked to his door and knocked on it once. There was no answer so she tried the door. It opened, revealing Dune completely naked and sitting on the floor. His red stained chin stood out against his pale skin. Without a word, she walked up to him and sat down across from him then touched his chin with trembling fingers. Instantly, he snapped his eyes open and grabbed her hand with unnatural speed then pulled her up as he got up as well. When the two were standing up, he embraced her and licked her face with his pomegranate stained tongue. Alex tried to turn her face away from him but it was impossible; she felt his tongue everywhere and could nothing to do about it. Dune licked her lips, softer this time, then kissed her fully on the lips. Alex could taste pomegranates while remnants of the seeds flew into her mouth without choking her. She wiggled in his embrace but he held on fast with no possible way of getting out of it.

"Dune," she said after pushing her face away from him, "Please let me go! You're scaring me." Dune's chin was a bright red and Alex couldn't help but stare at it as he stared at her with dead eyes.

"You've tasted the seeds," he said in a calm voice, "and yet you fear it now. Why?" He then released her from his embrace and walked to his bed and lay down, leaving Alex standing alone. She crossed her arms over her chest, causing Dune to chuckle.

"What the hell is wrong with you?" she asked with a horse voice then coughed. Some of the seeds were stuck in her throat. She coughed and fell to the floor while Dune just watched with eager eyes.

"Just swallow them, Alexandra," he said in a bored tone. "You've done it before. Swallow." Alex closed her eyes, trying hard not to puke, and swallowed. Instantly, the seeds went down without any complaints, leaving her slightly worn out and more than a little angry. She stood up on shaky legs and crossed her arms over her chest again. The robe was halfway on her body but she didn't care.

"You bastard!" she yelled. "You just sat there as I was choking; how could you?"

"I knew you wouldn't have died from the seeds," he said in a lazy tone. "I know you better than that, Alexandra." He rested his back against the headboard and crossed his legs as he smirked at her. This, thought Alex, was too much for her.

"Fuck you, you son of a bitch." She turned around and walked out of the room but Dune suddenly grabbed her arm and held her steady.

"Are you so afraid of what you're feeling right now, my dear Alexandra?" said Dune with a chuckle. He held her tightly against him and began to stroke her hair.

"Dune, let me go."

"No." Alex closed her eyes, wishing she was somewhere else, then opened them and gasped. There, in the hallway, stood the young woman from her dreams as clear as day. She still wore the grey dress while her skin was a dusty grey. She raised an arm towards her in silence while her face was passive and serene.

"Is she going, going down to the water?" said the woman in that same voice from the dream.

"I did not call you here," said Dune in an angry tone. "I did not call you here!"

"Not yet, yet, swirling faster down the river so dark and pale." Alex only stared at her while her mind screamed *she's not there! She is NOT there!*

"Who is she?" she asked Dune in a fearful voice.

"Someone that should not be here right now. I will give you what you need later," he said to the young woman. The woman lowered her arm and smiled sadly.

"This can not be, be further down the path. Do you have them?" Dune walked Alex over to the bed and set her down. Alex did not struggle; there had to be an explanation and she was going to wait for it. Dune then walked to the young woman and said something in a strange language to her. She nodded then walked down the stairs, leaving Dune in the hallway. He turned back to Alex and walked back into the bedroom then closed the door behind him.

"You ask questions," he said as he walked closer to her, "and you have tasted the seeds. How do you feel now?"

Alex placed a hand on her stomach. "I feel….okay. What was that woman doing here? She was in my dream a long time ago. Who is she?"

"She is of no concern to you right now, Alexandra." Dune laid next to her and began to stroke her hair. "I am sorry I was rough to you earlier; forgive me. Just seeing that woman made me feel…. uncomfortable. She wasn't supposed to be here right now."

"B-but I saw her in my dreams," stammered Alex. "I was by this glowing river and she stood by the cliff next to me, talking about really weird stuff."

"River?"

"Yeah…..but…this is weird, Dune. I want to go home. Does she live here?" Dune sighed; clearly, she was not going to let this go. He pulled her towards him and kissed her on the lips, now tender this time. His chin was still sticky from the seeds and, for the first time, noticed it. He got up and walked into his bathroom on the right side of the bedroom and closed the door, leaving Alex with more questions then answers. He still has yet to answer my question about that woman, she thought as she pulled her robe closer. He was so cruel to me earlier; how much of him do I really know? She smoothed out her hair and slid up the bed then crossed her legs. She wanted to leave but was unsure. At this point, she was unsure of a lot of things. She looked around at her surroundings; Dune's bedroom was simply draped in colours of cream, brown and red while a framed Chinese character hung over the bed. The plantation shutters were closed, cutting off the room from the rest of the world.

Dune came out of the room, still naked but no longer sticky with pomegranate juices. He got into bed with Alex and resumed stroking her hair. Alex noted that he now smelled like fresh linen.

"Sorry to have kept you waiting," he said as she stroked her hair, "Are you still angry with me?"

"You've managed to deflect answering most of my questions, Dune, so what do you think?" Dune chuckled as he stroked her hair. Alex glanced down and for the first time tonight, noticed his lean and slightly muscular body. In the past she wondered what he looked like naked and now that he was, she suddenly no longer cared. However, his hands felt wonderful through her hair. He continued to stroke her hair in silence, then moved the hand to her cheek.

"How can you do this?" she asked in a surprisingly clear voice.

"Do what?" The hand moved to her neck but still retained its tenderness.

"Be so tender to me, yet you showed a cruel side earlier. You let me choke on those damn seeds."

"You're stronger than that, Alex. I knew you wouldn't have choked. And, that was not cruel to watch you choke." The hand slid down to her chest.

"I don't know what to think anymore."

"Trust me, Alexandra. That is all you need to do right now. Don't ask questions but know this: I will not harm you, no matter what. As for my cruel side, well, even a rose has thorns."

"You're not making any sense." The hand now brushed lightly against her nipples. Alex sighed and arched her back. Dune pulled the robe away from her body, exposing her body to him while her eyes remained focused on him. He kissed her on the lips while his hand resumed caressing her body. Her arms reached up for him then pulled him closer to her, her dream of her skin touching his now coming true. His skin felt like alabaster, cold and impersonal, and yet she did not care. She no longer cared if he even spoke in riddles or was cruel to her. All she wanted at that point was him.

He slid her down on the bed so that they were lying next to each other while their hands explored each other. Alex closed her eyes and gave in to his hands and kisses, forgetting the woman and her fears surrounding her presence.

*****

Three hours later, the two laid amid sweat and sex stained sheets, their arms and legs wrapped around each other. Alex was asleep while Dune remained awake. He watched her slow breathing and wanted to touch her cheek but did not want to wake her up. He slowly pulled his right arm out from under her and propped up his head so he could get a better look at her. Her eyelashes were damp with sweat and they sparkled as she slept. To him, she was beautiful in this natural yet vulnerable position and he was glad to be a witness to it. He wanted to protect and love her while at the same time push her limits as far as possible, seeing what she would tolerate, then gently push them over the cliff without a second care. As far as he was concerned, she now belonged to him. She was his in every way possible and there was no going back from that. It was more than dating, more than cooing lovey dovey words to each other. She was now a part of him and he was grateful that it was her and not some idiot who was too dense to comprehend anything around them. No, he thought as he exhaled, she would understand and actually appreciate what he would give her during their time together. She would appreciate the pain and the love that would come soon after. It was his nature, after all.

Alex stirred around then blinked sleepily, wondering for a moment where she was then smiled as the images came to her. She blinked twice with now open eyes and looked up to find Dune staring at her. She smiled and yawned while cracking her jaw in the process. Dune chuckled and touched her cheek.

"What time is it?," she asked as she looked around.

"About 2:30 a.m. You've been asleep for an hour." He moved over to her and kissed her face. "Would you like anything to drink?"

"No thank you, I just want to get some rest."

He wrapped his arms around her and whispered, "Sleep, my dear. I'll wake you up later." She snuggled against his chest.

"Dune?" she murmured.

"Mmmm?"

"I love you." She fell back asleep while Dune remained awake with new thoughts. He smiled as he laid his head next to hers. Now there were no questions.

Morning brought in the sunshine and the beginning of a warm day. Each day, the temperatures rose steadily. No one even remembered that only a few months ago, winter held Memphis in its thrall. Alex felt the sun from the windows on her face and opened her eyes sleepily. She looked around and saw that she was alone in Dune's bedroom. The room smelled of last night and yet it was a comforting scent. She had no regrets as to what happened between them, only that she wasted so much time in getting to that point. A friend once told her that it took her three hours just to ask if they had any gum. She rolled off the bed and searched for her robe on the floor. Once she found it, she put it on and walked down the hall to the main stairs.

As she skipped down the stairs like a schoolgirl, a smile played on her lips as more thoughts of last night crept into her memory. She heard Vivaldi's Four Seasons playing from downstairs while the delicious smell of cinnamon wafted up to her. She reached the kitchen and found Dune in his robe in the kitchen whistling with the music while making coffee and fresh orange juice. She saw a plate of freshly baked cinnamon rolls on the table in the dining room with two settings for them. She had to smile; this was simple and yet very, very thoughtful.

"Good morning, luv," he said cheerfully as he walked out with a pitcher of orange juice in his hand. "And how are we feeling today?"

"Actually, pretty good," replied Alex as she sat down at the table. "These smell great! I take it these are your infamous homemade rolls?"

"For you, yes. I hope you don't mind a little Vivaldi," he said as he sat down across from her and poured juice for them.

"Of course not. He's my favorite classical composer."

"I had a feeling he was. Then enjoy it to your heart's content." He bit into a roll and smiled at the good taste. Alex took a roll and bit into it and smiled.

"Wow, you're a good cook!" She finished it off then had another. "Do you mind if I grab some coffee?"

"No, let me." He got up and poured a cup for her in the kitchen then brought to her with cream and sugar. She took a small sip and replied, "Even your coffee tastes great!"

Once they finished eating, Dune cleaned up the kitchen, shooing Alex out and telling her to relax upstairs in their room. Once she left the room, Dune walked into the den and found the young woman sitting in his chair while reading a book. He closed the door and strode over to her. The woman did not acknowledge his presence for several seconds as she calmly turned the pages, much to Dune's frustration. Fifteen seconds later, she closed the book and placed it on her lap then turned all of her attention to him. He crossed his arms over his chest and sighed.

"Why are you still here?" he asked in a weary tone. "I thought you would be gone by now."

"The Sleeper thinks, thinks of something, while I am not found."

"If you want them," he said, "then they are in the kitchen in the blue jar. I don't like carrying them around for so long inside of me. Not my style."

"But the grey is not for those who seek it, says the Sleeper."

"Please, do not come back until I tell you to. How long have you been here, by the way?"

"As long as the strings fold, folding downward into nothing." Dune sighed; sometimes, it was really hard to understand her. Sometimes he thought she talked like that on purpose just to confuse him, although she knew better than to do something as asinine as that. Dune turned around and let himself out of the room, but not before saying, "Charon, sometimes you really frustrate me." Charon said nothing but smiled then went back to reading. At least she understood that.

Alex sat on the bed and undid her robe. She lay down on the cool sheets, allowing her body to sink into the bed. For the first time in a long time, she felt completely relaxed. She got up and opened the shutters then lay back down on her stomach on the bed and watched a tree move sluggishly in the Spring breezes. For a moment, she envied that tree and its ability to move like that. She wanted her body to move without restraints then dismissed the idea. Sometimes, she spent too much time thinking about things rather than just doing them. It led her to more regrets than moments of joy. However, last night was not a regret, she thought as she slid under the down comforter. The scent of sweat came to her, causing her to bite down on the comforter while she shut her eyes tightly like a child about to blow out birthday candles.

"Is this a private party or can anyone join?" said Dune while he leaned against the doorframe. Alex opened her eyes and released the comforter from her mouth.

"Anyone can join," she said while laughing, "but I must warn you; it's a club full of freaky yet intelligent women." Dune grinned and entered the room while closing the door behind him. Minutes later, the sounds of their lovemaking echoed through the house, even while Vivaldi played downstairs.

Charon stood in the kitchen, holding the blue jar. She looked up at the ceiling and listened to the sounds then shrugged her shoulders.

Alex spent the day and next with Dune. He offered a sense of stability that, honestly, she had never felt before with Julian. Although Julian loved her, she felt a modicum of wariness, especially when he used to stay late at the gallery. But, all of that was over now, she thought one day while helping a customer. She was sorry that Julian was dead but not enough to waste her life in grieving for him. She had a life to live. And then, of course, there was Dune. She glanced over at him ringing up a customer while wearing his usual grin that just made everything better. How odd that, several months ago, I thought my life was pretty darn good, she thought. Now, I am no longer sure of anything, except that I love Dune. She shivered a little then began to laugh, causing her customer to stare at her in a strange way.

"Sorry, sorry," she said while waving her hands in apology, "I just thought of something really funny." The customer grinned then went back to trying to decide which CD he wanted, leaving her to continue with her thoughts about Dune.

The two spent more and more time together, of which Dune spent most of his time steadily coaxing Alex out of her hard and protective shell and back into the real world. He knew that she trusted him completely and he loved her for it. In a way, she was dependent on him and he liked that feeling as well. She needed a partner who would not run away from her at the first sign of problems, nor anyone who would treat her with little dignity and respect. She deserved more than a modicum of such things and he planned to give them to her and more. That was the least he could do. He did not, however, force her to move in with him, even though it would have been the right thing to do financially on her end. Although she did not have to worry about her finances, he still felt it was his responsibility to assist in any way possible.

Alex found herself wanting to be more out in the open, the effects of being shut in wearing on her already frayed nerves; thank goodness she had Dune, she thought while reading a book in her apartment one Sunday morning. Ever since Dune helped out more and more on many levels, she felt she needed some solitary time to enjoy the quiet comforts of her home. While it was true that her store was anything but work, she still looked forward to these moments. Dune, after claiming that her taking time off was a good idea, took over more and more of the duties, thereby freeing up her hectic world. Her couch sat against the living room wall with the windows, so the warm and not harsh sunlight felt good on her skin. She stretched and yawned then turned a page of her latest acquisition, a turn of the century French novel of pure literary decadence. One of the windows was open, giving her the sounds of city life without being too much, along with the sounds of the various birds in the area. She glanced over at her mug, realized it still had some of her Silver Needle white tea in it, then reached over and took a large sip of the lukewarm yet fragrant liquid. She sighed then leaned back into the couch and continued reading just as the phone rang.

Scowling a bit, she leaned over and picked it up from her coffee table.

"Hello?"

"Alex, it's me." The scowl disappeared and replaced with a large grin. She never tired of talking to Dune. "Sorry to bother you, but would you like to come over for dinner tonight? I figured you might want to do that since today is our one year anniversary-"

"Damn, I completely forgot," she replied as Dune laughed.

"No worries; I figured you did anyway. So, dinner tonight at my place? Say, around 7?"

"Sounds lovely, Dune. Do I need to bring anything?"

"Nope, I've got everything at my place. You can spend the night, if you'd like."

"Of course I would. Thanks. How's the store doing today?"

"Well, all of the magazine titles are stocked with new titles ready to be purchased. Customers have been steady, as usual. Hey, remember that girl that Phillip dated? The one with the purple hair?" Alex felt a lump in her throat but she swallowed it down. That was then and this is now, she thought.

"Yeah, I remember her."

"Yeah. She came by the store today. Hadn't seen her in forever. By the way, she cut off most of her hair; now, she looks like a pixie; her hair is short and spiky but still purple."

"Ah."

Dune coughed, not really knowing what to say. "Well, she said hello and hope that you're doing well. She's dating someone new."

"Really? What did he look like?"

"Nothing like Phillip, in case if you were wondering." Alex felt that same lump in her throat and this time did not swallow it down. She raised her hand to her face and felt tears sliding down her cheeks. Dune coughed again and mumbled a good-bye, knowing that she wanted to be alone at that moment. Alex hung up the phone and now allowed the tears to come. It had been some time and yet his death still bothered her. She placed her book on the coffee table then wiped her face with her shirt. Since his death, this was the first time she had ever thought and shed tears for him. It still bothered her that he died of a heart attack; it seemed so ridiculous and yet it was entirely possible. Although he was a smoker and a social drinker, he ate well with the occasional fast food binge. Maybe he was a perfect candidate for a heart attack, she thought. She quit smoking a while back with only sheer willpower and Trident Strawberry flavoured gum; the thought of coughing up lungs covered in tar was not high on her list of things to do in her life. It was good, also, that Dune was there as moral support but she did not need it for that terrible addiction.

Soon, the tears dried and her face tightened up somewhat, so she walked to the bathroom and washed her face with a warm and wet towel. After washing her face, she stared at herself in the mirror and was amazed at what she saw. It was like looking at a stranger and yet she smiled at the reflection. Gone were the puffy eyes and slightly chubby face. This face that stared at her was leaner, more defined, and more beautiful than before. She touched her face then touched the mirror. She looked and felt.....real. She looked down at her body and noticed that, even though she wore her usual baggy black yoga pants and an oversized shirt, she looked and felt better than ever before. She looked at her reflection in the mirror again and traced her face with her finger on the mirror then pulled back and walked into the living room. She did feel better, even after crying about Phillip. She stood by one of the windows and watched the city in full motion; people with places to go and things to do, while automobiles of every colour and shape zoomed or crawled by her apartment high rise. So many people on the go and yet how many of them were actually doing anything with their lives? How many of them were going through the motions of being productive when in reality were only spinning their wheels? She glanced across the street to the park and watched a couple walk along with their child in a stroller. Are they happy, she wondered? Did they get everything they wanted in Life, or did they just settle because they stopped believing in their dreams? She looked at them again and thought she could see them smiling at each other. Were they truly happy, or was it all for show?

Just then, the phone rang again, jarring her out of her morbidly intense thoughts. She grabbed the phone, checked the number and then smiled when she saw it was her bookstore.

"Hello?"

"Hey, sorry to bother you again, but I was wondering: would you like chicken or lamb tonight?"

"Huh, honestly, I would love chicken. Can't really do lamb, ya know. They're too cute."

"Well, so are baby chicks, my dear."

"Droll. Very droll."

"In fact, aren't baby chicks used as chicken nuggets?"

Alex laughed. "Okay, okay! I'm fine with chicken, goof."

"Chicken it is then, woman who loves goof. Bye." Alex hung up the phone and resumed her silent watch of the world outside for an hour with a smile stuck on her face.

Dune raced through the kitchen, making sure that everything would be ready for Alex once she arrived. He closed down the store an hour early, letting the customers know of their anniversary. Several of the customers clapped loudly while others gave him big smiles. Dune thanked them all profusely then raced home. Within minutes, scents of paprika, curry, and other spices mingled with chicken and steaming asparagus were all throughout the house. He wanted tonight to be perfect for them and for her.

Thirty minutes later, Alex arrived just as Dune placed a huge clay bowl filled with chicken stewing in a thick reddish sauce on the table next to the rest of the dinner's dishes. He grinned then grabbed and pulled her close to him. He kissed her on both cheeks then a long and lingering kiss on her lips while she wrapped her arms around him and deepened the kiss. When they pulled away, Dune said, "Happy anniversary my dear. Love you." Alex smiled and said that she loved him too then he proceeded to pull out her chair so she could sit down then placed her cloth napkin in her lap and pushed her closer to the table.

"I am your humble servant," he said as he whisked her plate off and began piling it high with a sample of all foods on the table, then placed it back in front of her. She picked up her fork and dug into the succulent chicken first. The meat practically fell off the leg bone as she skewed it with her fork then brought it to her lips. Dune sat across from her with his own plate while watching her take her first bite. When the chicken entered her mouth, it took Alex all of her willpower to not moan from absolute ecstasy of the flavours that now played with her tongue. The chicken melted like butter in her mouth while the various spices made themselves known to each of her taste buds. Each flavour nestled with the meat of the chicken, adding their own layer of enjoyment to her mouth. Alex closed her eyes and sighed with a very large grin on her face.

"I take it you like it?" said Dune as he speared a stalk of asparagus and devoured it whole. Alex only nodded her head then opened her eyes and resumed her exploration of his cooking. Each dish brought a different sensation to not only her mouth but her body as well. While the chicken brought about the sensation of sitting in something thick, spicy and warm, the asparagus filled her senses with thoughts of verdant gardens sprinkled with rain and sunshine while a hint of garlic teased and tickled her tongue every so often. The carrots with melted butter and brown sugar felt warm and toasty all the way down her throat and into her stomach, and the rolls felt like little yeasty pillows smothered in butter. Dune watched her every expression, knowing with pride that she did approve of his meal. He ate his food, enjoying the flavours and sensations as well, but nowhere near hers. Tonight, he wanted her to have it all.

When Alex sopped up the spicy juice from her plate with her second roll after her second helping of everything, she leaned back in her chair and patted her stomach.

"Now I've got a puppy stomach," she said in a slightly sleepy tone.

"Then I take it I've done well with dinner tonight?"

"Like you need to ask?" Dune got up and took their now empty plates into the kitchen and began to clear away the food from the table, leaving Alex to relax and digest the food in her stomach. Several minutes later after he cleaned off the table, Dune reappeared with dessert: two small but full bowls of homemade pomegranate ice cream. He set one in front of Alex, whose eyes were now wide with anticipation of enjoying this new temptation and then sat down with his own bowl.

"It's a family recipe," he said as he dug in with his spoon. Alex took a small spoonful of the ice cream and put it in her mouth. Instantly, her body welcomed the new sensation as she smiled widely.

"I've never had this before or even heard of such a thing, but I am so glad you made this tonight," she said as she took a larger spoonful of the creamy dessert and placed it in her mouth. Dune grinned and continued eating. After the third spoonful, Alex licked her spoon clean, placed it by her now empty bowl and said, "So, why are you really into pomegranates?" Dune halted with his spoon in mid stride up to his mouth; he placed the spoon in the bowl and smirked at her.

"Why bring this up now?" he asked.

"Well…..it's just that I've noticed you really do enjoy your pomegranates. Seeds, ice cream, jam, everything. So, are you vitamin deficient or something?" Dune closed his eyes and nodded no. "Are you mentally unstable and pomegranates are the only thing in the world that keep you mentally sound?" Dune smiled but shook his head no. "Are you-"

He held up his hand. "My dear, why is it so important to you? We're celebrating our one-year anniversary and, honestly, I don't want to talk about that. I want to talk about the lingerie I bought you that is upstairs in the bedroom, ready for you to wear it and for me to take it off you."

"I take it is pomegranate coloured?" she smirked. Dune only stared back at her, now with no smile or smirk. In fact, she thought, he looked quite annoyed with her. She gulped. "Sorry about the bad joke," she stammered, trying to get the evening back to a good night. "I was just trying to be funny."

"Oh yes. You certainly were funny." He got up and began clearing the table of their dessert bowls then remained in the kitchen for several minutes. Alex winced as he banged dishes and pots around. She felt bad that she asked him about it, but what was the big deal? So he liked pomegranates, so what? Everyone had a favourite fruit. She loved blueberries and strawberries and if someone were to make a joke about it, the last thing she would do would be to get angry with them. She almost got up to apologize to him but then remained seated. He was the one with the problem, not her. If he was pissed off, then let him do the apologizing. She would sit right here.

Dune returned to the table and sat down across from her with a blank look on his face. Alex stared right back; this was a fight she was going to win, no matter what. Instantly, she began thinking of how to even dump him and this relationship. If he is going to get pissy with me over some damn fruit, she thought as she stared at him in silence, then he can do it as a single man. I don't have time for this-

Suddenly, with lightening speed, Dune reached over the table and grabbed her arms, catching Alex completely off guard. She looked down with wide eyes and saw his hands tightly gripping her arms.....while he remained seated with a calm expression on his face. The veins in his arms bulged out and she could see hints of muscle in his abnormally strong arms. Now she was terrified.

"Dune," she croaked, "how......did you do that?" Dune said nothing but slowly got up, while his hands still pinned her arms, and began to grow taller. Alex watched in horrid fascination as her lover grew in size while glowering at her.

"You had to keep asking me," he said in a voice completely devoid of emotion. "You couldn't just leave well enough alone." He tightened his grip again, causing her to wince. She struggled against his grip but remained seated in her chair. She closed her eyes and took a deep breath then stared up at Dune. He looked to be at least seven feet in height and leaner than before. His eyes blazed with a cold blue fire that danced around in black sockets. She wanted to throw up. Gone was her lover, the man she trusted and admired; now before her stood a....thing. A freak of nature. She felt very small and very, very vulnerable. "Why couldn't you just leave it alone?"

"I....don't understand, Dune," said Alex in trying to regain some foothold in this odd conversation and turn of events while trying not to scream bloody murder. "What....the hell? What are you? Why are you so angry with me?" Dune closed his eyes for a moment then released her arms and walked over to her. She trembled as she felt freezing cold air emanating from his body. He held out his hand for her to take.

"You have given me no other choice, Alexandra. Take my hand."

"What are you going to do to me?"

"I am not going to hurt you. I promise." She looked at his slender and pale hand and sighed with frustration, fear, and slight anger. She looked back up at his now calm and eerie face and wondered just who or what he was. She reached out with her own hand, her fingers barely touching his palm, then retreated and sat on her hands.

"Dune," she said with a little more confidence than before, "what are you?" Dune said nothing but kept his hand out, patiently waiting for her to take it. "I don't understand."

"Take my hand and you will understand all of it." Alex slid a hand from under her and took his cold hand. Instantly, the room blurred and faded to black.

"Alex. Open your eyes. Don't be afraid. I've got your hand." Alex opened her eyes and found herself standing by a dark and sluggish river. She looked up and noticed that she was in a cavern of some sort then remembered that she still held Dune's hand. She turned to face him and screamed. There, holding her hand, was a seven foot tall humanoid dressed in a swirling grey robe that fell to the ground like dusty and very old cobwebs. On closer inspection, the robe turned out to be ghost-like creatures swirling around the humanoid's body, creating the effect of a robe, highlighting the mottled grey tone of its skin that looked to be wrapped around bones and nothing else. She then dared to look up at its face; it barely looked like Dune as its extremely long and narrow face stared down at her. The eyes, two dancing dark blue flames in black sockets, made Alex tremble. It wore a tall crown made of bones on its bald head and its ghastly smile revealed rows and rows of sharp and crooked teeth. She looked back down at her hand in its just as sense returned to her, giving her freedom to move. She yanked her hand away from the being and took several steps away from it in horror. She wanted to scream, cry or fall to the floor in a fit of complete insanity but instead stood and stared. The eerily beautiful figure turned towards her and, with arms open, walked towards her.

"You wanted to know more," it said in a deep booming voice, making Alex's eyes water and place her hands over her ears. "You kept asking me about that damned fruit. Now, I must show you." Alex closed her eyes as the tears finally slid down her face as she simultaneously willed them to stop.

"This can't be happening," she mumbled over and over as the figure now stood within inches of her. It gently took her hands from her ears and lifted up her chin.

"Alexandra," it said in a softer and lower voice, "look at me. What do you see?"

"She refuses to See, that which the Sleeper knows of," said a calm voice behind them. Alex turned to find the strange young woman dressed in a long grey dress standing behind her. Alex looked at her with now wild and pleading eyes then turned back to the figure then back at the young woman. Someone, she thought, needed to explain. Someone needed to help her.

"Charon," said the figure, "She asked about the fruit. I had to show her." The young woman only nodded then walked over to the glowing river, where a long rowboat suddenly appeared. She got in the boat, nodded at the two again and then turned away just as the boat began to move. As it did, a long stick shot up from the water and Charon grabbed it then used it to steer herself down the river. Alex watched all of this and suddenly, she knew. She knew everything.

She looked up at the dark figure, no longer afraid, and said in a voice that echoed all throughout, "You are Hades, God of the Underworld." Hades only stared back with a stoic face as the flames danced even more in their sockets. She smiled sadly and then everything went black just as Hades touched her shoulder.

"I'm sorry that I harassed you about the fruit," said Alex as she sat on the floor across from him in the library. She cracked her knuckles then winced as one of them hurt more than necessary, causing Hades to chuckle. She sucked on her knuckle then looked up at him, his now normal face, in wonder and slight horror. "I know that people love their fruit, but I thought you went way too far with it, so I had to know. Didn't think I would be facing a god from myths and legends of Ancient Greece." Hades chuckled again.

"Would you rather I revert back to my true self so you will feel more comfortable?"

"No thank you," she said while shaking her head. "If you don't mind, I'd like to talk to the human side of you."

Hades looked down at his human hands. "But….I am human, sort of. I, as with all of the gods, do have a human side. That is what makes us so understanding to the humans who continue to worship us." Alex closed her eyes tightly as a moment of madness tried to creep up from her stomach to her throat. She wanted to scream at him that she always knew the gods existed and that she wanted to worship him right then and there while laying rose petals at his feet. She had always had a curious streak in her ever since she was a child. She was the kid who read books rather than play video games or hang out at the mall. The more books she read, the more questions she asked. Her parents, although loving, never really knew what to do with her and her incessant questions so they gave her more and more books. Her questions disturbed them at times and they wondered if perhaps their priest at church needed to talk to her. Alex dreamed of gods and goddesses, creatures from beyond human imagination and worlds penned from the most brilliant of minds, hoping that perhaps her questions would be answered. She opened her eyes and forced herself to look into Hades' normal green eyes and smiled. Her questions were now answered.

"So, if you're here, then….where's Persephone?" He glanced away from her for a moment, but just long enough for her to catch it. "Wait," she said, "is she here on Earth with you?"

Hades shook his head no. "That is a long and complicated tale, Alexandra. Perhaps some other time." She jumped up and grabbed his arms with speed, causing him to widen his eyes at her in shock.

"No, damn it, you tell me now! So far, my whole world has just been turned upside down because of you, Dune...Hades, shit, what do I call you now?"

"Call me what ever you want," he replied softly. "It no longer matters." Alex released his grip but continued to stare at him until he gave in. She had a right to know it all, damn it; she loved him, even with the new knowledge. She resumed her spot on the floor with an expectant look in her eyes. Hades ran a hand along his face then began in a weary tone.

"Yes, it is true. I did kidnap Persephone and yes, I did commit rape once. The books were right on that point. However, they don't tell you why I did what I did. That is my own tale to tell. It happened a long time ago, of course, when I was summoned by my brother Zeus-"

"Hold it," said Alex while waving her hands frantically. "You said Zeus. Zeus, like in god with the lightening bolts? Leda and the Swan Zeus? Mount Olympus Zeus?" Hades nodded his head yes. "Whoa, I think I'm going to be sick." Alex held her stomach and tried hard not to throw up. Hades reached over to her and touched her face. Instantly, the sickness passed. She motioned with her hands for him to continue while still in amazement that Zeus was truly his brother.

"Zeus summoned me to Olympus in order to solve a problem of his. It seemed that he, during one of his dalliances with a mortal woman, got her pregnant. While that was not a problem, for he had many half-human, half-god children running about, this child would be born deformed and he could not have that. So, he sent for me to take both mother and child to my realm. In other words, have them both killed. I did as Zeus commanded, of course. When I was about to leave, I caught sight of the most beautiful creature there so I had to get a closer look. It was Persephone, daughter of the goddess Demeter. She was visiting her mother for a time in Olympus since she spent more of her time on Earth. When I first saw her, I knew I had to have her. She was something I had never had."

"What was that?" asked Alex.

"Tell me this: have you ever smelled a rose?"

"Of course, many times in fact. Why?"

"What was it like for you to smell a rose for the first time, after hearing so much about the flower?"

"Incredible," she sighed.

"Then you know how I felt when I first saw her. In my realm, I see only the consequences of humanity: suicides completed, premature deaths, natural deaths, everything. I have never seen humanity, or Life for that matter, on the other side when it is vibrant and beautiful. She was something I had never experienced in my realm and I felt, at that time, that I needed that. So, after I completed my deed with barely a lift of my finger, I snatched her away and carried her on my chariot to my realm. The rest of the gods were alarmed, of course, including Demeter, but I knew what I wanted. As we rode the chariot down to the Underworld, I remembered thinking that her skin felt so soft against my own dead and papery skin and it smelled of apple blossoms and sunshine. I could not wait to get her to my bed. She screamed and pleaded me to have mercy on her but I refused to listen. She beat her tiny hands against my chest and still I refused to listen. I wanted her in a carnal and primal way and I was not going to be denied.

"When we reached my home, I threw her into my room and did everything I could to her. Her cries later turned to muffled sobs then nothing at all. Her flesh yielded to my every desire, my every wish and yet I still wanted more from her. Since she was a minor deity, she could keep up with me and not crumble into dust. When I finished with her, I gently kissed her on the forehead and let her rest, for I would do it again soon."

"How could you be so cruel and yet so tender at the same time?" asked Alex with a note of disgust in her voice. "How could you?"

"I just did and have done with you as well. Whatever I do, I do without any doubt in my mind. No emotion shall run me; I control my emotions. I am a god, after all." Alex shook her head in disagreement with him. "Even though I wanted to feel that soft flesh against my own again, I did not. I raped her once. After leaving her to rest, I spent some time thinking about her while being the God of the Underworld. She was beautiful, yes, but there was something I wanted from her. I wanted her Life to have a sense of change in my own. I wanted her to love me. When I retrieved her later, she was stoic and refused to converse with me. She was so beautiful in my eyes that at times, while she sat near me, I would reach out and touch her golden hair or run a finger down her bare arm. She did nothing but stood there and look beautiful. She refused to speak to me, even when she ate the six pomegranate seeds at my table. I wanted her to be my queen not my slave, and yet she refused to do so. The story of her leaving for the months she did not eat the seeds is true; however, while she was gone, I realized that I no longer wanted her around me. I wanted a form of Life in my realm but she was too godly for such a request. She refused me by just being a deity and I soon realized my mistake in taking her. So, when she returned to my realm, I welcomed her as stoically as possible, then changed her into a statue while I myself left and traveled to Earth to think." Hades leaned back into his chair and closed his eyes. Now come the questions, he thought while waiting for her barrage. Alex sat riveted to the floor, stunned by what she had just heard.

"So....is she still down there as a statue?" she asked, to which he nodded yes. "How long have you been here?"

"Too long for me to remember, honestly. And no, she is not hurt or dead. She's a deity, after all; what seems like millennia to you may be only the blink of an eye to us. I told Zeus what I was going to do; he was never happy about what I did but still forgave me all the same. Dally with human women, yes, but never one of our own." He reached out with his now much longer arm and stroked the side of her face, leaving tingling sensations. "I want a queen, Alexandra. Someone who will sit at my right hand and preside over the Underworld as long as the days and nights continue to befall us."

"Why can't you just make Persephone change her mind?"

"Because I found someone much, much better for my queen." Alex's eyes widened in shock at his response. The tingling sensation on her cheek flared up for just a moment, causing her to cup it with her hand while her eyes were glued to the floor.

"Hades....," was all she could say to him.

"I give you a choice: you can say no and I will erase your memory. You will remember nothing of me and you will go back to your life as a bookstore owner and die of a natural death after a long life. However, when you die, your soul will only be a part of my realm and nothing more. I will see you, of course, but I will not do anything different towards you. You will be nothing more than fodder. However, if you say yes, I will prepare you myself for your escape from Final Death of your old life to be reborn into your new one with me. Once you die, you will arrive at the River Styx to ride with Charon to my realm. You will be made into a minor goddess with a foot in both the mortal world and the world of the dead. You can visit the ones you love here but they will no longer recognize you; in short, they will choose to not know you. This above all else: my love for you will never end, as I am not like my brother. I was always the moody one, so to speak."

Alex stared at him in silence then laughed out loud, sending Hades into confusion. When he gave her a questioning look, she said while trying to calm down, "Sorry, but it's just funny that you would say that. I mean, after all, you ARE the God of the Dead. You're surrounded by death all of the time, like the ultimate wet dream for a Goth."

"Actually that would be Thanatos. I am God of the Underworld, not Death itself," said Hades in a professor like tone, causing her to blush. "And yes, if you were wondering, I know him rather well. He's actually quite charming. Sometimes, the dead see me before they see him but it all works out in the end." Hades reached out and touched her cheek again and this time she did not flinch. He could feel her blood coursing through her body, her heart beating rapidly and her skin warming to his touch.

When he pulled back, she said, "Why me?"

"Why must you ask that? You know how I feel about you, what you have done to me since we've met. I love you. I know you love me as well yet I will understand your decision, no matter what it is."

"Can I have some time to think about this?"

"Of course. I shall give you 24 hours."

Alex sputtered in shock. "24 hours?!"

267

"My dear, I am going back to my realm. That is why you've seen Charon so much; she's been coming up here to gather souls to take back as well as give me pomegranates to keep me going, so to speak. They allow me to have a foot in both this world and my own." He stood up and stretched, causing every bone to pop in his body. Alex remained seated while staring at the floor. 24 hours. To choose between a mundane life and something bigger. Something greater. She looked up at Hades who looked down at her while he touched her cheek again with his elongated arms. She balled her hands into fists.

"You could be Queen of the Underworld, Alexandra, and my wife. You could be a goddess. I give you 24 hours. You will stay here with me to make up your mind." He walked out of the room, leaving Alex alone with her thoughts. She looked down at her balled fists and released them. In each hand was a small packet of dried pomegranate seeds.

"Will the Sleeper return?" asked Charon who appeared in Hades' kitchen just as he entered. Hades sighed and said nothing as he got out a bottle of water and took a long sip from it. Charon, ever the patient Ferryman, stood at the doorway waiting for him to respond. When he finished the bottle in two sips, he threw the bottle away, wiped his mouth then said, "I have given her 24 hours, Charon. After that, I will return home."

"The Sleeper knows, know that the tree is rotted inside, draining away and spiraling downward to an ether of black." Hades turned to face Charon and smiled.

"I know what I am doing, Charon. Trust me, I will return in 24 hours, with or without a Queen."

"Autumn rising, rising towards the new sun. The Sleeper must understand that He is missed." Hades placed a hand on her shoulder as a father would towards his daughter.

"24 hours. No more, no less."

Alex walked upstairs to the main bedroom after hearing Hades speaking to Charon in the kitchen. She did not want to disturb them and plus she had no idea what Charon was talking about. It sounded like poetry that had double entendre with every word. Plus, she did not want to face Hades yet. She had a lot of thinking to do with regards to his offer. As she reached the bedroom, she closed the door behind her and sat on the bed. She looked outside the window to the night sky and thought of the darkness she experienced while in the Underworld. The night of Earth was somewhat reassuring for her, for she knew what to expect and even the unknown was not as bad as most people would think. However, the darkness she experienced in the Underworld was colder, darker, and older with thankfully no souls or ghosts running around. That would have been too much for her. She lay on the bed and closed her eyes. Sleep was needed right now and she welcomed it greatly.

The sounds of birds chirping outside of her window woke Alex up. She blinked several times and realized that she was in the bed rather than on top of it. She rolled over and saw Hades sleeping next to her. She smiled then frowned then smiled again as she reached over and touched his cheek. It felt like a cooling piece of dead flesh as his eyes fluttered open. Rather than seeing the green eyes she was so used to, blue flames in black sockets met her own, causing her to tremble somewhat.

"You looked as though you needed rest," he said as he pulled her closer to him. His skin felt cold and slightly damp as it made contact with her warm and flushed skin. Her head rested on his chest while her ears listened to his heart beating slowly.

"When do I need to make up my mind?"

"I am leaving tonight. You have until then." Alex closed her eyes, wishing that this choice would go away all the while knowing that it would not. She had to decide and whatever choice she made would be one for eternity. She snuggled closer to him, pressing herself into his cold flesh, wanting to feel some sort of heat but knowing that it was a futile attempt. She, at that moment, wanted to be at home with a good cup of tea, a book, her husband reading on the couch with her and Phillip telling her tales of woe that made her laugh. She wanted her old life back but knew that could never happen, even if he erased her memory of him. She no longer had a husband nor did she have her friend Phillip. She felt a tear sliding down her face and onto his skin before it registered in her mind that she was crying. Hades lifted up her face and wiped her tears away.

"Hades-"

"Do you need to be alone for a moment? I can leave if need be."

"No, no, I'm fine." She looked into his flames, seeing nothing and desiring nothing as well.

"You have made up your mind, then?"

"Yes.....yes, I have. I choose to be your queen."

Hades smiled briefly then pulled away from her. "My love, I am glad although I would have understood if you chose to walk away from me." Alex nodded then wiped the new tears that slid down her face. "Why are you crying?"

"I don't know, actually. I just.....don't know."

"I understand, as strange as that sounds. It was not an easy decision to make."

"You're right; it wasn't easy to make at all. And yet, I feel as though I've made the right decision." She wiped her face once more with the sheet. "What about the bookstore? I completely forgot about that. What about my apartment, my things-"

"I will take care of everything, Alexandra. Once you do what needs to be done, I will take care of your life here." Alex nodded in mute agreement.

"So, what do I need to do?"

"Let's get dressed and I'll show you."

I still can't believe I made that decision. After he kissed me long and hard, we got up and proceeded to get dressed. My mind was going a million miles a minute and it took everything inside of me to keep from screaming bloody murder. I still can't believe I made that decision. Once dressed, I went downstairs. I still love him, even though I know what he is. I walked around the kitchen, looking for nothing in particular, when he entered the room, dressed in khaki pants, white shirt and loafers with no socks. His hair looked a little windblown while his normal eyes looked at me. He then walked over to me and embraced me. I felt his now warm skin against my own and I sighed. I loved him so much. When we pulled apart, he produced a small pomegranate from behind his back and I took it. Rather than the usual reddish coloured skin, this one was mottled grey with bluish spots. I looked at it for some time then up at him with a questioning look. What was I supposed to do with this, I thought.

"Eat this pomegranate," he said in a somber tone, "and you shall be saved from a Final Death. You must eat it all, including the skin." I sniffed it for a moment (it smelled like wet socks) and then I took a slow bite. It tasted foul and sickly sweet as the mushy skin gave in to my teeth yet I swallowed my first bite. I felt it go down my throat, burning and cooling at the same time. He just stood there, watching me eat, making sure I did not back down or out of what I had promised to him. However, he did not need to worry for I was not going to change my mind. All I had to do was look at him and my reasons for eating the pomegranate tripled. I closed my eyes and took another bite and noticed that this one was sweeter and less foul. When I opened my eyes, I noticed that everything looked hazy. I felt slightly dizzy but I still stood on my feet. He did nothing to support me; this was my decision, after all. My teeth tore into the skin while juice dripped down my chin and down the front of my clothing. I ate and ate, not caring how the fruit got in my mouth only that it did. Every bite got sweeter and sweeter and my eyes felt like lead weights in their sockets.

When I took the final bite, I chewed once then swallowed it all and wiped my sticky hands on my clothing. I looked up at him and felt like fainting. He was so blurry that I could barely make him out amongst everything else in the kitchen. He stood there, arms crossed, watching me still. I wanted to sleep, to fall down on the floor and sleep for hours, days, whatever. My eyelids grew heavy. I wanted to throw up but I had to keep the pomegranate in my mouth. The last thing I remembered here was him walking up to me and, while placing a hand on my now trembling shoulder, said, "This will not hurt at all." I heard the sound of coins falling and then everything went black.

Darkness, pure and eternal darkness. A sense of uncertainty mixed with fear. Perhaps he was wrong, she thought. Perhaps this was all a dream. She reached out with a shaking hand, searching for something, anything that would give her a sense of assurance. She took a step forward, surprised that she could walk then reached out. Nothing. She took another step forward then noticed that the darkness was not as dark. Another step. Brighter. Another step. Brighter. Her hands found something solid on either side of her and she almost screamed with joy. Rocks, stones all around her. She continued with more confidence towards the brighter darkness. As she walked along, arms now down at her sides, she felt something cold and wispy breeze by her. She stood rooted to the spot in fear, wondering what that was, when another wispy thing breezed by her, followed by another and another, until it felt as though she walked through cold spider webs. She reached out on either side, touching the rocks, and realized she was walking through a wide tunnel. Another wispy thing passed by her and this time she turned to her left to see just what it was. It was humanoid in shape but coloured a dusty grey with downcast eyes and several needles sticking from its arms. Alex wanted to scream but something else inside of her calmed her down. These are the dead, she thought as she walked along with them. A woman with bullet wounds passed her by on the right in slow and light steps, not once noticing her, while a young boy who walked on her left stopped and stared at Alex then walked up to her and kept up with her own pace.

"You are not dead," the soul said as it placed a cold hand on Alex's arm, causing her to stop. Other souls, now aware of this, stopped as well. They all looked at her with their dead eyes while some walked up to her and touched her. Their hands felt cold and dry, she thought while looking around.

"Why are you not dead?" asked an old man whose eyes were covered with a thin grey film. "You should not be here if you are living."

"I am here because I am Hades' Queen," she replied in a solemn tone. Instantly, all of the souls stepped back in reverence; some even bowed low to her.

"The Sleeper awaits, awaits through the glass, afraid to show hidden in stillness reigns," said a calming voice that surrounded them. Alex looked to her right and saw the river Styx churning slowly along while Charon, dressed in a long robe that hid her feet, stood next to an impossibly long boat on the riverbank. Alex walked towards Charon while the souls walked behind her, their hands still touching her while they whispered with spidery voices about her and her role as Queen. Alex walked up to the Ferryman then looked all around.

"I never realized how bright it was in here," she said.

Charon smiled sadly. "Welcome to the Underworld, fair Queen. Hades awaits," said Charon as she bowed low. Alex stood to the side as the souls got into the boat while each paid their two coins for their passage. Suddenly, Alex felt something on her eyes and touched them. There, on her eyes, were two coins. She looked around again and noticed that she could still see perfectly. She then looked at Charon who helped souls into the boat. Charon met her eyes and her questioning look.

"You wear the coins in order to be of both worlds, Queen. You will have the ability to travel the Earth but the coins will be invisible. Your coins, given by Hades himself, are for your eternal passage and your sacrifice."

"It was no sacrifice," she said as she too got in the boat. Charon looked around to make sure that everyone was in the boat, then got in and produced a long stick then pushed off from the bank. Alex stood towards the front of the boat while the souls gave her some room. The Styx churned along and every so often, Alex saw a face appear on the surface then disappear. Even the river is made of souls, she thought just as she felt a small hand touch her own. She looked down and saw the same young boy from before. The boy looked up at her then took her hand in his small one. Alex, not knowing what to say, welcomed his cold touch as she resumed staring forward. The tunnel held a faint glow for some time then it opened up to an incredibly vast area. It looked to be larger than three football fields with dark towers spiraling from the ground and dizzying into the sky, if there was one here. She saw grey floating and flying things all around the area, going every way, while lights dotted here and there, adding to the massive size of the place. One lone building, however, stood taller than the rest, and Alex instantly knew that it was Hades' manor. It is my manor as well, she thought just as the boat stopped quietly against a pier where several guards dressed in dark coloured togas stood waiting. Charon stepped out of the boat then stood to the side as the souls stepped out as well. Alex remained on the boat with the young boy while watching the souls led by the guards walk towards their new home.

Only one guard remained as he walked up to Alex and offered a hand to help her off the boat while Charon took the hand of the little boy. As Alex walked towards the manor, she turned and looked back at Charon holding the young boy, who raised his hand in a very mature manner and saluted her. Alex nodded once then continued her walk to Hades. She glanced at her guard and noticed he was covered in swirling darkness. She turned her focus towards her new home and her King, Hades.

Guards stood on every step leading up to the manor. The guard leading Alex stopped and turned to face the Underworld. With an unnaturally loud voice, he said, "All Hail, Queen Alexandra!" For one moment, everything and everyone stopped what they were doing and focused their attention to her. Alex turned to face the gathering masses and with one voice, they began to sing in a strange language. The song, painful and beautiful, haunted her ears. She wanted to cry yet she knew that it was a joyous song, one that they sang for her and her alone. It was a song from the Dead.

"My love, my eternal bride," said a deep voice behind her. She turned and saw Hades walking slowly down the stairs towards her. He was dressed in a swirling grey robe and toga while his bone crown stood firmly on his head. The flames in his sockets danced around with madness as he looked down upon his lovely bride. The guards suddenly went to attention as he passed by them. Alex could only stare at him walking towards her; this was now her King and husband. When he reached the bottom stair, she bowed low just as the song reached its crescendo then everyone fell silent. Alex raised up and saw that Hades held out his hand for her to take it.

"My Queen," he said in a solemn voice, "you need not bow to me. Take my hand and take your place by my side forever." Alex took his hand and the two walked back up the stairs while the denizens of the Underworld watched their new Queen take her rightful place.

When they were inside, Alex looked around in amazement, for the manor held a luxurious beauty that could be found nowhere else. The blues and blacks of the manor sparkled with lights not created by mortal hands. Small blush flames sat in large bowls, highlighting hallways and passages, while guards stood here and there, eternally waiting for their master's command.

"It's so beautiful," she whispered. "I thought it-"

"Was going to be dreary and dank?" answered Hades with a hint of a smile. "Come, let me show you to our room." He led her down one of the main hallways while Alex looked around like a child in complete wonder. This was her home now.

When they reached his room, the massive black door opened on its own, revealing a lush bedroom dressed in dark blue, black and silver. The mammoth bed sat in the middle of the room while here and there lay pieces of various art and statues. Alex walked in first, trying to take in everything with her eyes, until Hades placed his hands on her shoulders.

"There is something that needs to be done now," he said. Alex smelled cinnamon on his breath as it tickled her ear. He led her towards one of the statues; a young woman dressed in a simple toga. He walked up to the statue and touched it. Immediately, the statue came to breathing life as Persephone stretched her arms then looked at Alex curiously. Alex could hardly breathe; Persephone was so beautiful that it was eerie to look at her. Her long ringlet hair fell in waves down her back while her white peach skin looked soft enough to eat. Persephone walked up to Alex and touched her cheek.

"So, you are the one to replace me," she said with an angel's voice, "You are to be his Queen. Did he kidnap you as well?"

"No, I came here of my own free will," answered Alex. Persephone looked at her in shock then glanced at Hades who stood to the side. This was something she could not understand.

"Because of your choice," she said, "you have forever changed the Earth and all who dwell in it. Now that I am free to return to my home, there will no longer be four seasons. The world shall only experience two: Spring and Autumn." She raised a hand towards Alex and said as she began to fade away, "Farewell, Queen of the Underworld." Alex and Hades were now alone.

"It is time to take your place with me," he said as he placed his thin and cold hands on her shoulders while filling her nose with the scent of cinnamon.

Hades sat on his throne while presiding over the souls that entered his realm. Some of them had died of natural causes while others created their own untimely death. Each soul had to be presented to him before being claimed into the Underworld. Each soul had a story to tell and Hades patiently listened to them all. At one point, he turned to his right and met his flame eyes with Alex's coin eyes. She sat in her throne dressed in a black toga that fell to her sandaled feet as it complemented her now mottled grey skin. Her wavy hair fell about her face and down her back while her own crown made of elder branches and berries adorned her head. She looked down at the souls with a sad smile as she too listened to their stories. Her left hand sat on the arm of the throne. As she stared out into the vast realm, she felt Hades' hand cover her own.

TWO YEARS LATER

I can see them in the window of a restaurant, laughing and talking with another couple. They look good even though they were hit with a tragedy. I know it still bothers them but every day it gets a little better than before. That and they have their faith to guide them. I wish I could tell them that they really don't need it, but I would just be wasting words. They have their faith and I have my truth. I debate as to whether or not I want to step inside for a moment and talk to them, but I know they will never recognize me. Once she died, they moved on somewhat and I would be a complete stranger to them. However, seeing as how I am here for a couple of days and have nothing better to do, I decide to go in. The front door bell rings as I step in and look around. Not too many people are in the restaurant but that is fine with them. I can smell the delicious foods and my stomach begins to grumble, although I wonder if I am even hungry. He told me that even though I can eat the food up here, it was really not a necessary thing. I see the two couples sitting at a table and I walk over to them. Immediately, four pairs of eyes look up at me with a somewhat hesitant look. I smile and say hello and that I knew the one couples' daughter well when she was alive. They look at each other then look back at me with a smile. They ask me if I went to law school with Alex and I tell them that I did. They ask me for my name and I give them one, although in five minutes they will no longer remember it. I smile and ask them how they are doing since Alex's death (I was there at the funeral; Hades laughed when I told him that I wanted to attend it) and they reply with some answer that I know is not true. I know they are still hurting inside and that sometimes at night, the mother will cry silently into her pillow while her husband stares up at the ceiling. I smile and tell them that I moved to another town after law school but I came in for the funeral, to which they claim they now remember seeing me there (they did not) and that they appreciate my sentiment. They, along with the other couple, ask if I would like to join them for dinner, to which I reply no and that I have to be off, but it was good seeing them and to take care. The mother squeezes my hand and says with a watery voice to take care and love your parents. She says that because she remembers all of the fights she had with her, all of the times when she refused to understand her quirky daughter. I smile and wave good-bye then leave the restaurant while they attempt to reconnect with their earlier conversation. I walk along the street, past the restaurant and onward to another place, doesn't matter where. As I walk along the busy street with everyone else, I glance into a window and see my golden coins firmly on my eyes. No one else can see these coins; no one living, that is, and that is fine. I look up and feel that slightly warm, slight cold sun on my face and smile for I know that because of me, the Earth will forever be wrapped up in a Spring/Autumn package. As I look up, I can see Persephone dancing along the clouds in merriment; she retained her true self ever since leaving Hades' realm. I know that she still wonders just why I made that choice to be with him, but I know she will never understand it. Zeus' lightening bolts light up the sky every so often but it is too bright outside for the humans to notice. I continue to walk down the street, dressed in my long black and blue dress while my ink hair trails down my back in undulating waves. Several men stop to stare at me, for they've never seen beauty quite like mine. And I want to tell them, they won't until they die.

I am Queen and Goddess of the Underworld.

I am of two worlds.

The End

Discover other fine Kerlak publications at:

http://www.kerlakpublishing.com

CPSIA information can be obtained
at www.ICGtesting.com
Printed in the USA
LVHW111000100320
649524LV00001B/12